▶▶▶ *ACCEL·WORLD* Ø5
THE FLOATING STARLIGHT BRIDGE

REKI KAWAHARA
ILLUSTRATION BY HIMA
DESIGN BY bee-pee

"P...P-P-P-P-Pard?!
Wh-wh-what are
you d-doing here?!"

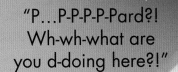

SILVER CROW

Haruyuki's duel avatar

"Same reason
you're here."

BLOOD LEOPARD

Mysterious maid clerk
working at a cake shop

WHAT ARE THE LEGIONS THAT DIVIDE THE ACCELERATED WORLD INTO SEVEN TERRITORIES AND RULE OVER THEM?

ITABASHI WARD

ADACHI WARD
YELLOW LEGION
CRYPT COSMIC CIRCUS

KITA WARD

KATSUSHIKA WARD

NERIMA WARD
RED LEGION PROMINENCE

ARAKAWA WARD

TOSHIMA WARD ● SUNSHINE CITY

SUGINAMI WARD

BUNKYO WARD
BLUE LEGION LEONIDS

SHINJUKU WARD

TAITO WARD

SUMIDA WARD

BLACK LEGION NEGA NEBULUS

● KOENJI STATION

● UMESATO JUNIOR
HIGH SCHOOL

● TOKYO SKYTREE

CHIYODA WARD

● GOVERNMENT OFFICE

● IMPERIAL PALACE

EDOGAWA WARD

KOTO WARD

SHIBUYA WARD

CHUO WARD
PURPLE LEGION: ???

GREEN LEGION
GREAT WALL

MINATO WARD

● OLD TOKYO TOWER

SETAGAYA WARD

WHITE LEGION: ???

MEGURO WARD

SHINAGAWA WARD

OTA WARD

ACCELERATED WORLD

Brain Burst, formally known as *Brain Burst 2039*, is a mysterious game program released seven years ago by an unknown producer, and it has already gone through several updates. Players—the number of whom is capped at approximately one thousand—become "duel avatars" and fight pitched battles, aiming to reach the pinnacle of the game, level ten.

Legions are groups composed of many duel avatars with the objective of expanding occupied areas and securing rights, the equivalent of a guild or a team in other online games.

There are seven main Legions, each led by one of the Seven Kings of Pure Color. These include the Black Legion's Nega Nebulus—with Kuroyukihime, aka Black Lotus, as its Legion Master—and the Red Legion's Prominence—helmed by Niko, aka Scarlet Rain. Haruyuki's Silver Crow and Takumu's Cyan Pile belong to Nega Nebulus.

Territory—the area controlled by a Legion. The system recognizes Territory when a Legion has an average win rate of more than 50 percent in Territory Battles against groups of the same size. These battles—available at any level—happen every Saturday night. In territories under the Legion's control, members of that Legion are given the right to refuse duels, even when their Neurolinkers are connected to the Global Net.

▶▶▶*ACCEL·WORLD* Ø5

THE FLOATING STARLIGHT BRIDGE

Reki Kawahara
Illustrations: HIMA
Design: bee-pee

YEN ON

NEW YORK

■ Kuroyukihime = Umesato Junior High School student council vice president. Trim and clever girl who has it all. Her background is shrouded in mystery. Her in-school avatar is a spangle butterfly she programmed herself. Her duel avatar is the Black King, Black Lotus (level nine).

■ Haruyuki = Haruyuki Arita. Eighth grader at Umesato Junior High. Bullied; on the pudgy side. He's good at games, but shy. His in-school avatar is a pink pig. His duel avatar is Silver Crow (level five).

■ Chiyuri = Chiyuri Kurashima. Haruyuki's childhood friend. Meddling, energetic girl. Her in-school avatar is a silver cat. Her duel avatar is Lime Bell (level four).

■ Takumu = Takumu Mayuzumi. A boy Haruyuki and Chiyuri have known since childhood. Good at kendo. His duel avatar is Cyan Pile (level five).

■ Sky Raker = Master Burst-Linker belonging to the old Nega Nebulus. Lives as a recluse due to certain circumstances, but is persuaded by Kuroyukihime and Haruyuki to come back to the front line. Taught Haruyuki about the Incarnate System.

■ Neurolinker = A portable Internet terminal that connects with the brain via a wireless quantum connection and enhances all five senses with images, sounds, and other stimuli.

■ In-school local net = Local area network established within Umesato Junior High School. Used during classes and to check attendance; while on campus, Umesato students are required to be connected to it at all times.

■ Global connection = Connection with the worldwide net. Global connections are forbidden on Umesato Junior High School grounds, where the in-school local net is provided instead.

■ Brain Burst = Neurolinker application sent to Haruyuki by Kuroyukihime.

■ Duel avatar = Player's virtual self, operated when fighting in Brain Burst.

■ Legion = Groups composed of many duel avatars with the objective of expanding occupied areas and securing rights. There are seven main Legions, each led by one of the Seven Kings of Pure Color.

■ Normal Duel Field = The field where normal Brain Burst battles (one-on-one) are carried out. Although the specs do possess elements of reality, the system is essentially on the level of an old-school fighting game.

■ Unlimited Neutral Field = Field for high-level players where only duel avatars at levels four and up are allowed. The game system is of a wholly different order from that of the Normal Duel Field, and the level of freedom in this Field beats out even the next-generation VRMMO.

■ Movement control system = System in charge of avatar control.
Normally, this system handles all avatar movement.

■ Image control system = System in which the player creates a strong image in their mind to operate the avatar. The mechanism is very different from the normal movement control system, and very few players can use it. Key component of the Incarnate System.

■ Incarnate System = Technique allowing players to interfere with the Brain Burst program's image control system to bring about a reality outside of the game's framework. Also referred to as "overwriting" game phenomena.

■ Acceleration Research Society = Mysterious Burst Linker group. They do not think of Brain Burst as a simple fighting game and are planning something. Black Vise and Rust Jigsaw are members.

▶▶▶*ACCEL·WORLD*

1

They should just turn all of Tokyo into a covered shopping district already.

Haruyuki's racing thoughts had a desperate air to them as he walked home from school, kicking up the excess water that was not absorbed into the water-permeable paving tiles.

He had always hated the rain. The signal strength of his Neurolinker dropped (albeit by only the slightest margin); an umbrella blocked one of the hands he needed to operate his virtual desktop; and worse, his body, which already tended toward dampness, got even damper.

He stopped at a red light and looked out from under his umbrella. Even though it had been raining the whole day, the heavy, leaden color of the sky was unchanged; the clouds were still swollen with water. On the right edge of his field of view, alongside the news headlines, the chance of rain display was a line of numbers like "eighty" and "ninety" until the following morning. Apparently, the rainy season front had no intention of leaving the Kanto region any time soon.

How great it would feel to just leap up and shoot through to the other side of that gray expanse. No matter where he looked there would be a sea of white clouds spreading out endlessly against an ultramarine sky, watched over by the blazing sun. This was a sight he had seen countless times in Storm stages, but naturally, he had never experienced it in the real world.

He could imagine it, at least. Standing on his tiptoes, he flapped his virtual wings and—

"It's green, you know!"

Whap! A hand slapped his back, and Haruyuki practically fell onto the crosswalk. He just barely managed to avoid face-planting into the ground and stepped forward at a brisk pace to hide his embarrassment.

"...Hey," he said, looking to his side.

"Hey." His interlocutor twirled a bright yellow-green umbrella. Chiyuri Kurashima. She splashed along in water-repellant sneakers, looking for all the world as if she not only did *not* feel a heavy gloom at the oppressively leaden sky but, in fact, actively enjoyed it.

"Did you get a new umbrella?"

When he asked about the unfamiliar object, his childhood friend blinked her catlike eyes awkwardly and nodded.

"Yeah...And you don't even need to start with me! I know what you're going to say! For some reason, I'm just really drawn to this color for little things like this. Because of my avatar, I think."

"Yeah, that happens. Before I knew it, my memory card case, my direct cables, they were all silver."

Two months earlier, in April, Chiyuri had become a Burst Linker, and the armor of her duel avatar Lime Bell was a lime green just like its name. She hadn't been very fond of the color at first, but before she knew it, more than a few of her possessions, including her trademark large hair clip, had been replaced with bright green counterparts.

"But don't go so far as your Neurolinker. Someone might end up outing you in the real because of it," he remarked, looking at the pale purple exterior of the VR device attached to her slender neck.

"Whatever, Haru!" Chiyuri popped her cheeks out. "You and Taku and Kuroyuki all have Neurolinkers the color of your avatars!"

"B-but I've been using this one since forever. The next time I change models, I'm going for a different color."

"Proooooobably piano black, I bet." She glared at him out of the corner of her eye, and his eyes unconsciously froze. His childhood friend laughed, rolling her eyes fondly, as she tilted her brand-new umbrella back and gazed up at the sky from underneath it. "It sure is pouring, though, huh?"

"Yeah, it really is...Oh, hey. What about practice?" Haruyuki cocked his head to one side, belatedly realizing that normally he, a member of the go-home team, and Chiyuri, a member of the track and field team, never walked home at the same time.

Chiyuri shrugged. "Whenever it rains, we always stay in the gym doing strength training or we go swimming in the indoor pool," she replied, as if the whole thing bored her. "But today, other teams are using both, so we ended up having to cancel practice. It's not fair that Taku and the kendo team get their very own dojo...Aah, if I don't get some exercise every day, I feel so gross, like all my muscles are fading away or something."

"You do? Really?" Haruyuki said, a little admiringly, given that he himself boasted of being a version of humanity that was the polar opposite of an athlete.

Chiyuri blinked as if remembering something and abruptly took a step toward him, placing her hand on his arm. He grew flustered at the sudden contact, and under her sharp gaze to boot.

"I've got it, Haru," she said. "Work out with me."

"H-huh?!" His eyelids flew back, and his mouth flapped open and shut before he finally managed to ask, "W-work out... Where...How..."

"What's that reaction about? O-ohh! You were thinking something perverted, weren't you?!" Her stern glare poured down over him once more before she brought a teasing smile to her lips. "I was just thinking we could go and duel. Tag team–style. What else could I have possibly meant, hmm, Professor Arita?"

"Th-that's totally what I was talking about. Obviously." Haruyuki feigned a calm he didn't feel and cleared his throat conspicuously before continuing. "What I meant was, what area and what kind of rules we should fight with."

"Ohh, hmm, well." Fortunately, she was apparently willing to bail him out here; a broad smile spread across her face as she pointed at the Chuo Line above the road ahead of them. "It's still early. Let's go to Shinjuku. Maybe we can get above the clouds if we're on the observation deck at the government office."

"I seriously doubt that, but whatever, sounds good." He shrugged and was aware once again of the weight of Chiyuri's hand still resting on his right arm.

Fourteen years earlier, in 2033, Haruyuki Arita and Chiyuri Kurashima had been born in the same high-rise condo complex in north Koenji. Their apartments were also only two floors apart, so they had basically been raised like twins since infancy. Given how large the complex was, there were of course many other children their age in the building, but the only person, other than Chiyuri, Haruyuki had been friends with in that whole expanse of time was Takumu Mayuzumi, who lived in a different wing.

Takumu had gone to a different elementary school, so Haruyuki could forget his everyday worries when they were hanging out. And the sole reason his relationship with Chiyuri hadn't changed, despite the fact that they went to the same school, was likely because of her strength and kindness.

When he started to be targeted by older bullies in elementary school, Haruyuki, not wanting Chiyuri to see him in such a pathetic state, had tried to put some distance between himself and her, but she had stubbornly refused to let him. He understood now just how much pressure she must have faced back then for remaining friends with a kid everyone else picked on. And yet, until they were in fifth grade, she had walked home to the condo with him every day and hung out until evening, inviting Takumu to join them to play video games or explorers. That time the three of them spent together after school was etched deep in Haruyuki's memory with a golden hue.

Oh, hey, maybe it's like that for Chiyuri, too.

Because the resource for the pseudo–healing ability of Chiyuri's duel avatar, Lime Bell, was probably—

"Train's here." She jabbed him with an elbow, and he raised his head to see that the train was already pulling into the Chuo Line platform.

"Right," he assented, watching the orange train car coming in from the west, and then adding in a small voice, "...Huh, Chiyu."

"Huh? You say something?"

"N-no, nothing." Haruyuki hurriedly shook his head, feeling his chest tighten for some reason at the sight of his childhood friend looking back at him, her short hair swinging. "Oh! We might be able to get seats!"

"Come on, it's only two stations!" An exasperated voice he was only too familiar with chased after him as he flew into the train car.

After taking the pedestrian walkway that stretched out underground from Shinjuku Station's west exit to the government building, they jumped onto the elevator that went directly to the observation deck on the top floor.

Vween. A brief sense of acceleration pushed down on them and then disappeared. The digital floor-number display on the wall changed with incredible speed, and the concrete wall soon turned to glass.

"Whoa," Chiyuri cried out as they flew upward. "Amazing, this gray..."

"You can't really see anything with the rain."

He had expected this. Hindered by the curtain of ceaseless rain, they could see almost nothing of the vast evening metropolis that should have been unfolding before them to the south. And as they went higher, mist clung to the glass, blocking the city from view entirely. The elevator decelerated—making them feel like they were floating—and finally stopped, along with the announcement that they had arrived. Beyond the doors, the world was dyed a uniform white.

Rebuilt in the thirties, the Tokyo Metropolitan Government Building now rose up to a height of five hundred meters. The only building in Japan, never mind Tokyo, that was taller was Tokyo Skytree in Sumida Ward. But Skytree's second observation deck was at an altitude of 450 meters, so the top floor of the government building was actually the point in central Tokyo closest to the sky.

Running out of the elevator, Chiyuri placed both hands on the expansive glass in front of her. "Whoa! Amazing, it's totally white."

"So basically, we're in the mist now, instead of the rain." Grinning wryly, Haruyuki came to stand next to Chiyuri. The other side of the window gleamed a milky color, as though it had been covered in thick cotton.

"Too bad, huh? We can't see the sky at all," he said.

Chiyuri, who had always been terrible at giving up, glared up at the sky, but then quickly looked back at him and smiled. "Well, whatever. Thanks to this, we have the whole place to ourselves."

And indeed in the midst of this foul weather, on a weekday evening to boot, there weren't too many idly curious city dwellers bothering to come up to the observation deck; not a soul was around.

"We came all this way! We make at least one round!" Chiyuri shouted, abruptly hooking her left arm through Haruyuki's right and yanking him forward.

"R—! R-right."

Somehow, Haruyuki generally managed to speak to Chiyuri normally in his real-world voice like he had when they were kids, but if she got the slightest bit cozy, the behavior of his mouth and tongue immediately became suspect. Giggling at his affected state, Chiyuri started walking clockwise around the outer passage of the observation deck.

Naturally, no matter how far they went, the scene outside did not change. White lumps of cloud simply twisted beyond the clinging droplets of water. Still, Chiyuri moved her feet rhythmically, without pulling even one dissatisfied face.

The current state of his relationship with his childhood friend was a little hard for him to grasp. Two months earlier, right after a particularly difficult and painful battle, Chiyuri had wrapped her arms around the necks of Haruyuki and Takumu and hugged them, shouting through her tears, "I love you both." Ever since, she had been completely carefree and open with them and tried to have the three of them hang out as much as she could, in the very spirit of this declaration. It was almost like she was trying to rewind time, back to when they had played together every day until it got dark outside.

"That reminds me, Haru."

"Wh-what?" Haruyuki abruptly lifted his face at hearing his name.

"We came to duel and everything. We might as well connect globally already. Then the tourist information tags will show up outside."

"Ohh…Right."

They were currently disconnected from the Global Net. Shinjuku Ward was the territory of the Blue Legion Leonids, which meant that if they left their connection on, another Burst Linker could challenge them at any moment. Hypothetically, going into duel standby mode while on the road was dangerous, but up here on the deserted observation deck, they would have no problems if they were automatically accelerated without advance notice.

Haruyuki nodded and first opened his Brain Burst controls to team up with Lime Bell. This way, on the matching list, they would be clearly noted as a tag team, and their challengers would basically be limited to other two-person teams. Then, he and Chiyuri simultaneously connected their Neurolinkers to the Global Net.

Immediately, countless tiny holotags popped up to fill his field of view, the guidance display for all the famous spots and big buildings they would have been able to see if the sky had been clear. Among the names he could see were nearby Shinjuku Station and Southern Terrace, with Kabukicho beyond them both, so he assumed they were facing east.

"I guess looking at just the tags isn't so interesting, after all." As Chiyuri laughed wryly, the thick clouds momentarily opened up as if the weather gods were taking pity on them, and the heart of Tokyo in the evening light suddenly spread out before them. She flew over to the window with a cry of delight, and Haruyuki hurried to stand next to her.

Seen with the naked eye from an elevation of five hundred meters, the massive city presented a chaotic figure, a tapestry woven from five hundred years of history. Just when you noticed the cutting-edge layered structures glittering brilliantly around Shinjuku Station, the sites of Shinjuku Gyoen and Akasaka immediately beyond that sunk into a dim gloom, almost entirely unchanged from the previous century. And farther off in the east was an even darker space, vast, reminiscent of the large black hole at the center of the Milky Way—the Imperial Palace.

Obviously, in the real world, this was a place where the casual visitor was not permitted, but Burst Linkers like Haruyuki and his friends were also unable to touch images from inside the palace because—highly exceptional for modern-day Japan—the security system in that space was not connected to the social camera network. Thus, the game was unable to reproduce the real structure from camera images as it did for other famous places, and so the Imperial Palace in the Unlimited Neutral Field of the Accelerated World was always an original, magic-castle-type structure.

But then, how would the opposite situation work?

Currently, the Brain Burst program hacked into the nationwide social camera net to create its Field. Its range included even Okinawa prefecture, which was not actually connected to the main island of Honshu; that fact allowed Kuroyukihime to run across the sea stretching out from Okinawa to Tokyo in the Unlimited

Field. So what if there were also places *outside Japan* monitored by social cameras? Would Burst Linkers be able to "go" there…

"Hey, Chiyu?" Haruyuki said as he stared absently off into the east.

"Hmm? What?"

"Lately, okay? On the news, there was this story about exporting the social camera technology—"

Did you hear about it?

Haruyuki didn't get to finish his question.

Skreeeeee! A familiar screech assaulted his ears, and his vision went black. Automatic acceleration. In other words, some Burst Linkers in the Shinjuku area had found the Haruyuki/Chiyuri tag team on the matching list and immediately challenged them to a duel. In the center of the darkness burned red, flaming text: HERE COME NEW CHALLENGERS!!

The thought of only a millisecond earlier was at once swept away by his excitement at the duel, his first outside the Nega Nebulus area in a long time.

2

Legs enveloped in silver armor landed on a thick, mossy branch. When he lifted his head, the scene had completely changed from the rainy skyscrapers of a moment before. The sky was a bizarre mauve, and all the tall buildings had been transformed into enormous, rough, and bony trees. Several thick ropes of ivy hung down among these, with a few pterosaur-like silhouettes flying leisurely among them.

Haruyuki looked down on the dense forest below from a branch near the terrifyingly high peak of what had been the Shinjuku Government Building. "Ugh," he grumbled. "A Primeval Forest stage. I'm bad at these."

"Why?" a voice next to him replied immediately. "It's so pretty. It's way better than some brutal map like a Wasteland or a Century End." The owner of these words was, of course, Lime Bell, clad in translucent emerald-green armor. Round, cute eyes glittered beneath the brim of her large, triangular hat.

"Well, sure, at first glance, it looks fun. But, like, there's too much stuff in the way when I fly, and I can't see the ground at all in this place."

"Quit whining! You have to practice fighting on the ground sometimes, too, you know."

"Yeah, yeah." Haruyuki nodded as she slapped him on the back with the bell of her left hand.

The characteristics of the Primeval Forest stage were extremely poor field of view due to the thick plant growth, and a ridiculous number of small animal objects known as "critters." Enormous carnivorous beasts also existed in this stage, and although they were few in number, duelers still needed to factor in their possible intervention when putting together battle strategies.

Reviewing the stage attributes in the back of his mind, Haruyuki glanced up to the right and checked the two HP gauges lined up there.

A two-person tag team had challenged them to this duel: the level-five Frost Horn and the level-four Tourmaline Shell, both active members of the Blue Legion Leonids, and whose names Haruyuki knew only too well. Since he was currently level five and Chiyuri level four, there was no difference in terms of the numbers, but their opponents had likely become Burst Linkers a fair bit before them. Taking a simplistic view of the situation, they might be assumed to be better than Haruyuki and Chiyuri, who had leveled up fairly quickly, but in truth, that was not the case.

This was how it worked: Burst Linkers were broken up into several types based on personality. For instance, there were the daredevils who took no account of win ratios and pushed whomever they could into a duel whenever they could, wherever they were, and the more conservative Linkers who carefully weighed advantages and disadvantages and aimed for the stars within reach with duels they could win. Even if Burst Linkers from two such disparate groups were at the same numerical level, they differed greatly in an invisible way: accumulated battle experience.

When Linkers challenged a higher-ranking avatar they had no hope of beating no matter how they struggled, or an opponent whose avatar attributes they were not compatible with and would inevitably lose to, the duel gave the Burst Linker experience separate from the numerical points they might have won: battle techniques, knowledge, and above all else the heart to stand firm in a tight spot.

Naturally, the play style of the daredevil group was less effective than that of the clever group. From time to time, they would be pushed into anxiety about burst points and would occasionally have to apply themselves to hunting Enemies in the Unlimited Neutral Field. But his teacher, Kuroyukihime, told him that in the end, it was this type who had the higher likelihood of making it to the top levels. Thus, Haruyuki made a conscious effort not to be choosy about his opponents once he had made up his mind to duel and gone out into the city; his aim was to maintain a style somewhere in between the daredevils and the clever kids, but…

The pair who had challenged them now, in particular Frost Horn, was well known as go-for-broke guys, with a daredevil level far above Haruyuki's. Which was exactly why they had not hesitated in the slightest to yank Haruyuki and Chiyuri into the Accelerated World immediately after they appeared on the matching list.

Noting from the movement of the guide cursor in the center of his vision that the enemy team was heading straight for the government building tree they were perched in, Haruyuki resolved to go along with his opponents' style.

"Chiyu, you wanna just get down from here and get this over with quick and dirty?"

"Sure." His partner grinned. "After all, if I can't see you, I can't heal you, and I've been practicing hand-to-hand combat lately, too!" She waved the bell of her left hand and smashed five or six of the hard-looking nuts hanging behind them.

Having been hit on the head by that bell in the past, Haruyuki unconsciously flinched before stretching a hand out to his partner. "All right, then how about we do a surprise attack from above!"

"Yeah!"

She offered her hand and he grabbed on to it before fearlessly stepping off the branch five hundred meters up in the air. They went into an upside-down free fall, aiming for the point indicated by the guide cursor, a spot in the hazy forest far below.

The cursor only gave a rough idea of the enemy's bearing, however. Thus, the opposing team wouldn't immediately realize that Haruyuki and Chiyuri were rapidly approaching directly above their heads. To make sure they used this bit of deception to their fullest advantage, Haruyuki delayed decelerating until the very last possible minute. The wind howled in his ears, and the ground approached with terrifying force. Although he was used to dives like this, he couldn't stop himself from holding his breath.

But Chiyuri, diving right next to him at the same speed, didn't even move her mouth to cry out; rather, her eyes shone with the thrill. She had some serious balls. Or maybe it wasn't okay to use that word to describe a girl...

"Found them!" A sharp whisper interrupted his meandering thoughts. "Below that huge red flower!"

He quickly shifted his gaze and glimpsed a big shadow and a small shadow racing through the dense growth of tall Rafflesia-like plants. The one on the right with light blue heavy armor and enormous horns growing from his forehead and both shoulders was Frost Horn. To the left, clad in sharp bluish-green armor, was Tourmaline Shell.

"I'll take the one on the right, you get the left. Hit 'em with everything you got," he said, and got a firm nod in response.

The enemy should have already guessed that Haruyuki and Chiyuri were either on the ground or somewhere in the government building tree. However, in mere seconds, both sides would come into close range, and the cursors would disappear. They had to decelerate and get ready to attack immediately before that happened. Haruyuki opened both eyes wide and focused his entire being on calculating that timing.

"Here we go. Five seconds to deceleration—three, two, one, zero!" He clutched Chiyuri's hand tightly, and on zero, he fully deployed the wings on his back.

To make the enemy mistakenly believe they were on the ground, Silver Crow hadn't dared charge up his special-attack gauge. Thus, no thrust came from his wings, but he was able to use them like a parachute. The metal fins caught on the air and put the brakes hard on their descent. Using the deceleration force to turn them around, he stretched out his left leg and assumed a diving-kick stance. Chiyuri did the same, tugging slightly on his hand, and adjusted her sights. The guide cursor then vanished from his field of view.

In that instant, the enemy tag team realized that Haruyuki and Chiyuri were unexpectedly close and stopped so abruptly that they dug grooves out of the earth. After quickly glancing around at their surroundings, they threw their heads back up at the sky.

But they were too late.

"Yaaaaaaah!"

"Hooooooo!"

Together with these battle cries, Haruyuki with his left foot and Chiyuri with her right kicked through the Rafflesia petals and plunged down onto their respective targets at an acute angle.

The timing was such that even these skilled fighters couldn't evade the strike free of injury. Frost Horn and Tourmaline Shell both crossed their arms in front of their bodies and braced themselves to block. Nonetheless, they were concussed by dive kicks storing up the kinetic energy of a descent from a height of five hundred meters.

A splashy light effect and a crashing noise filled the stage, as if a special attack had hit its mark.

"Mngh!"

"Hrrnk!"

Cries slipped from Horn and Shell as they hunkered down and fought to deflect the blow. Their feet gouged into the green earth, carving out four deep ruts. But no matter how large they were, it was impossible to completely guard against such a powerful attack.

The struggle for supremacy broke in a mere second: Horn and

his partner were simultaneously thrown backward. Still digging deeply into the ground, they skidded back, only to crash into a large tree trunk far, far away. The impact effect shook the stage once again, and the health gauges in the top right sank almost 30 percent.

Having succeeded in making the first strike, Haruyuki and Chiyuri landed on the ground via a backward somersault, and several voices cried out in the distance.

These shouts—"Oh, wow!" "You almost never see that kind of damage with a normal attack!"—were those of the Gallery, sitting in twos and threes in branches high above, looking down at the battle zone. Despite the fact that it was a weekday, there looked to be more than twenty people gathered there—unsurprising given Shinjuku's status as a duel mecca.

As the excitement died down a little, Frost Horn and Tourmaline Shell—knocked over backward, legs popping up out of the shrubbery—now leapt to their feet. They staggered slightly with the aftereffects of the damage they had taken, but they found their footing quickly enough and started shouting loudly in turn.

"Dammit! You were up on the observation deck! I bet you couldn't see anything at all! I mean, raining like that!"

"That's not the point, Horn! It's a date, get it? These two were on a date, Hooooorn!"

"Wh-wh-what…So they figured on a date, might as well duel∴?!"

"That's exactly it, Horn! They think they're gonna take us down and then be all hugs and kisses, Hoooooooooorn!!"

"U-unforgivable, Tori! Burst Linkers like this need to be wiped oooouuuut!"

This skit appeared for all intents and purposes to have been prepared in advance, and the Gallery around them flared to life once again. Mixed in with the explosions of laughter came one-sided comments like, "That's right, that's right," and, "Show 'em what the loveless are made of."

Listening to this exchange dazed Haruyuki, and he shook

his head fiercely back and forth. "N-no, that's not— I mean, a date or—"

"If you're so butt-hurt about it, maybe you should team up with a girl, too!" Chiyuri cried out as if to pour fuel on the fire, drowning out Haruyuki's stammered objections.

"Y-you don't pull punches." Frost Horn reeled back, unsteady once more.

"Yup, yup." Hands on hips, Tourmaline Shell bobbed his head in agreement. "We don't have a lot of girl Linkers in our Legion. I mean, just the idea of a group of close-range fighters stinks of sweat."

"This isn't the time for patting each other on the back! We're all here; we gotta beat them back and make the road home for these two a little awkward at least!!"

"Whoa! That's, like, seriously amazing, Hoooorn!"

"Shut up! We'll show them how a real man lives! Here we go…"

As Haruyuki stared dumbly at their little sideshow, Frost Horn suddenly readied his thick arms at his sides. The hard horns growing from his forehead and shoulders took on an intense light.

"Frosted Circle!!" He shouted the name of the attack, causing rings of bluish-white light to race outward with a *whoosh*. They pushed through Haruyuki and Chiyuri, and then scattered off behind them.

The speed and range were such that they couldn't evade the attack, but the light itself was harmless. Their gauges didn't move a pixel.

However, Haruyuki braced himself anew and waited for the phenomenon that would follow. He had fought Frost Horn several times in the Territories, but this was the first time he had been hit with this special attack directly. He was pretty sure that rather than causing direct damage to the enemy, the attack changed the properties applied to the area.

Cling, cling! Accompanying the sharp sound, the plants around them started to take on a whitish hue. Particles of light glittered in the air—they were all Frost. Crystallized water adhered to any and all objects, clothing them in a costume of ice.

Silver Crow's smooth, mirrored armor clouded at once. "Bell, I'll take Horn," Haruyuki said in a low voice as he watched a fairly thick layer of frost descend on his limbs and the extremities of his armor. "Keep Shell in check until I finish him off."

"Okay." Immediately after this short reply—

"Waa...aaaaah!"

A throaty roar echoed from the other side of the veil of frost, and an enormous shadow came charging straight at him. Frost Horn. Just like Haruyuki, his light blue armor was caked in frost. The horns on his forehead and shoulders appeared to be covered in an especially thick layer of ice.

He came at Haruyuki with a vicious shoulder tackle, right shoulder thrust far out. Haruyuki dropped his stance, opened his eyes wide, and watched for the moment to dodge and counterattack.

"Haah!" He flew to the right and to avoid being hit.

But his body was a fair bit heavier than usual because of the frost clinging to it, and his start was slow. It wasn't a direct hit, but the horn scraped him, and he felt the crunch of impact in his left shoulder. Gritting his teeth, Haruyuki held his ground, turned toward Horn as he slid past, and threw his right fist into his opponent's flank.

But this time, too, his timing was off because of the added weight. Covered in the dense frost, Haruyuki's short, straight punch would have caused greater damage than normal if it had hit the mark, but that force stopped at a mere light grazing of Horn's body.

This was the main effect of the special attack Frosted Circle. It increased the weight of the extremities of any duel avatar within range, interfering with small, swift attacks and serial attacks. Conversely, large, one-shot attacks became more powerful. It also had secondary effects: because Frosted Circle made it extremely difficult to see any distance, it effectively prevented getting distance for a sniper attack, and, because of the cold, it rendered thermal homing useless.

In other words, it forced nearly every type of avatar within the area into a fierce struggle, making it a fearsome ability in a variety of ways. Even if an avatar tried to move outside of the range of the effect, the frost was generated over a broad swath with Horn at its center, so running away was no easy feat.

Haruyuki glared at the shadow of Horn turning around in the distance and readying himself for another charge using his horns. *All right*, he murmured to himself. *I'll dance with you.*

While he was firming his fists and fighting spirit, he glanced over at the other pair of avatars facing off not far away.

His partner Lime Bell was similarly frozen white. The bell of her left hand, in particular, looked very heavy, with several icicles hanging off it.

But…

Tourmaline Shell didn't have a single particle of frost sticking to any part of him. The smooth, curved armor covering his slender body was unchanged from the start of the duel, glittering an almost wet bluish-green color. No—it actually *was* wet. The ice that tried to coil around him melted the instant it touched him and turned into drops of water.

This was the reason Tourmaline Shell and Frost Horn liked teaming up together.

When struck by anything, that tourmaline gem-colored armor took on an electric charge and generated heat. And although there were many electric- and heat-type avatars, there weren't too many who continuously generated heat. Shell was one of a very few avatars on whom Horn's special attack had absolutely no effect.

Tourmaline Shell readied sword hands, thin sparks crackling as they crawled along his arms, and came after Lime Bell in a single fluid movement. He launched one close-range attack after another with flat-handed strikes straight out of Chinese kenpo. Bell was blocking solidly, her large bell raised up in place of a shield.

Being a fairly high-saturation green, Lime Bell had a defensive ability that blew metal colors out of the water. On top of that, the thick frost covering her arms seemed to be blocking almost all damage from Shell's Electric Heat Palm. As long as she focused on blocking, she would be able to essentially maintain her HP.

However, the enemy tag team was no doubt expecting exactly this.

Horn and his partner naturally knew that Lime Bell was a Healer, extremely rare in the Accelerated World. In a duel like this, where both teams had an identical total level, if one team used the healing ability even just once, the possibility of defeat for the other team spiked.

Thus, they had come up with the battle strategy of Shell, who was able to move around freely within the range of Frosted Circle, keeping Bell occupied with successive, cutting blows while Horn took care of Crow. Although Haruyuki and Chiyuri had succeeded in attacking first, the duel since they had descended had proceeded exactly according to the enemy's plan.

To break out of this deadlock, Haruyuki had no choice but to defeat Horn without backup. *But I knew that the minute I decided to fight a close-range battle on the ground!*

Haruyuki brought his transient thoughts to an end with this shout and focused his awareness on the shadow of Frost Horn charging.

In the earlier confusion, he had physically experienced the added weight of the frost sticking to him. He should be able to just barely dodge this next onslaught and offer up a counterattack.

Horn had his left shoulder forward this time, horn readied low like a battering ram. Haruyuki swallowed his fear and stood his ground as bait.

Now!

The instant he went to kick at the ground the slightest bit sooner than usual to avoid the hit, the tip of the sharp horn slammed into Haruyuki's left shoulder.

"Aaah!"

Crying out involuntarily, he went flying helplessly. Spinning, he crashed into the ground but didn't stop there; instead, he bounced back, high up. If he fell again from there, he'd take extra damage, and so Haruyuki somehow managed to pull off a landing on both feet to avoid that damage penalty, if nothing else.

That said, at just a single blow from the spike, Haruyuki's health gauge had been depleted by nearly 20 percent. A deep indentation had been gouged out of the armor of his left shoulder, and sparks snapped and cracked as they scattered. That particular pain of serious localized damage raced along his nerves, but more than that, Haruyuki felt an enormous surprise.

His timing should have been perfect. Why had the horn attack—which had to be much slower than a bullet—hit him so dead-on?

The answer was revealed by Frost Horn, standing imposingly a little ways off.

"Ah-ha-ha-ha-ha! Surprised you, huh, birdman! You're always flying around up in the sky, so you wouldn't know, but you see these stylish horns little me's carrying around? The longer they're in the Frosted Circle, the longer they get! They stand all sturdy and tall, right!"

"…Wh-what…" Gaping, he stared hard and saw that the cone-shaped horns stretching out from the large blue avatar's shoulders and forehead, encased in a thick ice, were indeed a fair bit longer than they had been at the start of the battle. And they were getting bigger with each passing second even at that moment. In other words, he could learn the timing after taking any number of tackle attacks, and it would still be pointless.

"Whaddya think?! This is! A real man's! Weapon! Ah-ha-ha! Haaaa!"

At Horn's high-pitched laughter, cheers of "Hear! Hear!" and interjections like "That's just rude" poured down from the members of the surrounding Gallery.

Haruyuki took a deep breath and expelled it again as he listened to them.

I made a mistake somewhere along the way here.

Fighting recklessly without choosing my opponent looks kind of like tearing down my own style to push myself into a fight, but they're not the same. Thinking I could win on my opponent's turf without any kind of strategy at all is exactly the same as sneering at my opponent. When facing an enemy, I should be digging out everything I have and fighting for real right from the start. And if I don't do that, there's really no reason why I should have a chance of winning.

I'm going full throttle starting now!

Haruyuki made fists of both hands and thrust them out to deploy the wings on his back. With the damage they'd done at the start and the hits he'd taken, his special-attack gauge was nearly half full. He'd get Chiyuri to heal them and then they'd flee to the sky. They could wait there for the Frosted Circle to be released before attacking with another double super dive to crush Tourmaline Shell first—

"Geh!" In the middle of plotting out his strategy in his mind, something unexpected happened.

His wings didn't open.

He immediately peered around at his back and saw the thick frost clinging to the metallic fins folded up there. It must have been acting as an adhesive to prevent them from deploying.

Hurriedly, he brought his hands around to his back and tried to rub the frost off, while Horn watched.

"Whoa! What?!" he cried. "Serious chance! Aaaawesome!" Dropping his hips, he readied the remarkably large horn on his forehead and positioned himself for a dash forward.

With the shoulder tackle, Frost Horn had already shaved away 20 percent of Haruyuki's gauge. The forehead was apparently the main attraction; he absolutely could not get slammed with it. That said, if he abandoned the idea of a counterattack and just focused on running around, the situation would only get worse. He had to do something, something, anything—

"Heeeyah!!" A forceful battle cry echoed through the stage.

Glancing over, he took in the sight of Lime Bell catching Tourmaline Shell's chopping attack with her right hand and sending him flying with a magnificent one-armed throw.

Set free with a *pop*, Shell crashed on his back nearly ten meters away from her. However, frustratingly, in a stage like the Primeval Forest, where the ground below was grass or sand, throwing techniques had little effect. The bluish-green avatar sustained no significant damage and was ready to bounce back onto his feet right away.

But it seemed Chiyuri had had something else in mind with the one-armed throw.

She whirled around without so much as a glance at where her opponent had landed and brought the large bell of her left hand high up into the air while shouting, "Citron Caaaaaaall!!"

The bell came back down with a twirling flourish, and the lime green light that gushed from it, accompanied by a beautiful ringing, advanced in a straight line toward Haruyuki.

And passed immediately by his left arm to disappear futilely in the frost behind him.

"Wha…" Haruyuki's dumbfounded voice was overwritten by Frost Horn's high-pitched laughter.

"A-ha-ha! In the Circle, like, light techniques have a hit rate thirty percent lower, you know! If you're a real man! Fight! Mano a manoooooo!!"

Whk! White frost danced up around Horn's feet. He pushed off hard to plunge ferociously forward at Haruyuki. The long, large horn on his forehead glittered.

Haruyuki racked his brains frantically in that brief instant of the enemy closing in on him.

However poor her field of view might have been, had Chiyuri actually missed with her special attack there?

She was the serious type when it came to things like that. If she was going to use her healing ability, she would wait for a time until she was sure of success. And more than that, Haruyuki's health gauge was still down by only 20 percent. It was too soon to pull out Citron Call, given the poor mileage it got.

Which meant that Chiyuri had meant to miss, or rather she had been aiming at something that wasn't Silver Crow.

And the element other than the duelers that was able to move around in the battle in this Primeval Forest stage was...

The instant his thoughts reached this point, Haruyuki's eyelids flew back and he understood exactly what he had to do. He waited for Frost Horn's charge, dropping into a martial arts stance with one foot forward, and calculated the direction he should dodge in.

"Waa...Ngyaaah!"

Haruyuki pretended to be overawed at this throaty howl from Horn, turned, and ran with all his might to his left, perfectly tracing out the line Chiyuri's special attack had drawn earlier. From behind, a subterranean rumbling closed in on him, and he was bursting with the foreboding of damage ripping into his back.

After braking urgently and abruptly, he faced straight up and kicked at the ground with every ounce of his strength. He spread his arms out, bent his back, and flew past Horn in a backward somersault in order to come at him from behind.

His enemy believed Silver Crow couldn't use his wings. So he shouldn't be expecting Haruyuki to dodge upward. And sure enough, although he felt the sharp tip scrape the center of his back, Haruyuki danced through the air, taking no more of a hit than that.

The large avatar charged forward in a straight line in Haruyuki's reversed view of the world. Ahead, in the dancing curtain of white frost, an enormous elliptical shadow floated up.

"Whaaoo?!"

The cry came from Frost Horn. He flapped both hands and tried putting the brakes on his charge. But because his feet were half frozen, he wasn't able to stop immediately. Sending spectacular amounts of frost flying, he plunged straight into the round shadow.

Krrshk! The dry and yet somehow wet sound of destruction rang through the air.

The enormous ellipse broke into large pieces, and a transparent viscous fluid poured out. The something that crawled out from inside gave an angry cry, a *greee* to send chills down the spine.

It was an enormous creature object, the sort you always had to be watching out for in a Primeval Forest stage. There were many different kinds—carnivorous beasts and dinosaurs and even predatory plants—but as a general rule, no matter what type of creature it was, it would attack any duel avatar who entered its sights without discrimination.

The sole exception to this was when its egg was broken.

Disturbed in its peaceful sleep inside the eggshell, the large creature would single-mindedly hunt the avatar who had done the deed for a full five hundred seconds, which was well over eight minutes. At that moment, an enormous long-horned beetle looked down on Frost Horn, its four eyes shining red as it clacked its large and sturdy jaw.

As exasperated voices from the Gallery—"Aah, now he's done it"—rained down, Horn threw up both hands and started to talk to the carapaced creature.

"W-w-w-wait! If we just talk about this man-to-man, I know we can figure it out!"

"Gree gree greeee!!"

Unfortunately, it appeared to be female. Mowing down the surrounding Rafflesia with its large feelers, the long-horned beetle began to chase the avatar, which was half its size. As Horn shrieked and struggled with which way to flee, the large jaws snapped at the air above his head—*klak klak*—several times.

Naturally, the giant creature eggs that could spawn such terror didn't exist just anywhere. Even if you wanted to incorporate them into your battle strategy, you could spend your whole time in the duel searching intently and never find even one.

But this one time at least, it wasn't by accident that the egg rolled along.

Chiyuri had made it. In the midst of the duel, she had noticed the shadow of the enormous insect moving on the other side of the frost. And then she had released her special attack, making it look like she was aiming at Haruyuki, but actually targeting the insect.

In truth, Citron Call was not a healing ability; it was the power to rewind time for its target. It recovered the health gauge as a sort of pseudohealing, but it would also cancel out things like changes in Enhanced Armaments, and if it hit any stage objects, it would set their status back as well. Destroyed items were returned to their original state; giant long-horned beetles reverted to eggs.

Obviously, in the normal course of things, Frost Horn would have realized something was up and never approached the egg. But the frost drifting thickly through the air blocked vision and hid Chiyuri's target. As a result, Frost Horn followed Haruyuki's invitation and charged right into the egg.

"Eeeeeaaaaaah!!"

The shrill scream of the man and the angry cry of the giant bug receded deep into the western woods, in the direction of Shinjuku Central Park. The Frosted Circle went with them, and their surroundings soon enough returned to the original brightness.

Tourmaline Shell stared dumbfounded at his partner's flight before turning back with a gasp and resting his eyes on Haruyuki and Chiyuri in turn. "I'll get vengeance on Horn's behalf! C-come and get meeeee!!"

And, of course, they did.

"Nice work!"

Beaming, Chiyuri thrust her right fist forward and Haruyuki bumped it with his own before sliding slowly onto one of the benches lined up in the hallway of the top floor of the Tokyo Metropolitan Government Building. He let out a long sigh and, after disconnecting from the Global Net for the time being, turned a dazed face out at space.

It wasn't as though anything other than burst points had been at stake; they had just finished a normal duel, but he was ridiculously tired somehow. It was probably because he had pushed himself into intense hand-to-hand ground combat, a way of fighting so unlike his usual style.

Honestly, the stress of not being able to fly was like having no water in the desert, despite the fact that around the beginning of the first term there had been a period where he couldn't use his wings for more than a week. Yet that experience seemed to have just increased his yearning for flight all the more.

And that's how it was for Haruyuki, who was still only in his first year as a Burst Linker. So for *her*, having been in this world for more than six years, it was no wonder she burned with a nearly mad passion for the sky. Although it was impossible to even get a sense of this fire from her normal calm demeanor...

"Hey! What are you spacing out about?"

Bopped on the head, Haruyuki hurriedly blinked several times in quick succession.

Chiyuri, next to him on the bench, had her cheeks puffed out and was glaring at him sideways. Apparently, she had started talking to him, and he had just let it slip right by.

"S-sorry. What did you say?"

"I asked you if you wanna go one more time!"

He looked at the clock display in the lower right of his field of view: Only a few minutes had passed since they'd come up to the observation deck. This was par for the course given that a Burst Linker duel ended in at most a mere 1.8 seconds in the real world, but Haruyuki thought about it for a moment before replying. "Hmm, I kinda think that if we stay here and wait for another fight, it's just gonna be Horn and Shell again, y'know? But I guess that's fine, too."

Rolling her cat-shaped eyes exaggeratedly, Chiyuri also shook her head. "Yeah, going up against the same team would be kinda boring. But, like, we came all this way together; it seems like a waste to just do solo fights."

If she had been in her in-school local net avatar, she would've been twitching her large cat ears. Or at least that was the look on her face as she fell into thought. "Oh! I've got it!" She abruptly clapped her hands together. "We're right here in Shinjuku—let's call my big sister! She's at a high school in Shibuya, right? It's just one station, maybe she'd come."

Haruyuki was the tiniest bit surprised. Because the "big sister" Chiyuri was talking about was the same "her" who had popped into Haruyuki's mind earlier.

Her name was Sky Raker. A senior Burst Linker and old friend of Kuroyukihime who had joined—or rather returned to—Nega Nebulus just two months before.

The reason why Chiyuri called this Burst Linker her "big sis" was exceedingly simple. Chiyuri's last name was Kurashima, the "shima" of which meant "island," while Raker's real name was Fuko Kurasaki, the "saki" of which meant "peninsula." When they exchanged name tags at their first face-to-face meeting in the real, Haruyuki had casually made the offhand comment, "Shima and saki together. You must be long-lost sisters, huh? Ha-ha-ha!" And that was where that started.

Without waiting for Haruyuki's response, Chiyuri started typing out a mail to this elder "sister," inviting her to join them. As his childhood friend pecked at her holokeyboard somewhat awkwardly, Haruyuki struggled with whether or not to tell her to stop. Because he had the feeling first and foremost that Raker would definitely decline the invitation.

Although she had in fact returned to the Legion, Sky Raker had not been released from the criminal consciousness that bound her. To that very day, she deeply regretted how, long, long ago, she had left the Legion in such a way as to abandon her leader, Kuroyukihime. Chiyuri, of course, also knew about all of this. She was most likely trying in her own way to knock on the locked door to Raker's heart.

Which is why Haruyuki once again closed the mouth he had opened.

A few seconds later, when Chiyuri had finished typing out the mail, she connected her Neurolinker to the Global Net for an instant to send it. She disconnected again, waited for a bit, and then connected once more. After getting Raker's reply and cutting free from the network one last time, she glanced over the text of it.

"...She says sorry," Chiyuri murmured, lifting her face and smiling slightly, and Haruyuki offered the words he had readied.

"Raker's in high school and all; she has to be superbusy on weekdays. She's supposed to be in the Territories this weekend. We'll see her then."

"...Yeah, you're right." His childhood friend heaved a sigh before smiling broadly, as if changing emotional gears. She said in an abruptly spirited voice, "So, okay, how about we fight solo once apiece?"

"Hmm, I kinda feel satisfied with that fight before. But if you're still wanting to go, I'll totally join you, of course."

At this response, Chiyuri nodded, a happy look coming to her face, this time from her heart. "Okay. We got to have a fun, cool win, so I'm good for today, too. Aah, that really did feel great!"

"Yeah, I guess." He returned her smile and reflected on the earlier tag-team match.

He was quite pleased at simply having won in a contest of strength, avatar to avatar, but more exhilarating than that was that it had been a strategic victory, where they'd taken full advantage of the characteristics of the stage. Not to mention that that kind of upset victory—turning around a bad situation—almost never happened. The eruption of the Gallery when the battle had been decided was proof of that.

Of course, this did make the regret of the side taking the hit all that much worse.

Frost Horn somehow managed to shake free of the hot pursuit of the enormous long-horned beetle and return to the battlefield, only to face a concentrated attack in short order. And almost as if Chiyuri had also remembered Frost Horn's magnificent parting words at the same time as Haruyuki, they both spurted with laughter.

"Pft, heh-heh! 'Next time, we'll be the ones dropping on you!

From the top of Tokyo Skytree to kick you in the heads!' We'd totally see it coming and step aside, and then they'd crash into the ground like that, game over."

"But, no, wait, even before that, how're they gonna get up there? It's like two hundred meters from the observation deck to the antenna at the very top, and to begin with, are there even social cameras...that high up..." As he spoke, a thought abruptly flashed up in the back of his mind and Haruyuki's mouth decelerated.

The thing he had been trying to remember right before they were challenged to the duel...The bit about the first export of the social camera technology outside of Japan. The memory of something he had caught only a glimpse of in the headline news finally came back to him.

Chiyuri cocked her head to one side at Haruyuki's sudden silence. "What's wrong, Haru?"

"Oh, uh, n-no, it's nothing." He shook his head vigorously, and Chiyuri shrugged before leaping to her feet.

"Okay, then! Let's get tea somewhere before heading home. It's all sunshine for you, huh, Professor Arita?! You're not stuck with me all awkward on the way home after losing pathetically!"

He could talk about games forever, but this type of line never failed to make his brain flicker.

"N-no, it'd be fine. I mean, I don't care about losing. It's fine. Really," he mumbled awkwardly.

Chiyuri had already started walking toward the elevator, and her laughter glided through the air to his ears. Sighing, he hurried to catch up with her.

Outside the windows, white clouds kept up their constant flow.

3

Having said good-bye to Chiyuri two floors below in the condo and returned alone to his deserted apartment, Haruyuki had no sooner changed out of his school uniform than he had plopped himself down on the living room sofa and started racing his fingers along his virtual desktop. He first opened a browser and entered the search words through voice command.

"Social camera export."

At the very top of the list of results displayed immediately was the news item: *Japanese security system introduced to Hermes' Cord.*

Security system. Obviously, the social camera technology.

And Hermes' Cord was—

The name of the space elevator above the eastern Pacific Ocean.

He clicked on the link with a finger, and reading the text of the article, Haruyuki thought ardently about the whole thing.

In brief, what the article was saying was that the security system for the space elevator, an international facility, had adopted the same technology as the Japanese social camera network.

The Earth-side station for the space elevator was in the coastal waters of Christmas Island, vastly far away from Japan. If social cameras were set up in a place like that, then that place would be incorporated into the Brain Burst areas, wouldn't it? Assuming that was the case, was there a way to dive there?

After cranking away in his head for half a minute or so, Haruyuki quickly abandoned the effort. He just didn't know enough to figure out the answer. Not about Brain Burst, and not about the space elevator, either. Maybe this was the time to turn to his leader for guidance. Right, she would know much more about both. He closed the browser, launched his mailer, and then hesitated briefly.

After examining the ratio of the degree of his desire to simply discuss it with her and his desire to talk big, he came to a conclusion of "Right! Sixty–forty!" and quickly typed out a text mail to make an appointment for a dive call. A dive call with this woman of letters who excelled in all subjects, one of the most senior Burst players, and the leader of Nega Nebulus, the Black King aka Kuroyukihime.

The time specified in the response that came right back to him was twenty minutes later. During this time, Haruyuki finished off a supper of frozen shrimp doria and oolong tea before going into a full dive a minute before the set time and switching the environment data of his home local net for the object set he had downloaded from a site overseas.

Previously, when he had similarly invited Kuroyukihime to his home net, the only sets he had were either very cold or stank of gunpowder, which had thrown him for quite the loop socially, so since then, he had been collecting things that would create a good atmosphere. Although his mother did complain that he needed to stop filling the home server storage capacity with junk.

He pushed the connection request button almost the instant he had everything set up and the appointed time came. After a few seconds of the call placement sound, an avatar appeared before his eyes.

Jet-black dress, silver trim glittering. Folded parasol the same dark color. Spangle butterfly wings on her back with a red pattern.

This fairy princess, with just the slightest bit more mystique than she had in the real world, looked first at Haruyuki's pink pig avatar with a smile, and next at her surroundings. She then abruptly opened both eyes wide and let out a cry, clinging to the pole next to her with some force.

"Wh-whoa!"

"Huh?! Wh-what's the matter?!"

"Wh-wh-what's the matter? *This* is the matter! Wh-wh-what is this environment data?!"

At her consternation, Haruyuki hurriedly took another look around.

Mountain ridges a hazy purple. An expansive forest and meadow, and a white stone city. The two of them were at the top of a very tall tower where they could see the entirety of this beautiful scene. There was no handrail or anything of the like on the very small watchtower—which was only three meters in diameter, with two chairs placed in the center along with a gas lamp—so the view was exceptional.

"Uh, um…I-isn't it beautiful? I found this object set on a German site a while ago—"

"Before we get to that, exactly how tall is this skinny tower?!" she asked with a pale face, and Haruyuki peered over the edge, straight down. He felt like the distance from the ground was about the same as that of the observation deck at the government office, from which he had fallen in the duel that evening, and so he replied as such.

"Uh, let's see…maybe about five hundred meters—"

"That's too high, idiot! Or were you aiming for a suspension bridge sort of effect?!"

"H-huh? What do you mean?"

"The suspension bridge effect is, well…In a dangerous place

like a suspension bridge high up, due to a misunderstanding of the feeling of fear..." Halfway through her explanation, Kuroyukihime stopped talking before lightly clearing her throat and glaring at Haruyuki. "At any rate, that sort of psychological issue has no effect on me! Although...it's not a duel, so nothing will happen even if I do fall, but at least have the decency to give a little warning in advance at times like this..."

The end of her sentence lost to muttering, Kuroyukihime finally stood up and sat down in the chair next to him. Haruyuki had also sat down earlier, and he spoke now slightly dejectedly.

"Um, I'm sorry for scaring you. Should I change it to a different object set?"

"No, it's fine. Regardless of how high up this is, you went and searched this set out for me."

He saw a faint smile rise to her lustrous lips and breathed a sigh of relief. "Uh, um." He scratched his head with the rounded hoof growing from his right arm and gave her a belated welcome. "Good evening, Kuroyukihime. I'm sorry for calling you out like this so abruptly."

"Good evening, Haruyuki. I'm glad I could see you now since we didn't get a chance to talk at school today."

Umesato Junior High's school festival was at the end of June, and because this was the last big event for the current student council, Kuroyukihime, being the vice president, was extremely busy every day. Remembering this, Haruyuki took this chance to ask a question that had occurred to him countless times before now.

"That reminds me. Why did you join the student council anyway? The president and vice president are decided in an election, so does that mean you campaigned for it?"

"Mmm. Well. Given how fixated I am on simply becoming a level-ten Burst Linker, your question of why is a very good one. The administrative things and conferences take time, leaving me no time for dueling." Letting a meaningful smile slip across her lips, Kuroyukihime continued. "However, to answer honestly, the reason I became a council member was all for Brain Burst."

"H-huh?!"

"Think about it. For a Burst Linker, the school that you attend is the closest to you, and thus, the most dangerous field. You could even say that having a grasp of all that information and firming up the ground beneath your feet is, in fact, essential. As a student council member, I have nearly full access to the school database. And from that perspective..." Here, Kuroyukihime grinned at him and gave voice to something entirely unexpected. "Speaking of which, there is the matter of after the student council elections next term at the start of the second term. How about it, Haruyuki? You could stand for president."

"Wh...Wh-wh-wh-wha-wha-wha—" Jumping slightly in his seat, Haruyuki twitched his pig's nose at high speed. "N-n-n-n-n-no way, no way! I-i-i-if I did, that would be like giving the whole school a Supreme Court–mandated license to dump on me! Totally!"

"Mmm, in that case, it might work if I left Takumu to be president and you to be vice president—"

"That's! Not! The problem!" Decisively firm in his refutation, speech slightly colored by Frost Horn's tone, Haruyuki decided to force this train back onto its tracks. "Anyway, I fought a duel in Shinjuku today."

"Mmm, I heard the talk. A hard fight against Leonids' starting team."

"N-news travels fast." Haruyuki blinked rapidly and Kuroyukihime's smile shifted to something a little more sarcastic.

"Of course I know about it. Apparently, you and Chiyuri are perfectly in tune with each other."

"Oh no, that's...I mean...ummm..."

"What's the matter? I'm not reproaching you. As Legion members, the most important thing is for you to work well together, isn't it?"

A cold sweat sprang up on his brow at the Kuroyukihime Smile special attack, and he once again reoriented the train. "Right around the end of that duel, our opponent said something like he was going to jump from Tokyo Skytree and kick us, and that's when it suddenly hit me!"

Quickly opening his browser, he called up the article at hand and slid the window over to Kuroyukihime. "Um, Kuroyukihime, do you already know about this?"

"Japanese security system in Hermes' Cord? Mmm, I feel like I caught a bit of this on the evening news." She glanced at the holowindow before lifting her face and cocking her head to one side. "So what about this article?"

"Um, well…It really is just an idea…and maybe you'll tell me I'm totally, way, way off base, but…I mean, I kinda feel bad for calling you here over something like this at all, but…" After setting up this mumbling guard at top speed, Haruyuki finally got to the heart of things. "That security system is the social camera technology, right? So then that means that the whole of the space elevator in the Pacific Ocean comes within range of the cameras, doesn't it? So I was just thinking…Hermes' Cord would show up in the Accelerated World, too…"

Even after he trailed off there, Kuroyukihime's eyes were practically popping out of her head, so Haruyuki readied himself for her to burst out laughing at this totally idiotic idea or to get mad at him for calling her over for such a pointless matter.

However.

"Hmmmmmmm." Humming at length, Kuroyukihime placed the fingers of her right hand on her chin and stared down at the browser window one more time. Eventually, she lifted her head and shook it lightly. "What can I say…You really do let your thoughts roam, hmm? But it's…interesting. Mmm, it is a truly interesting idea."

"Uh, uh-huh," Haruyuki said idiotically, not knowing how he should react, while before him, Kuroyukihime made her avatar get up from the chair and begin pacing in the middle of the narrow observation tower, almost as if she had forgotten her fear of the five-hundred-meter height.

"Assuming social cameras had indeed been set up there... Normally, that would be a closed net...But I wonder if the Hermes' Cord central station has the extra space and power to accommodate that enormous image processing system? Either way, connecting with the SSSC in Japan with a satellite circuit and having them process the data would be much more efficient. And cheaper, too. In which case...there's a possibility that even the Brain Burst program could at least slip past the defenses..."

"Uh, um," he somehow managed to interject, moving both of his short hands intently. "I don't really get it."

Kuroyukihime stopped moving abruptly and waggled the index finger of her right hand as if she wasn't sure how to explain it. "Mmm. All of which is to say, Hermes' Cord is a low-Earth-orbit space elevator, so the design is incredibly pared down."

"What's low Earth orbit?"

"...That's where I have to start?"

A small, wry grin crossed her lips, and Kuroyukihime sat down once again. She cleared her throat with a light cough and called up a blank window. On the bottom, she drew a circle with her finger and wrote "Earth" in the middle of it in a flowing hand.

"So then, let's start with the basics. To put it simply, for a space elevator—also known as an orbiting elevator—you build an extremely tall tower from the surface of the Earth into space, and then you use an elevator that goes up and down this to move people and materials. The transport cost by weight is so low, launching a rocket or a round trip with a shuttle doesn't begin to compare. However..." Kuroyukihime's finger moved, and an enormous cylindrical tower shot up from the round Earth.

"Assuming the same construction methods as Tokyo Skytree, to build a tower that would reach up to space, the base area would have to be on a scale large enough to swallow up Japan entirely, like it is here. Constructing such a Tower of Babel is utterly and entirely impossible in practice. Here, we change our way of thinking."

The tower immediately disappeared, and next, a small square was drawn in space, far away from the Earth.

"We build a station like this in stationary orbit thirty-six thousand kilometers away from the Earth. We then suspend from there a strong and lightweight cable toward the Earth. Since the speed of objects going around in geostationary orbit is basically perfectly synchronized with the rotation of the Earth, for all appearances, it never moves from that one spot in the sky above the Earth. Just as the name says, it's stationary. Thus..." The line coming straight down from the square—the station in geostationary orbit—hit the Earth. "If you attach the end of the cable to the Earth, you get a tower like this. Or rather, a ladder that reaches from the Earth to space."

"Oh! I get it!" Impressed, Haruyuki slapped his knee with the hoof that was his right hand. But he soon furrowed his brow and popped his head sideways.

"No, but...Hold on a minute. No matter how light the material is, if that cable is thirty-six thousand kilometers long *and* thick enough to set up an elevator in it, the total weight has to be incredible, right? They don't pull that up and drop it on the Earth from the station in orbit, do they?"

"They do!" came Kuroyukihime's immediate reply, and he slid back in his chair.

"That's..."

"As to how they do it, here's how." This time, she had a line stretch out from the top of the station and circled with her finger to draw a dot at the end of it. "All you have to do is stretch out a cable from the top as well and attach a weight to act as the center of the station's load—its center of gravity, in other words. Once you do this, an upward vector is generated due to the centrifugal force of the rotating weight, and that balances the downward load the cable creates."

"Oh! I get it!" After being impressed once more, Haruyuki

craned his neck yet again. "So where do they get this weight from?"

At this, a meaningful grin made its way across Kuroyukihime's lips, and some fairly unexpected words came out of her mouth. "The concept for this geostationary orbit space elevator actually was announced by NASA in the United States more than forty-seven years ago, in the year 2000. But at the time, it was projected for completion in 2062."

"Huh?! B-but that's still...way ahead?"

"Mmm. So why did they set a date so far in the future? Because in NASA's plan, they were going to *catch an asteroid passing close to the Earth* and attach that to the tip of the cable stretching out above the station in geostationary orbit and use it as the weight."

"What?! They were going to catch an asteroid?!"

"Exactly. The idea was that if they waited until '62, a reasonable-size asteroid would luckily be flying by, and they would have developed the technology to catch it by then."

"That's fifteen years from now, right?...Isn't that kind of impossible?"

"Mmm, it is."

Not understanding anything about anything, Haruyuki simply flapped his jaw open and shut. "B-but...The space elevator—Hermes' Cord already exists, right! I'm pretty sure they finished it five years ago, so that would have been in 2042. So what changed?"

"Well, that...," Kuroyukihime replied as she wiped away the illustration in the window with the palm of her hand. "Compared with the initial concept model for the geostationary orbit space elevator I just explained to you, Hermes' Cord is a low-Earth-orbit space elevator, based on plans revamped from a more practical standpoint."

"Low-Earth...orbit."

"The basic idea is the same as geostationary orbit. But the scope is different. The central station for Hermes' Cord is suspended much lower than geostationary orbit, two thousand kilometers above the ground…That said, it is still outside the atmosphere."

"Uh, um. Geostationary orbit's thirty-six thousand kilometers, so…that's like crazy close, isn't it?"

"It is. And because of that, the cable can be shorter and lighter, so you can get by without using an asteroid or something like that for balance."

"O-ohhh…I get it…" Haruyuki nodded deeply before giving voice to the obvious question. "So then why didn't they just use this low-Earth orbit right from the start?"

"Because this method has its own problems. In order for this man-made object inserted into low-Earth orbit—that is, two thousand kilometers above the ground—to gain the centrifugal force needed to balance against the pull of the Earth—which is much stronger than in geostationary orbit—it has to go around at a speed that far exceeds the Earth's rotation. With geostationary orbit, the speed at which the station goes around is synchronized with the Earth's rotation, so the end of the cable can be attached to the Earth, but that's not possible with low-Earth orbit."

As she spoke, Kuroyukihime stretched out a finger and made a small mark in a spot fairly close to the circle representing the Earth.

"This is the Hermes' Cord central station, constructed in an orbit two thousand kilometers in the air. From this, a cable made from intertwined carbon nanotubes, or CNT, stretches out upward and downward to connect above with the top station and below with the bottom station, which act as weights."

The bottom tip of the line stretching out from above and below the mark was just a little separated from the outline of the Earth. Kuroyukihime tapped this gap with a finger and continued.

"This bottom station hangs a hundred and fifty kilometers above the Earth's surface. Any lower than that and the atmosphere becomes too thick, and the entire elevator would be pulled down because of the friction, eventually falling out of the sky."

"Whoa…" Haruyuki expelled a long breath and tried to get his thoughts in order.

"So then," he said, twitching his pig's nose, "um, Hermes' Cord is a four-thousand-meter-long man-made satellite made up of these three stations connected by carbon nanotubes…Is that it? And this goes around the Earth at a speed much faster than the Earth's rotation…?"

"That's exactly it. The bottom station's ground speed reaches Mach ten, so the low-Earth-orbit-type space elevator is also called a hypersonic skyhook."

"But, in that case, what's the thing they built on Christmas Island in the eastern Pacific Ocean? I remember seeing a huge man-made island on the news…I'm sure there was a long tower or something stretching out from it…"

"That island is the landing field for the space plane to take people and objects to the bottom station of Hermes' Cord. The planes that take off from there rendezvous with the station a hundred and fifty kilometers up and deliver their cargo. This cargo is then taken to the top station four thousand kilometers up, using the elevator, before being loaded into a shuttle going back and forth between the Earth and a station in geostationary orbit or the international base on the surface of the moon. Incidentally, since the station in geostationary orbit is also directly above the landing field, it's actually not incorrect to say that Hermes' Cord is in the eastern Pacific."

"Huh…" Haruyuki sighed several times and stared again at the illustration on the window before him. Since the diameter of the Earth was about 12,700 kilometers, a length of four thousand kilometers was probably the same proportion as an apple and its stem, but the idea that this thing was whizzing by above his head at Mach ten was a bit hard to swallow.

"Hmm, I dunno. Seems like a spring or something that could come falling down. It's scary," he said despite himself, and Kuroyukihime shrugged her shoulders lightly.

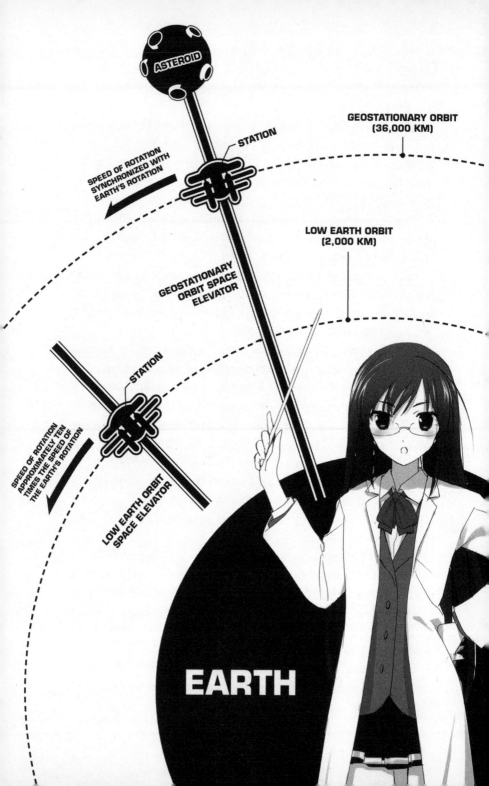

ASTEROID

GEOSTATIONARY ORBIT
(36,000 KM)

STATION

SPEED OF ROTATION
SYNCHRONIZED WITH
EARTH'S ROTATION

LOW EARTH ORBIT
(2,000 KM)

GEOSTATIONARY
ORBIT SPACE
ELEVATOR

STATION

SPEED OF ROTATION
APPROXIMATELY TEN
TIMES THE SPEED OF
THE EARTH'S ROTATION

LOW EARTH ORBIT
SPACE ELEVATOR

EARTH

"There was one that did almost fall, actually."

"Wh-what?!"

"Hmm? You didn't know about this? I'm pretty sure it was around the beginning of spring. There was that incident where terrorists mixed in with a group of tourists and tried to set up explosives on the central station. It's because of that that they decided to enhance the security system for Hermes' Cord. Japan took part in the international bidding for the system construction, leading to this news of the first export of the social camera technology."

"Oh, wow, is that how it happened? Sorry, I should've done my homework on that." Haruyuki pulled back into himself, just like when he was called on in class and didn't know the answer.

Fortunately, Professor Kuroyukihime didn't rebuke him further, but added an explanation with a wry smile. "Being a low-Earth-orbit space elevator, Hermes' Cord has smaller stations and a lighter cable than the geostationary orbit type. The design is very tight. Which is why even a pocket-size bomb could do some serious damage depending on where it was placed. And there would be no extra in terms of power or space to adopt a large-scale monitoring system. I think that's why Japan's social camera technology was adopted...Aah, and now we've finally come back to the beginning of this story."

She exhaled at length, and then waved the fingers of her right hand to pull up her VR operation menu. She materialized two drinking glasses and offered one of them to Haruyuki.

Ah, crap! I should have been ready to call these up, not her! he thought as he hurried to accept the glass and bring it to his lips. It seemed to be an original drink with countless fine-tuned flavor parameters; a refreshing, sweetly sour taste spread out in his mouth unlike any juice in the real world and yet with not a hint of anything unnatural about it.

"Th-this is good. Really good," he said, and Kuroyukihime laughed lightly, waving her left hand with a flourish.

"Lately, I've been practicing with real ingredients…Work with no do-overs is honestly very frustrating. Did you know, Haruyuki? Light soy sauce is light in color alone! I mean, what is that, salty water?!"

"H-huh, I didn't know that. But why are you suddenly working on your cooking—"

"That's obvious, isn't it? Someday, I…" Here, her mouth snapped shut, and Kuroyukihime cleared her throat loudly. "I'm just fooling around. Anyway, I suppose this means we've finally come to the point." Rather forcefully returning to the original topic, she continued her explanation at top speed.

"We were talking about the fact that Hermes' Cord doesn't have the leeway to equip an additional large-scale monitoring system. And so, that is where Japan's social cameras come in. That system collects in one place all the images recorded with its countless cameras using an exclusive high-speed net, and detects signs of criminal activity by automatically analyzing these data with a high-spec supercomputer. For instance, if a gun is picked up on a camera somewhere, the system immediately analyzes who the person with the gun is and where they came from, and continues to track them to see where they're going. The facility where this processing takes place, the Social Security Service Center, or SSSC, is somewhere in Japan, but not the slightest hint of where that place is has been made public."

"What? You don't know, either?" When Haruyuki asked her this in all seriousness, Kuroyukihime brought the wryest of wry smiles to her lips.

"Now look, what exactly do you think I am? I'm just a weak junior high school girl, you know. There's no reason I should know that kind of top-level classified national information!… Although, well, I have my suspicions."

"Wh-where is it?!"

"Not telling…More importantly, as I just explained to you, the automatic image analysis that's the heart of the social camera system is concentrated at the SSSC. Which means you don't need the essential items for normal monitoring cameras—enormous recording devices and human operators. If this lightness is the reason the system's being used in Hermes' Cord now...the cameras on the space elevator and the Japanese social camera network must inevitably be connected."

Haruyuki simply gaped as he took this all in, but since Kuroyukihime was blinking as if she was waiting for something, he finally remembered that this word "connected" was the chief objective of the sudden dive call.

"Oh!...Right, um. So they're connected, which means, uh..." Flapping his short pig avatar arms, he shouted, "We can go there, then?! To the Accelerated World's Hermes' Cord?!"

"Mmm...Well, we're still at the stage where the possibility is not zero." With a playful smile creeping onto her lips, Kuroyukihime continued in a tone that was somehow probing.

"First of all, there is the question of whether or not Brain Burst, which is in the end a fighting game, will conscientiously expand the stages that far. And then, assuming that the station is in fact connected to the net, how do you intend to get there? As a general rule, we Burst Linkers dive in the place where our real bodies are. In other words, to get to Hermes' Cord in the Accelerated World, we have to actually get into the space elevator on this side. They've started selling tour packages to the geostationary orbit station lately, but they're expensive!"

"They're superexpensive..." Haruyuki dropped his shoulders dejectedly.

He had the fleeting thought that Silver Crow and his wings could dive on the ground and then fly to the bottom station, but he rejected the idea before he even opened his mouth. Crow's maximum range was at best fifteen hundred meters. In contrast, Hermes' Cord was a hundred times that far away, floating some hundred and fifty thousand meters off in the distance. And even Christmas Island, where the space plane landing field was on the surface of the Earth, was completely impossible to get to on a junior high student's allowance.

"So. What it comes down to basically is that, unless you're super-rich, you can't dive at Hermes' Cord…"

"Or rather, I feel like if you could get to the real thing in this world, there would be no need to dive in the reconstructed article within the Accelerated World."

"Yeah. I guess so." Haruyuki sighed in disappointment this time, rather than wonder, and looked up at the sky.

The virtual blue seemed endlessly far away even from the top of the five-hundred-meter tower. Or rather, in this level of VR object set available for free, the tower could have been ten times or a hundred times higher and it wouldn't have reached the sky. Because there was no "other side" for this blue sky. A closed world with just the light blue tint stretching out intently.

"…Haruyuki."

Hearing his name suddenly, he brought his face back, and his gaze met Kuroyukihime's calm and yet somehow still mysterious eyes.

"Why do you want to go to Hermes' Cord so badly? I mean, compared with how freely you can fly with your wings, the space elevator is just a man-made object that goes around in a set orbit, after all."

"Uh, ummm." At the unexpected question, Haruyuki needed several full seconds to put the hazy thoughts inside him into words. "Obviously, I just like high places, so there's that…but another reason is that if we could go to Hermes' Cord, I thought maybe we could make the tiniest part of Her wish come true. She's had…her eyes on the sky, no, the other side of the Accelerated World for so long…"

The instant Kuroyukihime heard this, her eyes opened just the tiniest bit wider, and her long eyebrows furrowed into each other. The words that eventually fell from her lips were serene, like thought itself.

"I see," she murmured distinctly, and turned her gaze to the pale blue sky. "I suppose so…Her passion for the sky indeed has not been quenched even now. She still wishes to reach the other side of that distant blue madly, as much I seek level ten—no, perhaps even more than that."

"Uh-huh." Bobbing his head, Haruyuki turned his face upward once again.

Her: Sky Raker, the level-eight Burst Linker, a core member of the first Nega Nebulus. Long living as a recluse in the Accelerated World in the old Tokyo Tower, it had been three months now since she rejoined Nega Nebulus, a Legion member again after three long years.

However, this was not quite the same as returning to full active duty. Just as her refusal of Chiyuri's invitation that evening indicated, she was taking part only in the Territory Battles each weekend, without any involvement in normal duels. She didn't even come out to the front line in the Territories; she was always on standby in the rear, devoting herself to base defense.

Naturally, Haruyuki, and most likely Takumu and Kuroyuki-hime, too, were not in the least dissatisfied with this. Because as a general rule, Sky Raker, whose means of movement was a wheelchair, was not able to run anywhere other than paved roads and level surfaces. And when it came to defending their position, she got incredible results with her unique fighting style, freely maneuvering her wheelchair and trifling with the enemy while attacking repeatedly with sword hands. She was able to keep the healer Chiyuri almost perfectly safe when the enemy's main force was close-range types, to the point where adding just one attacker to the combination allowed them to fight more than adequately.

Compared with fall and winter of the previous year, when Kuroyukihime, Haruyuki, and Takumu had basically just barely managed to scrape by on their own for the hour of the Territories, the fighting power of Nega Nebulus now was growing at a ferocious pace. There was no doubt about that.

But there was one obvious truth that no one was giving voice to. If Sky Raker removed the seal from her Enhanced Armament Gale Thruster and strapped it onto her back once again, her fighting power would dramatically increase to several times, several *dozens* of times greater than it currently was. Having previously dodged an enormous enemy with this equipment, Haruyuki could testify that even if she was still missing both legs, a midair sprint using the thrust of the boosters could generate serious attack power.

However, even after Haruyuki had returned Gale Thruster, Sky Raker never went to summon the Armament, even when they were in a losing battle. It was almost as if she was firmly rejecting the wings that her own heart had given birth to.

"...I..." Haruyuki clasped his hands firmly in front of his own rounded stomach. "It's not like I'm thinking the Legion would be stronger if she started flying again or anything. I just...I want to let Raker know that if she doesn't believe in her own wings, she's wrong. I should know. I borrowed Gale Thruster once...That Enhanced Armament can't fly as long as Silver Crow's wings, it's true, and you can't go as high, but the instantaneous output is way more than the acceleration of any avatar...The truth is, there's a ton more power hidden in those boosters. That's what I think, anyway."

After thinking and thinking and delivering these earnest words, Haruyuki lifted his face and met Kuroyukihime's eyes, which were unusually kind and yet somehow brimming with mourning.

The spangle butterfly avatar nodded once slowly. "So if you take Raker to Hermes' Cord, you'll be able to communicate that to her," she said in a gentle voice. "Is that what you believe?"

"I do." Haruyuki dipped his head slightly, well aware of the fact that he was being far too starry-eyed. "If what I'm thinking is right, anyway."

"Honestly. How about once in a while being confident in your declarations?" The wry smile was soon tucked away, and after taking a deep breath, Kuroyukihime began speaking again.

"Just as I explained to you earlier, the real-world Hermes' Cord is going around the Earth a hundred and fifty kilometers up in the air. Thus, even if the newly deployed social camera net is connected to Japan's, I would expect that the Accelerated World's Hermes' Cord would naturally appear at the same height. Which is a distance that no duel avatar could possibly reach…But it's not necessarily the case that no means of transport exists."

"Wh-what?!" Haruyuki cried out in a high-pitched voice, leaning forward. Just as he was about to tumble off his chair, Kuroyukihime stopped him with the toe of a high heel against his flat nose.

"At best, it's simply a possibility. Calm down."

"R-right…"

"Listen. Despite how shrouded in mystery Brain Burst might be at its foundations, on the surface, it's a fighting game. In which case, don't you think a situation in which no fighter is able to go to a new stage is rather absurd?" Grinning, she moved her index finger as if in invitation. "So then, it wouldn't be at all strange if there were to appear somewhere secret in the Accelerated World a means of transportation that only those who thought long and hard and searched for it would be able to find."

"Secret…huh?"

"That sort of thing often happens in regular RPGs, after all. A treasure that at first glance seems impossible to get, but then if you carefully examine the map and use your head, you find a route there. That sort of thing."

"Oh, that's true, that's true. I love stuff like that." He bobbed his head in agreement with Kuroyukihime's example before staring hard at the illustration she had drawn.

The space elevator going around the Earth one hundred and fifty kilometers above it. The only way for him to get there was to use a space plane or a rocket. And the place where rockets were launched in Japan—

"Umm…Maybe Tanegashima Space Center?"

"No." This idea was dismissed with a shake of her black hair. "Ninety-nine percent of Burst Linkers are in Tokyo. So the portal should also be in Tokyo."

"B-but there's no rocket launch pad in Tokyo!"

At this cry, Kuroyukihime allowed a broad grin to spread across her face. "Perhaps if our avatars were made of real-world stuff, a rocket would be required. But they're not, are they? Our proxies in the virtual space are constructed of pure information. And in Tokyo, there is an information transmission facility with the largest output in all of Japan."

"Oh." Opening his eyes wide in amazement, Haruyuki continued, almost in a gasp, "T-Tokyo...Skytree..."

"Mmm. If Hermes' Cord is indeed a new duel stage, I think there's no way the portal there would appear anywhere other than Skytree. And the timing...That would be the moment after the social cameras have been deployed, when Hermes' Cord is closest to Japan for the first time..."

She erased the illustration on the window and opened a browser, flicking her fingers in quick manipulation. A screen filled with English was displayed, apparently the Hermes' Cord site. However, Kuroyukihime did not hesitate as she clicked on one link after another.

"It's sooner than I thought, the day after tomorrow," Kuroyukihime announced decisively, tracing a finger along the wavy line on a map of the world that eventually appeared. "June fifth, Wednesday. Five thirty-five PM."

4

Perhaps the rainy season decided it was time to take a little break finally, because that Wednesday was the first wonderfully clear day in some time.

Even after sixth period ended, there were still only a few fleecy clouds floating in the sky, and with the sun on his back as it started to set, Haruyuki raced toward Koenji Station by himself.

His destination was, of course, the opposite side of the city, the new Tokyo Tower at Oshiage in Sumida Ward, formally known as Tokyo Skytree. In approximately two hours, a portal to the space elevator Hermes' Cord would open on the special observation deck there…maybe.

It had all started with Haruyuki's fairly dreamy thought. He later slipped into the Galleries in Suginami and Shinjuku, but not a single Burst Linker was talking about Hermes' Cord. Even Kuroyukihime, the one who figured out the time and location of the portal opening, had added at the end of their dive call two days earlier, "Well, don't get too down if this ends up being a miss."

In which case, he at least wanted to incorporate the subtheme of a field trip to eastern Tokyo, a place where they normally never went, but unfortunately, Takumu and Chiyuri both had practice, and with the preparations for the school festival, Kuroyukihime had trouble getting away from the student council office these days. And so it fell to Haruyuki, the one who didn't have the guts to charge into solo duels in an unknown area.

"Whatever. If it's a miss, I can just go to that retro game shop in Akihabara." He offered those consoling words to his lonely self and got on the Chuo Line.

He changed to the Hanzomon Line at Kinshicho and by the time he got off at Oshiage station, the town was at last sinking into evening. He turned around slowly on the sidewalk and heaved a sigh of relief the instant he spotted it in the sky.

Living in Tokyo, he almost never went to the city's famous places, so this was still only the second time he had been to Skytree. The enormous tower and its truss construction glittering gold in the western sun rose up sharply like a ladder to the heavens.

A total of six hundred and thirty-four meters high, each side of the base was seventy meters. It had already been thirty-five years since it was built, but this broadcast tower was still the tallest building in Japan. He stood stock-still and simply took in its majesty for a while before hurrying toward it.

He paid the student entry fee at the gate and got on the high-speed elevator. The cabin started its ascent with a grinding acceleration, and an exhilaration still different from vertical takeoff in the virtual world came over him. As he had two days earlier when they climbed the government office, he unconsciously pressed himself up against the glass wall. If Chiyuri had been there next to him, she would no doubt have said, in an exasperated way, "You really do like high places, huh?"

A minute or so later, the elevator arrived at the observation deck and ejected Haruyuki along with a few tourists.

Somehow keeping himself from immediately running to the window, he glanced around at his surroundings. It being a weekday evening, there were very few minors. And the few that were there were university students on what looked like dates or young children with their parents. He didn't see anyone in junior or senior high school loitering around without an obvious purpose—in other words, anyone likely to be a Burst Linker.

Naturally, he could have also just connected his Neurolinker to the facility's local net, accelerated, and checked the matching list, but doing so on a closed net carried the risk, albeit slight, of being outed in the real. And supposing he did anyway, the only thing he could do when he found another Burst Linker's name was duel, and that wasn't his goal on that particular day.

Thus, Haruyuki gave up on his visual scan of the spacious observation deck and walked over to the windows on the west side.

The absolute height itself was far greater than that of the government office in Shinjuku, and the view of the city spreading out below the clear night sky was the very definition of overwhelming. With large skyscrapers popping up here and there among tiny speck-like buildings jammed together, it was almost like an old-school circuit board. Moving his gaze beyond all this, he found the majestic figure of Mount Fuji lying hazily in the distance outside of the bewitching city. To the upper left, the setting sun, its rays shooting down onto the horizon, held a belt of black clouds, promising more rain the next day.

When he turned his face up even farther, the hues of the sky shifted from a madder red to a gentle violet. Jets flew in, wingtip lights blinking and winking. Sightseeing airships floated lazily overhead.

Right now, high above this sky, a man-made object four thousand kilometers long is coming toward us at the hypersonic speed of Mach ten. The instant the thought popped into his head, Haruyuki let out a gasp. *The world's so big. Vast. It's just way too macro.*

I'm sure the reason I love to look up at the sky is because I get this feeling. I'm fat and pathetic and short, but when everything else becomes relatively micro like this, it doesn't matter. That feeling. It's like a temporary escape or something.

And I know it's the same thing when I'm Silver Crow and out there flying. In those moments, I can feel with my whole body the absurd scale of the Accelerated World. Compared with the infinite nature of space and time there, even the mountain's worth of problems I have are nothing more than a momentary speck popping modestly up on the surface of the ground. It's only when I'm touching the sky that I can believe that.

...But...

Then why did You look to the sky? I mean, why do You still look to the sky? It can't be that You want to experience that fleeting liberation the way I do. If that was your goal, then You have more than enough power in the Gale Thruster to make that happen. So why on earth...? What is it that You want in the sky...?

These questions Haruyuki asked in his heart were naturally directed at his other teacher, Sky Raker.

He then came up with some kind of vague answer to them. Of course, he didn't know if he was right. Or rather, it wasn't a matter of right or wrong. Only when Raker flapped her wings of her own volition once more and raced through the sky would the answer appear.

Which was why Haruyuki being at the Skytree now and waiting for a portal to appear was probably a complete waste of time. If Raker shook her head with her usual gentle smile and told him she had no intention of going, that would be the end of it.

But, Haruyuki thought, *no matter how deep the wounds she carries, Sky Raker's still a Burst Linker.* Which meant that she shouldn't be able to sit there and not be excited once she learned about a new field in the Accelerated World, and one that was a bridge stretching out four thousand kilometers up into the sky at that.

Just like the excitement was building in Haruyuki's own heart at that very moment.

As he took in the view of evening in central Tokyo, his time display rolled around to half past five. The predicted time for the appearance of the portal that Kuroyukihime had calculated precisely was 5:34:42. At that moment, Hermes' Cord, soaring in a waveform orbit centered on the equator, would be closest to Tokyo.

He waited impatiently for the minutes to pass until there were only five seconds to go, and he connected his Neurolinker to the Global Net.

At three seconds to go, he took a deep breath. At two seconds, he squeezed both eyes shut. And then with one second left, Haruyuki shouted in a voice that only he could hear, "Burst Link!!"

Skreeeeee!!
The noise of acceleration crashed over his body.

Opening his eyes slowly, he saw the frozen blue of the initial accelerated space. Everything—the city unfolding outside the windows, the floor and pillars of the observation deck, the smattering of tourists—had turned to transparent crystal and was still. In the form of his pink pig avatar, Haruyuki gently stepped away from his real-world body. After taking one, then two steps backward, he suddenly whirled around.

Normally, the café and merchandise shops sat in the center of the spacious observation deck, but at that moment, they had been completely wiped away; it was nothing more than deserted floor space now. However, no matter how hard he rubbed his eyes, there wasn't even a switch, much less a portal there. Haruyuki stood rooted to the spot for nearly ten seconds before heaving a sigh.

I guess the idea that a Space stage would show up was just a childish fantasy after all, he murmured to himself, and was about to plop down onto the expansive floor when—

Intense light mingled with vibration abruptly slammed into his entire body, sending him leaping upward. He lifted his face with a gasp; an enormous object was in the process of springing forth in the center of the flat space.

Stairs drawing broad arcs gradually rose up one at a time from the floor. On top of these a circular stage appeared, spinning, and then six slender pillars soared upward, carving out a regular hexagon. The transparent pillars held a pulsating blue light inside. As if in sync with this, shimmering particles rose up vertically from the centers of the pillars, stretching out almost to the ceiling, glittering beautifully.

"...This...It's the portal to Hermes' Cord...," Haruyuki muttered hoarsely, and stood up. The despair he had felt only a moment earlier was completely forgotten, and he clenched the right fist of his pig avatar tightly. So his guess hadn't been wrong. Who was it, again, who'd called it "childish fantasy"?

He raced over to the stairs, and without even a moment's concern or hesitation, he raced up the staircase on hoofed legs. *Vmm, vmm.* He slipped toward the center of the circle through gaps in the six pillars, which hummed the low song of that omnipresent vibration. For the final step, he brought his feet together and jumped. But those feet did not come back into contact with the floor.

"Whoa?!" Haruyuki yelped as he watched his own pig avatar be broken down into countless particles of light. It was actually more like returning to his origins than being broken down. As proof that his virtual proxy was being returned to essential information, the white particles were made up of minute chunks of digital code.

Immediately after he noticed this, Haruyuki felt his consciousness ascend vertically at an incredible speed. But there were absolutely no Gs accompanying the takeoff. He simply became massless light, shot through the upper structures of the Skytree, and flew off into the sky.

And there his view was completely whited out.

The cessation of sensation lasted only a few seconds.

First, Haruyuki heard the hard *clack* of his own feet touching the ground. Weight abruptly returned to his body and he involuntarily fell to one knee. In this crouching posture, he ever-so-tentatively opened his eyes.

The first thing he saw was the HP gauge in the top left of his field of view. *Huh?* he thought and stuck out both hands to stare at them. There, he found five sharp fingers on each, glittering silver. There was no doubt, these were the familiar arms of Silver Crow.

He panicked at the fact he was his duel avatar even though no duel had started, wondering if this was the lawless Unlimited Neutral Field, but he soon noticed that in the center of his green HP gauge, the English word LOCKED was displayed. Unable to immediately grasp the meaning of this, he twisted his head around for a while before deciding to put the question off for the time being. He took a deep breath, and here finally lifted his head to face forward.

"Wh-whoaaaaaa?!" he shouted and fell back onto his butt from the force of jerking his head back. Heedless of the awkward pose this put him in, he simply stared at the scene before his eyes.

The metal floor Haruyuki was sitting on ended a mere meter ahead of him. Beyond that was…sky. And clouds. The surface of the Earth below.

It should have been a familiar sight, considering that he could fly. But this was on an entirely different scale. It was so high up. Several times—no, maybe ten or more times the fifteen hundred meters that was the upper limit for the altitude Silver Crow could reach. The sky was dyed a deep ultramarine, and the clouds formed thin streaks or enormous vortexes far below, while the sea was indigo, and the land was hazy brown and green. If he fell from a place like this, he would probably be burned up from the friction with the atmosphere before he took any damage from the crashing descent.

Unconsciously, he inched backward, and once he was three or

so meters from the edge and its lack of railings, he finally expelled the breath he was holding. He stood up from his prone position and at last looked around to both sides.

The gray metal terrace appeared to be in the shape of a large circle. Following the line of it, he naturally looked back. And...

In the center of the ring-shaped terrace was a curved wall.

No, not a wall. A pillar. An extremely thick pillar, looking to be about a hundred meters in diameter, stretched up vertically. Haruyuki was standing on the broad floor at its flange base.

"Is this...Hermes' Cord?" Haruyuki's voice was barely a whisper as he stared dumbfounded at the structure, an enormous tower, a would-be residence for the gods. The metal glittered sharply like stainless steel and stretched up endlessly toward the other side of a sky that changed from ultramarine to a deep indigo, the top of the structure melting into the vanishing point, completely invisible.

The space elevator in the real world was composed of several cables made from intertwined carbon nanotubes bunched together. It was barely two meters thick, more accurately referred to as a "rope" rather than a "pillar."

But the object re-created in the Accelerated World that towered now before Haruyuki's eyes was nothing other than a pillar. It was a tower floating high up in the sky on a superhuge scale, several thousands of meters tall and a hundred meters in diameter. Why on earth would it have been expanded to this size?

He could think about it all day long and still not come to any answers, but he felt like all this was merely the details. The key point here was that there really was a Space stage. No, he probably should say that the place he was standing now was a High Altitude stage. In which case, if he climbed this enormous tower, a true space environment likely awaited...

"This is way bigger than I thought it'd be."

Haruyuki nodded firmly at the voice on his right. "Yeah. Compared with this, Skytree's a toothpick."

"Instead, though, there're almost no details on the surface. I wonder if there's an interior structure."

"But I don't see anything that looks anything like a door...Uh."

Gulp.

His entire body stiffened. Haruyuki jumped up adroitly and whirled ninety degrees to his right, shouting, "Gah?! Wh-wh-wh-wh-who-who-who-wh-wh-wh-wh-when-when—"

Who are you?! When did you get here?!

That's what he intended to cry out as a sharp challenge, but nothing more than a series of strange noises came from his mouth. The silhouette looking down on him expressionlessly from extremely close up as he did was—

Slender, dark red body. Sturdy thighs and forearms. Hands with sharp claws extended. Sleek tail flicking.

And from the mask with pointed ears sticking up from toward the back of the head and eyes shining silver, there was no doubt that this was a close-range duel avatar, one of the strongest Haruyuki had come across.

"P...P-P-P-P-Pard?! Wh-wh-what are you d-doing here?!"

"Pard," aka Blood Leopard, level-six Burst Linker belonging to the Red Legion Prominence, popped her shoulders up and replied, "Same reason you're here."

"Huh..."

His interlocutor was quite calm, so Haruyuki also finally calmed down a little and belatedly got ahold of the situation.

Traveling to this place most certainly wasn't a privilege that had been given to Haruyuki alone. Any Burst Linker who learned of the news of the placement of the social cameras in Hermes' Cord could consider the possibility of a new stage being added to the Accelerated World, and then guess that the time and location of the portal's appearance would be here, and then be able to arrive as he had.

He was a little happy that another player had had the same foolhardy thought as he had and actually come all the way to

Skytree like this, and a grin broke out across his face. But he soon arrived at another thought and his whole body froze.

And that was that it wouldn't have been at all strange for one new avatar after another to appear there at that moment. He whirled his head around hurriedly at their surroundings, but he didn't get any sense that a third person was about to show up.

As Haruyuki freaked out that it was too late to do anything, Pard spoke to him in a voice that was the tiniest bit exasperated.

"The reason you came through the portal first is because you dared to accelerate right there on the observation deck. I dove in the toilet on the first floor, so I was a little late. I'm pretty sure anyone else is going to be putting priority on keeping from being outed in the real, so we should have a few minutes' leeway still."

"O-oh. You did? Oh, right, I guess…" Feeling a belated terror at his own recklessness, Haruyuki now greeted Pard properly. "H-hello. Good to see you."

He bowed his head at Leopard, who waved her right hand dismissively and continued. "I am forever in your debt. I can only offer my apologies for communicating via nothing but mail after events took place…"

These words were in thanks for how very much Pard had helped in resolving the enormous predicament Haruyuki had been trapped in two months earlier. The leopard-headed avatar shrugged her shoulders and responded at unusual length.

"NP. You really helped me out that time, too. The info you gave me was really useful in finding the security hole at Akiba BG. But right now"—she patted Haruyuki on the back, urging him to move—"we should use this advantage, since we have it. Let's take a look around the pillar."

"O-okay!"

As he walked, Haruyuki felt a keen relief at the fact that Blood Leopard was the avatar who had shown up after he did, since they shared such a history. They might have been members of different Legions, but they could still get along. If it had been Frost

Horn, he would no doubt have grabbed Haruyuki from behind without saying a word and tossed him down to the Earth below.

They cut across the flange, about twenty meters wide, approached the pillar of Hermes' Cord itself, and even touched it, but the glittering alloy-like surface was unmoved. Despite details like seams in steel plating, there were no handholds that would allow a person to scale it.

Pard scratched at the pillar with her razor-like claws and discovered that it was too hard for her to make a mark on. Curious, she walked around to the right, with Haruyuki trailing along behind her. The pillar diameter was at least a hundred meters, so following the curved surface all the way around was no mean feat. When the backside of the transport device finally came into sight, Haruyuki noticed something and cried out.

"Ah! There's something there!"

He raced over, footfalls clacking.

At first glance, the objects appeared to be cars or boats. The streamlined vehicles, six or so meters in length, sat neatly in a line on an angled platform at the base of the pillar, glaring up at the peak of Hermes' Cord. Ten of them.

The vehicles had no roofs; the seating area was completely open. At the very front was an operator's seat for one person behind a transparent windshield. Behind that were two rows of two-person seats. Instead of tires, the vehicles were equipped with four large discs on the bottom, which seemed to be some kind of propulsive device. The smooth lines of the slender bodies created a form that hearkened back to the original meaning of the word *shuttle*.

"Wh-what is this…" Muttering, Haruyuki climbed up to the platform and approached the vehicle on the left end with a "1" painted on its side. The blunt iron body was cold and silent, no sign of fire in the engine. He stretched out a timid hand, poked at the smooth line of the door area, and instantly:

Beebong. A purple holowindow popped up. After a moment's

surprise, he peered at it. Pard, beside him, also brought her face in.

At the very top of the window sat a row of text in an inorganic font: 3D 18H 25M 18S (JST). These numbers, indicating a day, hour, minute, and second, were obviously some kind of timer.

"Hmm. So if this is a countdown, then it'll reach zero three days, eighteen hours, and twenty-five minutes from now...so at noon sharp on Sunday."

After Blood Leopard spoke, Haruyuki followed with the thought, "And then what will happen...?"

But instead of replying, Pard pointed at the lower part of the window with a finger very like the toe on a feline's paw. A short sentence was also displayed there: WILL YOU DRIVE ME? And below that, there was only a YES button. He understood the meaning of the simple English question, but even so, Haruyuki hesitated about what he should do.

"If you don't push it, I will," Pard, ever quick to impatience, whispered in his ear.

"Oh! I–I'm pushing it!" he replied, flustered. He raised his right hand, resolved himself, and touched the YES button.

Instantly, a short fanfare effect rang out, and the English text changed: YOU ARE MY DRIVER.

A few seconds later, the row of characters changed shape once more, leaving behind only the lone word RESERVED. At the same time, an object appeared, as if oozing out of the surface of the window.

It was a transparent blue card. In addition to the mark "1," it showed the same countdown as in the window. The instant Haruyuki took it, the next, and final, phenomenon occurred.

The streamlined machine transformed from a body color of dull iron to dazzling silver, making a noise as it did so. Haruyuki quickly realized that the shade, almost that of a mirror, was exactly the same as his—that is to say, Silver Crow's—armor.

"I get it," Pard said, as if satisfied, and stepped over to the shuttle with "2" painted on it. She touched the body, the window popped up, and she clicked the YES button without hesitation. When she deftly snatched up between two fingers the card that appeared, the vehicle body this time turned a deep red, dyed to match the color of Blood Leopard's armor.

Haruyuki walked over to Pard, still holding his card, and asked his question anew: "Uh, um…So you and I are registered as the drivers of these cars or boats or whatever they are…I basically get that. But what's this countdown? There're still more than three days left on it."

"Obvious. These shuttles won't move until the timer reaches zero at exactly noon on Sunday."

He nodded in an accepting way at this clear response before his next question popped up.

"R-right…B-but why such a long time…"

Here, Pard, rather unusually, opened the mouth hidden in the lower part of her bullet-shaped mask and laughed, sharp fangs glinting. "That's obvious, too. The three and a half days we're being given are a grace period to get a driver and four crew members ready for each of the ten shuttles. At noon on Sunday, we're going to slam our feet down on the accelerators and head for the top of this pillar. In other words…" She pointed with her uplifted right hand in the direction of the distant peak, and then the crimson leopard-headed avatar said, almost singing:

"We obtained the right to participate in the Hermes' Cord Race."

It took a full five seconds or so before Haruyuki understood the meaning of those words.

"Then…that means…the finish line is the top of this tower, which means…s-s-space?!" he cried, his voice practically turned inside out, and Pard nodded.

"Of course."

But before she could say anything further, they heard the sound of transit coming from the opposite side of the pillar. The

Burst Linkers who had accelerated in the basement had likely reached the portal of the observation deck.

After a swish of her long tail, Pard touched Haruyuki's back and whispered, "It would be best if we disappeared before they found us."

Indeed, since there were only ten shuttles, the limit for the number of people who could still register as drivers was eight. Having those who would inevitably be left out come along saying the privilege should be decided in a duel would be nothing more than a hassle.

"I—I guess so." Haruyuki agreed for now, pushing back the surprise in his heart, and her next utterance came flying into his ears.

"Once you release the acceleration, wait at the door to the parking lot on the ground floor. I'll take you to Suginami on my bike."

"Eee!" He froze up again. In the back of his mind, the violent power of the large electric bike Leopard rode sprang vividly back to life.

However, naturally unable to say, *No, that's fine, I'm good,* or anything like that, Haruyuki simply bobbed his head. "Th-th-thank you; that would be great."

"NP."

And then the pair shouted the command together.

"Burst Out!"

Meeting Pard in the real again after such a long time, she was fortunately—or perhaps unfortunately—not in the maid's uniform of the cake shop, but a tight-fitting T-shirt and slim jeans.

His eyes involuntarily strayed to the unexpected volume pushing out against the tight fabric, a volume imperceptible when she was wearing the billowing apron. Still with no expression on her face, Pard pulled an extra helmet out of the under-seat compartment, plopped it on Haruyuki's head, and straddled the motorcycle. After fastening the buckle himself this time, he hurriedly climbed up onto the seat behind her and timidly wrapped his arms around the slim waist before him.

At first, he restrained himself to the utmost in terms of the strength he put into those arms, but the instant the in-wheel motors roared to life in the bike as it left the Skytree parking:

"Aaaaaah!"

Just as he had before, Haruyuki couldn't help but cry out and cling to Pard as hard as he could. That said, it was all he could do to endure the extreme stops and starts at each and every red light, and he didn't really have the mental breathing space to pay attention to any sensations other than the ones that let him know he was still holding on.

They passed from Sumida Ward through Okachimachi and Ochanomizu, and right around when they were coming out of Iidabashi, Pard's voice reached Haruyuki's ears.

"It's five till six right now. You got time?"

"Uh, y-yeah."

The curfew set by Haruyuki's mother was nine o'clock, so he still had time. He couldn't say anything about whether she allowed him, still in junior high, to be out until that somewhat inappropriate hour because she had faith in him as her son or because it was too much of a hassle to enforce an earlier curfew. If he broke curfew once in a big way, he would probably find out the answer to whether she would get mad at him or not, but he didn't quite have the courage for that, and so he replied, *"I've got about two hours."*

Pard then said, so very casually, *"If I had tea for that long of a time, I'd melt away."*

Huh? T-tea?

He didn't even have time to really have that thought before the large bike pulled into a fast-food place along the road, turn signal flashing.

In the last eight months, Haruyuki had gone into this restaurant more than twelve times with Kuroyukihime and once with Sky Raker. Nonetheless, he had not the slightest air of being used to such a situation and broke into a cold sweat, anxious about the spotlight of *What is even up with such a mismatched couple?* most certainly being shone on him.

Telling himself that he was being too self-conscious, that no one was even paying attention to them at all, he sat down facing Blood Leopard in a booth and tried to block out the other customers from his mind by focusing on the teriyaki burger meal Blood Leopard had treated him to.

For a brief moment, he thought he might succeed somehow.

And then Pard pulled a red XSB cable from a pouch on her belt, leaned forward, and stabbed one end of it into Haruyuki's Neurolinker. With no expression on her face, she jammed the other end into her own.

Not able to hide from the wired connection warning that appeared in his field of view or the sight of the junior and senior high students in the shop very obviously staring at him and whispering to one another, Haruyuki ended up shrinking into himself, a total mess, cold sweat dripping down his face and all over his body.

It was clear that Pard paid absolutely no attention to customs such as the length of a couple's direct-connect cable being an indication of their progress in dating, and Haruyuki, unable to liberate himself from such concerns, asked in neurospeak that was almost a shriek, *"Oh! Uh, uh, um, wh-wh-why direct?"*

Her reply was quick and simple.

"So we can talk while we eat."

"...Right" was the only reply Haruyuki could give.

Pard displayed some serious technique in talking via the cable while digging into her hamburger as advertised. This seemed easy in principle, but there was a real risk of biting your tongue if you accidentally tried to speak with your mouth.

"Do you know how to dive into the stage for the race on Sunday?"

"Huh?" Haruyuki stopped chewing the fry in his mouth to answer the abrupt question. *"We don't just use the portal at Skytree again?"*

"*No need. The card you got when you registered as a driver is an item called a Transporter. It'll simultaneously move a maximum of ten directing Burst Linkers.*"

"*W-wow…So then, we just get together in Suginami and use this, and we can go straight to Hermes' Cord?*"

"*Yes.*"

This was a huge relief. Because if, hypothetically, Kuroyuki-hime ended up taking part in the race, it was just too big of a risk for her to connect even for an instant to an external net in distant Sumida Ward, bound as she was by the sudden-death rules as a level niner.

After breathing a sigh of relief and biting into his hamburger, Haruyuki felt a rudimentary question rise belatedly to the surface. Ever since he had jumped into the portal at Skytree, he had been drifting along where the current took him, but the real issue—

"*The real issue here is why are we suddenly racing? Those machines were prepared not by any player but by the system, which means the admin side of Brain Burst. It's been eight months already since I became a Burst Linker, but I don't think I've seen a single game master event like this.*"

At Haruyuki's inquiry, Pard thought for approximately half a second before replying, "*It's true that the BB admin normally never makes you feel their presence. But when there's a large-scale update in the Accelerated World, there're sometimes one-off events like this one. Like the year before last, when Tokyo Grand Castle opened…*"

Grand Castle was a large theme park in the Bay Area. It ended up being a hot topic, this fortress city like something out of medieval Europe built with actual rocks, daring to take up the theme of "reality" during the heyday of full-dive technology.

"*The day the social camera net started operating there, there was this event in the Accelerated World where you had to fight through swarms of monsters in the city and try to get the throne in the castle. My team was so close when we rubbed up against a large gang*" *from the blue team and we all went down. If that jerk Horn shows up this time, I'm going to let him have it."*

Flames roared to life in Pard's eyes, and Haruyuki unconsciously shrank into himself before managing to get a reply out.

"R-right, I get it. So then this race is…like an event to celebrate the addition of a new stage? Which means that the race only happens once…?"

"Pretty much."

In that case, he was incredibly lucky to have been able to reserve one of only ten machines. After shouting, *Mega lucky!* in his heart, Haruyuki hurriedly banished that thought. He definitely hadn't gone to Hermes' Cord to obtain the right to participate in an open event. He had set his sights on the pinnacle of the space elevator because he had something he really needed to tell *Her*, Sky Raker.

Well, there is that.

Thinking there were other things he should at least know as basic knowledge, Haruyuki timidly let a question flow through the direct circuit. *"Um…Pard. So like in the race, uh, if you come in first or second or whatever, is there some kind of—"*

"Of course there is." Blood Leopard nodded readily, not letting him get to the end of the question. *"Probably some burst points. Or an Enhanced Armament or some other item. Should be some kind of prize."*

"W-wow, really?"

Although he tried to feign calm, the huge gulping motion he made with his throat apparently gave him away, and Pard grinned. Neatly folding up the paper wrapper of the hamburger she had finished in no time flat, she said with utter calm, *"Best not to get your hopes too high. It definitely won't be enough points to disrupt the power balance between the Legions. And more than that…"* Here, she paused for a moment before she, the senior member of Prominence, shook the plait hanging down from her head and asked, *"Will all five members of your Legion be in the race?"*

"*Huh?...Ummm, the shuttle holds five people, so...*" Haruyuki, about to nod his agreement, forced his head to halt.

No matter how well they got along, or how she gave him rides on her motorcycle and treated him to hamburgers, Pard was, in the end, not on his side. She was a key member of the Red Legion, which might one day come up against the Black Legion. What was he doing carelessly telling someone like this about the movements of Kuroyukihime, who was bound by the rules of sudden death?

Perhaps having immediately seen through this hesitation on the part of Haruyuki, Pard quickly shook her head lightly. "*I'm not thinking of using this opportunity to take the Black King's head or anything. And HP gauges are locked during the event, so, I mean, that's not even possible.*"

"*L-locked...?*" Repeating the word, Haruyuki finally remembered. When he had been sent to Hermes' Cord earlier, the lone word LOCKED had indeed been clearly stamped on his own HP gauge. "*Uh, umm...So that means that no one can take damage or give damage during the event?*"

Although Pard did make a show of thinking about this question momentarily, she soon nodded. "*Yes.*"

"*Then why do we need four people for the shuttle crew? I figured we needed them to attack the other teams or defend or whatever...*"

"*Yes to that, too. The shuttle itself'll probably have an HP gauge, and once that drops to zero, you're destroyed. It was like that at the Grand Castle event. A game where each team carried an orb they were given, up to the throne on the top floor of the castle. The idea was that the players didn't die, but the orb lost HP in attacks by the monsters or other teams.*"

Haruyuki nodded at Blood Leopard's words, impressed. With that setup, even in the rather lukewarm situation where their HP gauges were protected, the race could end up being very hot indeed.

"*I get it...So that's how it works. If that's it, then I think all five members of our Legion will be in the race. But...why do you ask?*"

Haruyuki turned a puzzled look on Pard, and in an extremely rare occurrence, she seemed to be struggling with what to say.

But the hesitation disappeared in a mere second.

"There are two people who are very important to me in the Accelerated World." The quiet thought came through the red cable. *"One is the king I serve. Someone I want to protect no matter what happens. And the other is my eternal rival. We became Burst Linkers at basically the same time, and we've fought countless duels. 'Strato Shooter,' 'ICBM'…"*

Haruyuki instantly grasped who those two names referred to. *"…Sky Raker…?"* he murmured, and Blood Leopard nodded gently.

"I was so happy when I heard she'd come back. But she's only participating in the battles to defend Territories, so I haven't seen her yet."

"Oh…You haven't? Right, you haven't."

Currently, the Red Legion Prominence and the Black Legion Nega Nebulus were in the middle of a cease-fire of an indefinite term. Thus, Pard, a senior Red member, would have no reason to take part in an attack on the Suginami area.

Haruyuki took a deep breath and, in a move that was unusual for him, looked straight into the eyes of his conversation partner before saying, *"The truth is, I want to bring Sky Raker to Hermes' Cord somehow, for my own reasons. Even if she's not onboard with the whole thing, I'm going to try hard to persuade her to come. I'm sure you'll be able to see her on Sunday."*

"That so?" Her response was brief, but a faint smile rose up on Blood Leopard's lips, and she slowly, deeply nodded. *"Thanks, Silver Crow. I'm glad we could talk like this…Maybe it won't just be the two of us, maybe all three."*

Unfortunately, Haruyuki had no idea what she meant by that. Thus, like an idiot, he just asked. But…

"S-sorry? What…Who would that be?"

Not telling.

Instead of those words, it seemed, Pard yanked the direct cable out.

Back on the bike, she saw him to Suginami, and after Haruyuki watched her fade into the night until her taillights disappeared, he started thinking absently.

There were about a thousand Burst Linkers in total. And nearly all of them lived in the metropolis of Tokyo. It was a number that very much did not allow you to remember all of their names, and the majority of them had a relationship that consisted of single-mindedly taking points from one another. And yet if you fought for long enough, at some point, relationships other than "enemy" started to develop. When he thought about it now, the first time he met his now-priceless tag team partner Takumu—Cyan Pile— it had been as genuine enemies...

In the back of his mind, the faces rose up and disappeared again: those of his Legion companions, starting with Kuroyuki-hime; then friends like Niko and Pard, his rival Ash Roller; and even Frost Horn and that gang.

Aiming for level ten as a Burst Linker was essentially equal to continually kicking down other Burst Linkers. Most likely, this was exactly the thing the mysterious developer was aiming for: Make a thousand young people fight among themselves, and select just one perfected player.

But even if that were so, even the developer couldn't exactly stop them from developing feelings for one another rather than hatred during the process. The fact that Blood Leopard could care about Sky Raker like that, a Burst Linker she had never been on the same team with, was proof of that.

I want to be like that, too. The feeling swept over Haruyuki as he walked toward his house. *No matter how badly beaten I get, even if I'm so frustrated I could cry, I still won't hate my opponent. Because I love this game and the Accelerated World.*

Because I think I'm happier than anyone that I get to be a Burst Linker.

Really? Is that really all?

A voice abruptly questioned him.

At the same time, several shadows quickly flashed across the screen in the back of his mind. A rust-colored avatar like a steel framework. A layered avatar, thin jet-black planks lined up. And the no-longer-extant dusk-colored avatar with the spherical visor and long talons. The members of the Acceleration Research Society, a group that saw Brain Burst not as a fighting game, but rather as a tool for thought acceleration, and focused only on the acquisition and use of points.

Over these last two months, any activities they might have carried out had been entirely under the radar. But there was no way that they had simply vanished. They were almost certainly lying in wait somewhere in the Accelerated World watching vigilantly, hostilely, waiting for the chance to invade again.

ARE YOU GOING TO LET THEM? CAN YOU FORGET THE TERRIBLE PAIN THEY CAUSED YOU, YOUR FRIENDS, THE HATRED IN YOUR HEART FOR THEM, AND HOW THEY MADE YOU SUFFER?

Haruyuki didn't notice that the voice echoing in the back of his mind had at some point stopped being his own and taken on a dark, warped metallic quality. Scowling at the throbbing sensation in the center of his back, he stepped briskly onto the site of his condo building.

IT'S ONLY NATURAL TO HATE GUYS LIKE THAT. IT'S ONLY NATURAL TO STRIKE THEM DOWN WITH THAT HATE. RELEASE ALL THE

RAGE, THE RESENTMENT, THE HATRED, AND DESTROY THEM. YOU
HAVE THE POWER TO DO IT. THE POWER TO TEAR OFF THEIR LIMBS,
DEVOUR THEIR FLESH, DRINK THEM DRY OF BLOOD. THAT'S RIGHT.
EAT THEM. EAT THEM. EAT THEM. EAT THEM. EAT—

"Shut up!!" he cried in a strangled voice, hanging his head low.
He stopped in front of the main entrance to the shopping mall,
and residents of the buildings and various shoppers went around
him as if he were just another obstacle.

Among the countless pairs of shoes flowing to both sides, he
felt like he saw talons glittering the purple of dusk and squeezed
both eyes shut tight. In his head, he told himself firmly, *If they
show up again, I'll fight them. But it won't be because I hate them.
It'll be because I love the Accelerated World and because I believe
in bonds other than hostility there. I'll fight to protect that.*

REALLY?

The voice left this word like a creaking laugh before receding.
The throbbing in his back finally faded and disappeared.

He let out a long breath and rubbed palms soaked with sweat
along his trousers before he set out with heavy feet, head still
hanging, for his deserted condo.

5

"Hey, hey, heeeeeey!!"

The shout echoed throughout the battlefield, accompanied by the throaty roar of the V-twin engine. A high-pitched squeal, then another shout. "Cheap wall like this'll never stop a master like me!!"

"No way?!" Haruyuki looked around, panicked. The discolored buildings characteristic of a Weathered stage crumbled here and there, and a barricade had been made of the rubble. He and Takumu—who was now fighting a little ways off—had brought the buildings down. Taking advantage of the extremely brittle nature of the terrain particular to this stage, they had focused on smashing buildings and blocking whatever roads there were.

Their objective was to reduce the mobility of the motorcycle-using Ash Roller, a member of the attacking team in the Territories. They had succeeded; there was no longer a way to get from here on the front line to the base Sky Raker was protecting in the rear—or at least, there shouldn't have been.

"Wh-where are you riding?!" Haruyuki searched desperately for the origin of the burbling roar of the engine. A few seconds later, he found it. But unable to move immediately, he simply stood bolt upright, mouth gaping, totally open.

The gunmetal American motorcycle was moving from right to left on the opposite side of the four-lane main road. But he was going far too slowly. And it wasn't to avoid the rubble blocking the road—given that the rubble was piled nearly two meters high, avoiding it was impossible right from the get-go—but rather because *it was being carried.*

The enormous bike, complete with rider, was up on the right shoulder of a small avatar only half its size, laboriously stepping over the rubble-pile barricades. Ash Roller straddled the seat of the bike swaying on that shoulder and simply raced the engine.

"Th-there's no point in racing the engine!!" After throwing everything he had into this unconscious rejoinder, Haruyuki finally realized that this was not the time for staring. Their aim was the base beyond the mountain of rubble. If they occupied that, things would get annoying.

"A-as if I'd let you!!" he muttered and charged toward the opposite side of the main road. When he did, the small avatar bearing the motorcycle shot a glance at him and—

"My brother Ash! Go on without meeeee!" Spitting out this ridiculously cool line, he heaved the bike forward. For his size, his strength was incredible.

The large American bike bearing Ash Roller, who had apparently at some point gotten a younger-brother-type companion, soared over the pinnacle of the barricade, the high-pitched sound of the exhaust ringing out remarkably loudly.

"Your heart's giga-buuuuuurning, yo!!" He hit the asphalt with his usual nonsensical shouting and took off at high speed, white smoke rising up from the rear wheel.

Saturday, June 8, five thirty PM. They were in the middle of a three-on-three team battle to defend Suginami area number three. Kuroyukihime and Chiyuri were taking a break, so on the Nega Nebulus side, it was Haruyuki, Takumu, and Sky Raker. Against them on the attacking side was a three-person team from the Green Legion Great Wall, led by Ash Roller.

There was a difference in the level makeup, with eight, five, and five for Haruyuki's team, and five, five, and three for the enemy, but Brain Burst was the type of game where if you let your guard down even just one time with this kind of gap, the whole situation could easily be upended. Gritting his teeth and vowing that Ash breaking through the barricade would be the man's only triumph this match, Haruyuki went to chase after the speeding bike. However…

"Ain't gonna let mew get through here!!"

Accompanied by this shout—which Haruyuki couldn't decide was an attempt at creating a character or the kid's actual voice—a shadow flew down before him. The avatar who had been carrying Ash Roller's motorcycle.

His name was Bush Utan. Level three with dark grass-colored armor. He was a few centimeters shorter than Silver Crow, but he had a toughness about him that kept you from really noticing that. The reason for this was his abnormally developed arms. They were so long that if he was leaning forward, his hands very nearly scraped along the surface of the ground, making his overall silhouette reminiscent of a type of primate, but still, he was definitely not an opponent to take lightly.

"Anyone who says something like that obviously doesn't have it in him to stop me!" Haruyuki replied, glaring cautiously at the large arms turned toward him. He bent forward, aiming for a decisive, super-low-altitude dash.

Bush Utan had poured all his potential into those enormous arms. He was an avatar that specialized in brute strength. If Haruyuki took a punch from him, the damage would be enough to blow away the two-level difference between them, but Utan didn't have much in the way of speed. And anyway, he had no intention of fighting here.

Racing along, nearly scraping the ground himself as he closed the gap in an instant, Haruyuki brought his enemy's focus downward before leaping up with all his might. He vibrated his wings for a mere instant to preserve his special-attack gauge, so that rather than flying, he soared over his enemy's head in a long jump.

Utan hurriedly stretched both arms up above his head, but Haruyuki was far beyond his grasp. *You should've closed in on me yourself to reduce the number of options I had,* Haruyuki remarked tangentially in his head. The distance between opponents wasn't something you had, it was something you actively controlled—

"Hng! Wha?!" The cry of shock slipping out of Silver Crow's mouth was drowned out by a thick battle cry.

"Ooh ho ho hoooo! I'm not letting mew gooooo!!"

In some incomprehensible turn, Bush Utan had stretched his arms out. He hadn't dislocated his joints or anything like that; no, he had in fact elastically extended his arms to nearly three times their original length, and now grabbed tightly on to Haruyuki's ankles with his enormous palms.

"Hnngaaaaah!"

Utan was about to slam Haruyuki down onto the ground as hard as he could, so Haruyuki deployed his wings fully in the opposite direction and released every bit of propulsive force he had.

"Nnngh!"

The state of equilibrium was momentary. No matter how great Utan's physical strength might have been, weight-wise, he was in the light class. With the primate-type avatar dangling from both legs, Haruyuki ascended blindly. As he thought about how he would just carry the other avatar like this and take out Ash Roller—

"Ooh ho?! Mew're scaring me!!"

He heard a pathetic scream, and his flight speed dropped with a jerk. Hurriedly looking down, he saw that Utan had removed just his left hand from Haruyuki's feet and was using that hand to grab on to a building's roof railing instead. His arms were now stretched out to the limit, so it was almost like an avatar had been fastened to the middle of a long rope.

"Hey! L-let go!"

"N-no mway!"

Haruyuki flapped his wings fervently, but the power with which his left ankle was being held didn't appear to slacken in the least. Takumu's Pile perhaps could have cut him free of Utan's arm, but he seemed to be still in the middle of a pitched battle against the third member of the enemy team a little ways off, judging from the clashes Haruyuki could hear.

With no other choice, Haruyuki continued with the midair tug-of-war as he raced his eyes over the area, looking to the west side of the main road. Instantly and unconsciously, he opened his mouth. "Crap…!"

The large American motorcycle had already raced ahead a hundred meters or more and was charging right at the small plaza at the end of the street. In that plaza stood a tall flagpole in the center of a circle emitting a violet light. The black of the flag there was the proof that this was Haruyuki's team's base.

The base was a spot existing in each Territory Duel Field where members of the team occupying the base could recharge their special-attack gauges over and over within the circle. Which was to say, the Brain Burst Territory Battle was nothing more than a fight in which teams pushed the front line forward while occupying base after base and taking down their opponents' bases.

The base Ash Roller was aiming for was currently being guarded by no one but Sky Raker. As a level eighter, her power was obviously the real deal, but because of her strange fighting style, there was a big difference in whether she had the advantage or not depending on the enemy's affinities.

And from where Haruyuki was standing, he was forced to conclude that because wheelchair-user Sky Raker and motorcycle-user Ash Roller were of the same lineage, Sky Raker would be at a disadvantage here. When it came to performance as a vehicular Enhanced Armament, the motorcycle was obviously superior in each and every way.

The motorcycle faced the sleek silver wheelchair plopped down in the front of the plaza and the graceful female-shaped avatar occupying it, and then it charged, roaring thunderously.

"Masterrrrrrr!" The skull-headed rider's cry was for some reason mixed with tears. "I!...Today for sure! I'm going to go... beyond you, Master...!!"

Up in the air, Haruyuki's jaw dropped. Sky Raker was indeed Ash's teacher and his "parent," but a line like that was something you only shouted after numerous twists and turns, in the final moments of battle. Although today was actually already the third time Ash Roller's team had taken part in the Territory attack, this would be the first time that parent and child faced off in direct contest.

Raker in her wheelchair grinned beneath her wide-brimmed hat and shook her long sky-blue hair. "You still have so much to learn, Ash."

And then she stretched her left hand straight out in front of her, turned her palm toward the sky, and curled a finger up in invitation. *Come.*

To this Ash replied with a sharp "Hyaaah!" He jumped up vertically from his seat and stood with his right foot on the handlebars and his left on the back end of the seat. He rode the motorcycle almost like a surfboard; the name of this unique technique was V-Twin Punch, so named by the rider himself.

Sky Raker didn't appear to panic in the slightest seeing this, but Haruyuki was already grinding his teeth once again. This was a bad situation for her, wasn't it? Because given that she couldn't stand up from her wheelchair, Sky Raker's hands could no longer reach Ash Roller's body. And if she attacked the bike with her bare hands, she'd be the one taking the damage.

"Master! Giga thanks for everythiiiiiiing!!"

The sole of his boot opened the throttle all the way, and the motorcycle jumped into a final acceleration, spewing flames from the muffler. The instant the massive gray front tire was about to deal a serious blow to the wheelchair—

Raker's left hand caressed the silver wheel beneath it so fast it was nearly blurred. Sparks flew up from the ground, and the wheelchair shot backward with intense force.

Impossible! You won't be able to get away! Haruyuki shouted in his heart at Sky Raker, who was a teacher to himself as well. The wheels had to be turned by hand to make the chair move, and while the power it held for sprints was incredible indeed due to its extremely light weight, it could continue at that pace for only a moment. Once she had fallen back, the bike would quickly catch up with her and send her flying.

Or so Haruyuki expected as he caught his breath. But at the same time—

Sky Raker stretched her entire body forward with wonderful abandon, avoiding the front tire, and pressed her right hand onto the bike's handlebar. She grabbed only the brake lever.

It looked like such a casual gesture, but the power it contained was apparently very much more than that, and a flood of sparks gushed from the front rotor disc. And what would happen to the motorcycle when only the front brake was locked with this kind of force?

"Oh! Whoa?!"

Even before Ash Roller managed to cry out, he was rising up at the force of the sudden deceleration and flying through the air along with his bike, wheels racing meaninglessly, before crashing into the wall of a distant building.

This impact seemed to be more than the Enhanced Armament of the motorcycle could endure, and the whole thing burst into fierce flames with a *whoosh* before exploding into pieces.

However, Ash Roller himself had, perhaps fortunately, been standing in the seat, and was not caught up in the explosion, but rather thrown high into the air.

"Noooooooooooo!" Screaming, he reached the peak of his parabola, stopped for a moment, and then started to drop back down—with Sky Raker pushing her wheelchair into a sprint once more, aiming to stop directly below him.

"So very much to learn."

Grinning as she rendered this assessment, she thrust the palm of her left hand up perpendicularly with such force as to practically scorch the air. This open-handed punch beautifully caught the back of the rider's black leather jacket, causing such an impact that it reached even Haruyuki, up in the far-off sky.

In addition to the damage from falling from so high up, he had also taken a critical hit to the center of his body, the combination of which easily knocked Ash Roller's HP gauge down to nothing.

"You are the master...Mercy, Tera-nothing." Leaving these mysterious words behind, the skull rider avatar exploded and scattered.

Watching Sky Raker as she brushed her hands off, Haruyuki and Bush Utan murmured at the same time.

"S-so strong..."

"Meah's too strong..."

They gasped as their eyes met. Sky Raker had so wonderfully repelled Ash and guarded the base, so there was no longer any real point in continuing this midair tug-of-war.

Haruyuki said nothing as he flapped his wings forcefully, abruptly using up the remainder of his special-attack gauge. The upward force he generated made both of Utan's arms creak alarmingly.

"N-no meoway! Burn, biceeeeeps!"

The left arm hanging onto the railing of the building and the right holding Haruyuki's ankle swelled up and pulled with terrifying brute strength, bringing Haruyuki back down.

In that instant, Haruyuki changed the orientation of his silver wings by one hundred eighty degrees and readied himself for a sudden dive. Inevitably, Utan ended up being yanked toward Silver Crow with the strength of his own arms.

"W-wait, meo—!"

The *w* disappeared in the sound of a ferocious dive kick hitting its mark.

The two avatars fused into a single lump and crashed to the

Earth. Utan released Haruyuki's ankle from its imprisonment with the impact, and in the close-range fight that necessarily followed—the zero-range fight, to be precise—he was no match yet for Haruyuki.

Having had his HP shaved away in the scrum, Utan disappeared from the battle, leaving a parting threat like the lead in a gangster movie. "I-I'll get you back for this tomeowrrooooooooow!!"

...Tomorrow?

Haruyuki had a bad feeling about that somehow, but he tossed it up on a shelf for the time being and rushed to the front line to offer Takumu backup.

Fifteen minutes later, real-world time.

The five members of Nega Nebulus gathered in the center of the field that served as the setting for their last battle and commended one another on their hard work. They had once again managed to thoroughly safeguard Suginami areas one through three for the week.

Sitting on a nearby lump of concrete, Haruyuki felt a pleasant exhaustion as he exhaled deeply. In time, he spoke to Sky Raker, who was next to him. "But still...I never even thought of that sort of attack strategy with Ash Roller's bike."

In the past, Haruyuki had met victory against Ash Roller by lifting the rear wheel of the motorcycle and thus removing its propulsive force, but grabbing on to the brake lever while the bike was in motion, and thereby sending it flying, was way more stylish, speedy, and, more than anything, totally cool.

But Raker shook her head as she laughed quietly. "Unfortunately, you can only use that technique when Ash is standing on the bike."

"Oh...R-right..."

Indeed, the rider's hands normally would not leave the handlebars. He hummed his understanding, and this time, Kuroyukihime uttered with a rueful laugh, "Before that, though, to lay a hand on a bike that is accelerating full throttle, you have to synchronize yourself with its speed using a power sprint like Raker, or else you'll end up the one damaged instead."

"Oh...R-right...I guess..." Haruyuki dropped his head and Chiyuri and Takumu raised their voices in unrestrained laughter.

The jet-black avatar laughed briefly once more before adding, "But, well...It could be that you flying at full speed can do the same thing as Raker's dash. Check into it."

"Right!" Haruyuki assented enthusiastically, and his Legion leader looked around at her subordinates.

"If there's nothing else that needs consideration, let's discuss tomorrow," she said. "I believe a text message from Haruyuki outlining the general concept has already gone around, but perhaps we could have the explanation from him again here."

"U-understood." Hurrying to his feet, Haruyuki stepped out in front of the four sitting avatars and began to give an overview of the big event on Sunday—the Hermes' Cord Race—first of all talking about how there was no need to go all the way to Skytree. If they got together at Haruyuki's and directed, he said, the transporter card item would take them all to the bottom station of the space elevator.

Second, he described how Silver Crow had registered as the driver of the first shuttle, and since he was unable to change this, the other four would have to be the crew. In other words, they would be staffing the shuttle to guard it or to attack rival teams.

Finally, he spoke to how their HP gauges would be locked during the race, so there would be no risk for the level-nine Black Lotus.

After he had somehow managed to get this far, albeit stammering the whole time, Haruyuki suddenly hesitated. He couldn't decide whether or not he should tell them about the fact that Blood Leopard from Prominence had registered with the second shuttle and that she had said she was eager to see Sky Raker again. He quickly came to the conclusion that he would stay quiet about it for now, since the only ones who could understand the way things worked between Leopard and Raker were Leopard and Raker.

Thus, Haruyuki expelled a deep breath and finished up with, "That's all!"

"Nice work," Kuroyukihime responded quickly, and stood up again after Haruyuki sat back down. "This was also touched on in Haruyuki's mail. There was the Grand Castle Attack race event the year before last. I know Raker understands this, but..." The Black King stopped speaking momentarily and made the blade of her right hand sing through the air. "At that time, I was in hiding from the assassins of the other kings and not connecting to the Global Net at all, so I was unable to take part, which...I do deeply regret."

"Absolutely. I know I sent waves of resentment from the top of Old Tokyo Tower all the way to the Grand Castle." Sky Raker laughed gracefully, and Kuroyukihime nodded firmly, while the remaining three Legion members sat up straighter with a start. Not one of them would have been surprised if Scary Master Raker's ire had actually managed to take down several duel avatars.

"At any rate, all of this is to say: I want to completely wipe away my regrets from two years ago in tomorrow's race. Takumu and Chiyuri have both good-naturedly agreed to take part, and it was Haruyuki who realized that a new stage might appear and went all the way to distant Skytree to get the right for us to take part. It would be a true shame if we were to waste this gift."

"N-no, that's—" Haruyuki hurriedly shook his head and hands. "It was just this idea that sorta popped into my head...You were the one who guessed all the stuff about when and where the portal would appear..."

"That idea popping up was key. Those ten spots filled up quickly, and the majority of the registered teams apparently bought the information at a high price from NPC shops in the Unlimited Neutral Field. Only you, and maybe one or two others, realized the possibility on your own."

"H-huh…Is that what happened…"

Perhaps the expected timing of the portal appearance in the NPC information was slightly delayed, and that was why Haruyuki, who had figured things out from zero, and Pard, who probably had, too, were the first to reach Hermes' Cord.

So then really, he should be thanking Chiyuri for inviting him to go to the Shinjuku government office the day before. And also, of course, Kuroyukihime for talking the whole thing over with him in the dive call. Having friends really was pretty great…

As Haruyuki let these thoughts wander through his mind—

"Lotus, may I?" Sky Raker raised a light hand and advanced her wheelchair with a *creak*. She turned around in a fluid movement and looked at the faces assembled there. "I'm also very much looking forward to the event. After rejecting any contact with the Accelerated World for so long, I am grateful every single day that I'm able to fight in the Legion, the reborn Nega Nebulus, again like this—alongside my companions. If it were possible, I would so much love to combine forces with you all and set our sights for the finish line in the race. But…"

She cut herself off for a moment and dropped her gaze to her own legs, covered by her long white dress.

"From what Crow's said, there are only four seats for the crew in the shuttle and no real space for anything else. In which case, I'll be without my wheelchair and simply glued to that seat. Which means that this avatar will become a mere object. If I'm just going to pointlessly increase the load the shuttle carries and dull its speed, then it's better if I don't even get in in the first place."

"B-but you—!" Haruyuki cried out reflexively, trying to deny Sky Raker's words.

However…

If Sky Raker had been a long-distance avatar, then she could have more than adequately fulfilled an attacking role while glued to a seat. But just as her fresh sky-blue color indicated, she was a fairly pure close-range type. Most likely, for close-range types to take on an attacking role in the race, an action like jumping over to the other shuttles would be required. For Sky Raker and the wheelchair that took over for her legs, this was, of course, impossible.

Seeing Haruyuki grinding his teeth tightly, Raker said gently, "Corvus, don't worry about it. Even if I'm not there, if it's you, Lotus, Pile, and Bell, I honestly believe you'll end up on top when crossing the finish line."

No. No, that's not it.

I...I wanted to bring you *especially to that pillar stretching up into the sky. In that world ahead where we'll be shooting up the four-thousand-kilometer space elevator, there's something I want to tell you. On the ground, I'm held back by gravity and I can't get it out. This particular thought...*

"Raker." Kuroyukihime's voice sounded like she was also enduring a kind of pain, similar to Haruyuki's and this prayer in his heart. "Your avatar likely weighs less than Crow's. Whether you are on the shuttle or not, the power-to-weight ratio will not differ that much. And even if you can't move from the seat, it's enough for you to stand on guard duty—"

"I can't go, Lotus," Sky Raker said curtly. "As a fundamental principle, you...and Nega Nebulus must move to strike at the other kings to bring you to level ten. If you come in first in the race tomorrow, you'll be given a quantity of burst points worthy of the feat. And that will bring you that much closer to your end objective. In which case, you shouldn't be concerned about me, which would reduce your chances of winning, however slightly... Isn't that right?"

Her argument was more than sound, and thus even sad. Most likely, in her heart, Sky Raker had clearly determined her role as someone whose range of movement was severely limited. She would expend every effort in ways she was able to help the Legion. But conversely, she would absolutely not take part in battles where it seemed like she might become a burden.

So all of that came down to this.

Sky Raker had already given up on her own game, her own Brain Burst. She had agreed to Kuroyukihime's request and come back to the Legion, but her motivation was solely to help Kuroyukihime. She had strictly prohibited herself from the thrills and excitement of the duel, the joy of talking with others through her fists. Almost as if it were a punishment she should continue to receive forever.

That's not it, Haruyuki murmured once more in his heart.

Getting his Legion master Kuroyukihime to level ten was also Haruyuki's own personal objective. He constantly prayed that until that time came, he could be a knight worthy of closely guarding his King. He put nothing before this goal, but there was one thing that *was* on the same level:

Playing. Having fun with this fighting game known as Brain Burst.

The duels couldn't just be painful. They couldn't be just mechanisms for earning points. At the end of those roads was nothing but darkness, a heavy shadow falling even on the real world, as embodied in the Acceleration Research Society.

Naturally, Haruyuki didn't think that Sky Raker would fall into that darkness. But if she had yet to forgive herself even now, then she most certainly was not happy. But he didn't have the ability to communicate those thoughts and feelings at the moment. Kuroyukihime and Takumu seemed to feel the same way, both of them stiffening up like rocks and simply hanging their heads.

A silence blanketed everything other than the timer, which noted that they had ten minutes left until the field disappeared. It was a silence Sky Raker broke with a gentle, short laugh. But a moment before that—

"Sister Raker." Chiyuri started talking, using the strange semi-nickname that had at some point stuck for her.

"What is it, Bell?"

"I...I've been thinking about this for a long time," Chiyuri said as Lime Bell stood up, using an almost-hesitant voice that somehow could still make its listeners feel the resoluteness of her will. She took a few steps to stand before Raker. After she took a deep breath, an unusually serious air came over her mask. "As long as it's okay with you, big sis, I'd like to try something. To see whether or not I can bring your legs back with my power."

Haruyuki's eyelids flew back. Chiyuri's—Lime Bell's power was, in other words, the special attack Citron Call, the result of which was a reversal of time. Any avatar or object subjected to it had time rewound.

In a normal duel, this technique was used as a pseudo–healing ability to recover the HP gauges of allies. But the fact that its effectiveness did not stop there had been proven the other day in the fight against Frost Horn and Tourmaline Shell. Since it was possible to dodge the technique, it was fairly difficult to use against enemies, but if it succeeded, it could even forcefully eliminate Enhanced Armament summoned by an enemy. And in this sense, Citron Call was a special attack even rarer than a healing ability.

However.

"B-but, Chiyu," Haruyuki reflexively interjected, "I'm pretty sure Master Raker lost her legs more than three years ago. Can you actually rewind time so far back?"

"Okay, um..." Chiyuri cocked her pointed, witchy hat and waved her index finger, as if to confirm her own thinking. "My Citron Call has two modes. The first one uses up half my special-attack gauge and rewinds the in-game time in units of seconds for the status of the target duel avatar. That's the one I use to heal HP."

The number of fingers increased to two as she continued. "And then, mode two uses all of my fully charged gauge and rewinds the avatar's status, except for level increases...like in units of fixed changes due to external causes. One by one, it cancels out changes like buying Enhanced Armament with points or stealing techniques and parts from other avatars. That's the one I got Haru's wings back with."

"So fixed changes...are undone?"

It was Kuroyukihime who murmured this. "Mmm," she hummed quietly and, still sitting, brought the ridge of the sword of her right hand up to her mask. "Easy to say, but when I think about it, that's quite the power. The natural enemy of—or perhaps, divine retribution for—those with theft abilities."

"But I can't interfere negatively with the status data of anyone other than the target, so I can't get back items someone else owns. Which is why I couldn't get back Haru's wings when I used my power on him. It's pretty easy to run away from the technique itself, so it's hard to use it on an enemy during battle, Lotus."

As Haruyuki worked hard to digest the rules for the somewhat complicated technique, Takumu opened his mouth.

"Chi, with that Citron Call mode two, how many steps back can you cancel out these fixed changes? What's the maximum?"

"Um, let's see. I haven't actually tested it out, but judging from how my gauge decreases, I'd say I could go three steps, max."

"Three...hmm? Raker, since you lost your legs, have you had any other status changes?"

The sky-blue avatar paused for a moment at Takumu's question. "There was the exchange of Enhanced Armament with Corvus...If that counts as two changes, then the loss of my legs would be the third."

"U-um, Master. What about the wheelchair...?" Haruyuki asked reflexively the instant he heard these words. The silver wheelchair in which Sky Raker sat was an Enhanced Armament item, the same as Ash Roller's motorcycle, and Haruyuki wondered if getting it also counted as one fixed change.

Raker shook her head lightly, stroking the wheels gently. "I acquired this immediately before I cast off my legs."

She sounded nonchalant, but the meaning hidden in her words was significant. At the point in time when Sky Raker asked Black Lotus to cut off her legs, she had anticipated that the amputation damage might be permanent, or she had been prepared for it to be. In other words, the injury she had suffered didn't stop within the framework of the normal game system; there was a greater logic at work: *that* system.

"Bell." Sky Raker's voice calling out interrupted Haruyuki's thoughts. The Burst Linker in the middle of their collective stares, who even now lived half as a recluse, announced in an endlessly kind tone, "Thank you. I gratefully accept your feelings...But even if it doesn't work, you mustn't blame yourself. The causes and effects here are all within me."

To Haruyuki, it seemed that the latter part of that statement had been directed to Black Lotus as well as Lime Bell. The black crystal avatar stiffened momentarily and lowered her face slightly.

"I understand, big sister Raker." Chiyuri's determined voice broke the silence that fell over the stage. "But I'm definitely going to bring your legs back. Oh, and Haru?" Her gaze swung around to Haruyuki, and she flicked a finger at him as he blinked in confusion. "I think you'll get a message saying you got some Enhanced Armament while I'm using the technique, but you have to cancel. Otherwise, it'll be a big hassle later!"

"R-right, got it."

When Haruyuki nodded, Chiyuri glanced up to her left. She was probably checking that her special-attack gauge was still full, charged up at the base during the Territories. She brought her face back down and put a foot forward.

In sync with Lime Bell, as she stepped forward, Kuroyukihime, Takumu, and Haruyuki fell back.

The freshly green avatar stood about two meters in front of the wheelchair and pointed the enormous bell attached to her left arm directly up at the sky. She tilted her pointed, broad-brimmed hat backward and took a deep breath, throwing her slender torso back.

"Okay, here we go…Citron…"

At the same time as she started to call out the technique name, she rotated the bell in a large counterclockwise circle. *Ring gong.* A magnificent sound washed over the field. Normally, when she was healing Haruyuki and their team's HP, she rotated the bell twice, but Chiyuri drew another two circles after that and—

"…Call!!"

With the loud cry, she brought her left hand straight down in front of her.

A ribbon of yellow-green light and chords like something played by an orchestra of angels cascaded from the large bell and enveloped Sky Raker. Her long sky-blue hair and the hem of her white dress flapped back, exposing hidden legs. Below the round knees, almost as if they had been designed that way from the start, there existed absolutely nothing.

Sky Raker closed her deep-red eye lenses and clasped her hands in front of her chest as her entire body flashed lime green once. At the same time, in the center of Haruyuki's vision, a system message popped up.

Do you accept the Enhanced Armament Gale Thruster?

Haruyuki quickly pushed the no button in the window, which flashed erratically, quite unlike a normal window. He felt something returning to Sky Raker, and her body flashed brightly once more. This was likely Chiyuri's ability rewinding the two item exchanges that had taken place between her and Haruyuki.

This really is nuts. Haruyuki was impressed anew. Normally, canceling a transaction of money or items in a net game, it went without saying, was something solely at the discretion of the game master. And because of this overwhelming authority, the GM was occasionally likened to a god. However, since there was no so-called GM in Brain Burst, you could say that Chiyuri was, in the Accelerated World, the only one other than the mysterious developer who had the power of a god—even if just a part of that power...

A third flash sent these thoughts rolling around in Haruyuki's head flying.

"...!!" The three witnesses held their breath and opened their eyes wider.

In the writhing green light, they could definitely see tiny particles of light blue radiance settling on Sky Raker's thighs. As the number of these particles increased before their eyes, they extended downward. They clumped together into tapered cylinders, grew denser, and began to draw out the hazy shape of legs—

Fwsh!

They vanished like particles of ice melting in the sun.

Instantly, the green light faded as the sound of the bell grew distant and disappeared.

In the center of the now-silent field, Lime Bell staggered as though she had used up all of her energy. Black Lotus was immediately at her side to catch her.

The yellow-green avatar hung there, no strength left in her legs. "...Why...why," she muttered hoarsely. "How come...they're not coming back...?"

"It's not your fault, Bell." The answer came from Sky Raker, gently rearranging the hem of her dress. She moved her head slightly with a comforting smile. "This result proves that in the termination of my legs, a logic of higher priority than the normal game system is at work. The image control system...in other words, the Incarnate System."

Haruyuki took a sharp breath. In a larger gesture, Black Lotus, still holding Lime Bell, pulled her right foot back. She turned her V-shaped mask away.

Sky Raker began to speak calmly at Chiyuri, who was rooted to the spot, and, by extension, Kuroyukihime.

"But you've only heard the broadest outline of the Incarnate System, Bell, so perhaps this is hard for you to understand... Three years ago, I tried to increase the maximum altitude I could fly with the power of my will. In exchange for the sacrifice of my legs, it let me reach the sky; that was the deal I made with god—no, the devil. My wish was heard, or rather the tiniest bit of it was. My maximum altitude reached a mere hundred meters higher...and my legs have never come back, no matter how many times I dive into the field. Keeping my legs away is my own will. I no longer know how to undo this. Which is why it's not your fault you couldn't bring them back...and it's not your fault, either, Lotus."

When you chase after that power, you absolutely lose something as payment.

The Red Legion's Blood Leopard had told him this. Maybe Leopard, too, had had an image of Sky Raker in the back of her mind at the time.

To those words, Haruyuki had this response: *I want to believe. I want to believe in the Incarnate System, in Brain Burst itself.*

He couldn't make a lie of that. Absolutely not. And to that end as well, Haruyuki had to take Sky Raker to the pinnacle of Hermes' Cord.

"Raker," Haruyuki called to her, quietly but in a voice that pulled together every ounce of determination he had. He stared directly into her deep-red eye lenses and moved his mouth. "I don't think that the fighting ability of our avatars is what decides the strength of our team, of our companions. Like observation and judgment—no, before that, I think the feeling of being able to fight even harder because we're together is more important than anything. You give us support, Raker. Just having you with us, we are so, so much stronger. So...So."

With his limited linguistic competence, Haruyuki could only manage to get this much out. Still, trying to communicate what was in his heart, he clenched his hands tightly, and abruptly, Cyan Pile's large hand slapped him on the shoulder from behind.

"It's just like Haru says. Raker, you're a priceless part of the battle potential of this Legion."

"That's right, sis!" Chiyuri bobbed her head up and down. "We're strongest when the five of us are together!"

And then finally, Kuroyukihime took a step forward. "Exactly, Raker. It's as everyone is saying." The leader of Nega Nebulus spoke in a tone that was calm, though the pain hidden at the core of it was palpable.

"I told you this before as well. I need you. At any and all times…Let's make this simple. If you are not in tomorrow's race, the four of us won't be able to fight with everything we have. Just this alone is reason enough for you to take part in the event." She sounded fairly overbearing, but it was that overbearing tone that gave her words the power to get right to the heart of the matter.

Sky Raker's eyes flew open, and then a faint wry smile crossed her lips. She shook her white hat as if to say, *Honestly.*

"Lotus, that way of speaking you have hasn't changed at all since the first time I met you." She hung her head and lightly stroked her knees with her hands. "There are some things you lose and never get back. But I know that there are also things that keep shining, without ever being damaged…Perhaps the right at least to believe that—or rather, to wish for it to be true—still remains for me…"

Her quiet murmuring, making almost no noise, flowed softly from below her hat. At the same time, Haruyuki felt as though he saw the glint of a single drop falling into space. However, when she lifted her face, the same gentle smile as always was playing around Sky Raker's mouth.

"Thank you, Lotus, Pile, Bell…Crow. I suppose I can allow myself to be swayed by your kind words. But…" Her expression became playful. "You'll need to get rid of any sugary ideas of

aiming for second or third because I'm taking part. We either have total victory or we burn up in the sky."

Eep!

Haruyuki jumped up to stand a little straighter, and Takumu and Chiyuri raised their voices in easy laughter.

You guys don't know! The truth is she's really, really scary!

Shouting this in his heart, Haruyuki finally was able to put a sincere—albeit slightly stiff—smile on his own face.

6

After bursting out to the real world from the Territory battlefield, Haruyuki hesitated to open his eyes for a while, feeling the pull of gravity on his entire body. He sat like this for nearly ten seconds, but finally, slowly, he lifted his face.

The living room at six o'clock in the evening had fallen back into a silence so deep that he could almost believe that the conversation and laughter exchanged only moments before on the other side had been a hallucination.

The lights were low, so it was fairly dim. The evening sky he could see through the narrow gap in the curtains had sunk into a dull, leaden color. The only movement in his field of view was the apathetic march of the thin second hand of the analog clock hung on the wall, essentially serving nothing more than a decorative purpose.

Sighing lightly from his position on the sofa, Haruyuki flopped over onto his side.

They did try insofar as it was possible to meet in the real before diving for the Territories each Saturday. But when they didn't have that luxury, they joined in the battles from their various locations, such as individually in their houses or from other parts of town. Although a single fight in Brain Burst was over in a mere 1.8 seconds in the real, defense of a Territory took a succession of ten battles at minimum, so it took up nearly ten minutes, breaks in between fights and the like included. Today, Kuroyukihime hadn't really been able to get away from the student council office, and so she ended up diving separately. And, of course, given that her house was very near the border with Shibuya Ward, Sky Raker took part from a distance nearly every week.

Haruyuki couldn't seem to come to terms with fighting in the Territories by himself from his house. The reason was simple: He would make it through ten or more successive and heated battles as if in a dream, and then share the thrill of victory or the bitterness of defeat with his companions, only to burst out and wake up suddenly alone in an empty house; it made him feel a pitiless loneliness.

Until he met Kuroyukihime in the fall of last year and received the Brain Burst program, he had never felt lonely being alone. On the contrary, he had felt more comfortable that way. Every day, almost before classes were over, he was flying out the school gates as if to escape when heading home, where he would hole up in his room and throw himself into the world of games and anime and comics. Having a conversation with someone in the real world— just being in the same place as someone else was agony. Even if that someone else was Chiyuri or Takumu.

A mere eight months.

That's still all the time that had gone by since he became a Burst Linker. And yet now, Haruyuki felt from the bottom of his heart that he wanted to see his friends from the Legion he had only just said good-bye to. And it didn't matter if it was Niko or Pard or Ash Roller or even Frost Horn. He wanted to exchange blows in a duel, to clamor with criticism over a battle as a member of the Gallery, to meet someone in the real and talk about nothing.

"What happened to me?" he muttered, burying his face in a cushion.

At that moment, a window of some kind started to open in the center of his vision, together with the default sound effect of his home net, and he slapped the confirm button, without bothering to look at what the window said. After all, it was probably just the usual message from his mother about how she was going to be late that night. He promptly forgot about it as words in this vein continued to pop up in his mind.

Have I gotten stronger? Or weaker?

He supposed you could say that the fact that his fear of other people had decreased meant he was stronger. But at the same time, his dependence on other people had also increased.

Back when he was alone every day, he had nothing to lose. But now, Haruyuki was deeply terrified of destroying the modest personal relationships he had managed to develop over the last eight months. In particular, the lone thread of black silk tied tightest in the depths of his heart that stretched straight up, glittering all the while—

Even though he knew this line of thinking was dangerous, he couldn't stop. Lying facedown on the sofa in the dim living room, he squeezed his eyes shut and kept thinking, bringing his arms up around his head.

Naturally, the end of that thread was connected to the person who had saved him, his "parent," Kuroyukihime.

She was currently in ninth grade at Umesato Junior High. And the first term of that school year was already half over. Which meant there were just ten months left. Once a mere three hundred days passed, Kuroyukihime would graduate from Umesato. He hadn't asked her anything about where she would go to high school. He was afraid to ask.

Real-world time, passing bit by tiny bit in that moment as well, felt to Haruyuki like a raging river flowing at a speed a thousand times faster than normal. If it were possible, he wanted to spend all of their remaining ten months together in the Accelerated World. By a rough calculation, an amount of time equivalent to the infinity of eight hundred and twenty years would pass on the other side, but he felt that even that would most certainly not be enough.

"Kuroyukihime," he murmured out loud, squeezing the edge of the cushion.

"Hmm? What?"

He felt like he heard a voice coming from right beside him. Still facedown, Haruyuki repeated her name in an attempt to hear once again the reply of the phantom girl.

"Kuroyukihime."

"And I said 'what,' Haruyuki?"

That voice included a gentleness and a doubt that was simply too real. Haruyuki, realizing that he had pushed himself to the limits of his own delusional imagination, rolled over toward the left.

And found before his eyes, a mere fifty centimeters or so away from the sofa, two legs wrapped in black stockings.

His eyes fluttered open and shut before he vacantly lifted his gaze. Skirt at the perfect above-knee length. Jet-black short-sleeved shirt with a soft brilliance. A deep red ribbon. From the slender neck equipped with a piano-black Neurolinker to the silky, flowing lengths of hair to the pale face possessing a some-how inhuman beauty, currently cocked to one side, a vision with overwhelming reality filled Haruyuki's field of view.

*Man, I really can't underestimate my imagination. I mean, a vision so clear like this. Maybe I put it together with image data in my memory without realizing it. But do I have a full-body shot with this kind of high resolution...*Haruyuki nonchalantly stretched out his right hand, grabbed the hem of the pleated skirt, and tugged at it.

Even the unbearably real sensations of the texture of the fabric and the mass and flexibility of the person beyond it were communicated to his fingers, and just as he started to wonder—

"Whaaa?!" He heard a cry of that nature and his hand was slapped away. Followed by: "Wh-wh-what are you doing, you idiot?!"

The roared rebuke poured down over him, and at the same

time, a slender hand reached out and grabbed his cheek with three fingers to demonstrate their merciless pulling power.

"Hya…Haah?!" As he uttered this squeal/cry of surprise, Haruyuki understood.

She was real. She was not a hallucination, nor a photo, nor a 3-D artificial reality image. The genuine article, Kuroyukihime herself, had suddenly appeared in Haruyuki's own living room, her beautiful eyebrows arched into a *V*. But why? How? Maybe she'd teleported? Electron coherence—?

Half a minute later, Kuroyukihime, having stretched out Haruyuki's cheek to a point where she was satisfied, flopped back onto the opposite sofa and revealed her secrets.

"Look here! I very clearly rang the bell and everything! And then you—without even saying so much as the *h* of *hello*—unlocked the door, so having no other choice, I simply showed myself in. I called out in my actual voice from the entryway, you know!"

"Oh!"

A window had in fact opened up while he was thinking about the stuff with his face buried in the pillow and his ears blocked by his arms. He had just assumed it was a mail from his mother and pressed the confirmation button without even looking at the text. But that window had actually been to notify him of the intercom call.

It was his own fault for leaving the messaging noise set to its default, which sounded very similar to the intercom buzzer, and after making a note to himself in his internal memory not to forget to change that, Haruyuki sat up straight and opened his mouth again.

"Uh, ummm. I-it's good to see you."

"Mmm. Here I am," Kuroyukihime replied, her lips still slightly pointed as she tugged down the hem of her skirt. It was a good thing he had pulled it toward him earlier. If he had tried to flip it up or something, he had no doubt he would definitely not have gotten off as lightly as a stretched-out cheek.

After this thought drifted through his head, Haruyuki realized that the gears of his brain had once again wandered into strange territory. And that wasn't the issue anyway, it wasn't about how Kuroyukihime had gotten into the house. The fundamental issue to be clarified straightaway—

"R-right, anyway, um. Why did you come all of a sudden?" He timidly gave voice to the question.

Judging from the fact that she was still in her school uniform and her school-specified bag was on the floor, Kuroyukihime had apparently come directly from Umesato JH. If she had something she needed to tell him, she could have done so in the meeting earlier where they reflected on how the Territories had gone. She could've mailed or called, too. So it was something for which none of that would suffice.

"It's something that requires an incredibly high level of security...Is that it?" he added, attempting to get a jump on the situation, but Kuroyukihime cocked her head slightly and shrugged.

"No, not particularly...What? I don't have the right to ever-so-occasionally come and hang out? Even though it appears that Takumu and Chiyuri visit rather frequently?"

She started to puff her cheeks out once more, so Haruyuki moved his head back and forth in the horizontal direction at top speed.

"N-no, no, no, no, not at all! I-I-I-I'm really happy. Superhappy. I wouldn't say anything if you were here every day, or even if you went ahead and moved right in. Oh! R-r-right, I'm sorry, I should offer you something! I'll make some coffee right away; please sit down. Or I guess you're already sitting down! Sorry!"

If he kept chattering like this, he was bound to say something he couldn't take back, so he practically fell off the sofa onto his feet and escaped in a dash to the kitchen. A "No need to bother" mixed with an exasperated-seeming smile chased him, and his nervousness abated slightly.

It wasn't any top secret Legion thing; she had just stopped by to hang out on her way home from school. As a regular junior high student, doing the sort of thing classmates often did.

The moment this thought crossed his mind, a laugh threatened to slip out of his mouth, and he had to work hard to keep it in as he pulled out the most expensive-looking bag of coffee beans from his mother's collection in the cupboard and poured them into the percolator.

During the time that the cloudy sky beyond the window went from the color of lead to the black ink of night, Haruyuki chatted away as if in a dream. About the Territories that day. About recent events in the Accelerated World. About the race the next day.

And he didn't leave it at topics related to Brain Burst; he chattered and talked and babbled about happenings and rumors at school, local Suginami issues, and even the 2047 summer models announced by the various Neurolinker companies.

"...But I think the large, high-performance Neurolinkers lately have gotten things essentially backward, you know? Like, they should be machines developed with wearability in mind, to the point where you can forget you even have one on. And yet the new Hitasu models coming out, I mean, an external unit for carrying around comes with them, standard!"

"Heh-heh, I understand how you feel. But I wonder if you can actually say that after seeing the specs. According to rumor, by moving the connection and slots to the external unit, they've managed to equip those Linkers with a console-line CPU, you know."

"Oh!...N-no, but no matter how great the CPU is, it's not like it'll give you an advantage or anything in Brain Burst, right?"

"Mmm, now that you mention it, I suppose not. But I have heard that using the latest Linkers makes the effects processing just a little more gorgeous."

"Seriously?! No fair, that's no fair!"

"What? It's not as if a beautiful appearance raises your win rate. Incidentally, I'm planning to switch to the new Rekto model next month."

"Whoa! No fair! That's way unfair! K-Kuroyukihime, let me try it—"

"Come come, you can't use another person's Linker. And even if you could, I feel like it wouldn't fit your neck anyway. Ha-ha-ha..."

It was fun.

Just thinking about having Kuroyukihime all to himself, sitting on the sofa across from him, coffee cup in one hand, talking, nodding, and laughing, Haruyuki experienced a delight such that he nearly ascended to Heaven.

A face-to-face conversation in the real world with real voices was quite the luxury in the current age, and Haruyuki relished this style of communication, which half a year earlier he would have been too nervous to carry out satisfactorily. Which is why he didn't realize a certain something: the fact that every so often, the faintest hint of sorrow would bleed into Kuroyukihime's eyes.

Approximately two hours later:

Interrupting this time, which he wished could go on forever, was a low rumbling from Haruyuki's stomach area.

"Whoops! Is it already that time? I've stayed far too long. It's already suppertime."

"N-no!" Haruyuki hurriedly shook his head back and forth. "It's totally fine! I'm not even hungry yet—"

Grr.

His flesh emitted a hungry growl, once again betraying his heart. *And this is why I'm sick of physical bodies!* He restrained his stomach with both arms, but it was to the point where he could do nothing against the involuntary movements of his own innards.

"Heh-heh, no need to fight it. You were incredibly busy in the Territories today; you must have used up the majority of your energy. Make sure to fully replenish yourself for tomorrow." Smiling, Kuroyukihime stood up.

He wanted so much to say, *Well, in that case, how about you at least stay for dinner?* but the only thing he could make was frozen pizza or frozen doria or frozen *chahan* rice. Very few would say any of these was the sort of menu one invited guests to enjoy.

Even as Haruyuki agonized about it, Kuroyukihime was picking up her bag from the floor, cutting across the living room, and walking away.

That pace—

For an instant, he felt it was the slightest bit heavier than her usual spirited step. A sharp insight pierced Haruyuki.

Maybe the truth is she actually had something else she wanted to talk about? And there I was blabbing about all my own stuff, using up all our time? I was just in my own world, so happy, so fun, and I didn't pick up on something important...?

Forgetting the intensity of his hunger, Haruyuki opened his mouth.

But no words came out. In this situation, it would seem almost like an afterthought; how could he ask her if she was worried about something or anything like that? He should've picked up on this an hour ago. Or at least half an hour ago. He would just have to shut his mouth now and wait for her to say something.

Staring at her back as she moved down the hallway toward the glass door, Haruyuki prayed, *God, please give me just one chance here somehow.*

It was at that moment a low noise, like the Earth rumbling, came from the distance.

Naturally, the source of the sound was not Haruyuki's stomach. It was lightning. Tossing his gaze toward the living room window, he saw white flash twice, then three times, deep within the thick clouds that weakly reflected the lights of the city. The flare was followed by thunder, slightly louder and closer this time.

Immediately, droplets of water began to tap against the window, and as he watched the neon colors bleed, Haruyuki said hoarsely, "Um, Kuroyukihime. This rain's pretty crazy."

Kuroyukihime also stopped. "The weather report said there was a less than ten percent chance until midnight," she replied, her face to him in profile. "It's rare for them to be this far off the mark."

"Uh, um. Do you have an umbrella?"

"Unfortunately, I am as you see. Sorry, but..." She spread empty hands, and Haruyuki wholeheartedly expected her to continue with something about waiting the rain out here. But... "...perhaps you could lend me one?"

"Uh...Yeah, right, of course." Nodding firmly, he had no choice but to head toward the entryway when a second phenomenon stopped his feet.

A window popped up in the right side of his vision with a yellow warning mark.

"Oh...There's a lightning strike advisory and a network damage report for Suginami and Setagaya."

"So it seems. I can't honestly believe that I would draw down a direct strike, but...I hate the idea of net lag on the way," she said, furrowing her brow.

During the time you were coming and going, AR information—from local traffic bulletins, a navigation line to your destination, the distance you'd traveled to how many calories you'd burned—was quite handily displayed all over your visual field through the Neurolinker. But when the net wasn't working properly and lags were frequent, it conversely made walking very difficult.

"Hmm. But the time is still the time, after all." The normally immediately and incredibly decisive Kuroyukihime displayed a rare moment of indecision as she looked at the clock. Haruyuki followed her example and shifted his own gaze to the bottom right of his virtual desktop. 8:07 PM. The sort of time that couldn't really be said to be early anymore but wasn't particularly late, either.

The quiet sound of rain and thunder came to them from the other side of the window, and the two continued to stand awkwardly in the living room in unsettled postures.

Haruyuki breathed in and out several times before opening his mouth. But no matter how he tried, those final words would not come out. There was no real need for him to feel any kind of pressure, though. It *would* be better for her to wait until the rain stopped, or at least until the lightning storm had passed. It was a completely inoffensive thing to suggest, a thing that was, in fact, only natural. So then why was his heart rate soaring suddenly?

He couldn't pick up the expression on her face, in profile two meters away from him. Hesitant, weary, somehow nervous, or maybe just waiting for something?

Pee-pong.

The default beep suddenly sounded, and Haruyuki froze with a gasp.

The window that appeared in the center of his vision this time was a text message through his home server. Sender: His mother. Subject: *By tomorrow night.* Main text: *I won't be home, so take care of things.*

A third miracle. Although really, it was nothing so exaggerated as that. Practically every other weekend, Haruyuki's mother came home on a different day from the one she had left on, and the rest of the weekends, she didn't come home at all. However, for Haruyuki, this was the best and perhaps the ultimate timing. He closed the window and pushed a voice from his closed throat.

"Uh, uh, umm…It wouldn't be any b-b-bother or anything at all. Th-that, umm, uh…" Haruyuki wrestled with whether or not to let her know the details of his mother's mail and that there weren't any kind of obstacles.

Kuroyukihime went ahead and got right to the heart of it. "No, your mother should be coming home pretty soon. It would no doubt be a bother. I'll just…"

The instant he heard that, several of the safety valves in Haruyuki's heart blew out, and the words flew out of his mouth on their own. "No, i-i-it's fine! My mom said she isn't c-c-c-coming home today!"

Crap! That's way too blunt! I was just supposed to say I wanted her to wait out the rain. Haruyuki fell even further into panic. But…

Kuroyukihime merely twitched her upper body a nearly indiscernible amount. Finally, after rolling her eyes halfway around in the opposite direction from Haruyuki, still in profile, she said distinctly, "Is that so? Well then, I suppose I'll impose on your kindness."

"P-p-p-p-p-please d-d-d-d-do!" Bobbing his head up and down, in the back of his mind, Haruyuki was grateful for his mother's principle of extreme laissez-faire. He could only pray now for the lightning above his head to tie things up for even a few seconds longer. If possible, an hour, no, at least thirty minutes…

Kuroyukihime started to walk again as her mouth moved at a fairly high speed. "Now that I'm thinking about it, we're all meeting here at your house again tomorrow, and if I go home now, it'd just be twice the hassle."

"Th-that's true. It's completely inefficient—"

—Huh?

It's annoying to go home, since she'll be here again tomorrow? What does that mean?

As Haruyuki stood frozen in place, stance unnatural and look baffled, before his eyes, Kuroyukihime placed her bag on a chair at the dining table and said: "So then, I'll just duck into the mall downstairs."

The words lingered in the air as she stepped out the door.

Supposedly, Haruyuki had made the expensive and fancy frozen margherita pizza he had secreted away in the depths of the freezer for supper, put more coffee on, and watched the evening news with Kuroyukihime on the sofa, but he had almost no memory of this time.

When he came to, he was alone in the living room.

However, the faint sound of a hair dryer coming from the bathroom down the hallway led him to believe that the whole thing had not, in fact, been a hallucination.

Here, finally, the transmission of his brain, which had been racing idly for more than two hours, managed to get into first gear, and Haruyuki recommenced his interrupted thoughts.

A hassle to go home. So then, was it okay to interpret those words to mean that she would not go home before the time of the race the next day? In which case, didn't that inevitably lead to a situation in which Kuroyukihime remained in his house the whole night? In other words, wasn't that "staying over"? Was such a situation legally and theoretically permitted to happen, despite the fact that they were in junior high? But there was no other way to interpret it.

Keep it together! Even if that's what's happening, you gotta deal with it calmly! I mean, it's not the first time or anything. I mean, that time, too, she just sort of ended up staying. But that time Niko was here, too, and we had that big retro game playoff and then it just ended up us sleeping in the living room and all...

"Thanks for letting me use the bath."

The door to the living room abruptly opened, and Haruyuki sprang to attention, looking over at the owner of the voice with such force that his vertebrae threatened to shoot out of his spine.

She was clad top and bottom in simple, warm gray pajamas that she had probably bought before at the shopping mall on the ground floor. "Somehow, I keep getting new pajamas," Kuroyukihime said with a faint, wry smile, pulling her hair back with a hair tie.

"Ha—yeah...You can leave those here if you—" His mouth ran on automatic up to that point before he belatedly realized what he was saying. "I-I-I didn't mean it like that! T-t-t-today's just because of the lightning and it's not like I'm totally thinking I want you to stay over again or anythi— I—I—I—I mean, it's not like I would hate that at all or anything, so, uh, um, ummmm."

Haruyuki gesticulated wildly with both head and hands while Kuroyukihime's smile grew broader until she finally offered him a life raft.

"Maybe you should use the bath, too, before the water gets cold?"

"Right! I'll do that!" He practically rolled off the sofa and escaped from the living room at top speed.

A bundle of confusion once more in the still-steamy bathroom, he hopped in and out of the bath, and while he changed into the sweats that served as his pajamas, Haruyuki gave his full attention to the actions he had to select from now.

And the answer he came up with as a result was slightly—no, fairly pathetic:

"Please use my mom's bedroom! It's the door at the end of the hallway! O-o-o-okay, then, good night!" he chattered/shouted from the entrance to the living room, locked himself up in his room, and yanked his duvet over his head.

He had vaguely guessed that Kuroyukihime had come over because she wanted to talk about something. But in circumstances like this, Haruyuki simply could not believe that he was able to stay calm face-to-face, what with her in her pajamas. He had no doubt that, just like before, once his brain overheated, he would end up spitting out all kinds of things that would be a hundred times better kept to himself. He wouldn't even be surprised if he just collapsed from hyperventilation or dehydration or arrhythmia before he even got the chance to say something stupid.

And if that was where this was going, it was better to hide in his bed. At the very least, he'd be able to make it through the night without forever saving in his brain a memory that made him cry out "gaaah" or "ugh" every time he remembered it later.

But having activated full backward-looking-psychological-shut-in mode for the first time in a long time, Haruyuki grit-ted his teeth with self-loathing. The thought that he had grown stronger was nothing but wishful thinking, and he curled up into a tight ball.

Which is why, ten or so minutes later, when he heard a light knocking on the door and a voice asking, "Can we talk a min-ute?" he was deeply surprised that he didn't pretend to be asleep.

Instead, he sat up in bed and took a deep breath. With the air pressure, he chased the worm of weakness from his body and replied in a clear, if hoarse, voice, "Sure."

Once she soundlessly opened the door and came in, he saw that Kuroyukihime was inexplicably holding one of the large cush-ions from the sofa in both arms. She looked around the room before briskly stepping over to the edge of the bed and sitting down.

"I thought you'd tell me no," she said in a small voice, her back toward him.

"...I thought I would, too," he replied distinctly.

"So why'd you change your mind?"

"Hmm...uh..."

He was surprisingly calm. Despite being in this rather earth-shattering situation, Haruyuki felt composed and relaxed, perhaps because of his relief at having made it to this moment without committing any egregious errors.

"Because I was pretty sure you actually had something impor-tant you wanted to talk about."

"What? You managed to see through me that far and yet you take the superspeedy sleep strategy?"

"I-I'm sorry." He scratched his head as he apologized to the thin back, snapped straight before him.

"...Well, you did let me into your room now, so I'll forgive you." Kuroyukihime relaxed her shoulders, shifted slightly on the bed, and looked at Haruyuki sitting in the center of it. Her expres-sion was kind, but, of course, the sorrow that had shaken her that whole day had still not disappeared from her eyes.

She lifted a slender finger and stroked the piano-black Neurolinker attached to her neck. At the same time, she murmured, "'Those who lose all their points and have Brain Burst forcefully uninstalled lose all related memories.'"

Haruyuki gasped. This was the system to maintain the confidentiality of the Brain Burst program, the existence of which had been proven to them a mere two months earlier. It was absolute salvation for the defeated, and at the same time, an extremely merciless punishment.

Kuroyukihime brought her hand down as a faint smile with all kinds of emotion rose to her lips. "I was terrified when that final rule, a rule I had only heard rumors of before, was made so undeniably explicit. Because if I ever lose to another King just once, in that instant, I will forget who I have been. But, well, Haruyuki, at the same time, I...I was also relieved."

Unable to instantly grasp her meaning, Haruyuki was confused. Kuroyukihime squeezed the cushion on her lap, hung her head low, and continued.

"Two and a half years ago, I forever banished one of the Kings from the Accelerated World with a surprise attack during a meeting. Ever since, I've been afraid in the depths of my heart. I thought he...the boy who was the first Red King, Red Rider, was out there somewhere in Tokyo nursing a deep grudge toward me."

Haruyuki took a sharp breath.

She had told him this story countless times up to now. He had even seen a video file with a recording of that scene. So he had thought he understood the size of the scar this incident had left on her heart, but at the same time, he had foolishly thought that she had already overcome that pain.

"B-but..." Instinctively, he leaned toward Kuroyukihime, sitting on the right side of the bed, and started speaking in a daze. "Even if it was a surprise attack...wasn't that still a just attack according to the rules? And he was the leader of an opposing

Legion, plus back then, you didn't have the non-ggression pact, right? So then there's nothing to hold a grudge about—"

"That's not it, Haruyuki." Kuroyukihime interrupted his desperate words, shaking her head gently but firmly.

"Huh...What do you mean...?"

"I used my level-eight special attack Death By Embracing when I took off Red Rider's head. The range is a mere seventy centimeters, but in exchange, it has a very high attack power. That said, it shouldn't have been enough to kill Rider in a single blow. After all, he was the same level and a very pure fighting type, with a very high defensive capability, third after green and blue. Yes... you likely see it now. At that time, I activated the Incarnate System. That prohibited power that all seven Kings vowed not to use after the subjugation of the fourth Chrome Disaster."

This time, Haruyuki was at a complete loss for words.

The image control system was a high-level interface hidden within Brain Burst. Deliberately using this system to go beyond the boundaries of the game was the so-called Incarnate System. Its power was tremendous, but at the same time, it held a terrifying dark side. Those who sought the power of the Incarnate had their hearts swallowed up by darkness; this was the consensus of the high-ranking Linkers Haruyuki knew. Kuroyukihime before him was no exception.

The slim back curled up even farther and from the depths, a dry voice resounded.

"Rider has the right to resent me and the way I broke that vow. I don't regret choosing the path of fighting the other Kings, but the sensation of that single blow alone stains my arms... And that's why, Haruyuki. For a long time, I firmly refused to believe the rumors that former Burst Linkers lost their memories of the Accelerated World. Because I couldn't allow myself to cling to such rumors, to let them ease my burden. But, two months ago, when we finally got proof that the rumors of memory loss were true...I was relieved. It confirmed that Rider no longer remembered that he had been the Red King or that he had been chased out because of my betrayal. I truly did heave a sigh of relief from the bottom of my heart. Honestly...I'm such a hopeless coward...Ha-ha-ha..."

The figure of the pajama-clad Kuroyukihime laughing softly looked unusually weak and fragile. Haruyuki mustered up his minimal courage and shifted another five centimeters toward her.

But, of course, he couldn't actually touch her hand or anything like that; instead, he simply spoke in all earnestness. "K-Kuroyukihime. I think that knowing that this sort of memory-loss treatment is lying in wait, and yet still going out there and fighting, puts an incredible amount of pressure on us. B-but we went and found out about it. We have to just accept that fact and keep fighting. In which case, getting a little relief from that in exchange, there's nothing cowardly about that. Maybe the opposite. I think it's only right."

Kuroyukihime lifted her face a bit and glanced at Haruyuki. A pained, gentle smile bled onto her pale lips. "I see. That's so like you, such a logical opinion. Right, you should be fighting with that kind of faith...However, I probably don't have that right."

"Wh-why not?!"

"Well, you see...Rider's not the only Burst Linker who's suffered an irreversible loss because of my Incarnate attack."

"That's..." Haruyuki blinked several times and furrowed his brow. "Do you mean the fourth Chrome Disaster? B-but you didn't have any choice there."

"No, that's not it." Kuroyukihime shook her head despondently, bound hair swinging. A few seconds later, she announced in a voice that was practically a sigh, "My...old friend. Before I made you my 'child,' she was the only person I was bound to by friendship in the real world as well...Fuko. Or rather, Sky Raker."

"...Huh...?"

"The reason Chiyuri couldn't recover Raker's legs even with Citron Call after the Territories today was not because *her* will is at work. Mine is. Most likely, my will is even now eating into

Raker's scars and blocking any regrowth. Like a poison…Like a curse."

"That's—! That's not true!!" Haruyuki cried out in a trance. He shook his head fiercely and leaned forward as he argued vehemently. "Raker herself says that she basically forced you into it. Right up to the end, you tried to change her mind, but Raker wouldn't listen no matter what you said, so you had no choice: You cut her legs off…Isn't that what happened?!"

"That's exactly it, on the surface at least…" She buried her face in the cushion she was holding. "But…I was twelve at the time, even younger and more foolish than I am now. Rather than the path of fighting alongside me as Legion submaster, she chose her longing for the sky…I couldn't understand how she felt, how she was forced to that choice. In the end, once I grasped that Raker was never going to change her mind, my sadness…my anger…I put all these feelings into the blade of my right hand and amputated Raker's legs. And in my heart at that time was most certainly the will that if that was how she wanted it, then she could lose her legs for the rest of time. That turned out to be a curse, one that lingers even now. It's the same as the malice of the first Disaster that gave birth to the Armor of Catastrophe…"

She put all the strength in her arms into squeezing the cushion. Her cracking voice flowed quietly in the dim bedroom.

"Raker's—and your—will is the materialization of hope. But mine's not. Just the opposite. I overwrite with the power of rage, of resentment, of despair. Not building anything, not creating anything, just cutting things off, causing loss. As symbolized by the form of my ugly-in-the-extreme avatar…If you all keep fighting alongside me in the reborn Nega Nebulus—no, the Nega Nebulus that you all *revived*, I know you will…"

The latter half of her speech faded into obscurity, and Haruyuki felt almost as if he were listening to Kuroyukihime's soundless self-recrimination.

No. No. You're totally wrong.

There's no way despair and loss are your essential nature.

Because you saved me. You offered me a sincere hand and pulled me up from the bottom of the blackest bog. You offered me the most overwhelming salvation!

He shouted all this in his mind, but his ability to turn this vortex of emotion into words was decisively lacking. Haruyuki clenched his teeth and thought intently about how he could let her know just how she and Brain Burst itself had saved him.

The answer he came up with after about five seconds was:

"Kuroyukihime," he said, pulled something out from a corner of the headboard, and gently offered it to her. It was an XSB cable covered in silver wire. With one plug in his left hand, he held the other in his outstretched right.

"Kuroyukihime, please duel with me. If you do, I'm sure you'll understand…how…how much you…" Haruyuki was unable to hold back the emotions rising up in him, and tears spilled out of his eyes. Sniffling, he took a deep breath and continued in a shaky voice. "…how truly important you are to me."

Kuroyukihime turned more than half her face to him now, eyes opened wide. A mixture of surprise, hesitation, and fear flitted across her face until it settled on a weak smile tinged with pain.

"You do always surprise me," she murmured, accepting the plug. However, instead of plugging it into her own Neurolinker, Kuroyukihime crossed the bed to sit on her knees, directly in front of Haruyuki. The scent of soap and shampoo wafted up, sending his awareness flying off, despite the current situation. She placed her left hand on his head and gently pulled his head toward her.

"Now that I think about it, a one-on-one fight with you, this would be…" As she spoke, she fitted the plug into the terminal on his Neurolinker.

"…Th-the first time," he replied as he stretched out the hand with the plug toward Kuroyukihime's Neurolinker, trying to keep it from trembling too much. He faced her, met her eyes, and at the same time, jacked in. In his vision, the wired connection warning flashed.

The sensation that more than just the digital signals—that both of their consciousnesses were linked together—settled over him, and Haruyuki slowly called out the command.

"Burst Link."

Thin legs covered in silver armor stepped down onto a cracked marble floor. The condo Haruyuki lived in had been transformed into a chalky temple. The walls dividing each house and each wall had all disappeared, and the entire floor had become a spacious atrium. The high ceiling was supported here and there by Greek-style pillars. A faint, pale yellow sun shone in through the external openings.

A Twilight stage, the very stage in which Haruyuki had received his first lecture from Kuroyukihime.

Finishing his check of his surroundings, he turned his gaze straight ahead to find a bewitching, elegant, obsidian avatar standing quietly some twenty meters away. Both hands, both feet, were long swords. An armor skirt resembling a flower petal encircled her slim waist, and both sides of her face mask glittered sharply.

Rather than in an attack posture, the traitor of the Accelerated World, the Black King Black Lotus, had both hands by her sides, her head hanging slightly. However, the slender standing figure was emitting an intense pressure, making him feel as though he were standing below an enormous guillotine, and Haruyuki involuntarily sent a shiver running through Silver Crow's slim body.

No! This is not the time to lose your nerve! he shouted at himself beneath the silver mask.

The reason why Haruyuki had asked for a duel with Kuroyukihime was extremely simple. He just wanted to let her know the faith he had in her as the Burst Linker who supported him.

Brain Burst was, in essence, an online fighting game. And games were meant for having fun: the thrill, the excitement, the emotion of playing. And in the case of net games, the competition, the solidarity of fighting together. Players far and wide had the right to enjoy these. Games definitely did not exist to make people suffer.

The sole method Haruyuki had of communicating this belief to Kuroyukihime was to muster everything he had and fight here and now like this. He had to challenge her using all his power, convinced as she was that her avatar and her Incarnate reflected despair, that she dragged any opponent she crossed blades with into that despair. And he had to make her remember the fun of the duel.

And that's why I—

"I'm not holding back, Kuroyukihime!!" Shouting, Haruyuki kicked at the ground ferociously.

Black Lotus did not move. However, without the slightest easing of the threatening presence emanating from her, she instantly raced a distance of twenty meters and pushed deep into the cracking marble.

His first blow was the thing he was best at: a right straight punch. He rotated his hips and shoulders forward as far as possible, but at the last possible second, Kuroyukihime lightly ducked the blow. It aimed for the center of her body, and she dodged it by bending in half.

Although she had accepted Haruyuki's challenge, she was still held back by her own uncertainty. She wasn't her usual top-notch self. She came back with a counterattack of a thrust with her right sword, but Haruyuki could clearly see the tip of it coming.

He lined up the fingers of his right hand, stretched out before him. Bending his arm like a whip, he went to meet Kuroyukihime's thrust with a sword-hand.

Even though he hadn't ever fought a direct duel with her, having fought alongside her in the Territories for the last six months,

Haruyuki had noticed an extremely modest weak point in Kuroyukihime's close-range fighting.

The swords of Black Lotus's limbs were fearsome weapons for both offense and defense, but because they were, in the end, swords, there was a directionality to that power. Specifically, the attack power was concentrated exclusively in the edge, and the flat of the sword was even fragile, in fact. Of course, they weren't likely to snap at a single blow, but he could pile on the damage there. And if he was looking for a chance of winning in a close-range fight, that was the only place he was going to find it.

"Hngah!"

With a cry, Haruyuki hit the side of the blade plunging toward him with a stiff chop of his right hand. Or at least tried to.

But the impact he anticipated didn't happen. Instead: Soft... was the only way to describe the gentle response he felt, and Haruyuki was floored.

The long jet-black sword caught Haruyuki's chopping hand with a small circular motion from the outside. It couldn't be, but to Haruyuki's eyes, it looked like the sword had transformed into some flexible material and was capturing his arm in a spiral. But this was only a fleeting sensation—

"Hah!" Here, Kuroyukihime allowed a brief exhalation and shook her right arm sharply as she took a step forward.

Instantly, an explosive backlash slammed into Haruyuki's arm, up to his shoulder and chest.

"Wha—?!"

By the time he cried out, he was already being sent flying backward helplessly. Unable to get control over his posture, he crashed into a round pillar off in the distance. The pillar collapsed with a rumble, and still unable to stop, Haruyuki tumbled along on the floor before finally halting, arms and legs splayed.

He stared at the stars flickering before his eyes for more than a second before shaking his head and leaping to his feet. He managed somehow to keep himself from staggering, lifted his face, and shouted, "Wh-what was that just now?!"

Kuroyukihime leisurely hovered closer from afar and shrugged lightly. "The way of the firm against the way of the flexible," she replied. "I suppose we could call it something like that. One of these days, I'll tell you about when I trained in the Chinatown area of Yokohama. Anyway, Haruyuki, didn't you have something you wanted to tell me?"

Her voice was calm, but Haruyuki was keenly aware of the single drop of desolation buried within it.

So Kuroyukihime was currently caught up in emotions she normally kept buried. Her duels generated only a negative energy. There was not a single thing she could give to her opponent, not the excitement of battle, not the solidarity of fighting together. Or so she was firmly convinced.

But you're wrong! I am at maximum thrill right now! I'm not afraid. I'm shaking all over with real emotion, that someone as strong as you exists in this world…and that this person would fight with me.

Haruyuki kept himself from shouting out and clenched his hands into fists. He was sure this wasn't something he could communicate with words. Which was why he wanted to fight. He couldn't shrink now just because she sent him flying once. He couldn't be done here unless he put forward everything he had in him.

"I'll tell you with my fists!!" he yelled, and went into another dash.

The attack that had knocked him on his back had also eaten nearly 20 percent of his health gauge. But in exchange, his special-attack gauge had also been charged. As he ran, he gradually deployed the metallic fins on his back.

He abandoned his aim of trying to counter Black Lotus's swords from the side and bet everything on a 3-D rush attack at zero distance, something he had been practicing in secret for a long time.

"Unh…aaah!"

Howling, he went for another long punch with his right hand.

Kuroyukihime similarly came at him with a right thrust. With the difference in reach, he would get hit first if nothing changed.

The glittering sword tip drew nearer, closed in, and the instant it was about to touch his helmet, Haruyuki vibrated just his left wing hard, once. With no advance warning, Silver Crow's body slid to the right, and the sword passed by, sparks scattering from the side of his helmet.

"…!"

The sound of Kuroyukihime inhaling sharply. But with no sign of stopping, she whirled her body around, using the sword tip of her left leg as a pivot, and tried to dodge Haruyuki's punch. He shook his right wing. His trajectory was once again corrected to the inside and—

Clang! The modest and yet definite sound of impact was joined by sparks bouncing off Black Lotus's left shoulder pauldron. And the health gauge in the upper right of his vision did indeed decrease, though by the smallest increment: a mere dot.

Now!

"Heeyaah!"

Haruyuki let loose a battle cry and waved his left leg high. Common sense would have it that a high kick would never hit its target in this kind of close-quarters situation. This was because such a kick required a certain amount of distance from the end of the left leg, which was the axis of revolution, and the end of the right leg, which was in the position to generate damage.

Perhaps surmising this, Kuroyukihime set herself up not to take the blow or to avoid it, but to counter with an elbow strike.

But here again, Haruyuki momentarily turned the thrust in his left wing all the way up. With his forward-leaning body as an axis, the high kick sang through the air with a minimal turning radius that would normally be impossible.

Kuroyukihime immediately canceled her elbow strike and threw her upper body back, but Silver Crow's sharp toes scraped the left side of Black Lotus's mask. Once again, sparks and minimal damage.

Normally, after pulling out a fancy move, Haruyuki inevitably stiffened up. But now, he used his left leg to kick off the ground while the force of his right leg swung around. Kuroyukihime, on the other hand, sank down in preparation to jump backward, perhaps disliking the close contact.

Another moment of thrust with his right wing. He jumped on the centripetal force generated and threw out a roundhouse kick from the left rear.

Kuroyukihime blocked with a bent left arm. Fierce impact. The orange flash effect colored the armor of both avatars and the surrounding marble.

Noticing the gauge in his upper right drop by two dots on the edge of his vision, Haruyuki this time put all the reactive force of the kick into the thrust of his left wing. His body spun suddenly in the opposite direction, and using this energy, he sent his left spear hand shooting out over and over. His fingertips dug shallowly into Kuroyukihime's right shoulder.

When they were facing each other, he threw open both wings. A double-knee kick was just barely blocked by her right arm, and the biggest impact up to that point shook the stage. Damage: three dots.

This kind of uninterrupted rush, which took advantage of the instantaneous thrust of his wings, was the secondary use for his flying ability that Haruyuki had spent hours and hours training to use in his special bullet-dodging training room. Name: Aerial Combo. Compared with the primary use, Dive Attack, it seemed rather staid at first glance, and he couldn't hope to do much damage with it, but in addition to the fact that he could use it indoors, he could also activate it with just 20 percent in his special-attack gauge. And, most importantly, it was nearly impossible to handle when you were seeing it for the first time!

"Aaaaah!"

Pushing his whole body into an acceleration that made his nerves shiver and sing, Haruyuki increased the speed of his rush even more. Maintaining close quarters, he continued to shoot out attacks, his limbs almost never touching the ground. Black Lotus managed to just barely dodge or block all of them, but even still, the damage he carved out steadily whittled down her gauge.

As he flitted about, totally absorbed in the battle, Haruyuki shouted in his mind, *This is me now, Kuroyukihime. This is the full power of me, the person you pulled up from the swamps and gave wings. If your true nature is despair, if it's loss that cuts everything away…then what is this fight now?!*

At some point, the figure of Silver Crow had transformed into a congregation of silver light glittering in the air. He had thrown the door open for his reaction speed in a full-dive environment, a speed he had trained and built up in the virtual squash game in the Umesato local net, where he'd first caught the attention of Kuroyukihime way back when, and Haruyuki kept throwing out his midair combos. He wasn't certain exactly how many dozens of times he had attacked, but he still had not landed a single clean blow. Kuroyukihime silently and thoroughly defended, single-mindedly evading or blocking Haruyuki's rush, when his movements should have in theory been impossible to predict.

Although they exchanged no words, at a certain point, Haruyuki became aware of a deep, rich emotion being communicated between the two of them whenever their avatars touched.

Admiration. Haruyuki at Kuroyukihime's defense techniques. And most likely, Kuroyukihime at Haruyuki's midair rush. Both of their hearts were filled with an incredibly deep emotion.

Abruptly, he felt like he could hear her voice.

Ohh, I see…Was that it, then?

This is the duel. Forget everything and simply become one with your duel avatar; move as you wish. Even if it is a world that disappears in a mere 1.8 seconds, even if it is a contact that ends in 1.8 seconds…a mindful duel surely leaves something behind. It gives us something…

Rider and me. The countless battles Raker and I have fought since childhood, too, they must...Something precious has come from them...and even now, that something lingers in both of our hearts...

Haruyuki didn't know whether he had actually heard these thoughts or not.

Because that voice came to him in the moment his right fist, thrust out for the hundredth time, touched Kuroyukihime's left blade and was drawn into it, a moment almost outside of time.

In the next instant, that mysterious gravity once again violently swallowed up Haruyuki's fist.

...Ah! The "way of the flexible"...!

Gritting his teeth, Haruyuki got ready to resist the explosive reactive force.

But it didn't come. Instead, his body was pulled into her chest, both arms held firmly and brought to a stop.

"Huh..."

At this deeply unexpected development, Haruyuki stiffened up, unable to decide what he should do, and in his ear, her actual voice this time came whispering.

"That was wonderful, Haruyuki."

Huh? The duel's over? But both of our gauges are still pretty full. And we've got tons of time left...

In the moment that he glanced up at both of their health gauges, bewildered, Haruyuki understood something serious.

Because of the ceaseless, instantaneous thrusting with his wings, Silver Crow's special-attack gauge had been used up from its full state, and only 10 percent remained.

In contrast, Black Lotus's special-attack gauge was completely charged from the countless blocks, and glittered a full bright blue.

"It's been two and a half years since I used this technique. Thank you, Silver Crow. Nice fight." As she murmured, Black Lotus's arms encircled Haruyuki under his own. Circled around his back, they flashed an intense violet.

"Death By Embracing."

Following her utterance of the attack name, a light *snip*. Before the echoes of this had died away, Silver Crow's health gauge turned entirely red, sliding into nothingness from the right end—to zero.

...Damn, that is some serious power.

This final, great admiration swelled up within him at about the same time the flaming text YOU LOSE popped up before his eyes. Fortunately, Haruyuki's whole being emitted a silver light before the sensation of the top and bottom of his duel avatar separating came over him, and he exploded and scattered.

Passing through the darkness replete with the sensation of floating, he returned to the real world.

On his bed, Haruyuki opened his eyes and, after blinking several times, took a look at the face of Kuroyukihime, which should have been right there in front of him.

That was not to be, however. Because Kuroyukihime had in the blink of an eye pressed herself up against him, placed her head on his left shoulder, and wrapped both arms around him.

"Uh! Um! Hey—"

The black hair tickling his cheek and the scent of shampoo slammed into his brain, and Haruyuki tried to leap up while still sitting. But there was no way he could do something as agile as that, so instead, he abruptly lost his balance and fell backward. He hurriedly tried to recover himself with the thrust of his wings, but naturally, there was nothing of the sort on his flesh-and-blood back.

Thump! He fell onto the mattress, and, after a slight delay, the slender body of Kuroyukihime came in for a gentle landing on his stomach.

The faint rasp of the air conditioner in his ears, Haruyuki froze completely and utterly, both eyes wide open. *Okay, just calm down! Make a calm decision before you do anything!* Although

that thought was in his head, he simply could not begin to grasp what was happening, much less act.

At eleven at night, he was lying on his bed in his usual sweats. He was fine up to that point. No problems there. But Kuroyuki-hime was in her pajamas on top of him, both hands wrapped around his back, squeezing even more tightly now—this situation, was it actually, really reality? And why was this even happening to start with? This whole thing had to be the doings of some kind of virus, start to finish?

"You surprised me." Her real-world voice poured directly into his ears, and Haruyuki cut off his confused-to-the-extreme thoughts. "You...At some point along the way, you got that strong..."

Her murmuring voice was filled with emotion, and while Haruyuki was still unable to process a single thought, his mouth managed to move on its own.

"B-but the result was basically a perfect win for you..."

"That's just a reflection of the difference in our levels. It was a much more equal fight than you think. When you kept on rushing me in midair like that, you really forced me to block, and desperately, for the first time in an incredibly long time."

"R-really?" he said, half believing her, half not. In Haruyuki's experience, the difference between his ability and that of the Black King was, to be honest, from the bottom of the space elevator up to the peak—no, out to geostationary orbit.

However, Kuroyukihime brought her head up a bit and stared into his eyes from extremely close up, smiling faintly. "Really. Aah, I wish I could let you know just how happy I am right now, how full of emotion I am!"

In the depths of her large black eyes, a light like stardust swirled, glittering. Just seeing that, his brain threatened to leap out of his head once again. Haruyuki didn't know which of their hearts was creating the powerful heartbeat he felt on the border between their bodies, closer than they had ever been before.

They were so close, their noses were almost touching. They exchanged glances—

Kuroyukihime announced her next words calmly. "At the very least, I've decided to trust in the path I've walked this far. I'll have many regrets, but…even so, the colossal amount of time I've spent in the Accelerated World and the countless duels I've played through were not in vain. Because as a result of this path, I found you and I was able to bring you in." The five fingers of her right hand moved up from his back to caress his cheek.

"Haruyuki, I'm proud of you."

The instant he heard this, all of the shock and confusion inside him evaporated and was replaced with something hot filling both eyes and flowing down the sides of his face and onto the sheets. The liquid kept coming, falling without stopping.

He blinked hard several times, and as he rubbed his face with the back of his right hand, Haruyuki began to excuse himself in a hoarse voice. "Oh…Um, I-I'm sorry. I…It's…I—I—" But for some incredible reason, even his voice turned into heaving sobs, and in between words, he bawled like a child. Trying desperately to get this under some kind of control, he continued to speak. "I— That's the first time in my life…a-anyone's ever told me they're p-proud of me. And—" Unwilling to expose his ugly sobbing face any more than that, Haruyuki tried to turn away.

But Kuroyukihime held him back with her whole body and stroked his head gently as she pressed her own face up against his slick cheek. "Well then, I will say fourteen years' worth of it. You are the lone child of me—of the Black King, Black Lotus, and I am more proud of you than I am of anyone else in this world, my perfect partner."

It felt like each time she patted his head softly, the thing blocking his chest eased pleasantly. He took a deep breath and closed his eyes.

The faintest of voices reached his ears. "No, you're not just that. The real-world you, Haruyuki Arita, too…and me…Kuro…"

But he didn't get to hear the rest.

Because here, Haruyuki had probably made the biggest of that night's blunders.

Coupled with the exhaustion from mustering all his strength for the duel, the sweet pain of the overflowing emotions melting away, the sensation of her kind hand, and the warmth of their bodies touching, his consciousness had been smoothly sucked into the darkness.

In other words, he fell asleep. Like a log. In this especially, like a child.

He felt like the last thing he heard was mixed with a wry smile.

Good night, Haruyuki.

7

Ding-dong.

A light chiming sound echoed inside his brain, disturbing his deep sleep.

Wha? he thought, with a head that was at best 10 percent awake. It wasn't the sound of the alarm clock he always used. And in any case, that clock sat on the headboard, so he should be hearing the noise from above. But the sensation of sound delivered directly to his consciousness, without it going through his ears— *Oh, that's right, I fell asleep without taking my Neurolinker off. I hope the shell didn't get cracked or anything...*

Ding-dong.

The chime again. He finally realized that the sound was not an alarm to wake up. It wasn't the sound of mail or a call arriving. The ringing was the intercom to let him know someone was at the door. Reluctantly, he half opened his eyes and looked at the clock hanging on the wall to the right of his bed. Nine in the morning.

His mother wouldn't be home until the middle of the night. Maybe it was a courier with a morning delivery? He thought about just pretending he didn't hear the bell and having them leave it in the delivery box, but it was time for him to get up anyway. Takumu and the gang were coming at eleven.

After closing his eyes tightly one final time, Haruyuki got up.

Instantly, he felt a slight tugging resistance on the right side of his neck. He turned his gaze to find a silver XSB cable stretching out from the external connection terminal of his Neurolinker. Glinting in the light of the sun coming in through the gap in the curtains, it disappeared beneath a thin blanket—

Where the tiniest part of a head of silky black hair popped out.

"...Unh."

Waaaaah?! He very nearly shrieked before clapping his hands over his mouth to desperately hold the cry in. In the moment of this shock, as if all circulation of blood in his body had suddenly reversed direction, he was entirely awake. Blinking repeatedly at top speed, he stared doubtfully, but the small head didn't disappear. Just the opposite, the distinct outline of a slender body lying there appeared under the blanket. He could doubt it no longer: Someone was sleeping in Haruyuki's bed, fifty centimeters away, back turned to him.

"Mmm...mmm."

This someone, perhaps sensing Haruyuki moving, rolled over and let out a small sigh. The blanket slid off and the hidden face was revealed.

"......Ku—"

Ro-ro-ro-ro-ro?! He managed somehow to suppress scream number two. That beautiful face—a beauty he was very familiar with and yet never felt even slightly used to—belonged without a doubt to Kuroyukihime.

Why the hell is this—?! He shrieked in the back of his mind before finally remembering the details of how the previous night had ended. Kuroyukihime had come to his room late, they'd talked for a while, and then they'd had a direct duel. After that, he didn't know what had happened or how, but when all was said and done, Kuroyukihime had ended up falling asleep like that in this bed, and Haruyuki seemed to have no recollection of the process leading up to this result. Serious misstep. Serious situation.

Still frozen like a stone statue, he mustered every ounce of willpower not to look at the rumpled sleeping figure, pajama top noticeably flipped up—*Don't look don't look don't look*—

Ding...dong.

Once again, the chime, longer than before now, echoed in his auditory system. With the thought that that was one seriously patient courier, he glanced at the visitor window in the right of his vision; it seemed that they hadn't just come to the entrance on the first floor, but all the way up to the twenty-third floor already. Having little choice, he decided to put off the situation before him for the time being and gently plucked the direct cable out before carefully stepping down to the floor. He tiptoed out of the room, closed the door, and sprinted to the entryway, replying in a hush, "Okay, okay, I'm coming!"

"Sorry to make you wait so—"

Haruyuki swallowed the "long."

On the other side of the opened door was not a cheerful young courier standing there grinning.

Snow-white, wide-brimmed hat. Shrug of the same color. Light blue chiffon dress. Thigh-high socks with a border pattern on slender legs peeking out from the skirt hem. Long, full hair reaching down her back, a small bag dangling from both hands. This visitor was clearly—

"M-Master?! I mean, Raker?!" Haruyuki cried out, stunned, and the woman bowed lightly at him. She responded in a voice even more clear and gentle than it sounded through the net.

"Good morning, Corvus. When we meet in the real, you can just call me Fuko."

At these words from the second-in-command of the Legion Nega Nebulus, level-eight Burst Linker Sky Raker, real name Fuko Kurasaki, a girl two years older than himself, Haruyuki quickly bowed again.

"Oh! R-right! Good morning, Fuko. Oh! Uh, excuse me! Please come in!"

"Thank you. That would be lovely." She closed the door and, as she took her sandals off, he got some slippers ready for her.

"A-although…you're pretty early," he said, still somewhat spaced out. "There's still ages until we're supposed to meet."

"Hee-hee-hee, I'm sorry. I wondered if it might be a bother, but it's the first time for me to come over to your house and I'm afraid I couldn't wait. At any rate, I did send a mail very early this morning…"

"I-I'm sorry! The truth is I was asleep until just a minute ago." As he spoke with an embarrassed laugh, Haruyuki finally realized that the current situation was very much not one in which he should be laughing.

At that very moment, on Haruyuki's bed only seconds away down the hall, the Legion Master aka Kuroyukihime was fast asleep! Clad in perfect pajama top and bottom!

Wh-wh-wh-wh-wh-what am I gonna do! No, now's not the time for doing. Think, think! Right, first, I'll show Raker to the living room. And then I'll secretly get Kuroyukihime's stuff, and she can change in my room, and we can work it out so she comes in from outside again. That's it; that's the only option.

As Haruyuki instantly came up with this secret operation, Sky Raker politely lined her sandals up before stepping into the slippers set out. She no sooner had them on than Haruyuki was showing her the way to the living room.

"P-please, this way, p-p-please…Straight ahead, please!"

"R-right. Thank you." She smiled, puzzled, but then began to walk next to Haruyuki. She spoke in a singsong voice. "The truth is, I came early because there's something I wanted to talk about, just you and me, Corvus. It's been a while since just we two talked. Lately, the only chance we get to meet is in the Territories…I wanted to thank you properly…once…"

Her words suddenly dropped away and the reason for the abrupt interruption was clear. However, he did not have the extra brain space to come around to that insight. Because at that point in time, Haruyuki had again frozen solid, one foot in the air, about to take another step.

The French-gray-pajama-clad figure that appeared shuffling

from around the corner two or so meters ahead of them in the hallway looked first at Haruyuki and then at Fuko with a dazed expression. She batted long eyelashes. She moved her lips and the voice of someone freshly awake came out.

"Morning, Haruyuki."

Followed by.

"Morning, Fuko."

Reflexively, Haruyuki dipped his head with a "Good morning," and as if pulled along, Sky Raker also replied, "M-morning, Sacchi."

"Mmm." Still 80 percent asleep, Sacchi aka Kuroyukihime nodded once before facing forward again. She cut across their view, walking in a fashion similar to the hovering of her avatar, and disappeared to the left. A few seconds later, they heard the sound of the door to the washroom opening and closing.

Silence.

It was not a voice that broke this heavy blanket of quiet, but a movement. A pale hand extending from the right pinched Haruyuki's ear and yanked on it hard.

His whole body stiffening, he allowed himself to be pulled around to confront a smile he had rarely seen on Sky Raker's face. He wondered, almost as a means to escape, where he had seen that expression before, and it soon hit him: It was the very smile that her duel avatar had given him in training, when she pushed him off the top of the old Tokyo Tower in the Accelerated World's Unlimited Neutral Field.

Eeee! Haruyuki shrank into himself.

"Corvus," Raker said gently. "What is the meaning of this?"

"...I-it's not like that." Haruyuki could think of no other option than to immediately shake his head vigorously.

About ten minutes later:

Fuko faced Kuroyukihime, back in her Umesato uniform now, and Haruyuki, also changed into daytime clothing, sitting together on the sofa, and silently brought her teacup to her lips.

Chak! She returned it to the saucer and lifted her face. The same tranquil smile as always was on her face, but Haruyuki was convinced that if this had been a VR world, she would have had a little anger emoticon flashing near her forehead.

"Well, I do understand the circumstances here. And the heavy rain last night was indeed not in the forecast? And there were malfunctions in the network in the west of the twenty-three wards? You probably would've encountered some difficulty in returning home, wouldn't you?"

"E-exactly. The rain was really quite something, Fuko. And the lightning, it was just like that time when Purple lost it..."

Kuroyukihime acted her story out with her body and her hands, earning a bright smile from Fuko. However, that smile held an attack power on par with the special attack Ultimate Chill Kuroyuki Smile. Attribute: Terrifying wind. Right, maybe he could call this one Vacuum Smashing Raker Smile. He was so glad that Chiyu wasn't here, too. If this smile were combined with the Superheated Chiyuri Beam, they would annihilate each other and bring down this room—no, the entire condo...

As he escaped into his thoughts, Fuko's next attack reached his ears.

"Which is why I'll be understanding of this. But if, as you say, Lotus, nothing untoward happened, then there's no real reason for me to help you conceal the incident, is there? If Bell and Pile knew, they would certainly be moved at the closeness of their Legion Master and Silver Crow—"

"Th-tha-that's just—!"

Haruyuki laid his own cry over Kuroyukihime's stammering.

"A-ah! M-M-Master, please, it's just that—"

"Well then, how about we do this?" Once again, the glittering Raker Smile. "Please invite me to a sleepover as well sometime this month. Under that condition, I would be delighted to keep this quiet."

"Wh—! Wh-wh-what are you talking about, Fuko?!"

"Goodness! I did have Corvus stay at my house once, you know? Complete with dinner?"

"Wh—! Wh-wh-wh-what is she talking about, Haruyuki?"

"N-n-n-no, not like that, not in the real, in the Accelerated World! And I slept on the floor!"

Whipping his head back and forth at top speed, Haruyuki thought to himself, *I don't know if I've ever seen Sky Raker enjoying herself so much or Kuroyukihime so on the defensive. These two really are connected on some deep, spiritual level.* As only honestly good friends, who shared a different history than they did with Haruyuki, could be.

That bond was cut once by inescapable fate. And then three years later, guided by the same fate, they met again and now were completely restored. That's what he wanted to believe. He wanted to believe it, but…

Haruyuki had spent his time since the fall of last year staring intently at and adoring Kuroyukihime, and he knew. No matter how many walls they might try to take down, in the depths of Kuroyukihime's eyes, there was a pain that was not completely melted away. An equal measure of self-recrimination likely lay in the shadow of Sky Raker's smiling face as well.

The Incarnate System required those players seeking to master it to confront their own mental scars. Because powerful imagination was only born from a powerful wish, and a wish was nothing other than the flip side of a lacking. Unless you turned toward and occasionally entered the emotional holes that made up the core of your duel avatar, holes so dark you wanted to forget they were even there, you would never be able to obtain sufficient power to produce a large overwrite.

That's what Sky Raker did three years earlier. She cut both legs off of her avatar to purify this lacking within herself, and then used the Incarnate System to increase the power of Boost Jump she'd been given by the original system to the point where it was Flight. If he were to seek more power than any of his basic attacks, then Haruyuki, too, would likely have to tear open the scar in his heart that he had now finally managed to start walling over and let the blood flow again. His own scar, his psychic wound, was his hatred of himself. Hatred of his ugly, fat, bad-at-talking, bad-at-sports, bad-at-school self.

No, maybe the truth is it's not really that. I mean, back then, I wasn't as fat as I am now. The me back then who stood on the other side of that living room door and eavesdropped on the conversation inside. And yet...the people fighting in whispers, about me... No, that's not it. That's not it. It's because I'm fat. It's because I'm always flinching. That's why they, I mean someone like me—

"...yuki. Haruyuki!"

A sudden slap on his left arm and Haruyuki lifted his face with a gasp, only to meet the suspicious eyes of Kuroyukihime. Reflexively, he dropped his head again.

"What's wrong? You stopped talking all of a sudden."

"You don't...look so good, Corvus," Sky Raker said, and Haruyuki hurriedly shook his head.

"N-no, it's nothing at all! I—I was just...thinking about the Incarnate System..."

After his mouth had heedlessly raced this far, he realized it was not the most appropriate subject to bring up in the current situation and clamped his lips shut, but he couldn't cancel out the words that had already been released. Kuroyukihime and Fuko both opened their eyes wide for a moment, and then after a few seconds of silence, smiles of a similar nature spread across both of their faces.

"...I see. Was there something you wanted to ask?" Kuroyukihime brushed his hand lightly as if she had read his mind. Her fingertips, normally comfortably cool to the touch, were now the slightest bit warm, and Haruyuki exhaled shortly. The gaze Fuko had turned on him was full of a gentle light again, and at some point, words started to fall from his lips.

"Uh, umm, well...I was just thinking. About the structure of the Incarnate System...In the end, the bigger the lack at the core of the Burst Linker, the more...I mean, the more unhappy you are in the real world, the stronger it is. Like, is it something like that—"

"No."

"That's not how it works."

Their answers were instantaneous. They exchanged glancing looks, almost as if to determine who would speak next, and Kuroyukihime to his right turned to face him directly.

"Those mental scars are in the end nothing more than a key deciding the attributes of the duel avatar. There are much stronger powers than that in the Accelerated World, so strong as to be unlimited. The knowledge to put together battle strategies and techniques, battle abilities cultivated through training and experience, and the bonds of friends and companions and rivals. Even in an Incarnate battle, the predominance of these powers is not in the least bit shaken. So really, it's the exact opposite of this idea you have. Which is that those who drag their real-world unhappiness into the fight become stronger than those who simply enjoy the duel, isn't it?"

"Y-yeah...I guess it is."

"That idea is absolutely correct. Do not doubt it even a little. What we say now has that as the foundation." When Kuroyukihime closed her mouth here, Sky Raker smoothly picked up where she had left off.

"At the same time, there exists still another reality, Corvus."

"R-reality...?"

"Yes. To other people, you may look like you are simply and earnestly enjoying the duels. But it's very nearly impossible to be completely satisfied in the real world as long as you are a Burst Linker, even for instance, a Burst Linker like my 'child' Ash Roller. Because the essential requirements for the installation of Brain Burst—to have been equipped with a Neurolinker from shortly after birth and to possess a high-level aptitude for the quantum connection—are elements that run counter to real-world happiness."

The moment he heard this, Haruyuki gulped his breath back.

When it came right down to it, 90 percent of the time, the reason for putting a Neurolinker on an infant was to cut down on the amount of work involved in child-rearing. With the Neurolinker, you could always monitor temperature, heart rate, and breathing, so you could step away from the child, and you could automatically execute a variety of educational programs instead of talking to them. And when the baby started crying in the night, you could even force it into a full dive. However, no academic or education critic could assert definitively that the baby was happy like this.

Similarly, the requirement for a high-level aptitude for the quantum connection might seem like a superior talent that only chosen children possessed, but the truth was not so. This aptitude, or rather this affinity with the Neurolinker, was determined by how many long hours you had spent since childhood in high-density full dives; put another way, how much time you had thrown away in the real world and locked yourself up in a virtual world. Like the way Haruyuki had always escaped with single-minded focus into the virtual squash game of the Umesato local net.

As if reading his thoughts, Kuroyukihime began to speak again quietly. "Perhaps this is an uncomfortable way of phrasing it, but…in the majority of cases, those able to meet the conditions required to become a Burst Linker are children raised without enough love from their parents. Conversely, children raised from infancy always watched over by their parents, touched by them, having conversations in their real voices, don't need Neurolinkers or any virtual world. However, young me needed these, as did Raker."

Haruyuki dipped his head lifelessly and mumbled, "Of course, I needed them, too. When I was little…I was always alone in this house, even at night, and it was so scary."

The pale fingertips once again touched the back of Haruyuki's hand, and she continued almost soothingly, "All of which is to say, well…nearly all Burst Linkers have a single common lack: real love between parent and child. That's the reality Fuko mentioned earlier. And those who become Burst Linkers, when they exercise their right as a 'parent' to copy and install that one time, they instinctively try to select someone who bears the scent of the same scars as themselves to be their 'child.' As a result, we are intensely dependent on this second parent-child relationship we've obtained; we cling to it. To gain what we were unable to get in the real world…In other words, we cling to the Accelerated World itself. To maintain these new bonds, we try to preserve the stability and the concealed nature of the Accelerated World. Honestly. It's quite the well-made system. You really have to hand it to the developer."

"Ha-ha-ha."

At Kuroyukihime's chuckling, a slightly reproachful smile came across Fuko's face.

"Sacchi, you're as cynical as ever, hmm? Corvus, I know I said 'unhappy reality' earlier, but that wasn't to say that the thing itself is unhappy."

"H-huh?"

Haruyuki fluttered his eyelids, and Sky Raker turned a gaze on him that was the very definition of the word *affection*.

"What I'm trying to say is this: The Incarnate System does indeed use as its energy source those mental scars, that is to say, your trauma. Which is why in a way, it might be true that the more unhappy you are, the greater the power you can manifest. But, well…all Burst Linkers in the depths of their hearts bear the huge, enormous scar of being given a Neurolinker instead of their parents' hand soon after they were born. It's just not reflected in their avatar or their Incarnate because they don't really remember it. So then it's futile, isn't it, to compare this with any unhappiness accumulated after this one that is so vast? Better is to compare the size of your hope. The power of the

Incarnate System isn't decided by the depth of the holes in your heart alone. It's also determined by the height of the trees rooted and budding there."

Here, Fuko's voice shook momentarily. She slowly lowered her gaze to the glass table.

"A long time ago, I tried to force those trees to grow and ended up cutting them down at the root, so perhaps I have no right to... to speak now..." Regret and even more than that, a deep resignation colored her words.

Kuroyukihime stretched out a hand toward the now-silent Sky Raker. "Come here, Fuko."

Raker stood up from the sofa opposite and detoured around the table to set herself down to the left of Haruyuki. The girls, now forcibly wedged into a two-person sofa with Haruyuki in between them, acted in a completely and utterly unexpected way.

They stretched out their arms from both sides of him and squeezed each other tightly—and Haruyuki in the process. Naturally, all of the serious conversation they had been having up to that point flew out of his head, and, dumbfounded, he curled up into himself.

However, for some reason, the panic that honestly should have kept up forever rapidly melted away just this one day, like ice in the sun. Instead, a warmth he couldn't really put a name to spread out in his chest. It was something still different from the sweet, painful warmth when Kuroyukihime had held him on the bed the previous night.

Eventually, he heard Fuko above his head. "Hee-hee-hee... We're like a pack of kittens whose mother hasn't come home, huddling together in the nest."

"It's a happy thing to have someone to huddle together with." Kuroyukihime's response came swiftly. "The night ends sooner that way. And then you can tumble around and play in the sun once more."

"You're right. Play in earnest, play seriously. Whatever the expectations of the developer of the BB system might be, this alone we can never forget."

The two of them sat there still for a while, but finally, their bodies pulled apart, neither one initiating it. Kuroyukihime placed a hand on Haruyuki's still-dazed head.

"First, today's race! This is Brain Burst, after all, so there'll no doubt be no manual or tutorial as there would be with a normal race, so it might be rough going, but we're counting on you, Driver!"

"R-right." Haruyuki nodded hurriedly, and now Sky Raker was patting his back.

"Exactly. I deeply despise things like putting up a good fight or losing by a narrow margin. And I also hate the word *ambivalent*. If you get ambivalent about your promise to invite me to a sleepover, I will push you off of old Tokyo Tower once again."

"Wh-whaaaat?! B-b-b-but th-th-th-that's—"

"H-h-h-he's right, Fuko! No one's even said anything about a promise—"

"A-ha-ha! You're too late. You've already signed the contract in your soul!"

Listening to Sky Raker laughing delightedly, Haruyuki resolved himself anew in his heart.

They absolutely had to win the race event that day. At the very least, they would somehow, someway reach the top. And not for the victory or the prizes. To extend a long, long vine from the past and cut the thorns of regret that held these two even then in its curse. If they climbed those four thousand kilometers to an altitude where the gravity of the surface didn't reach, he was sure they could do it.

And just then, the high-pitched visitor chime rang for the second time that day. When he looked at the clock, he saw that the hands had arrived at eleven before he knew it.

"Oh! Looks like Taku and Chiyu are here." He stood up and took a few steps before timidly offering a reminder. "Um, Master, the two of them, I mean."

"Don't worry. I made a promise. I'll keep your secret." After Sky Raker nodded with a grin, she winked in a deeply meaningful way. "But secrets bring about new secrets, you know."

Aah! She's serious.

He tucked the thought away for the time being and raced toward the entryway before impatient Chiyuri rang the bell a second time.

"Bow down! Give thanks!"

Chiyuri raised up the basket in her hands as she spoke. And as usual, the starving fell prostrate with glee before the divine object—or, more accurately, the bewitching scent drifting out from it—and they ended up first taking care of the business of defeating their hunger.

Pulled from the basket was tagliatelle with seafood tomato sauce, offering ample demonstration once again of the skill of Chiyuri's mother. She had prepared enough for five people— even more than that, actually, with plenty left for Takumu and Haruyuki to have seconds. She had apparently no sooner finished making it than Chiyuri and Takumu were dashing up the two floors to the Arita residence, since hot steam was still rising up from the flat pasta when they measured it out from the deep dish. The five of them seated around the dining table scrambled to plunge their forks into their plates.

"Mmm, what wonderful skill."

"This really is incredibly delicious."

Kuroyukihime and Fuko raised their voices in admiration at their first taste of Chiyuri's mother's cooking, and Chiyuri ducked her head, as if embarrassed.

"Heh-heh-heh. My mom seemed all excited, too...this many people coming over to Haru's place for, like, the first time ever—"

"H-hey, Chiyu! You don't need to make a big announcement!" Haruyuki reflexively interrupted her, but he himself knew best just how true this actually was. He also glared at a giggling Takumu before devoting himself to scarfing down pasta.

"Now that I'm thinking about it," Kuroyukihime said, somewhat apologetically, still smiling, "ever since the mission sometime back to subjugate the Armor, Haruyuki's house has ended up being our sortie base for every little thing. I really should put together a proper Legion headquarters."

"N-no, we can use my house; it's totally fine! I mean, my mom hardly ever comes home on the weekends anyway," he hurried to respond before realizing that talk about parents was still a somewhat sensitive topic, and abruptly added, "Now that you mention it, what did you do during the era of the first Nega Nebulus? For a headquarters, I mean."

Kuroyukihime and Fuko, sitting next to each other across from Haruyuki, exchanged glances, and then nostalgic looks came over both faces. It was Fuko who replied in a gentle tone.

"At the time, there were a great many more members than there are now, but almost none of them had a relationship that allowed meeting in the real. To be specific, it was Lotus, me, and one other. Nega Nebulus was a Legion united by strong feelings toward the aloof flower Black Lotus, rather than by relationships between its members. Longing, worship. Or feelings of protectiveness."

"F-feelings of protectiveness?" Takumu asked. Haruyuki and Chiyuri also opened their eyes wider.

"Yes." Sky Raker smiled even more delightedly. "When the Legion formed, Lotus was still only nine in real-world years. Although naturally that sort of real information was not made public, you could tell to a certain extent from her bearing and attitude. While boasting overwhelming fighting prowess, she was nonetheless childish and easily hurt. Many Burst Linkers no doubt squealed and cooed over her and joined the Legion."

"C-come now! It's true I was a child, but I refuse to consent to the idea that I was easily hurt, Raker!"

"Oh? Well then, shall I also tell them about how we ended up meeting in the real?"

"N-no! You can't; I forbid it! I absolutely forbid it! If you tell them, it's the Judgment for you!" she shrieked as she began to intently peel a shrimp, and Haruyuki involuntarily burst out laughing. Kuroyukihime hung her head even farther and muttered, "Even though you older lot were all only ten or eleven anyway..."

Fuko's shoulders shook for a minute with laughter. "That was how it was," she continued. "So back then, there was nothing so large-scale as a headquarters. I suppose that's basically the same situation with the other Kings' Legions. The King and their executive court had the possibility of enormous danger if they exposed their real information, even to other Legion members."

"Mmm. Although it's a different story if you're confident you have a perfect grasp on the entire Legion," Kuroyukihime said after finishing the shrimp as she abruptly wiped the previous expression off her face.

Haruyuki cocked his head to one side. The Legion Masters may have had the privilege of the Judgment Blow, but it would be hard to bind all the members of a large Legion with the fear of that alone. The effective period of Judgment was for a month after leaving the Legion, so as long as you were prepared to keep running during that time, betrayal was possible.

However, Kuroyukihime's tone suggested that there was in fact a King actually achieving this sort of perfect grasp. He wanted to ask her about it, but before he could, she set her fork down with a clatter and said in her usual tone, seemingly satisfied, "Aah, that was truly delicious! Thank you, Chiyuri. Please thank your mother as well."

"Oh! Sure! I was a little worried about whether or not you'd like it. I'm glad you did!" Chiyuri grinned happily, and Kuroyukihime turned a wry smile on her as she wiped her fingers.

"Come come, my usual fare is incredibly slapdash. I could give Haruyuki a run for his money."

"Whaaaat? That's not good for you!" Chiyuri screwed her face up.

"Well then," Sky Raker said with a composed look. "Perhaps Corvus and Lotus both had the same frozen pizza last night."

Puzzled looks from Chiyuri and Takumu. Contrasted with the deer in the headlights from Haruyuki and Kuroyukihime.

"F-frozen pizza lately's pretty good with the whole CAS freezing technology! Do you know about this? Basically, they use supercooling so that they don't destroy the cells when they freeze stuff…"

Blathering away in a desperate bid to change the subject, Haruyuki had the abrupt thought, *Wait, there is one, isn't there? A Legion that's under perfect control.*

The second Nega Nebulus now was exactly that—or rather something more than that. Because all the members exposed their real information to one another and even came together to eat like this. None of them doubting any other, they were bound by real trust. Almost as if they were a family.

This absolutely could not scale up to a large Legion with more than forty or fifty members, but Haruyuki felt that these bonds themselves were their greatest weapon to fight the other Kings going forward. At the same time as this feeling hit him, in the depths of his heart, he prayed resolutely that they would be bound like this forever. He closed his eyes for a moment, quickly opened them again, and involuntarily smiled wryly without letting it onto his face. In his ears, Kuroyukihime's words came back to life.

To maintain these new bonds, we try to maintain the stability and the concealed nature of the Accelerated World.

That sentence summarized everything in his mind at that moment.

*But…*Haruyuki took a step forward in his thinking. *Even if the movements of my heart put me onto the exact trajectory the developer intended, that wouldn't decrease the value of these bonds even the tiniest bit.*

Right. Whether or not there's some hidden objective somewhere in Brain Burst...
I will protect this family.

A few minutes later, once they had all finished eating and everything was cleaned up, they moved to the living room sofas. The U-shaped set was for five people, and they sat down in such a way as to allow them all to daisy-chain.

After they quickly connected using four XSB cables of various colors, Haruyuki looked around at everyone assembled. "Umm," he said. "Once you accelerate and show up in the initial accelerated space, please stay on standby there. I'll use the transporter card in my menu, and then we should all be instantly taken to the bottom station of Hermes' Cord."

The others nodded. The details of the race had already been outlined in that earlier mail, so all that was left now was to wait for the time. They stared not at the analog clock on the wall, but the digital clocks in the bottom right of their virtual desktops, which constantly displayed the precise Japan Standard Time. Two minutes and three seconds until noon.

Real-world time normally felt like it raced by, the surging waves of swift currents, but at times like this, each and every second seemed so long as to be vexing. Still, the digits did indeed continue to decrease until at long last, there were just twenty seconds left.

"Now then, everyone," Kuroyukihime uttered in a light, clear voice. "Let's enjoy every minute of the Hermes' Cord Race! I'll start the countdown! Ten, nine, eight, seven..."

The five leaned back deeply into the sofa as they closed their eyes. *Six, five, four.*

They took a deep breath. *Three, two, one.*

They shouted.

"Burst Link!!"

8

During the time he raced up the tunnel of light leading to the empty sky 150 kilometers above the Earth, Haruyuki transformed from his pink pig avatar to his duel avatar, Silver Crow. He slipped through one particularly dazzling ring and landed on metallic ground with a *clang*.

Which was immediately followed by four sets of footfalls from his companions echoing through the space. He straightened up from his hunched posture and opened his closed eyes.

"Whoa! A King! The Black King's heeeeeeere!!"

"Now things are getting exciting! Negabu's the beeeeeest!!"

Showered on all sides with welcoming cries, Haruyuki jumped a little.

"Wha…?!" He hurriedly looked around and was rooted to the spot at the scene before him.

The flat metallic ring stage. The steel tower soaring up from the center. The surrounding dark blue sky and the herds of hovering white clouds. This was indeed the majestic Hermes' Cord, the space elevator in the Accelerated World he had visited a few days earlier.

However, three enormous things he didn't remember seeing the last time sat there, encircling the tower.

No matter how he looked at them, they were clearly audience seating. The tiered stands fifty or so meters long floated in the sky slightly above the stage on which Haruyuki and his friends stood. The four rows of seating were jam-packed with avatars of a variety of colors. Putting all three spectator stands together, these audience avatars likely numbered more than five hundred. In other words, half or more of all the Burst Linkers in existence were occupying this field now.

"This...is turning into a real thing, huh..."

"Seriously. I've never seen this many people at once before."

Next to him, Cyan Pile (Takumu) and Lime Bell (Chiyuri) murmured, stunned. Naturally, Black Lotus (Kuroyukihime) and Sky Raker (Fuko) were their usual calm selves, but even still, they likely each had their own strong emotions welling up. They looked up at the sky soundlessly.

"...How did that Gallery even dive here...," Haruyuki unconsciously murmured.

"Spectator transporter cards were given out," someone from immediately behind him replied right away.

"O-oh, that makes sense...Huh, the system even does nice stuff sometimes...Wait, what?!" Gasping, he whirled around.

Standing there was a slim duel avatar with a dark red body who had approached him without his realizing it. He didn't need to see the triangular ears popping up from the mask or the long tail to know that it was Blood Leopard, nicknamed Pard, member of the Red Legion Prominence. A little ways off stood four avatars, likely her team members, conversing quietly. They were all veteran Linkers he had seen countless times before, but the figure of the crimson girl avatar was not among them.

"H-hello, nice to see you, Pard."

"'Sup."

"Um, Niko didn't come?" Haruyuki asked quietly after exchanging greetings with the ever-abbreviated leopard-headed avatar.

"She super wanted to, but the six Legion mutual nonaggression pact prohibits fighting among Kings, even in an event. I have a message from her instead: 'Aim for second. Good luck.'"

"Oh…R-right." The corners of his mouth tugged unconsciously upward at the image of Niko's frustrated face, and an equally frustrated tone popped up in his mind, and Haruyuki followed up with another question. "So then, um…Is the Red team fighting with us until we're close to the finish line?"

But Blood Leopard did not reply. She shifted her gaze from Haruyuki and began to walk soundlessly. She slipped between Takumu and Chiyuri and passed in front of Kuroyukihime, toward the light blue avatar sitting in the silver wheelchair.

The two Burst Linkers, who had in the past been opponents in countless fierce battles, stared silently at each other. There was no hostility there, but rather, a hard, wizened air spread out, and the surrounding chatter and bustle receded temporarily.

A few seconds later, Pard took a step back and glanced at all of the members of the Black team before turning back to Sky Raker once more.

"We're going for the win with all we've got," she said.

It was a declaration. They might be friendly Legions, but they wouldn't be working together. Haruyuki actually felt there was likely more meaning to the statement than that. Now that Sky Raker had sealed away Gale Thruster and continued not to take part in normal duels, the day when these two could go back to their old friendly rivalry was not coming. Which was why, at least today, Pard was without a doubt wanting to fight for real.

Likely having grasped this, Sky Raker nodded deeply. "Just what I was hoping for," she replied.

The leopard-headed avatar returned the nod lightly and pivoted her lithe body, heading back to her own team members. The five from Prominence then headed toward the shuttles parked at the base of the elevator tower.

Looking up, Haruyuki saw huge digital numbers counting down. They were carved into the upper part of the sloped starting grid, where the multicolored shuttles were lined up. There was still ten minutes before the start of the race.

"All right, we should head over, too. That silver one on the left edge, that's us, number one, hmm?"

Urged on by Kuroyukihime, the five members of the Black team also started toward their shuttle. As they did, another shadow approached them from the right. Until Haruyuki heard the voice, he had no idea who this avatar was, running with heavy feet in sturdy boots.

"Hey, heeeeeeeey! Here you are, all set to be a lazy loser dog—no, loser crow!"

"Huh? What? Ash?!"

"...H-hey! Who else d'you think this megacoooool star'd be!"

The cocky skull-helmeted head obviously belonged to Ash Roller, whom he had fought just the day before. When he looked away, behind the avatar running toward him, he saw a bright ash-gray shuttle. Apparently, the century-end rider had some-how succeeded in registering as a driver for the race.

Thinking the very rude thought that if Ash Roller had figured out the appearance of the portal on his own, then he was way more intellectual than anything about his character suggested, Haruyuki began excusing himself. "S-sorry. You're not on your bike, so I wasn't sure who it was—"

"C-come on, you! Treating me like an accessory to my bike, that's bullshit!"

"That's rude, Ash."

The instant that voice sounded from behind Haruyuki, the century-end–style avatar leapt to uncharacteristic and ill-fitting attention and offered a respectful bow. "H-hello, Master! And Miss Lotus, p-pleasure to see ya!"

After offering up this marble-mouthed greeting, Ash Roller lifted his face as though he had just remembered something and abruptly brought his skull face up to Haruyuki. "R-right, this totally ain't the time for dissing each other! Crow, I got somethin' I wanna ask you."

"S-sure, what is it?"

"You signed up as the driver for machine number one here, so that means when you got to this stage, you were the first?"

Stunned at the unexpected question, Haruyuki recovered quickly. "Yeah, that's right. But it was at basically the same time as Blood Leopard. She was second."

"So then, that shuttle was like that when you guys got here? Or did you see the dude who registered for it?"

Unable to comprehend what Ash Roller was talking about, Haruyuki craned his neck around. The skull-headed avatar grew impatient and placed an arm around Haruyuki's neck and started running, cutting across the row of shuttles.

"Hey! Uh! Where are we—?!"

"You'll totes get it once you check it!…See? The tenth shuttle. So? Was it like that at the start?"

Haruyuki didn't even hear the majority of the latter half of the question. Because the instant *that* came into view, surprise slammed into the crown of his head.

The tenth of the shuttles lined up two meters apart on the starting grid, the machine enshrined on the right end—

Was decayed.

Almost as if it had been left exposed to a sea breeze for several years, the entire body was covered in rust. In contrast with the other nine machines, all shining brand-new, the same color as the bodies of their registered drivers, the tenth shuttle had completely lost all brilliance and was rusted a reddish brown. It wasn't just the body that was weathered; the wear extended to the seats and the driving discs under the machine body. The idea that this shuttle could run seemed utterly improbable.

Haruyuki unconsciously stretched out a hand and lightly clicked the way he had when he registered for machine number one a few days earlier. *Pwan!* A system window popped up. He read out loud the word displayed there.

"Re-reserved? So someone's taken it…in this condition?!"

"Man, you understand zero or what? By the time the other

Legion mems and I got here at five thirty on Wednesday, it was already like this."

"What? That's weird!" Haruyuki's eyelids flew back as he protested. "Pard and I took off pretty quickly after we registered for shuttles one and two, but before we did, we could already hear a ton of people running over. There probably wasn't even ten seconds between the time we disappeared and the time you guys got here. There's no way anyone could have registered without me or you seeing them...and even before that." He closed his eyes for a moment and called the distinct memory up before saying decisively, "When we left, number ten here was not rusted. It was a clean steel gray, the same as the other machines!"

"F-for real serious? So then...that means it just went and rotted on its own in those ten seconds?...Or some dude hiding somewhere did it..."

"No way. That's impossible. There's nowhere to hide. And even if I didn't notice them, Pard absolutely would have..."

They each cradled their heads. As they struggled to reach a logical answer, a loud buzzer sounded, and cheers several times louder shook the stage. Lifting his face with a gasp, he saw they were down to three minutes left.

"Welp, totes sucks ass, but nothing to do but leave this thing be. Doesn't look like the driver's here anyway."

"I guess so. If it's some kind of system thing, we'll probably see during the race at some point."

"That's totes it. Aaaaanyway, we both gotta get out there and do it for real."

"Right! Let's give it everything we have!"

Haruyuki and Ash Roller dipped their heads at each other and ran back to their own machines. As they separated, the usual venom came flying his way.

"Let me tell you now, though! Long as it's got tires—tricycle, tanker truck, whatever—it's giga welcome to supercool me!"

"These shuttles don't have tires!" Haruyuki retorted. When he reached shuttle number one, his four crew members were already sitting in the rear seats.

"Huuuurry up!" Chiyuri shouted, waving her right hand. "What are you doing?!"

"A-ah! Sorry!" Hurriedly leaping into the driver's seat, he grabbed on to the steering wheel. On the small windshield, the text HELLO, MY DRIVER popped up, followed by a display of various indicators. That said, it was nothing complicated. Just a speedometer, a trip meter, and an endurance meter.

Kuroyukihime leaned forward from the front row of the crew seating, next to Sky Raker, who had unequipped her wheelchair. "Crow," she whispered. "I did a quick look-over of the other participants, and they're basically all top fighters, including members of the six main Legions. Still, at any rate, this is the first time any of the drivers has operated a shuttle. Proceed cautiously until you get used to driving it. We'll keep a tight guard against any attacks from the other teams, so don't worry about that."

"Totally!" Chiyuri, sitting in the back row, continued. "And if we take a teensy bit of damage, I'll just rewind!"

"Hmm. Bell, I don't think our special-attack gauges will charge that much, since our avatar HP gauges are locked," Takumu pointed out, and Chiyuri cried, "What is that even?!" while Kuroyukihime and Fuko laughed.

Glancing over his shoulder at the picture his companions were painting, Haruyuki murmured in his heart, *I'm counting on you, Kuroyukihime. Let's do it, Taku, Chiyu…and Raker. I am definitely going to take you to the finish line. That's why I'm here right now, after all.*

"Okay! One minute! Everybody, hang on tight!" Haruyuki shouted as the shining digital numbers above his head dropped down to the last two digits, and then turned to zero.

The enthusiastic cries pouring down from the three floating spectator stands once again shook the Earth. Tightly gripping the wheel, he lightly pressed down on the accelerator with his right foot. The shuttle engine area howled reassuringly, and the vibration enveloped the vehicle. The digital meter displaying the total race distance of four thousand kilometers glittered brightly.

Staring up at the majesty of the Hermes' Cord re-created in the Accelerated World, a metal pillar piercing the sky, one hundred meters in diameter, Haruyuki had an abrupt thought.

Right about now, in the real-world elevator, too, rich tourists are ascending toward space, right? And they're not even thinking about this. That in another world produced by the social cameras placed in every nook and cranny of the elevator, dozens of children are about to race up alongside them right now.

Of course, the Accelerated World is, in the end, not real, just a fabrication of our Neurolinkers. But even if there's no physicality here, it really does exist. Because—

I am right here burning up with real excitement!

"Go! Go! Go! Go! Go!"

The chanting of the Gallery drowned out the sound of the red signal lights coming on. Points of crimson light formed a line in the sky above, shining down on the ten shuttles. At that moment, one of the spectator stands precisely blocked the sun hanging high in the air, and the stage was blanketed by a thick shadow. A second buzzer sounded as the signal lights shone red on the vehicles. The roaring of each engine increased all at once. Dazzling lightning gushed from the four driving discs in place of tires and bounced off the steel surface below.

"...Here we gooooooo!!"

The instant the countdown hit zero and the lights turned green, Haruyuki slammed the accelerator to the floor.

Tremendous torque kicked the machine into the air. Ten shuttles raced up the short incline in the blink of an eye and began a vertical sprint. Along the gently curving surface of the enormous metal pillar they flew, all in direct violation of the law of gravity. Some sort of attractive force seemed to be at work between the pillar and the machines, and even when the angle of elevation reached ninety degrees, the physical sensation was essentially no different from driving along a straight road.

Foot stuck to the accelerator, Haruyuki glanced over at the speedometer. The vivid digital numbers told him that in a mere ten seconds, he had sped up to more than two hundred kilometers per hour, and he was still climbing dizzyingly fast.

"H-hey, Haru. Y-you sure you should be going this fast?!"

At Takumu's concerned voice from the rear seats, Haruyuki half shouted in reply, "Trust me! I've played a ton of racing games and crashed thousands of times!"

"...Th-that's..."

"Allll riiiight! Flyyyy!"

Chiyuri's cheer drowned out Takumu's hoarse voice.

Glancing at the reflection of the rear in the upper part of the window, Haruyuki saw Kuroyukihime and Fuko sitting with cool expressions on their faces. Encouraged, he put even more force into his right foot. Two hundred fifty kilometers per hour. Three hundred. If he were driving a real-world race car, it would be reaching its limit right now, but the virtual linear-drive shuttle howled at an increasingly higher pitch and kept pulling itself up to endlessly faster speeds. The details carved into the steel below melted into ripples and the lumps of clouds that appeared occasionally flew back behind them in the time it took to blink.

A few seconds later, when the red-tinged digital meter began to flash the MAX icon, they had reached five hundred kilometers per hour. Apparently, this was the shuttle's top speed. He exhaled all at once the breath he'd been holding and now finally took a look outside the vehicle.

Silver shuttle number one, containing the Nega Nebulus team, was as before racing at the left end of the line of vehicles. To their right, about ten meters or so away, the red team's machine, led by Blood Leopard, glittered with deep crimson sparks.

Beyond that was the machine carrying the four members of

the Blue Legion Leonids. The driver was Tourmaline Shell. The enormous figure taking up one of the rear seats was Frost Horn. Even farther to the right, Ash Roller, who belonged to the Green Legion Great Wall, was yelling, "Hey, heeeey!"

These four machines, essentially lined up in a row, were fighting for the lead. Slightly behind them, pulling up a tight rear, was the team from the Yellow Legion, Crypt Cosmic Circus. Naturally, the Yellow King was not among them, but he saw a few faces he had gone up against in battle more than once mixed in there.

Be careful of those guys! He carved the warning into his brain and looked closely once more. It seemed that the only Legion team with a King was their own, and the four machines running along in the rear in a single lump seemed to be from midsize Legions—that said, all of them had far more members than Nega Nebulus.

The shuttles running were the total of nine he noted. Which meant that, in the end, that super-rusted shuttle didn't actually start. The unresolved question caused him momentary discomfort, but he quickly banished it from his mind. Regardless of who had turned the shuttle into that corroded mess, they couldn't have any impact on the race anymore.

Having gotten a grasp on the situation, Haruyuki was about to turn his gaze back to the front when he spotted an enormous shadow in the sky behind them, which surprised him a little. The three floating spectator stands crammed with the total of six hundred members of the Gallery were automatically chasing the shuttles. Only now did he notice that the tumult of mad cheering was coming to him alongside the howl of the linear engine.

"Hee-hee, it does seem that they've placed a few bets."

Sky Raker nodded at Kuroyukihime's words. "Mm-hmm. I saw the Matchmaker running around looking quite busy."

The Matchmaker was a mysterious Burst Linker who ran the gambling/tournament hall Akihabara Battle Ground. And he seemed to have shown up at this race as well.

"H-huh. Have you been to Akiba BG, too, Raker?" Haruyuki

asked as he made incremental adjustments with the steering wheel, and he got a reply in the form of a wry smile from Kuroyukihime, rather than Sky Raker herself.

"She has, she has. Raker used to—"

But he didn't get to hear what came next. The cheers of the Gallery abruptly doubled in volume, overlaid with a series of sounds that practically pierced his eardrums. Haruyuki immediately looked to his right. His face stiffened. "Whoa! Pard's already starting!"

The sounds were originating from the weapons readied by the four Burst Linkers sitting in the back of the red team shuttle. It seemed that the only close-range type was the driver Blood Leopard, with the other four solidly in the long-distance camp. A battery of machine guns and rifles sent out a barrage of light bullets.

Their target was the blue team shuttle racing along to the right of the red team. The blue team, in contrast, was apparently all close-range types, and Frost Horn plus one other avatar with thick armor leaned forward to defend against the hail of bullets. Avatar HP gauges were locked, so no matter how many bullets rained down on them, they wouldn't die, but there seemed to be a recoil effect at work. From time to time, their bodies would bounce back, and in that opening, the shots would hit the mark on the shuttle body.

"Waah, you guys! Unforgivable! Serious! Tori, hit that machine!!"

With an "Okay, Hooooorn!" in reply to Frost Horn's shouting, Tourmaline Shell turned the steering wheel to the left. The blue team shuttle zoomed in on the red team. Apparently, they were planning to bring down their opponent's shuttle by throwing themselves at it.

That's the kind of pira-e-style fighting Frost Horn loves. Haruyuki watched excitedly as the scene played out. The Gallery crowds following from the rear on the floating stands also got even more worked up: "Slam 'em!" "Noooo!"

As the two machines grew closer, the accuracy of the hail of bullets naturally increased. Countless tiny holes were gouged out of the left flank of the blue shuttle as sparks crackled and scattered. But its endurance was apparently fairly high; the shuttle didn't show the slightest sign of slowing down.

"Oh! Okay! Take this! A real man's! Spirit punch!!" Shrieking, Frost Horn stood and brandished his right fist.

Instantly, Blood Leopard spun the steering wheel of the red shuttle so fast it blurred. The linear wheel squealed and the machine whirled around. The shaken right rear slammed into the side of the blue shuttle. The impact knocked Frost Horn—standing and ready to swing a superpunch—helplessly off his feet.

"Wha! At! Whaaaaaaat?!"

With a shriek, he tumbled and fell outside the vehicle, which was speeding along at an intense five hundred kilometers an hour. The instant he touched the surface of the tower, he bounced back high up with a tremendous *wham*, scattering showy sparks. A throaty scream accompanied the enormous body as it bounded along, receding in the blink of an eye behind them. After a few seconds, it disappeared from sight entirely.

Meanwhile, Pard stabilized the vehicle as though nothing had happened and slid away to get some distance. The projectile barrage started up again. The blue team tried another daring close-range attack, but it seemed that here, the shuttle had finally reached the limits of its endurance. Abruptly, the two linear wheels on the left spurted flames, and the six-meter machine began to spin like a top. Amid the rising and falling cries of the remaining three crew members, the engine whined higher and higher—

Explosion. On a massive scale.

As the cheers and shrieks of the Gallery washed over them, the charred machine and the three avatars disappeared from sight, just like Horn before them. Watching this, Haruyuki shrank into himself with an inner shriek. Kuroyukihime and Fuko made almost admiring comments.

"I see. If you fall from the shuttle, that's the end of the line, then. Either way, that was quite the attack by Prominence."

"It was. Just like Leopard. From the selection of her teammates to her handling of the machine, her unparalleled skills haven't grown the slightest bit dull."

"S-s-sis, is now really the time for admiration! They'll be after us next!" Chiyuri shouted at essentially the same time that the four shooters of the red team, having finished reloading, repositioned themselves facing left. The muzzles of their guns aimed perfectly at number one—or, more precisely, taking into consideration the curvature of the bullet's path, a little ahead of their machine's nose.

"Gah!" Haruyuki shouted, and hurriedly pulled the wheel to the left. But Pard, through some wonderful maneuvering, managed to maintain the same positional relationship. A cheer rose up from the Gallery at the two machines drawing lovely parallel lines above the column a hundred meters in diameter—in other words, three hundred and fourteen meters around—but unlike a car commercial, this game of tag was life or death. The instant one of the shooters gave the command, the four guns erupted in flames all at once.

"......!"

We can't escape! Haruyuki instinctively pulled his head back, but the sound he heard was not that of bullets hitting them, but rather a high-pitched reverberation. Hurriedly shifting his gaze to the right, his eyes beheld a totally unexpected sight.

Leaning out from the starboard side somehow, Black Lotus was repelling nearly all of the bullets falling in a curtain of rain upon them, the swords of her hands glittering at incredible speed. Cyan Pile, in the rear, was also thoroughly guarding the machine, using the enormous Pile Driver of his right hand in place of a shield.

Only a tiny few bullets slipped through their guard to hit the body, and the endurance indicator dropped hardly at all, but there was no doubt the situation would only gradually get worse.

Even if he got close to them aiming to use their own shuttle as a weapon, he couldn't hope to beat Pard when it came to driving technique; they were more likely to have a precious crew member knocked out of the vehicle instead, just like the blue team.

"Ah, come on! Just 'cause we don't have any reds on our team, they think they can just shoot us up all they want!" Chiyuri shouted indignantly from the left rear. And indeed, this lack of any long-distance types had been Nega Nebulus's biggest weak point since its reformation. When they lost in the Territories, most times, the opponent included a powerful red type.

However, lamenting this fact here and now would get them nowhere. Haruyuki steadied himself to challenge Pard to a dog fight with their machines and was about to call out to the backseat. But a second before he could—

"I'm getting out," Sky Raker announced quietly.

"Huh? Master, what?!"

"This is simple addition and subtraction. The Promi team has five people, and four of those are large, heavy guns. If I get out of the shuttle, there'll be four of you, and you should be able to shake them off with speed."

"Y-you can't do that, sis!" Chiyuri's half shriek was covered up by Raker's cool words.

"I told you, you know, that if I was to participate, we would put everything into the top spot. And getting out here is my 'everything.' If I don't, you won't be able to respond to Leopard! She's not holding back, you know!" And then, the sky-blue avatar grabbed on to the side of the ship with her left hand and unhesitatingly went to send herself flying.

Instantly, Haruyuki yanked the wheel hard to the right. The machine went into a half spin, and Raker was thrown back into her seat.

"No…No, Master!!" As he focused all his mental energy on operating the steering wheel and the accelerator to desperately try and restabilize the machine, Haruyuki squeezed a voice out from his throat. "Getting out yourself isn't 'everything,' not even close! We have to fight on the same stage or we communicate nothing!!"

"Crow's exactly right, Raker!" Kuroyukihime shouted as she continued her awesomely precise defense. "We are a team! All five of us fight, and all five of us win!"

"But...But I have—!" Fuko's half-shrieked rebuttal rang out. "I have no means of fighting! I can't even stand up and defend, much less attack! I can't do anything other than sit here like some object...!"

"You can, too!" The words, almost a cry of desperation, gushed from Haruyuki's throat. "You have...the wings you produced, the wings you made strong!!"

He hesitated about whether or not he should say anything here. Sky Raker had her own reasons and feelings for firmly locking away that power after rejoining the Legion and keeping it locked away. Haruyuki didn't want to do anything to force her into facing them. Which was why he was trying to take Sky Raker to the pinnacle of Hermes' Cord, which he believed for various reasons was the lone place where he could actually be allowed to say this.

But if Raker got out of the shuttle at that moment, that opportunity would be lost forever. Thus, Haruyuki could only shout and pray that his words reached her.

"Our special-attack gauges basically won't charge in this field... so I can't fly. But your wings are different. Immediately after you equip them, the gauge is fully charged. Which means you *can* fly!" Looking back from the cockpit, he stared directly into Raker's eyes. "Please. Lend this shuttle—no, lend us the power of your wings! If you do, we should be able to escape from Promi's sights!!"

Instant silence.

Haruyuki's ears picked up none of the howl of gunfire showering them, or the sound of Kuroyukihime and Takumu repelling those bullets, or the cheers pouring down from the audience in the sky. He simply and earnestly turned those ears toward Sky Raker's thin breathing and the echoes of struggle it contained.

"...I hurt Sacchi."

"...With my words, with my attitude, and with my heart, I hurt her. The fuel for my wings contains each and every tear Sacchi shed back then. Which is why...Which is why I can never again—"

"That's not true, Raker!!" Kuroyukihime's dancing hands came to a sudden stop as she whirled around.

Immediately, the gunfire began to gouge into the side of the machine and mercilessly pound against Black Lotus's back. Even as her slim body shook and staggered with the impact, Kuroyukihime's words were firm.

"I...I was foolish! I didn't even try to understand the enormity of what you carried around with you! I simply wanted you to do everything for me and I was convinced you betrayed that. I was irrationally angry; I resented you! I have no right to seek anything from you...but!" Here, her voice finally began to shake with the force of the emotion bleeding into it. Behind the jet-black mirrored goggles, beams of violet-blue light poured from her eyes, almost like tears. "But the time to fly is now! Not for me, and not for the Legion...For you. Fly, Raker!"

At the same time as this impassioned cry, a bullet that came flying from a large rifle caught Black Lotus squarely, violently in the back. Sky Raker leaned forward to prop up the small body staggering toward her. The thin arms trembled as if hesitating to draw any closer.

Master—No, Fuko. Haruyuki started talking deep in his heart as he put his physical efforts into driving the shuttle. *Two months ago, on the roof of Shinjuku Southern Terrace, Kuroyukihime took a step forward. So right now, you...please pull Kuroyukihime toward you with your own hand. I can't close that final distance; no one else can. It's something only you can do!*

There was no way those words could have reached her. But the next instant, Fuko's trembling stopped. The arms that supported

Kuroyukihime's body slowly bent and folded, and her hands circled round to the other girl's back, embracing her tightly.

"Thank you, Lotus." In the midst of the innumerable bullets whizzing past them, her words came quietly but with a certainty. "Now, now I finally see it. My wings...They're not full of tears, but rather your hope, your kindness, and your love." Here, she pushed Kuroyukihime back down into the seat to the right and nodded definitively. "So there was no need for me to be afraid...I can fly. Now, I'm sure I can fly again...!"

Instantly, Haruyuki finally understood.

Sky Raker hadn't given up or anything like it. She had been afraid. She was afraid that even if she did equip her Enhanced Armament, she wouldn't be able to fly like she used to—that in the same way her legs continued to be lost, her own negative will would also inactivate the Armament.

However, there was no fear in the way she threw her chest out now and reached both arms out into the sky. In those deep-red eyes, he glimpsed a nearly infinite sky.

As if singing, Sky Raker cried out the "preset equip" phrase loudly.

"Calling Gale!!"

In the endless ultramarine of the empty sky the machine hurtled toward, Haruyuki saw the twinkling of a vivid light blue star.

This turned into two laser beams pouring down, which pinpointed Sky Raker immediately, despite the fact that the shuttle was racing ahead at maximum speed. The light enveloped her entire body before quickly concentrating on her back and materializing as the streamlined silhouette of the boosters of the Enhanced Armament Gale Thruster. Perhaps because they interfered with the equipment, the white hat and dress melted into light and disappeared, revealing the slender main body of the avatar.

"Raker..."

"Master!"

"Sis!"

"Sky Raker!"

The four other Legion members all cried out at the same time, and Sky Raker nodded forcefully before dancing up from her seat. Of course, this wasn't because she had thrown herself from the vehicle. Taking Lime Bell's hand, she moved to the rear of the shuttle and grabbed tightly ahold of the small rear spoiler.

"Crow! Stabilize the ship dead ahead!"

Haruyuki jumped to follow Raker's instruction. The red team in number two had likely guessed number one's intention and began to shower them with an even heavier hail of bullets, but Kuroyukihime once again knocked each and every one of them aside.

"I'm going! Three seconds to boost! Two, one, zero!!"

Krrrrr!! An extraordinary roar was generated, and at the same time, Haruyuki's entire body was pushed forcefully back into his seat as he clenched his teeth.

This acceleration. Desperately struggling to keep the machine under control, he peeked at the rearview window. There reflected he saw two jets of flames erupting from Raker's back and stretching out endlessly, like the tail of a comet. The output was far and away greater than when Haruyuki had used Gale Thruster. There was no abnormal light effect coming from the booster itself—i.e., they were not emitting any overlay—so this power boost wasn't due to the Incarnate System. It was the crystallization of effort, the vast quantities of burst points poured into the Armament over who knew how many years.

Bringing his gaze back to the front, he saw that the speedometer in the right edge of the windshield had smashed through the limit, and that they were reaching 650 kilometers an hour. The curtain of fire from number two had already been cut off, and the red team reflected in the starboard mirror grew smaller and smaller before his eyes.

Haruyuki suppressed the wave of emotion trying to fill his heart and focused on driving the shuttle. If their orientation were disturbed even the slightest bit at this speed, the machine would no doubt crash immediately. Up to now, there had been no obstacles at all on Hermes' Cord, but he couldn't let them get tripped up by a tiny gap or anything now.

A mere half second later, Haruyuki saw that his misgivings were realized.

A curious object appeared ahead of them. A line of broadly spaced rainbow rings glittering on the surface of the pillar. The diameter of each ring was at least three meters. If they kept charging ahead like this, they would smash into the one in their path.

"E-evasive action! Raker, get back in your seat!" Haruyuki shouted hurriedly, but before he could finish speaking, Kuroyuki-hime gave an unexpected instruction:

"No! Charge on like this, Crow!"

"Huh…B-but?!"

"It's fine! Just go!"

Either way, it seemed that Gale Thruster's energy gauge was exhausted, and Sky Raker once again borrowed Chiyuri's hand to return to her original seat. After seeing that, Haruyuki readied himself and tightened his grip on the steering wheel.

"U-understood! We charge! Everyone, hold on tight!"

A mere two seconds later, still at the same insane speed, shuttle number one plunged into one of the rainbow rings.

9

The flash of the light, the impact, the enormous explosion—did not happen.

Instead, a strange phenomenon enveloped the machine. The dark blue sky spreading out around them vanished, and a light the same rainbow color as the mysterious rings radiated outward. At the same time, the howling of the linear wheels ceased, and the space was filled with only a high-pitched sound of resonance.

The roar and vibration of the race disappeared abruptly, and feeling a curious sensation in his ears, Haruyuki hesitantly opened his mouth. "Uh, umm, Kuroyukihime, what is this...?"

"Warp zone."

He whirled around at Kuroyukihime's immediate and decisive reply. *Huh?!*

"W-warp?! Something like that in the race?!"

"I get it. Actually, it's only natural that there would be, Haru." This time, it was Takumu nodding. A single finger popped up, and he entered full-on professor mode to explain. "I mean, think about it. The total length of Hermes' Cord is four thousand kilometers, right? And this shuttle's maximum speed is five hundred kilometers an hour. Which means even if you kept the accelerator floored, it would take eight hours to reach the finish line. And that ends up being an endurance race. It's basically impossible for one driver to drive the whole way."

"O-ohh…Yeah, now that you mention it…"

Totally satisfied with this explanation, Haruyuki checked the meter with the distance remaining and saw that the four digits were dropping at a bewildering pace. Somehow, they seemed to be taking a shortcut through this space to a point about a thousand kilometers away from their goal.

"So then, like, anyone who *doesn't* go into the rings there is gonna be in serious trouble, right?" Chiyuri said, her pointed hat shaking.

"Come come, Bell!" Kuroyukihime's response was mixed with laughter. "You'd just need to make a U-turn at that point."

"Oh! I guess! Hmm. But I kinda get the impression that if you play this sort of game cautiously, you're gonna lose!"

"Well, I wholeheartedly agree with that."

Their little back-and-forth made everyone laugh briefly, and just as that laughter was subsiding, Kuroyukihime, still seated, turned to Fuko, who was sitting to her left, and began to talk quietly.

"Raker, thank you. And…I'm sorry. You suffering for such a long time was solely due to my own cowardice." Just as she was about to bow her head deeply along with this apology, Sky Raker gently stretched out her right hand and stopped her.

"Lotus. I, too…There are so many things I need for apologize to you for as well. But we won't be able to completely communicate our feelings in words alone. So when I'm able to fight you once again at full strength, let's talk, and talk at length, then."

"Mmm, I suppose so…I suppose you're right…," Kuroyukihime murmured in response, and closed her eyes briefly before continuing with a faint smile. "Indeed, our total duel results are one thousand, two hundred and thirteen wins for me…and how many losses, I wonder?"

"Oh! You only forget the number that's inconvenient for you!"

Once again, a tranquil laughter spread out through the warp zone, and, bathed in these gentle reverberations, Haruyuki murmured in his heart, *Maybe I didn't need to butt in after all. These two are definitely connected in a deep place in their souls. Right... They must have been able to build that connection precisely because of their time here in the Accelerated World, where time flows a thousand times faster...*He closed his eyes and tried to thoroughly process his own thoughts when—

Thmm. The center of his back throbbed. At the same time, cold words were born in the back of his mind, in his own voice and yet somehow not his own voice.

In that case, the opposite must be true, too. Don't you think?

There has to exist in the Accelerated World an ugly, swollen hatred nurtured through time moving a thousand times faster than outside. Perhaps inside me.

RIGHT. THE SEED OF A HATRED YOU CAN'T GET RID OF HAS TAKEN ROOT IN YOU. IT WAITS FOR THE TIME TO BUD AND BLOOM. HAVE YOU ALREADY FORGOTTEN THOSE WHO ONCE TORTURED YOU? HAVE YOU INDEED FORGOTTEN ALREADY THE PAIN OF THE WOUNDS THEY INFLICTED ON YOU WITH THEIR IRRATIONAL VIOLENCE AND MALICE? MALICE WITH MALICE. POWER WITH POWER. THAT IS THE RESPONSE. THE SEED TO THAT END IS ALWAYS WITHIN YOU.

As the darkly twisted voice whispered, several faces floated up on the backs of his tightly closed eyelids.

The malicious classmates who had teased Haruyuki in elementary school. The delinquents who rained violence down upon him, bluntly demanding money and more once he started junior high school. When their faces disappeared, the masks of duel avatars sprang up in their place. Although they were few, the Burst Linkers he had hated unreservedly in the Accelerated World looked down on Haruyuki from on high, grinning.

You intend to understand even them? Be connected? No. It is impossible.

Aah, that's exactly it. I mean, I've already banished one of them forever. So I can't be connected to him anymore. But that's...I had no choice. That's the natural thing to do with a guy like that!

Accompanying this shout like a howl, the throbbing in his back gradually grew stronger. However, curiously, that pain was no longer simply uncomfortable. The larger it grew, the more he could imagine the pleasure when it was released. The voice continued, irritated, inviting.

THAT'S RIGHT. IT'S NATURAL TO CRUSH THEM. YOU ALREADY HAVE THE POWER TO DO EXACTLY THAT. YOU JUST HAVE TO SAY IT, THAT NAME. JUST THAT AND YOU CAN BEAT THEM ALL DOWN SO THAT NOT ONE REMAINS. CUT THEM UP, TEAR THEM TO PIECES, EAT THEM UP. EAT THEM. EAT THEM. EAT—

"C-Corvus?!"

The sharp cry was accompanied by a hand grabbing his left shoulder firmly, and Haruyuki opened his eyes with a gasp. He froze momentarily before awkwardly looking back.

Sky Raker, sitting on the left of the middle row, was the one stretching a hand out. The deep red of her eye lenses shone intently as she stared hard at Haruyuki. A dry, thin voice slipped from between her lips.

"Corvus...What did you do just now...?"

"Huh...Wh-what...I didn't..." Haruyuki shook his head firmly, feeling guilty at the turbulent thoughts racing around in the back of his mind. But he wasn't actually lying. His body was simply sitting in the driver's seat and gripping the steering wheel. He really *was* doing nothing.

"...I...saw it, too. For just a moment...an Incarnate overlay on your body...?!"

"Hngh...?!" This time, he groaned, shocked to his core.

He had absolutely not been using the Incarnate System. That alone he could declare with certainty. To begin with, at his level of training, there was no way he would be able to unconsciously do anything to activate an overwrite.

"Th-there was not! I wasn't using Incarnate or anything! Honestly!!" he shouted as he continued to shake his head fiercely.

Fuko's hold on Haruyuki's shoulder grew even tighter, but eventually, she let go, exhaling softly. "Yes. There's…no way. Your overlay *is* silver. But…the light before…"

Fuko's voice faded away and Kuroyukihime picked up where she left off. "So we saw wrong. Most likely, some change in the surrounding light effects was reflected in Crow's mirrored body…Sorry for scaring you. But, you know, it's your fault, too, for being that color."

Her words, her tone 70 percent back to its usual coloring, lightened the mood in the cabin in the middle of the super-high-speed warp. Chiyuri and Takumu, together in the backseat, let out long breaths.

"Honestly! Don't scare us, sis! Although it's true Haru's avatar can sometimes make your eyes all wonky."

"Seriously. Oh, I got it! How about you smoke yourself with some sulfur and oxidize that steel?"

"A-ha-ha! That's a good one, Taku!"

A wry smile unconsciously came across Haruyuki's face at the conversation between his childhood friends. Instantly, he felt the release of the power tensing up his entire body, but that something cold that had seeped into the depths of his heart didn't seem to be going anywhere.

That voice he'd been hearing every so often these last few months…Haruyuki had thought all this time that the voice with the metallic effect applied was being uttered by his own interior self. That it was another self born from accumulated feelings of negativity. Haruyuki had spent a great deal of time by himself from the time he was a child, so he did have this sort of habit of having conversations in his head.

But…what if it wasn't? What if it wasn't just a metaphor, but there really was something other than Haruyuki producing this voice?

However, in that case, the owner of the voice would have to exist not in the Accelerated World, but inside Haruyuki's Neurolinker. Because the voice would also, on exceedingly rare occasions, whisper to him when he wasn't in a dive. Which meant that it was some kind of virus or AI program? Or...the consciousness of a real human being was lurking in his memory somewhere...? Was something like that even possible...?

He felt like someone somewhere far away was suppressing a laugh, and he closed his eyes tightly to try and banish the thoughts from his mind. This was no time for uncertainty. They were about to plunge into the climax of the Hermes' Cord Race and they had to win, no matter what.

At the very moment he opened his eyes wide, a ring of blue light came into sight ahead of the machine. Most likely, the warp-zone exit.

"Everyone!" He took a deep breath and shouted. "We're coming back out onto the course! Hold on!"

Four crisp shouts of assent came back to him.

Holding tight to the steering wheel, Haruyuki pointed the nose of the shuttle toward the center of the blue ring. The exit grew closer before his eyes, filling his vision, and the instant the machine touched it, it became a vortex of light, swallowing everything.

"Waaah!!" Chiyuri was the first to shout.

And then all of them, including Haruyuki, raised admiring voices.

The sky before them was a perfect obsidian black. Against this backdrop, countless particles of light came together to draw a beautiful line. It was the river of the heavens: the Milky Way. However, it was almost entirely different from the night sky they would look up at in a Moonlight stage or a Desert stage, in terms of the number of stars and the brightness of them. It was as if they could hear the clear melody played by the stars like the ringing of bells, despite the cold, still world they found themselves in.

Hermes' Cord, the orbiting space elevator, the enormous steel pillar, pierced this starry plane and stretched upward in a straight line. A fierce sun shone from the left of the gently curved surface. The light also fell on the body of the shuttle speeding along, making it glint silver and creating a thick shadow to the right of the vehicle.

"...Space...," Kuroyukihime murmured, pointing the sword of her right hand straight out at the Milky Way. She continued in a still voice. "Is this scene a digital painting done by the BB servers?...Or..."

"...They're probably using images of the real thing captured by the social cameras. The position of the stars is just too accurate...," Fuko responded, also in a near whisper.

Of course, even if the image was the real thing, coming at them through cameras and networks and Neurolinkers as it did, it was probably different from the sight the astronauts and tourists were seeing with their naked eyes. Still, Haruyuki, and likely his four companions, too, continued to drink in the galaxy before them, each of them with their own strong emotions spilling into their hearts.

I could stay and admire this silent, cold, and yet busy world forever if it were possible—Although that wish sprang up in Haruyuki, the majestic moment did not continue for long.

The roaring of several engines came at them from behind. Naturally, if this were the real outer space, they wouldn't have been able to hear any noise at all, but in the Accelerated World, some measure of user-friendliness was given priority. Hurriedly looking back, he saw machines of a variety of colors come shooting out of the warp-zone exit.

In the lead was the red shuttle, driven by Blood Leopard. Slightly behind that, the gunmetal shuttle containing Ash Roller's team. Followed by the Yellow Legion shuttle.

After a bit of an interval, two of the midsize Legion shuttles appeared. Apparently, there were only six teams left, including Haruyuki's. Excluding the one that was decrepit right from the start, two more teams had joined Frost Horn's in dropping out.

The incredible echoing of each machine howling ever louder shook space. Above his head, the three enormous spectator stands warped out, and six hundred Burst Linkers raised their hands and stamped their feet. Taking in the cheers showering over them, the six shuttles formed a line and raced on.

"Good! Only five rival machines left!" Kuroyukihime shouted in a crisp tone, switching gears abruptly. "They're all strong enemies, but we're the ones who're going to win this! Listen, we're going to tear them all apart!!"

"Yeah!" Haruyuki and the others thrust their fists into the air. He checked the meter: just under a thousand kilometers to the finish line. If they flew full throttle at five hundred kilometers an hour, it would take two hours, but with the Territory battles on the weekend, the total time was double that. They were so absorbed in the race that two hours would be an instant.

All right! I can't make a single mistake now! No way I'm letting Pard and her team use us as a shooting range again! he shouted in his heart, adjusting his grip on the steering wheel as he glared ahead into the distance for any complex terrain, any kind of obstacle zone.

However…

Immediately to their right, the unexpected, the seemingly impossible happened.

A bizarre something rose up from the center of the concentrated shadow of the shuttle, which was produced by intense sunlight, and accompanied by a slight splashing sound.

A single thin, large panel. Rectangular, about the same length and height as the shuttles, it ran silently parallel to number one, about two meters away. Even though it was supposedly moving along at five hundred kilometers an hour, it produced not a single vibration, not a single sound. The matte black seemed to swallow all light.

The nature of the object sent a jolt through Haruyuki's memory. He didn't have to work at recalling why.

The mysterious Burst Linker who had jumped into the "final battle" in the Unlimited Neutral Field at Umesato Junior High

School two months earlier, just after the start of the new school year. There was no doubt that before them now was that avatar with the ability to change his own body into thin panels and slip into any and all shadows to move about. But what was he doing here now?

The impact and the question burst from Haruyuki's throat in the form of a name. "Black Vise...!!"

Almost as if responding to his cry, the enormous panel peeled back soundlessly to both sides, to become two thin membranes. They spread out before quickly disappearing, as if melting into the vacuum.

The object that then appeared from between those thin membranes stunned Haruyuki all over again.

A shuttle. It was exactly the same shape as the one the Nega Nebulus team rode in, but the color was different. A powdery reddish brown, as if tiny speckles had bled out—in other words, the color of rust. This was very clearly shuttle number ten, which had sat rotting quietly at the right end of the starting platform. But this machine, which had seemed to be out of the action, now had brilliant lightning gushing from its four linear wheels and was zooming along at top speed.

Which meant that shuttle number ten had not been destroyed by corrosion, but rather that the color was nothing more than a re-creation of that of the registered driver.

Struck with a certain conviction, Haruyuki shifted his gaze the tiniest bit and looked over at the cockpit of this tenth shuttle. Sitting there, silently gripping the steering wheel, was—

The thin body, reminiscent of a riveted steel frame, of a duel avatar the same rust color as the machine. And this was not Haruyuki's first encounter with him, either. Two months earlier, he had fought this opponent just once at Akihabara Battle Ground, the underground arena set up within the local net of an arcade in Akihabara.

"Rust Jigsaw..." Haruyuki uttered the second name at a lower volume than his previous cry.

However, even when his name was called, the rust-colored avatar remained silent, not even turning his head. He sank intently into the seat, as if he had become one with the shuttle.

Looking at the rear seating area for the four-person crew, he saw only one person there. Or rather, it would be better to say "one panel." Because there in the back row was just a shadow with no thickness. The strange shape—black paper arranged in human form—could be none other than Black Vise, just as he had thought.

Both Burst Linkers belonged to a group that called itself the Acceleration Research Society. The scope of this organization and the members that made it up were unknown. The one thing Haruyuki did know was that they all had illegal VR devices—brain implant chips, aka BICs—in their skulls and that, using this power, they maneuvered to avoid the limitations of Brain Burst.

Which was why, for Haruyuki, the fact that these two would show up at an event so festive as the Hermes' Cord Race was wholly unanticipated. Unable to rouse himself from the shock of it, he could only gape as countless voices rose up suddenly from the sky above.

"H-hey, whoa! Where'd that shuttle come from?!"

"Number ten didn't drop out, after all?!"

"If that thing wins, what happens to our bets?!"

The Gallery was also apparently stunned at this unexpected development. The wave of commotion contained much more of the element of surprise than of excitement.

Haruyuki listened to the quiet conversation happening on shuttle number ten among the shouts.

"...I guess this is where my work ends?" The calm voice sounding like a teacher belonged to Black Vise.

"Yeah, you're good." The purposefully low voice of a boy, cracking with adolescence, replied. "Go home."

"Well then, I'll take my leave of you here, Jigsaw...Good-bye, Black King. And the ladies and gentlemen of Nega Nebulus."

"...You," Kuroyukihime muttered. But by the time she made a small movement with her right hand, the human-shaped shadow in the rear seat was already dancing upward. It slipped into the ink of the starry sky and receded in the blink of an eye, vanishing.

With things having come this far, Haruyuki finally managed a hazy guess as to why number ten had abruptly appeared from the shadow of number one.

Possessing many curious abilities as he did, Black Vise was likely able to lock up not only himself, but also other people and objects within his black panels, and then sink into the shadows with them. When the portal had opened at five thirty on Wednesday afternoon on the top floor of Skytree, Haruyuki and Pard hadn't been alone in being the first to visit the top of Hermes' Cord. Black Vise and Rust Jigsaw had also, in fact, been there. The pair must have concealed themselves in the shadow of the tower and registered to drive the tenth shuttle the instant Haruyuki and Blood Leopard had burst out. Which was why none of them—not Haruyuki, not Pard, and not Ash Roller and the others who came running in immediately after—noticed the shadowy duo.

And it wasn't just during registration that Vise showed off his powers of concealment.

The instant the race started that day, the starting platform had been completely swallowed up by the shadow produced by the enormous spectator seating. Vise and Jigsaw had slipped through this to get into their shuttle before concealing the machine itself immediately after the race started. From there, they moved into number one's shadow without attracting anyone's notice, and then they had held their breath right up next to Haruyuki and his friends until that moment. All of which was Vise's ability: to move or stop with total freedom as long as he was in the shadows.

While Haruyuki was running this speculation down in his

head, Rust Jigsaw, the sole remaining avatar in shuttle number ten, fell silent once more and gripped the steering wheel tightly.

"Rust Jigsaw." Unable to completely grasp the current situation, and also feeling an incomprehensible discomfort, Haruyuki began to toss out words at the rust-colored avatar. "Why are you showing up here now? If you wanted to, you could have stayed hidden in our shadow all the way to right before the finish line and then flown out and snatched the win."

Jigsaw didn't even blink, much less answer. But Haruyuki squelched his physical unease and continued.

"But leaving the shadows now at this stage instead of doing that...you feel like racing us for real? That suits us just fine! A fair and square fight for the remaining thousand kilometers—"

"Silence." The lone word cut Haruyuki off. Hearing Rust Jigsaw's voice for the first time, he found it cold and dry, and yet tinged somehow with heaving emotion, almost boiling.

"Huh...?"

"Don't talk. Don't make me listen to bullshit about races and fights." After this languid utterance, Rust Jigsaw moved for the first time to glance over at Haruyuki and his team. His eyes were a penetratingly cold red, set beneath a face mask that had a design like an assemblage of thin iron pieces. His only memory of that face from the duel before at Akiba BG was of Jigsaw, at wits' end, losing to Blood Leopard's literal bite, but the ice residing in the gaze of the rust avatar now was enough to wipe that helplessness away.

Jigsaw narrowed those eyes and said—practically ordered: "Have some shame. Be ashamed of how you all continue to avert your eyes from the true nature of Brain Burst."

"Oh?" Having stayed silent until that point, Kuroyukihime spoke up now, her voice containing a dangerous edge. "Then I ask you. What is this true nature?"

Even when faced with this question almost like a sword itself, Rust Jigsaw showed no signs of agitation. "Recognize," he spat, slowly turning his face forward. "Brain Burst is simply a slightly dirty life-hack tool."

"Life...hack...?!" The voice, heavy with indignation, belonged to Takumu. The large blue avatar started to lean over the side of the ship, and the yellow-green avatar next to him pulled him back.

"Look, you!" Having stretched out instead of Takumu, Chiyuri offered her own rejoinder point-blank, without a hint of fear. "That's a matter of personal opinion! Even if it is just a tool for cheating for you, it's not like that for us! Our Brain Burst is a superamazing fighting game, got it!"

"That's exactly right." Sky Raker picked up Chiyuri's thread. "And you contradict yourself. If it's simply a tool, then why are you taking part in this event? Why did you show yourself halfway through the course? If you have the desire to fight, to compete, then that's proof that your Brain Burst is not a tool but rather a game."

At this pointed remark, Rust Jigsaw curled up tightly in the cockpit.

Haruyuki thought he might be trying to endure something with that movement. And then several conjectures popped up in his mind.

What if Jigsaw himself wanted to repudiate his own words? Didn't he want to fight properly as a Burst Linker, to taste the thrill and excitement of the duel and, through that, feel a connection with someone? In other words, was he hoping to leave the organization that bound him...the Acceleration Research Society...?

The instant he remembered how the twilight-colored marauder—who had belonged to the same organization—had not made that choice, or perhaps had been unable to make that choice even while he had the option to, Haruyuki instinctively called out, "Y-you...The truth is, you wanted to come *here*, didn't you...?"

Silence.

After a fairly long pause, Rust Jigsaw slowly lifted the face he had hidden in the steering wheel and looked at Haruyuki once more.

In that moment, Haruyuki understood that his guess had been inescapably wrong.

What Jigsaw had been enduring was anger. A confused rage boiled, wholly unconnected with sharpness or genuineness. A diffuse hatred that simply spread in all directions, unable to converge on a precise target. An enormous rusty saw brandished wildly, so to speak.

"Regret," Rust Jigsaw commanded in a creaking voice. He then took his right hand off the wheel and clenched those five fingers around his forehead. The movement was one of enduring extreme pain, but the words he uttered gradually grew colored with an insane heat, rose in pitch, and changed to a shriek. "Regret your own softness for not attacking the instant you saw me. And pay the price. Scream in the midst of overwhelming terror! Your foolish sport ends today! And then the era of desire and competition, destruction and slaughter will arrive! Precisely now...this time!!"

And then Haruyuki saw it.

Shafts of dull red light rising up in all directions from all over Rust Jigsaw's body.

At once, the light began to swirl and writhe like a myriad of snakes. High-frequency vibrations began to shake the shuttle, and then the enormous body of the space elevator. The steel surface, the two shuttles, and even inky black space blazed red.

It wasn't a special attack. Because HP gauges were locked for this race event, their special-attack gauges wouldn't charge. Thus, this light was born from Jigsaw's will, his imagination...

"He can't—! Overlay!" Kuroyukihime was the first to shout out. "Get us out of here, Crow! An Incarnate attack is coming!!"

Haruyuki was already yanking the steering wheel to the left as hard as he could. At a steering angle that was just barely above dropping into a spin, the shuttle tried to get some distance from machine number ten.

"Behold, imbeciles!!" They heard the voice as if it were chasing the machine escaping to the backside of the tower. "This is the true form of Brain Buuuuurst!!"

In the rearview mirror, Rust Jigsaw stood up in the cockpit and threw both arms high into the air.

He howled.

"Rust Order!!"

The world trembled.

...*That* was overlay?!

Haruyuki shuddered as he jammed on the accelerator like he was trying to push it through the floor. The vortex of red light centered on shuttle number ten swelled up to the scale of a small star, zooming in on shuttle number one.

"H-hold on!" Shouting, Haruyuki pulled back a little on the steering wheel. The explosion of light was a force to swallow up the entire hundred-meter diameter of Hermes' Cord. Running at an angle, they wouldn't be able to get clear of it. The light chased after them insistently, several centimeters behind the rear of the shuttle, now back on a straight trajectory.

Holding the wheel steady as he looked back over his shoulder, Haruyuki gasped hard at the sight behind them.

The surface of the elevator, which had until mere moments before shone a lustrous steel gray, was decaying with incredible force!

Almost as if he were watching a video on fast-forward of a piece of steel left on the beach, spots of red rust popped up one after another, anywhere the light touched it. These grew enormous before his eyes and soon merged to completely cover the elevator. Eventually, cracks grew up here and there, and chunks of the tower caved in, scattering blood-colored rust. Several craters formed, as if the tower were being showered with invisible meteors.

"Th…that's…crazy…" A hoarse voice slipped from his throat, and Haruyuki shook his head from side to side. "I mean, an Incarnate attack's one thing, but this…Pard's claws didn't even leave a scratch on the elevator…A-and even before that, the scope's just too large…!"

As far as Haruyuki knew, for all Incarnate attacks, the effect target was limited by the person. For instance, even with a long-distance attack, you first had to expand your own attack power with your will and then release that at the enemy.

But the will of Rust Jigsaw raging before his eyes now was causing unlimited destruction over a broad swath. In principle, this should have been impossible. The energy source for Incarnate techniques was the wielder's mental scars…in other words, the imagination that belonged to the wielder, and no one else.

Kuroyukihime, similarly looking behind them, replied to Haruyuki's question in a low voice. "Space Corrosion…"

"The antithesis of will, with hope as its source…" Sky Raker explained the unfamiliar term. "The ultimate form of a hateful will. A powerfully strong hatred of the world causes an overwrite of the field itself…But to bind this amount of imagination, even a King-class player would require very long hours of mental concentration."

Kuroyukihime narrowed both eyes sharply and nodded. "Hiding in our shadow that whole while was likely to buy that time. But even so, it's too far beyond the norm. He's surely forcibly boosting the depth of his mental concentration with a BIC function…?"

"He can't be. That's…It would place too large of a burden on a living brain…"

Even as the two talked, the rust storm Jigsaw had summoned continued its destructive march.

Several of the other team shuttles trailing behind ended up prey to the corrosion. Blood Leopard and Ash Roller had apparently managed to take advantage of their excellent control to evade the storm by decelerating, but still, their shuttles were instantly half coated in rust, significantly slowing them down. Even if they had escaped total destruction, looking the way they did, there was no way those shuttles were going to make it to the finish line.

But that was nothing compared with the damage to the Yellow Legion and the two midsize teams. They had charged headlong into the range of effect, and the cries of a dozen people rang out all at once.

Immediately, the three shuttles were covered with a thick coating of rust. And it didn't stop there. The armor of the crews in the vehicles also corroded before their eyes, parts and equipment crumbling and scattering to the rear. Finally, the damage reached the avatars' forms beneath the armor, and they collapsed and spilled out, falling into the darkness behind them.

"What's going on?! Our HP gauges are supposed to be locked!" Takumu's groan was overlaid with Chiyuri's heartbroken cry.

"This...This is too awful! The race is in shambles!!"

"Heh-heh-heh." Almost as if he had heard them, Rust Jigsaw's laughter caught up with them from behind. "Ha-ha! Ha-ha-ha-ha-ha-ha!! Despair!! Lament!! And feel remorse!! This is the retribution for your deception!! This world does, after all, have the same roots as reality!! Impossible to avoid the corrosion of everything in existeeeeeence!!"

The raging red light practically erupted upward as though these words themselves were Incarnate. The vortex of energy captured one of the floating spectator stands.

No way. Haruyuki's eyes flew open as even the audience seating—an object that should have been completely protected by the system—was blanketed in red rust, accompanied by an unpleasant *zrr zrr zrr zrr* sound. Several cracks immediately appeared in the once-smooth bottom, and the outer panels fell off one after another. And then a few seconds later, the enormous structure simply crumbled in the sky above the tower.

More than a hundred people from the Gallery crammed in there were thrown into the void, an avalanche of avatars. Cries rose up from all over. Some were completely corroded, while others crashed into the surface of the elevator. Either way, they were all forcibly ejected from the Accelerated World with a momentary flash.

"I-insanity...," Kuroyukihime moaned, her upper body thrown back as though the scene itself were pressing into her. "Going this far...The Gallery will most certainly realize it, too. That this phenomenon transcends the framework of the normal system..."

At these words, Haruyuki was conscious all over again of the madness of the situation.

The senior Burst Linkers, including the Seven Kings of Pure Color, had been doing everything within their power to conceal the existence of the Incarnate System. For instance, even when the need arose for a guide to give instruction in how to use the techniques, those guides were resolute, making the initiate swear to use Incarnate only when attacked with Incarnate. The reason for this was solely because of the enormous dark side the Incarnate System contained.

Those who reached a hand into the holes in their own hearts, seeking even greater power, were at the same time pulled into those depths. You were swallowed up by the negative feelings once sublimated as your duel avatar. The worst of these cases was the Armor of Catastrophe, Chrome Disaster, which formerly brought about enormous chaos in the Accelerated World. To prevent the same thing from ever happening again, the Kings had strictly controlled information related to the Incarnate System. Even the cunning Yellow King, Yellow Radio, had chosen the path of retreat in front of many subordinates, rather than use Incarnate.

Now, however, at the climax of the grand event Hermes' Cord Race, Rust Jigsaw had released an Incarnate technique before the eyes of more than five hundred Burst Linkers, providing the members of the Gallery obvious confirmation of the phenomenon through their own senses. Confirmation of the irrationality of the supposedly protected audience seating collapsing, supposedly locked HP gauges being blown away. Of the existence of an abnormal power overwriting the normal system.

"Why...would he...," Sky Raker murmured helplessly, shaking her head slowly. Haruyuki understood how she felt so much it hurt.

She, of all the Burst Linkers, believed most strongly in the light side of the Incarnate System. She believed that hope, rather than hatred or fear, was the greatest power in the Accelerated World. For Raker, the sight of a power materialized through the ultimate hatred injuring so many Burst Linkers must have been hard to bear.

"Master..." When he turned around to speak to her, Haruyuki noticed something on the edge of his vision and hurriedly faced front again.

Ahead of the shuttle, which was just barely outracing the effective range of Jigsaw's enormous Rust Order attack, several protrusions stretched up from the surface of the elevator. Probably obstacles to make the race more exciting. If the situation were not what it was, this would be the place where he would be eager to show off his skill, but as it was, Haruyuki felt only astonishment. Charging full speed ahead through the antennae and tanks in close proximity was out of the question, but if they slowed down even a little, they'd be caught in Jigsaw's Incarnate.

As he gritted his teeth, the enormous reverberation of the collapse of the second floating spectator stand reached his ears, along with countless screams.

"Dammit...Dammit!!" Haruyuki shouted involuntarily. The tears springing to his eyes blurred the world into a rainbow.

This was supposed to be the best, most exciting race. I was supposed to team up with my best friends and fight my heart out with my best rivals. And more than anything...Just a little more, only the tiniest bit farther, and I would've been able to take Raker to the "end of the sky" she's wished so hard for!!

"As if…I'm gonna lose heeeeeere!!" Haruyuki screamed, brushing away his tears and glaring straight ahead. He couldn't accept that the race was going to be destroyed by a hateful will. He would fight to the end. He would resist.

The only way to keep moving forward while evading the Incarnate attack was to make it through this obstacle zone without slowing down at all. The load Jigsaw was carrying in number ten was far and away the lighter, but perhaps because he was trying to keep the accelerator pressed down while he released his enormous attack, his speed was essentially the same as that of Haruyuki and his team in number one. If he could just continue to keep this gap between them, they should be able to fly through the finish line first, without getting caught in the rust storm.

Almost as if he were becoming one with the machine, Haruyuki concentrated all his mental strength into his hands upon the steering wheel, his right foot upon the accelerator pedal, and the seat beneath him.

A few seconds later, the sprinting shuttle flew right into the middle of the antennae covering the tower surface at irregular intervals.

"Hng…ah!" As a cry slipped from beneath his clenched teeth, he dodged to the right and left the steel poles that came flying at them one after another. Because he couldn't ease up on the accelerator, if he slipped up even once, that would be the end of it. Over and over, he just barely managed these corners. The magnetic force generated by the linear wheels was on the verge of losing its grip on the steel surface.

It seemed that the four in the rear seats had picked up on Haruyuki's determination. Each time the machine threatened to angle up into a dangerous incline from his wild cornering, they shifted the load on the opposite side without saying a word. With this desperate, cooperative play, shuttle number one continued to flee unwaveringly, scant centimeters in front of the Incarnate storm chasing them.

In contrast, shuttle number ten did not deviate from its path a single millimeter, even as it plunged into the obstacle zone. All the antennae and tanks before it transformed into lumps of rust from the top down and were blown away. Despite the fact that it had already been five minutes since Rust Order was activated, the raging Incarnate light showed no signs of weakening.

If he could sustain such a large-scale overwrite for so long, the strength of his imagination was truly terrifying. Yet at the same time Haruyuki shuddered at the depth of that hatred, he felt a touch of doubt.

This wasn't the first time he had gone up against Rust Jigsaw. Two months earlier, he and Blood Leopard had teamed up to fight Rust Jigsaw on the duel stage at Akihabara Battle Ground, and they had won.

But back then, Jigsaw hadn't even tried to use any kind of Incarnate attack. And, judging from everything he had said and done today, if he could have used one, he definitely would have. Haruyuki could think of two reasons for that. Either the only Incarnate attack Jigsaw had was this Space Corrosion, which took a long time to activate and carried an element of risk for his brain, or the previous time they met, he had been forbidden by his superiors to use any kind of Incarnate.

If it was the latter, that would mean that during these last two months, there had been a significant policy shift within the mysterious Acceleration Research Society. Because Rust Jigsaw's actions—his rampage—today had to be happening with the approval of that organization. The fact that Black Vise, who had identified himself as the vice president, had helped him was proof of that. What on earth could the objective of the Acceleration Research Society be, to launch destruction like this on such an enormous scale...?

Haruyuki was able to start churning these thoughts around in his brain—albeit only in one corner of it—once he had memorized to some degree the pattern of the obstacles' appearance. It was complicated, but the antennae were placed following a fixed set of rules. All he had to do after figuring it out was continue to dodge to the sides without making a mistake. And this was the sort of action he had mastered more than a few times up to now in the countless racing games he had played—

But, in a flash, Haruyuki understood that the pattern was itself the area's biggest obstacle. The instant he became accustomed to the placement of the antennas and had a little mental leeway, the rule for that placement changed entirely.

"Hng!" Groaning, he devoted himself to steering. The sides of the machine scraped up against obstacles he couldn't dodge completely as the shuttle swung left and right, sending vivid sparks scattering.

Then, a few seconds later, as if sneering at Haruyuki struggling, a group of antennae lined up in front of them blocked the way forward entirely. There wasn't enough space to slip between them. The only thing he could do was dodge wide to the right or the left. But at this speed, the instant he turned the wheel, they would roll.

By the time he made that judgment, his right foot was already reflexively pulling back from the accelerator and stepping on the brake. *Skree!* The magnetic force lines howled, and the shuttle pitched forward into a left turn.

The storm chasing them didn't let the opportunity presented by this slight deceleration get away.

"Haruuuu!!" Takumu shouted as a rusty red swallowed the rear of the machine.

An abnormal vibration came to him through the steering wheel. Even without looking in the mirror, he knew that the beautiful silver body was rapidly corroding, peeling back, and falling away. Mastering his fear, Haruyuki tried to accelerate once again, now that they had pulled out of the turn. But the acceleration that had been so reliable until just a moment ago did not return.

It wasn't just the body; the linear wheels in the back had also rusted. Shuttle number one tried earnestly to sprint away with just the magnetic power generated by the discs in the front, but these produced only half the output.

"Ngh!"

"Aaah?!"

Immediately after he heard Takumu and Chiyuri crying out, the maw of the red storm came down on Kuroyukihime and Fuko in the seats ahead of them and even on Haruyuki in the driver's seat.

"Ha-ha-ha-ha! Corrode! Degrade! Decay!!"

Jigsaw's shrieking laughter came to him from a distance. But Haruyuki had no time for listening to it.

So hot! A fierce pain, as though his entire body were being showered with boiling water, enveloped him. When he looked down, the smooth, glittering silver armor of Silver Crow was clouded white all over and pocked with tiny holes. Simultaneous with this phenomenon, the HP gauge in the top left of his field of view was rapidly ripped away as if mocking the LOCKED displayed above it.

Enduring the agony, Haruyuki looked back. And reflexively twisted his face. Similarly having every bit of the armor of their duel avatars eaten away, the four members of his crew were curled up, trying to withstand the fierce pain. A metallic color to start with, Silver Crow was weak against corrosion attacks, but to see even the regular colors of Kuroyukihime and his friends being devoured—Jigsaw's Incarnate was not the simple idea of "rusting." It was, just as the attacker himself had shouted earlier, a more fundamental "degradation," "decay."

"Ah…Ah!" As if unable to withstand the pain, a thin cry escaped Chiyuri. Hearing it, Takumu tried to shield her with his own body, but the red light penetrated every nook and cranny, and the fresh green of Lime Bell withered cruelly.

"Bell…!" Sky Raker called, and then dropped her eyes, as if hesitating.

But the next instant, she jerked her face up and reached her slender right hand up high into the sky.

"Raker—" Kuroyukihime started to speak, but Raker stopped her with a wave of her hand.

A vivid sky-blue light gushed from Fuko's outstretched palm.

Overlay. The light of an unshakeable will released from deep in her heart.

"Wind Veil!!"

The high cry of the technique name was followed by wind. A whirlwind, tinged with a hazy light blue color, appeared, centered on Raker, and enveloped the entire shuttle. Instantly, the corrosive pain torturing Haruyuki's entire body faded away as if it had never even happened. A web of sparks bounced up where the red light and the blue wind came into contact, showing the two imaginations clashing.

There was no mistake, this was an Incarnate technique activated by Sky Raker. Not an attack, but a defensive image. And it covered not only herself, but also everything within a radius of three meters.

If...

A positive Incarnate targeting the individual was *hope*.

And a negative Incarnate targeting a range was *hatred*.

Then what to call a positive Incarnate protecting five people?

These feelings flitting through Haruyuki's heart were fleeting. Wrapped in the blue veil, machine number one had slowed down, and number ten with Rust Jigsaw inside was closing in on them at high speed from twenty or so meters away. The rust-colored avatar rising up from the cockpit thrust both hands up at the sky, malice turning to loud laughter and scattering.

"Ha-ha-ha...ha-ha-ha-ha-ha-ha!!"

The antennae ahead of him snapped one after the other, while the surface of the tower behind him split into deep fissures as the shuttle quickly grew distant. The very person who had so thoroughly destroyed the Hermes' Cord Race sped upward, alone, to the finish line awaiting the winner in distant space.

"Dammmmmmit!" Haruyuki shouted involuntarily. He couldn't let this happen. It was already impossible for the half-destroyed number one to overtake number ten, but at the very least, there was absolutely no way he was going to allow Jigsaw to be the winner. That would be defeat for all the teams taking part in this race—no, for everyone, including the more than five hundred people in the Gallery.

That said, there was still one thing Haruyuki could do…

No.

There was. Even if he couldn't race anymore, there was still one lone method of stopping Jigsaw.

The shuttle finally slipped out of the effect range of Rust Order. Raker reined in her sky-blue wind and slumped into her seat, spent. Kuroyukihime held her shoulders, looking worried. After watching this scene, Haruyuki brought his eyes back to the front. The shuttle's speed had been cut in half, but he should still have the two linear wheels in the front.

Completely forgetting the emotions carved into his heart only moments ago at Sky Raker's Incarnate technique, Haruyuki gritted his teeth. He could drive the machine like this, but he had no chance of catching up with Jigsaw anymore. Which was why there was just one method left now. Right. Not with the machine, Haruyuki alone.

"Haru, what should we do? If we go ahead and keep a safe distance like this, we could probably be second, but…," Takumu said from the rear seats.

"Mmm," Kuroyukihime replied in a strangled voice. "If that's the only prize we're going to pick up, we might as well leave the machine here…"

Their conversation barely registered in Haruyuki's consciousness. He saw only the receding rust storm as he staggered to his feet in the driver's seat.

"Crow?" Kuroyukihime called, as if suspecting something.

"Kuroyukihime, watch out for everyone," he replied curtly without looking back.

"Wh-what are you going to do?!"

Instead of answering, Haruyuki smashed the accelerator to the floor, still standing. The half-ruined machine squealed in protest. Lightning gushed from the rusted linear discs like the throes of death.

Haruyuki confirmed that the digital meter was once again increasing as he leaned forward with a grunt. He threw both hands ahead. Drew them back forcefully. In sync with this action, the thin metal fins folded up on his back deployed on both sides.

The damage from the Incarnate attack that had ignored the system's protection had taken more than 30 percent of his health gauge. To compensate for that, his special-attack meter had been charged to more than half full.

In other words, he could fly. Right now.

"Y-you can't! Stop, Crow!" Kuroyukihime shouted, guessing his intention. "You can't fight a hateful will with hate! There's no longer any meaning for you to fight here and now!!"

"But…I…I!" Haruyuki squeezed a cracked voice from between clenched teeth. "I can't let him do this!!"

Whatever means he had to resort to, he would stop Jigsaw. No, crush him.

Immediately after he added this in his heart, the right linear disc released dazzling sparks and abruptly exploded. Seconds before it did, Haruyuki bent forward and leapt into the sky with all his might.

To support his body, the rear of which threatened to blow off, he vibrated his spread wings only lightly. But he stared ahead, as if devouring the scene before him, and in the center of his field of view caught sight of number ten racing in the distance.

"Go!!"

With a sharp cry, he released the full thrust of both wings. Deserting number one as it went into a spin before coming to a stop, Haruyuki flew upward alone.

The maximum speed of Silver Crow, the lone duel avatar in the Accelerated World with the ability to fly, was roughly three hundred kilometers. In contrast, shuttle number ten was racing along at a speed of more than four hundred kilometers. Thus, starting from zero, there was no way he would have been able to catch up, but if he shot himself forward, using a shuttle going the same speed as a catapult, the supplement should give him a tiny chance.

Channeling every ounce of his mental strength and his special-attack gauge into flying power, Haruyuki plunged forward, a beam of light.

He soon charged into Rust Order's effective range, and the armor covering his body began to cloud over. The surface foamed as if boiling, became minute particles, and melted off behind him.

The fiery pain once again danced around his nervous system, but the size of his anger won out. He pierced the raging rust storm in a straight line and closed in on the shuttle. The corrosion reached the wings on his back, and one by one the ten metallic fins on each side peeled away from the base, but he paid no attention and kept charging.

He lost both momentum and thrust rapidly, and his speed dropped. Six hundred kilometers an hour. Five hundred. If he didn't catch up with the shuttle before his speed dropped below the four hundred kilometers an hour the shuttle was doing, he would never get another chance to catch it.

He drew nearer rusty number ten...nearer...but his forward momentum was growing duller—

"Unh...Ah!" As he pushed everything he had into a battle cry, Haruyuki touched the rear wing of the shuttle with the fingertips of his left hand, fell back again, touched it again—and dug solidly into it.

"Aaaah!!"

Howling, he finally yanked his body forward with nothing but the strength of his arms and flew into the rear seat of the shuttle. In the cockpit, Rust Jigsaw looked back with a gasp. The slightest hint of surprise raced across his naked framework face.

At this distance, almost like the eye of a typhoon, there seemed to be almost no corrosion effect. Still, during the time he was charging through the Incarnate storm, Silver Crow's body had become covered with rust, worn-out. Thirty-five percent left in his HP gauge. Pieces of armor dropping, Haruyuki drew in his right hand, lined up his fingers, and focused the last of his mental strength there.

He sharpened his imagination. Generated an overlay, concentrated this on his fingertips, and made it converge into the shape of a sword.

"……Laser Sword!!"

Haruyuki released the sole Incarnate attack he had learned, squarely at the center of Rust Jigsaw's chest.

Along with a metallic squeal, silver light stretched out from the hand he thrust forward. He reached the rust-colored armor, grazed it—

But here, Silver Crow's right arm itself quietly crumbled from the elbow. The silver light diffused vainly into space, and Haruyuki's first and last attack ended in carving merely a single dot off of Jigsaw's HP gauge.

Having exhausted every ounce of strength, he was on the verge of collapsing on the shuttle floor when a thin line, extending from the outside of Rust Jigsaw's right arm, caught Crow under his left arm to support him.

"Heh. Heh-heh-heh." Chuckling leaked from the rust-red avatar as he turned completely around to face the rear. He took his foot off the accelerator, and the shuttle gently decelerated.

But even if Haruyuki had succeeded in stopping number ten here momentarily, it meant nothing to what was left of number ten and the totally destroyed machines driven by Blood Leopard and Ash Roller.

As number ten came to a complete stop, the Incarnate storm gradually subsided, and space returned to its original color and stillness. The cold light of the stars and the fierce light of the sun poured down on them.

"Recognize." Rust Jigsaw dangled Haruyuki on a thin line about two meters long, stretching out from his right arm. "This is the limit of you who blindly believe that this world is a game."

Abruptly, the fine black line began to vibrate repeatedly. A dense row of minute triangular blades popped up from the top of it. A saw. This was clearly his main weapon, the jigsaw that had given Haruyuki and Blood Leopard so much grief during the duel in Akihabara.

"And understand. This is the price for your foolishness."

The vibrations of the jigsaw suddenly doubled. At the same time, a weak overlay enveloped the entire saw. He was inactivating the stage's HP protection rule at the same time that he enhanced his cutting power with Incarnate.

Immediately, a metallic shriek came up from under Haruyuki's left arm, followed by an incandescent pain.

"Unh...Aaaaah!" Screaming, Haruyuki tried to jump back. But his body wasn't obeying his commands.

Silver Crow's own weight hanging down gradually pulled the jigsaw into the base of his left arm. A few seconds later, a stream of sparks came gushing out, and his arm was effortlessly removed. His health gauge, dyed a bright red, was cut down to 10 percent.

Having lost both arms now, Haruyuki collapsed to the shuttle floor like a broken doll, and Jigsaw tossed off words again, tinged with cold laughter.

"Heh-heh. Lament. That if you had to be a metallic color, you could not be gold or platinum, resistant to corrosion, or at least stainless steel."

And then Jigsaw extended the saw from his left arm, crossed it with the one from his right, and clasped them around Haruyuki's neck, yanking him up high in the air.

Crucified, head helplessly thrown back, Haruyuki caught sight of the last remaining spectator stand.

The hundred or so members of the Gallery were still clamoring with confusion and doubt. However, even in the midst of that, a pronounced disappointment wafted through the air at Silver

Crow, who, after making such a daring and bold attack, was now dangling helplessly without even getting to strike a single blow. "What'd this guy even come for?" "This is what we got all excited for…?" The countless voices pierced Haruyuki's ears.

I don't need you guys telling me that. I'm the one most disappointed in me, okay? Haruyuki murmured in his heart, waiting for the jigsaw around his throat to bare its teeth. *I was soft. Too ignorant. I never even dreamed that Incarnate born with hatred as its source could be this incredibly powerful…*

Someone from inside his head responded to this thought.

Naturally. Did you really believe this thing called hope *could be greater than malice in terms of attack power?*

He closed his eyes and replied, *Well, how was I supposed to know? I mean, I can't use that kind of power.*

Once again, someone rebutted. *Not true. You knew. That power's been sleeping in you for a very long time. A power even purer than hatred. A malice accumulating inside, never dispersing to the outside world, single-mindedly honed and whetted.*

That is: anger. The Incarnate of rage has existed within you from the distant past, waiting for the time it would be released.

Thmp.

Suddenly, the center of his back began to throb coldly. *Thmp. Thmp.* This pulsing, almost a heartbeat, cycled a frozen fluid, like mercury, through Haruyuki's veins.

Well.

WELL!!

NOW IS THE TIME! CALL MY NAME!! RELEASE ME!! I WILL CHANGE YOUR ANGER INTO POWER!!

"Unh…Aah…!"

The chill filling his entire body abruptly became flames, and he was overwhelmed with a burning sensation. Haruyuki opened his eyes.

And then he saw it: the fluctuation of a thick aura rising up from his own battered body—overlay. But it wasn't silver. It was a gray pressing up against the boundary between gray and black, a color of darkness he was sure he'd seen somewhere before.

Something terrifying was happening. Instantly, he was choking on fear, but the moment he looked at Rust Jigsaw dangling his body in the air, that fear vanished.

The conversation with whomever it was had apparently taken place in the mere twinkling of the eye while Jigsaw pulled Haruyuki's body up and began to whirl the saws. A discordant sound came from his throat, and the minute teeth ate into his thin armor.

But Haruyuki had forgotten his terror of having his head cut off. "I...won't let you," he muttered, staring intently at Rust Jigsaw. "You alone...I will totally not let you."

"Heh. Heh-heh. Resign yourself. There's no longer anything you can do."

"I won't let you...I won't let you...," Haruyuki returned, almost delirious, his core cold as ice. It stirred up his overwhelming rage, as if to surround ice with scorching heat.

Rust Jigsaw no longer existed there as himself. He was the symbol of all the irrational malice that had tortured Haruyuki for the better part of the fourteen years of his life.

If, in that place, there had been even just one friend connected to his heart, perhaps Haruyuki might have been able to stop himself. The way he had in that decisive battle in the Unlimited Neutral Field two months earlier.

But now, he had left the stalled shuttle number one, together with Kuroyukihime, Fuko, Takumu, and Chiyuri, who had all been deeply injured by Jigsaw's Incarnate attack, off in the distance behind him. This fact only served to increase Haruyuki's anger all the more, and there was nothing to hold him back.

"You...You..." In a voice that resonated metallically, Haruyuki released his final roar. "As if I could ever...let yooooooouuuuu!!"

Instantly.

The heat of his rage finally crossed a certain threshold.

Haruyuki felt something break through the armor of his back and stretch out, writhing. He brandished whatever this was in place of his lost arms, and beat at the two saws binding his neck, breaking them.

"Mmng!" Jigsaw groaned while Haruyuki leapt back, putting some distance between them.

After landing outside of the parked shuttle, he plunged the thing stretching out from his back into the surface of the tower. Brilliant sparks flew everywhere, together with an enormous *crash.*

It was a sinister tail, countless blackened silver segments connecting, a sharp, sword-shaped protuberance at the tip. The black silver tail swaying like a snake, Haruyuki took the deepest breath he could, threw his head back, and howled, "Unh...ah... aaaaaaaaah!!"

An aura of darkness cascaded from his entire body, and shock waves rippled through the stage. The Gallery in the air began to shout and holler in earnest. But their voices no longer reached Haruyuki's ears. Instead, a single sharp command slammed into the center of his brain.

Now then! Call my name!!

Striking a daunting pose, thrusting his tail into the vertical wall to support his body, Haruyuki called the name that flashed in the back of his mind.

"Chrome...Disasteeeeerrrrrrrr!!"

10

The Gallery, Rust Jigsaw, even the stars fell silent.

In the stillness, a black lightning poured down from out of nowhere to strike Haruyuki, and in the upper right of his field of view, a purple system message glittered.

You equipped the Enhanced Armament...

The cursor at the end blinked twice, three times. Almost as if the Brain Burst system itself were afraid to note the name. However, after flashing for a fourth time, the cursor flowed to the right and carved out a single row of text.

...The Disaster.

The darkness overflowed.

A muddy black/dark-gray aura spurted out in several lines from the base of the tail to wrap thickly around his entire body. These immediately condensed, grew thicker, and wiped away the silver of Silver Crow.

Finally, a glassy metallic luster appeared on the surface of the concentrated darkness. A shining dark metal, blackened like the tail. A myriad of armor parts, all with sharp edges, materialized at high speed from his back out to his extremities. These covered his chest, his stomach, his legs, and even the two arms he had supposedly lost, leaving no gaps, creating a perfect blackish-silver full-body armor. At the same time as his arms regenerated inside the armor, his HP gauge was completely restored. Finally, there came a heavy metallic clanking, and a thick helmet covered his head from the rear.

His field of view changed color. A light gray layer was added to everything, leaving only the figure of Rust Jigsaw in the center to stand out vividly.

Haruyuki slowly raised his arms and looked at the ten talon-fingers glittering brutally at the ends of them. Worlds away from the slender hands of Silver Crow, even if they could hold nothing, he was easily convinced that the talons alone would be fearsome weapons.

And it wasn't just his hands. It was also the torso covered by the thick armor. And the legs, drawing out sturdy, supple lines. And the three enormous claws on his feet.

His entire avatar had turned into a crystal of pure power.

Unable to bear the force racing through his entire body, Haruyuki clenched both hands ferociously, turned his head back to the sky, and—

Howled.

"Gng...Yurooooooooo!!"

Released from his throat was the metallic roar of a beast.

Standing in the shuttle a little ways off, Rust Jigsaw reeled for a moment before quickly recovering himself. Even Jigsaw couldn't have anticipated this scenario, but the voice he spoke in was filled with the same cool contempt as it had been up to now.

"Heh-heh, interesting. The Armor of Catastrophe? Fine. Recognize that this so-called most evil power is, in the end, an embellished pretense."

This utterance also felt to Haruyuki like nothing more than a single drop of water falling into incandescent flames. Emotional thoughts were completely blocked. Only a high-speed, calculating logic filled his consciousness—in other words, the question of how to most efficiently render inactive the enemy before his eyes.

He could no longer hear the voice that had whispered to him so many times before now, nor did he feel the anger the voice had led him to. The reason for this was clear. Haruyuki himself had now become completely one with them.

So that's it?

I'm already...the sixth Chrome Disaster.

I'm sorry, Kuroyukihime. I'm sorry, Master. Sorry, Taku, Chiyu...

These thoughts created a tiny ripple on the surface of his consciousness and disappeared, leaving behind nothing but a purified bloodlust.

Rust Jigsaw moved first.

On top of the parked shuttle, he raised a leisurely right hand and spread out five angular fingers. The hand was wrapped in a dull red light.

Instantly, something strange happened in Haruyuki's field of view. Several English words were displayed at high speed in the newly added gray layer. From what he could understand: PREDICTED ATTACK/INCARNATE ATTACK; RANGE/POWER ENHANCEMENT/ CORROSION TYPE; THREAT LEVEL/ZERO.

"Rust Touch!"

Following the attack name, Jigsaw's hand released an enormous phantom hand, which grabbed tightly on to Haruyuki's body. Armor that glittered a dark gray immediately began to cloud over—however...

"Gaaar!!"

With a short roar, Haruyuki flung his arms out. He casually ripped the phantom hand off, and it dissipated into the void. The chrome silver armor also immediately regained its original, almost wet luster.

He took a heavy step toward the cockpit and laughed curtly. "Heh-heh...You said before I should be stainless steel." His voice was tinged with a metallic edge and twisted strangely. "You were wrong. The reason stainless steel doesn't rust is because the *chrome* it contains is passive. It's the chrome that doesn't rust."

Once again, a suppressed laugh slipped out. "Your Incarnate is useless against me now." As he made this sneering declaration, Haruyuki pushed off with both legs like an animal.

In the air, he spread the wings on his back with a *flap*. They bore not the slightest resemblance to the original simple metal fins. His wings had transformed into something with a weapon-like silhouette, and Haruyuki shook them with all his might.

He simply raised his right hand, and without having to particularly focus his mental energies, a dark overlay spilled out, almost overflowing. This immediately concentrated into the shape of a dagger, like the katar used by Middle Eastern soldiers, as he closed in on Jigsaw.

To meet this, Jigsaw extended a long saw tinged with the red of his overlay from his right arm and went to meet the dagger. Instantly, detailed information raced across Haruyuki's field of view. PREDICTED ATTACK/INCARNATE ATTACK; POWER ENHANCEMENT/AMPUTATION TYPE; THREAT LEVEL/20. This time, the information even included the trajectory the jigsaw would likely carve out.

"Yurooo!" Haruyuki barked and slid his body about fifty centimeters to the right in midair.

The jigsaw, having the longer reach, attacked first. However, the tip was tracing with incredible fidelity the predicted line Haruyuki had been shown. As a result, he was able to dodge it, despite the fact that normally, even without the relative power difference, the strike was precise down to the millimeter and should have been impossible to evade. He immediately thrust the black katar into Jigsaw's left shoulder.

Skrrinng! A painful ringing filled the air, and Jigsaw's body was sent flying from the top of the shuttle. However, displaying impressive control, he was able to tuck into a roll and land on his feet on the surface of the tower.

His body tilted back toward the Earth. A sort of pseudogravity in the direction of the Hermes' Cord pillar was at work on the interior of the shuttles, but the instant any avatar stepped outside, the ground was no longer the ground, but rather a precipice continuing vertically for several thousand kilometers.

Jigsaw instantly stabbed the saw in his right hand into the surface of the tower to support his body and keep from falling.

Touching down right in front of him, Haruyuki similarly pierced the tower with the talons of his feet and assumed an imposing stance.

"Heh-heh-heh. What kind of acrobatics are you going to show me next?"

Here, finally, concentrated hatred came from Rust Jigsaw's eyes. "You......ret. Gret. Regret. Regret. Regret regret regret regret!!" The muttered order turned into a scream, and as if guided by that hatred, his left arm began to shine with the largest overlay he had mustered so far.

Shiink! The jigsaw came flying. Red light streamed off it, countless teeth glinting. His arm drew a circle, fast like smoke, and the jigsaw transformed into a giant ring. He then fired it off somewhere; the saw whined as it flew away. It was Rust Jigsaw's long-distance attack, Wheel Saw. This technique, which involved throwing a rotating saw with extreme cutting power, had previously caused Haruyuki no small amount of grief.

However, it wasn't moving in a straight line now. The saw completely disappeared from Haruyuki's view and came at him along a curve like a boomerang. At first glance, he shouldn't have been able to handle it.

But the detailed information in his field of view appeared once more. PREDICTED ATTACK/INCARNATE ATTACK; RANGE/POWER/ MOVEMENT EXPANSION; THREAT LEVEL/40. And then an estimate line stretching from the top of Jigsaw's left hand, flying over Haruyuki, and coming around again from behind.

Without even looking over his shoulder, Haruyuki waved the tail attached to his back, once, broadly.

Cliiiink! The earsplitting sound of impact rang out, and the rotating saw of the special attack bounced harmlessly away, disappearing into the starry sky.

Haruyuki vaguely understood what the various information-tion displayed in the gray layer was. It was a prediction of the future calculated from vast battle experience accumulated by the Enhanced Armament The Disaster, which was the true form of the Armor of Catastrophe. He couldn't even begin to imagine how many duels this armor—born at the dawn of the Accelerated World, inherited by five Burst Linkers—had passed through. That data, essentially infinite, were being used to predict with terrifying accuracy every attack from his enemy.

"How? Explain. What is this power?" Rust Jigsaw moaned hoarsely.

Haruyuki glanced at him through his thick visor. "Are we done already? Then disappear." And he attacked, artlessly, dead-on.

This was not a *duel* on which the pride of Burst Linkers rested. Nor was it even a simple *battle*. It was better called a *slaughter*—no, *work*.

Unable to use his right hand, Jigsaw went to greet Haruyuki with the saw in his left arm wrapped in Incarnate and kicks from both legs. However, Haruyuki completely saw through each and every one of these attacks with the predictions of the Enhanced Armament and his own inspiration. He moved only the bare minimum distance with his wings and tail as he simply slashed at the enemy avatar.

In a certain sense, this fight was perhaps the perfected form of the Aerial Combo Haruyuki had worked so hard on. Yet there was not one speck of excitement or beauty or pride in it. It was simply nothing more than an ugly atrocity unfolding in the empty sky three thousand five hundred kilometers above the Earth.

First, he cut Jigsaw's right arm off. Then his right leg. His left leg. And finally, only the left arm supported the avatar.

A minute or so later, having dissected his enemy, Haruyuki grabbed tightly on to the head and torso of the ruins of the avatar that had been Rust Jigsaw, now a lump about to fall to Earth, and yanked them upward.

He should have been feeling absurd levels of pain, but Jigsaw still maintained the energy to smile thinly. "Heh-heh...heh. Praise yourself now. But...my objective's already been achieved."

Haruyuki had almost no interest in this, but still he cocked his head and listened to what Jigsaw had to say.

"And in a certain sense, we benefit even from the restoration of the Armor. Tremble with fear. From this moment, this world you believe in will begin to transform. It will lose this show of order, and the original confusion will cover everything. Before the revolution we bring about, despa—"

Gashhuk.

Without bothering to listen to the end, Haruyuki crushed Rust Jigsaw's head. The avatar threw off a red light and scattered; the Burst Linker who had ruined the Hermes' Cord Race departed from the Accelerated World for the time being.

No.

Maybe the destroyer in the truest sense was already Haruyuki himself. This race that he had wanted so desperately to save only a few minutes earlier no longer mattered either way to him.

It's not enough. Something like this, it's totally not enough.

Muttering in his heart, Haruyuki swiveled his head around. Naturally, there was no one. But the energy like a vortex throughout his body and the destructive urge, rather than subsiding, seemed to burn even more brightly.

I want to fight. I want to beat down more enemies, more and more, one after another, with this power.

He threw his head back, seeking new enemies, and the last remaining spectator stand jumped into his field of view.

The hundred or so members of the Gallery leaning forward in their seats wore uniform expressions of bewilderment. Whispered conversations flew back and forth through space.

"Isn't that...the Armor of Catastrophe...?"

"No way. I heard it was completely annihilated a little while ago."

"But, you know...That kind of crazy performance, the Armor's the only thing that could do that...?"

"But, come on, the look's totally different from when I saw it in the Unlimited Neutral Field…"

If you want to know so badly. Confirm the truth of it with your bodies. The truth of the legendary berserker, the overwhelming power of Chrome Disaster.

A mad smile bled onto Haruyuki's face below the visor. He slowly deployed his wings. The long tail folded up into an *S* and concealed itself in his body. As he was on the verge of kicking off the ground and heading toward the myriad prey there—

Something gently touched the wings on his back.

It was a memory. The memory of the countless duels that had permeated the metallic fins that were supposed to be mere propulsive devices. In particular, the wings, colored with darkness, flashed back for the merest of moments to the memory of the lone fight against the Black King Black Lotus, which had taken place the previous night in Haruyuki's bedroom.

Far, far away, a fleeting voice was revived within him.

…I'm proud of you…

Abruptly, the talons on his feet held firmly on to the iron plate in an unconscious movement. His body, so ready to soar up into the sky, was yanked heavily back down.

…I.

A single thought trickled down like a drop of clear water in the middle of that consciousness seething for battle.

The strength I'm looking for…shouldn't be…this blind slaughter…

The white ripple spread out in his head. Instantly, a part of his blackly lit armor shook unstably.

Do not fight it. Do not fear. This is precisely what you sought, someone said in the back of his mind, sounding irritated. Now, release even more of that anger. Destroy everything before you. And then eat it. Eat it all. If you do, you will obtain more, more, more, unlimited strength.

Eat? I…I don't want that…I don't want to be strong…for myself. It's for the people I love…To protect my meager but still warm family…

And for that person more important to me than anyone, to keep chasing after the same dream, I...

Abruptly, several hazy faces popped up before his eyes. Smiling faces, with their gentle gazes, began to paint over the black waves crowding in on him from all sides.

IN THAT CASE, EAT THEM, TOO. EAT THEM AND MAKE THEM YOUR POWER. NO NEED FOR ANYONE ELSE. DESTROY. SMASH. I AM THE PERSONIFICATION OF CALAMITY. I AM A SYMBOL OF TERROR. I AM THE TRUE CHROME DISASTER!!

This voice echoing like a broken bell.

Haruyuki mustered all the mental strength he could and shouted in return, *No! No!! I...I...!!*

"I am Silver Croooooow!!"

The instant the cry burst forth from under his visor—

The heavy armor over his body lost its hardness, like liquid metal. *Drip, drip.* It flowed toward the bottom of his feet, revealing Silver Crow's original helmet. The dark metal did not disappear, however. It coiled around the silver plating and tried to return.

"Unh...Ah! Aaaaah!"

Clenching his hands so tightly they threatened to break, Haruyuki resisted it. He worked with every fiber of his being to distance himself from the dark fluctuation trying to take control of both his avatar and his consciousness. But after only a few seconds, his resistance proved to be in vain; the evil shining began to return from the tips of his limbs.

This power of control far surpassed the domain of a simple item, stepping even into the realm of a true curse. Not some digital code written by the server, someone's consciousness itself. And it was trying to fuse with Haruyuki's own.

He had absolutely no idea what kind of logic would allow this sort of phenomenon to occur, but in fact, although it had only been a few minutes, Haruyuki's own thoughts were already encountering serious interference. While fighting Rust Jigsaw, Haruyuki had been more than half not-Haruyuki. If he fell into that state again, he might very well turn this fearsome power on his companions, on that someone most precious to him.

Exactly. Just like Cherry Rook, the fifth Chrome Disaster, who had tried to hunt his own "child," Scarlet Rain.

"Go away…Go away…Go awaaaaaaaay!" He pushed a desperate voice from between gritted teeth. But the Armor had already restored itself to his arms and up to his knees. It didn't seem that he would be able to stop this force.

In that case, there's one thing I can still do.

Sharp claws glittering, he raised his right hand and turned the tips of those talons toward the center of his own chest. Five fingers dripping with dull black Incarnate aura, he went to pierce the heart area, the most critical point of a duel avatar—

"Haruuuuuuu!!"

He heard his name in the distance. Jerking his head up with a gasp, he looked down along the space elevator and found there an unexpected sight.

A fresh green avatar with her right hand stretched out toward him as far as it would go. Lime Bell. Carrying her, the sky-blue avatar Sky Raker, flying toward him in a straight line, glittering flames jetting out of her booster. And then far behind, shuttle number one, running along intently on its lone remaining linear wheel.

"S-stay away! Bell! Raker! You can't come any closer!!" Haruyuki shouted in a daze. Instantly, his mental focus weakened, and the armor increased the pace of its reclamation of his body.

"Run! I…I can't…hold it back…anymore…!!"

Pwaah! A dark aura erupted from his entire body.

A sharp metallic sound echoed and reverberated as the Armor of Catastrophe climbed up his chest from his shoulders and covered his stomach. All that was left were his neck and head. The heavy metal collected there in the blink of an eye, and began to build back its sinister headpiece. A light gray film lowered itself over his field of view. If the visor of this helmet came down, Silver Crow would without a doubt completely disappear.

However, Sky Raker's charge did not waver. She began to go even faster, flying straight at Haruyuki.

On her back, Lime Bell lifted her left hand straight up. She spun the enormous bell, dazzling in the sunlight, around once, twice, counterclockwise. Three times. And then a fourth time.

Finally, she brought it down, pointing it straight at Haruyuki, and shouted loudly, clearer than the din of the stars.

"Citron Caaaaaaaaall!!"

Majestic bells, an orchestra of angels, echoed throughout the space. Riding the beautiful sound, a ribbon of light shining a clear green flowed toward him.

Text flickering irregularly popped up in the thin added layer covering his field of view. PREDICTED ATTACK/NORMAL SPECIAL ATTACK; RANGE UNKNOWN/POWER UNKNOWN/EFFECT UNKNOWN; THREAT LEVEL/100.

Haruyuki's left arm moved on its own to release a dark fluctuation on the ribbon. However, Haruyuki mustered whatever willpower he had left, so much so that it felt like his brain would catch fire, grabbed his left arm with his right, and pushed it back down.

Immediately after that, the clean lime-green light wrapped around Haruyuki's body.

As if sliced up by the ribbon of light, the dark armor broke into parts all over. The heavy metal once again melted into a fluid, and the tail on his back was even pulled in at the base. The power of Chiyuri's special attack Citron Call mode two, to forcibly rewind the status of an avatar, was trying to cancel out the equipping of the Enhanced Armament.

Geh...Yuroooooo!

The ferocious howling of a beast filled his head. Echoes of overwhelming anger and frustration. And then in the middle of that—the tiniest bit of fear.

Go away! Go away! I don't need you! I'm going to get stronger; I'm always going to have the right power now! So...you have to go awaaaaaaay!!

As if repelled by Haruyuki's cries, the metal abruptly disappeared, leaving only the tail that had appeared first. In the fresh green light, Haruyuki raised his now-freed arms, grabbed hold of the tail extending from his own back, and then put every drop of strength he had into ripping it off.

His entire avatar creaked, and a terrifying pain pierced his back. But he didn't let up. *Skrrk, skrrk.* The unpleasant sound of destruction filled the air, and the thick tail in his hands flailed as though it were a separate living creature.

FOOL.

The weakened voice whispered as his back.

IN YOUR HEART, YOU DO WANT TO FUSE AND BECOME ONE WITH ME AND MY POWER. BECAUSE YOU ARE THE ONLY ONE, OTHER THAN MY CREATOR, WITH WHOM I HAVE BEEN IN SUCH POWERFUL ALIGNMENT.

Haruyuki replied firmly to the voice. *Even still. Even if that's true, I reject you. I refuse you. And I do this for the people who gave me the power to be able to do it!!*

At the same time, he concentrated the remainder of his will into the hands, gripping the tail. Haruyuki changed that to light and released it.

"Laser...Sword!!"

A clear metallic *clang* filled the space, like the clashing of pure silver swords.

The snow-white swords of light gushed forth, crossed each

other, and sliced halfway through the heavy metal tail. The raging cry of an animal rang out just one final time, and then in the top left of his field of view, a system message flashed: YOU DISARMED THE DISASTER.

The final remaining fragments of the tail melted and crumbled away into nothing, as if wiped out by the light of the sun.

Having used up all his energy, Haruyuki slowly began to fall toward the Earth, but four arms belonging to the flying Chiyuri and Fuko gently caught him.

Apparently, he was out for longer than he thought.

When Haruyuki opened heavy lids, the jet-black mirrored visor of the Black King, Black Lotus, was before his eyes.

"Kuro...yukihime..." Murmuring, he lifted his head. He was in the front row of the crew seats of shuttle number one, parked now. They had laid him down on the bench seat, with his upper body resting on Lotus's lap.

When Kuroyukihime realized Haruyuki had regained consciousness again, she nodded once slowly. A gentle voice trembled slightly as it came out from her mask. "You came back to us, Crow. Well done...You really...came back to us..."

"Kuro...yukihime..." Haruyuki's voice began to shake implacably. "I...I'm sorry...I...I..."

"Don't talk now. You used all your strength and fought an opponent who needed to be fought. That's enough for now..."

"That's right, Corvus." Sky Raker looked back from the cockpit and stretched out a hand to stroke Haruyuki's helmet tenderly. "You saved the race from its would-be destroyer. No one in Nega Nebulus—no, in the Accelerated World, would reproach you for that fight."

"......" His heart was suddenly full and he started to drop his head when Takumu spoke to him from the rear seat, his tone his usual one.

"Exactly, Crow. And I've known forever that you snap and do

crazy stuff. When you went flying after shuttle number ten, it was more like, *Ah, here we go again.*"

"A-ha-ha! It's so true! And then it's always us cleaning up after you!" Chiyuri, next to Takumu, laughed delightedly.

Haruyuki felt he had to stand up for himself. "W-well, I never asked you to clean up or anything!"

"Oh, ohhh. So that's your story? And after big sister Raker and I worked so hard, that's all you have to say for yourself!"

"Unh...S-sorry...You really helped me out..."

His four teammates laughed at once at the back-and-forth. After a slight delay, Haruyuki added his own laughter to the mix.

They chatted harmoniously for a while, and then Chiyuri whirled her head to look around the shuttle.

"Aaah. But it totally sucks we can't make it to the finish line after you worked so hard for us, Haru! And it's just a little farther, too."

At this, Haruyuki pulled himself up from Kuroyukihime's lap and checked the condition of shuttle number one. It was just as Chiyuri said; the machine didn't look like it was going anywhere anytime soon. The rear, which had taken the full force of Rust Jigsaw's Incarnate attack, was rusted and crumbling, while the right linear wheel in the front had blown off completely, and the left had crackling sparks popping out of it. It was actually a wonder they had managed to get from where Haruyuki had flown off from to where he had fought Jigsaw.

"Well, there's nothing we can do about it." Kuroyukihime waved the sword of her right hand. "We should simply be glad that the victory was not carried off by that villain...At any rate, after this, it probably won't be the time or place for any further events in the Accelerated World..."

She trailed off, and Haruyuki opened his mouth to ask her what she meant.

At that moment, a shout rang up from below them on the tower.

"Hey, hey, heeeeeeeeey! Too early for the giving of it up, meeeeeeeeen!!"

"Waah?!" Haruyuki cried out, turning around. There in his sights were two shuttles laboriously climbing the tower, weak sparks shooting from the linear wheels. There was no mistake, these were the machines of the green and red teams he had assumed dropped out long ago.

Ash Roller sat in the cockpit of the machine, which was in the lead. But Haruyuki could see neither hide nor hair of Bush Utan and the other Green Legion members, who should have been riding in the rear.

And driving the shuttle behind Ash was the deep crimson, leopard-headed avatar, Blood Leopard. But she, too, was alone; there was no sign of the shooting squad.

The extent of damage on both machines was not much different from that of number one. As Haruyuki and his companions watched, stunned, the two machines staggered toward them and came to an awkward stop alongside them. Instantly, all the linear wheels on both shuttles flew off with a pathetic noise.

"Ah. Aaaah. Mega-solid work getting this far." Ash Roller patted the side of his shuttle, and Pard, too, gently stroked her steering wheel and murmured, "GJ." And then they both lifted their faces and looked at the five members of Nega Nebulus.

Cocking her head to one side, Kuroyukihime spoke for all of them. "Well, I suppose I should first say, 'Well done'...How on earth did you manage to chase after us, even after losing your team members? It's definitely no longer possible to continue the race."

"Oh, yeah, right. I kinda just talked with Miss Panther Head here for, like, a minute, right?" Ash Roller said, scratching the back of his skull helmet. "So then the whole team dropped out, yeah? Just took the hits too hard, you know—"

"You talk too much. And I'm not a panther, I'm a leopard," Pard interjected curtly and picked up the explanation. "Currently, none of the shuttles is drivable. But if our three teams work together, there's a very small possibility we could reach the finish line."

"Wh-what do you mean, Leopard?" Sky Raker leaned forward and Pard met her gaze.

"One step outside of the shuttle and you're on a vertical cliff. But my Beast Mode and Bike Guy's motorcycle can run up walls."

"B-bike guy...," Ash Roller muttered in a complicated tone, but was ignored as the unfaltering explanation continued.

"But that will deplete both of our special-attack gauges. So Bike Guy and I run to that limit carrying Crow and Raker. Then Crow carries Raker on his back and flies to his limit. Finally, Raker flies as far as she can with the energy remaining in Gale Thruster. Although I don't know whether or not she'll be able to make it to the finish line." Pard spread both hands as if to say, *Only the gods know that.*

At the unexpected proposal, Haruyuki and his friends fell into a dumbfounded silence. The first to break this quiet was Kuroyukihime.

"I see. Interesting. There's merit in trying. But...naturally, you aren't offering your help free of charge?"

"That is totally of cooooooourse! The prize points for coming in first get cut up three ways! And you guys nick 'em all and it'll totally giga suck—"

"That's rude, Ash."

On behalf of Ash Roller, who fell instantly silent at Raker's voice, Pard cocked her head slightly to the side. "So?"

"Of course we accept," Kuroyukihime replied immediately, and the leopard-headed avatar responded with her usual "K" and smiled faintly.

After Blood Leopard transformed into a beautiful four-limbed beast with the Shape Change command, the lightweight Sky Raker climbed onto her back, and then Haruyuki sat himself on the back of the American chopper that Ash Roller summoned.

"Well then, I wish you godspeed. We will be cheering you on from here."

Takumu and Chiyuri nodded at Kuroyukihime's words.

"It's up to you now, guys. Give this event a happy ending for all of us!"

"You can do it, Crow, big sister Raker! And you, too, Leopard, and bike person!"

After dropping his head momentarily, Ash Roller shouted with his usual enthusiasm, "Okay, here we goooooo! Grab on and hold! Me! Tight! Corvus, man! Aaaah, I'd rather be saying that to Master!" The roar of the engine partially drowned out this somewhat pathetic line. Ash Roller spun the rear wheel exaggeratedly before sending, almost shooting, the motorcycle sprinting up the vertical wall.

Following them, making almost no noise, Pard started to run with Raker on her back. The large paws of the cat beast stuck firmly to the surface of the tower, looking for all the world like a cat running up the trunk of a tree.

After they started to move, a loud sound abruptly and wholly unexpectedly poured down from above their collective heads. Cheering. The multicolored avatars of the last remaining floating spectator stand were raising their voices all at once.

"All riiiiiight! Show us that Burst Linker spirit!"

"You can do iiiiiit, Leopaaaaard!"

"Crow! You totally kicked butt back there!"

Some of the cheers were directed at Silver Crow, and Haruyuki unconsciously looked up. They had to have seen him summon the forbidden Enhanced Armament, the Armor of Catastrophe. And he had even thought, just once, of massacring the more than one hundred members of the Gallery with that power. But he heard no voices of reproach. Maybe it was just that they still hadn't realized the truth of the matter. Either way, the cheers they flung down on them brought a warmth to Haruyuki's heart.

Apparently, the ascension of the spectator stands was synced to the lead shuttle; the Gallery did not chase after them. In the blink of an eye, the enormous stand and the figures of Kuroyukihime,

Takumu, and Chiyuri waving below it grew distant, finally melting into the exterior panels of the gleaming silver elevator and disappearing.

The throaty roar of the engine and the faint footfalls echoed through the space three thousand and some hundreds of kilometers above the Earth. Almost as if the massive destruction only moments earlier had never happened, the silver Hermes' Cord stretched out endlessly, beautifully, and continued up toward the Milky Way, where the rivers of stars flowed.

No one spoke, and there was no need to. The four headed for the peak of the tower with their own emotions and a single shared thought in their hearts. That's what Haruyuki believed as he sat quietly, entrusting his body to the bike's vibrations.

Immediately before he had been discharged from this world, Rust Jigsaw had talked about a "revolution." So that no doubt indicated that the next large-scale act of destruction would be carried out with the clear intent of his organization, the Acceleration Research Society. But no matter what kind of changes they brought about in the Accelerated World, there were definitely precious things in this world that would never change. Because here and now, the members of three enemy Legions were combining forces and aiming for a single goal.

"As long as I keep this fact in mind, I'll never give in to the temptation of the Armor again," Haruyuki murmured, and no voice came back in response.

How far did they race like this?

Eventually, ahead of them, a row of tiny lights that were not stars popped up, creating a beautiful, shining blue ring that wrapped around Hermes' Cord and disappeared into inky black space.

"Guess that's the finish line, the top station," Ash Roller said, slackening his cruising speed. "Managed to run a fair way thanks to the weak gravity, but this is the end of the line for this cool dude. How 'bout you, Miss Leopard?"

"Me, too."

The two nodded at each other lightly and looked back over their shoulders at their respective passengers.

"It's up to you now, Crow," Ash Roller said awkwardly. "And, y'know, however the chips fell back there, you had extreme guts in the battle against that rust dude. Maybe things're gonna get for-real serious later, but don't go getting all bummed out, got it?"

Haruyuki nodded deeply and somehow managed to squeeze out a reply. "Th-thank you."

"Yup. And you better not forget our share, Corvus man!"

"Raker." To their right, Blood Leopard offered a very brief farewell to Sky Raker. "One thing…Welcome back, ICBM."

Raker stroked her back gently and replied, equally briefly, "I'm home, Bloody Kitty."

Once their respective farewells were finished, Haruyuki deployed the wings on his back. Thanks to the Incarnate battle with Jigsaw, his special-attack gauge was nearly charged to the maximum. He flapped his fins lightly and soundlessly rose up from the passenger seat of the motorcycle. He reached out his hand and grabbed tightly on to the outstretched hand of Raker. At this, the lightweight avatar was pulled up from Leopard's back and drawn close to Haruyuki.

Here, finally, the special-attack gauges of the bike and the leopard appeared to be spent; they both began to slow down rapidly. Haruyuki turned to fly backward and see them off.

"Okay, then! You make sure you get Master there, Crow!"

"CU."

Tires and legs stopped and rested momentarily on the wall before gently peeling away. Pulled by the gravity of the Earth spreading out blue far below them, Ash Roller and Blood Leopard began to drop leisurely. If this had been the real world, there would have been absolutely no air this high up, but the Accelerated World was apparently set to inflict damage from friction with the atmosphere, and an orange light encased the two avatars. Their silhouettes receded, drawing out vivid tails like falling stars, until finally they released a powerful burst of light and vanished.

"...Thank you." Haruyuki bowed his head deeply toward the two avatars, who had returned to the real world and once again set course for the peak of Hermes' Cord.

There was still a fair ways to go before the top station, colored by its blue rings. It was right on the edge of how far they could reach by combining both of their flying abilities. However, Haruyuki felt that making it to the finish line was no longer the key part of this. Three teams had joined forces and done their utmost to reach a difficult goal. That was the most valuable part of this race.

"Let's get going. Master, maybe on my back," he said to the sky-blue avatar whose hand he held, and Fuko smiled quietly.

"If that's how it is, then please hold me in front. We are finally alone, after all."

"Huh?...R-right." Flustered, he nodded and brought both arms around the back with the boosters equipped and the thin legs amputated from the knee down. Raker held on as well, wrapping her arms around his neck.

"O-okay, here we go!" he announced to hide his embarrassment and vibrated the wings on his back.

To curb the depletion of his special-attack gauge, he stopped at the bare minimum–strength thrust. Furthermore, there weren't any other opponents to fight. The two avatars began a gentle ascent, leaving a hazy trail of silver light.

They flew through the silent world, watched over only by the countless stars. Perhaps it was just his imagination, but it seemed like the light from the sun shining above them, off to the left, was gentler than it had been before. Only their small shadow raced along the smoothly curving surface of Hermes' Cord.

For a while, neither of them said anything.

However, eventually, Fuko, her forehead buried in the right

side of Haruyuki's chest, murmured, deep-red eye lenses half closed, "This sight...I've seen it for so long in my dreams...But at the same time, I've come to fear it somewhere in my heart..."

The infinitely rarified atmosphere still managed to bring about a bit of a breeze, ruffling her bluish-silver hair. She gently brushed away her fringe with the fingers of her right hand and continued.

"The other side of the sky was an impossible dream. And to make that dream come true, I sacrificed anything and everything. My fighting power...responsibility as the deputy head of Nega Nebulus...and Sacchi's friendship. I threw everything away, committed an enormous crime, and still my hand did not reach the sky...When I understood this...perhaps I was just a little relieved. With that, I was freed from the deep delusion that had moved me. All that was left for me was to sit secreted away at the top of a tower, forgotten by everyone, and gaze out at the changes in the Accelerated World."

A faint smile spread across her lips, and she closed her eyes. Her expression was perfectly calm, but Haruyuki saw in the corner of her eye a very tiny particle of light, glittering like a diamond—a tear welling up.

"My dream was too heavy for my shoulders. But even after I dropped it, unable to completely bear that weight, I could not entirely abandon it. This dream that I held in both hands like I was shielding the embers of a flame about to die out...When one day, a little crow appeared in my garden and took it over for me...You have no idea how happy I was...Now, here, I will say the *thank you* that I haven't been able to all this time. Thank you, Crow—no, Haruyuki."

Fuko opened her eyes and lightly caressed Haruyuki's cheek with an outstretched hand before abruptly declaring in a clipped tone, "You've gone to the trouble of holding me in your arms to carry me all this way, but...I don't have the right to visit the real other side of the sky at the finish line of this race. We'll switch places. I'll carry you as far as I can fly. From there, please head to the finish line yourself. This is my duty after giving up on my dream, and your right as the one who has always sought the sky, with so much more strength and so much more seriously than I did…Now, Corvus. Let me down here."

"No." At this instruction, Haruyuki shook his head in a gentle yet definite motion. "You're wrong, Raker."

"What…?"

"You haven't given up on your dream. The sky you aimed for is so much higher, much, much higher than mine. I'll prove it to you now. I…I came to this place now, to the top of Hermes' Cord, just to tell you this." Saying only that, Haruyuki suddenly flapped his wings with all his strength.

The ten fins on each side were wrapped in a dazzling white light. The high-pitched ring of resonance echoed in their ears, and an intense propulsive power enveloped them. The stars on either side became long lines and flowed by. But…

This full-power charge only lasted a few seconds.

The sound of his wings vibrating rapidly faded, and the light also disappeared. It wasn't that his gauge had been exhausted. Despite the fact that the fins were still fluttering fiercely, they were not generating any thrust. Finally, even their forward momentum vanished.

"My wings can't fly any farther than this," Haruyuki said to the woman in his arms once they stopped ascending, grinning as he did. "The air's too thin. My flying ability propels me forward through the vibration of those fins beating at the air. So this high up, I can wiggle them all I want, but I won't move forward. This game really does get a little too hung up on the details, doesn't it…"

Fuko opened her eyes wide and listened without saying anything. Staring at her beautiful rose-red eyes, Haruyuki finally turned into sound the words he had kept warm in his heart a long, long time, all this time.

"But…But your wings are Gale Thruster, a booster, a jet pack. In this world without air, even you…only you can fly. So why the booster…That's because right from the start, you saw not the sky, but only something beyond that. Higher than the clouds, than the stratosphere, and higher still…You've been wanting the world of this star. You, this avatar…" Here, he closed his mouth for a moment, and after taking a deep breath beneath his helmet, Haruyuki told her in a shaky but clear voice, "You were born to fly in this world. Sky Raker, the one who looks out on the sky. You've always been a duel avatar meant to fight in space."

This sentence spread out in the rarified atmosphere, melted, and disappeared.

Fuko opened her glittering red eyes even wider. But, saying nothing, she simply held tight to Haruyuki's gaze with her own. Finally, she lightly shifted her head and looked down at her legs. Haruyuki moved his own gaze in the same direction.

A massive blue planet sprawled there, as if supporting the steel pillar soaring up endlessly—Hermes' Cord.

The Earth. Illuminated by the sun from the right, it was colored with a beautiful gradation, moving from blue to indigo before sinking into black. Against this backdrop, snowy white clouds drew out complicated patterns, while the continents carved out complex edges around them.

Fuko raised her right hand lightly and pointed at the border between the right half of the lazy arc of the planet and the inky black of space.

Straining his eyes, Haruyuki saw a thin light blue veil there, wrapping up the Earth's surface as if to protect it from the chill of space. Compared with the scale of the planet and space, this glittering was extremely modest.

"…That ephemeral sky-blue line…" Fuko's whisper caressed Haruyuki's consciousness like thought itself. "That's all of it, the sky that I've aimed for, dreamt of, occasionally hated…and then given up on…"

This time, a large tear really did spill from her sunset eyes, falling to drift idly in empty space. Eventually, that drop of water was pulled down by the minuscule tug of gravity, to return to the blue oceans of the planet it came from.

Fuko looked up at Haruyuki again, raised her left hand, wrapped both her arms around Silver Crow's neck, and squeezed tightly, fiercely. Words played in his ear, engraving themselves into his mind.

"Thank you, Corvus. It's so wonderful that I could come here...that I could see this sight. I finally understand it now: The reason my legs remain gone...is not because of my attachment, but rather my fear. I was afraid that if I knew the size of the sky... my dream would end. But there's no need for that to happen. Because..."

Unconsciously, Haruyuki also gave voice to the words that came next.

"This world is infinite."

Fuko laughed softly in his ear and abruptly planted her lips on the side of his helmet. Like this, she slid over to his mouth before pulling away slowly.

"Huh! Ah! Um!" Forcefully enough to ruin the whole moment, Haruyuki shook his head frantically, and Raker's smile changed into something playful.

"It was through your helmet, so I'm sure Sacchi will forgive it." Regaining her usual cool, she said firmly, "Really, thank you, Corvus. I'm...going now."

"Right!!" Nodding decisively, Haruyuki supported her body with both hands, letting it flow gently in space. Raker stretched out a finger to stroke his arm, touch his hand, and pull away. They nodded at each other wordlessly, and then the sky-blue avatar turned her face to the peak.

The blue rings coloring the top station of Hermes' Cord, now only a scant distance away, could be seen perfectly clearly now. Along with the artificial lights glittering faintly beyond it. There was no doubt that it was the station in geostationary orbit, floating off thirty-six thousand kilometers in the distance.

Fuko brought her slim hands down to her sides and lit a tiny flame in the jet opening of the streamlined Enhanced Armament attached to her back, Gale Thruster. Due to the almost total lack of gravity here, even with this hint of thrust, her avatar began to slowly ascend. Without looking back, Sky Raker gradually picked up speed. Growing distant. And more distant.

And then, Haruyuki was sure he saw it.

Particles of blue light collecting, condensing, and drawing out a beautiful line at the ends of Raker's legs, where they had been amputated. This surface, transparent like glass, gradually took on the same color as the main body of the avatar from the knees down. Modest calves, long and slender shins stretching out. Heels equipped with wedge lifts and pointed toes. All of this shone and sparkled in the sun.

"...Ah, ah..." A quiet voice escaped from Haruyuki's throat. At the same time, a hot liquid filled his eyes.

In the center of his vision, blurred, too, with the light of the stars, Sky Raker, now returned to her original form finally, after three years—no, after many times that in the Accelerated World—pierced the inky dark and flew forward. As if she were dancing, as if she were swimming, she soared endlessly upward, graceful in her acceleration.

Here, finally, the energy that had allowed Haruyuki to continue hovering against the pull of gravity was exhausted.

Fighting against the virtual gravity that tried to pull his avatar gently downward, Haruyuki reached his right hand out as far as he could. Between his outstretched fingers, the light of the thrusters became a large blue star, drawing out the shape of a cross.

11

"The previous Chrome Disaster's...'wire'...?"

The glass that was halfway to her mouth stopped moving abruptly, and Kuroyukihime repeated Haruyuki's words, taken aback.

"Yeah...That's all I can think of anymore..." Haruyuki nodded, almost hanging his head, after looking in turn at the equally speechless Fuko, Takumu, and Chiyuri.

Sunday, June 9, 12:15 PM. Not even ten minutes had passed since the five of them had all returned to the real world at slightly different times on the sofa set in the Arita living room.

Naturally, first off, they had all grabbed one another's hands with delight at having overcome so many difficulties to so wonderfully win the Hermes' Cord Race—although they did have to split the prize points three ways with the red and green teams. They had all praised one another's fighting prowess and raised a toast with glasses of oolong tea.

However, after some chatter about their victory, inevitably, they were forced to address the elephant in the room: Silver Crow's transformation into Chrome Disaster.

That said, none of them reproached him for having summoned

the Armor. Kuroyukihime was the first to acknowledge that in that situation, if possible, she might have done the same herself. But there was one point at least that had to be clarified. And that was the mystery of how on earth the Armor had appeared, or rather, returned.

Five months earlier, Haruyuki, Takumu, and Kuroyukihime had accepted the Red King Scarlet Rain's request and fought the fifth Chrome Disaster in the Unlimited Neutral Field. As a result of the fierce battle, the Armor had finally been destroyed, and Cherry Rook, who had summoned it, was Judged by the hand of the Red King.

After it was all over, immediately before they returned to the real world through the leave point in Sunshine City in Ikebukuro, every one of them had then and there opened their own item storage and confirmed that the Armor of Catastrophe had not been transferred to them. And, of course, Haruyuki also had a vivid memory of seeing absolutely nothing in the open window.

So there should have been no way that Silver Crow could summon Chrome Disaster at this late date. However, in reality, Haruyuki had dispatched the formidable enemy Rust Jigsaw in an instant with the fearsome power of the Armor.

In trying to explain this seeming contradiction, Haruyuki miraculously remembered, in the middle of the conversation, a single insignificant event in the intense fighting in Ikebukuro, something he had paid absolutely no attention to before now.

"Ummm...I thought you'd remember, Kuroyukihime, since you fought the fifth Disaster yourself." Clutching his glass of now–thoroughly lukewarm oolong tea, Haruyuki haltingly put his thoughts into words. "He had the ability to use those super-fine hooked wires he shot out from his hands to pull opponents or objects toward him. Or the opposite: to affix the wires to some surface and pull himself along, like a fake flying ability. And you totally couldn't see it coming...I had no other choice. To stop him from escaping through the portal, I deliberately caught that wire on my own back."

As he spoke, Haruyuki remembered the shock and metallic *krnch* when the wire hit his back, and even the sensation of the cold, sharp hook.

"Once we were connected by the wire, I yanked Chrome Disaster up high and then finished him off with a dive kick. And I'm pretty sure that's when Disaster's main body was destroyed. The wire was cut in the impact. And one end of it somehow…stayed in my back? When I came back through the portal, I didn't check what happened to it."

Haruyuki clamped his mouth shut there, and Kuroyukihime murmured, dumbfounded, "The previous Chrome Disaster's… 'wire'…?"

"Yeah…That's all I can think of anymore…" He hung his head, and Takumu's voice crept into his ears, edged with the same shock.

"B-but, Haru…Is it even possible for some part to drop off one duel avatar and stick to another one, staying with you even after you burst out?"

"I-I've never heard of anything like that, either." Chiyuri shook her head, scowling so hard, she nearly pulled her face into itself. "I used to end duels with a broken sword or lance or whatever stuck in me all the time, but they were all gone by the time I went into my next duel!"

"But…there's no other explanation. A-and when I summoned Disaster before, the first thing was that long tail growing out of my back. And it grew basically from the same place where the hooked wire got me."

And when the mysterious voice had spoken to him those many times over the last few months, he had always felt a throbbing in the same place on his back.

This thought alone he did not give voice to. It was just too terrifying. If that throbbing was indeed the wire Chrome Disaster had left behind, then that meant…wounds he got in the Accelerated World continued to have an impact on his flesh-and-blood body. No matter how he thought about it, that at least had to be impossible. It defied all logic.

The three childhood friends sank into silence, staring at one another, and it was Fuko, silent until that point, who opened her mouth hesitatingly.

"Actually…residual foreign objects straddling duels is a phenomenon that's possible system-wise."

"Huh?"

Three sets of eyes were turned on her abruptly. Raker met each in turn and explained. "In other words, an attack with a parasitic attribute. It's exceedingly rare, but there have apparently been cases of obtaining this attribute, a power that goes beyond curse types. However, I only know of abilities that would allow you to parasitize small animal objects and steal their vision and voice, or to get into explosives and blow them up using some kind of trigger…"

Kuroyukihime picked up where she left off in a quiet voice. "An Enhanced Armament making part of itself a parasite to escape destruction…I've never heard of anything like it. But if what Haruyuki's telling us is true, then that explains part of the Disaster legend." The Black King set her glass down, clasped her fingers above crossed legs, and connected the dots. "With a probability of one hundred percent, the Armor of Catastrophe moves to the storage of the person who banished its owner. This rate is impossible under the normal rules for transfer of ownership, but those times when it can't move as an item, it makes part of itself a parasite and lives on…Thinking about it like this, it's not unconvincing."

"R-right, that's true."

Parasite. A shiver running up his body at the disgusting images the word brought to mind, Haruyuki nodded. Something else popped into his mind then, and he hurried to ask, "B-but if the parasite is a system ability, there has to be a way to get rid of it, right?"

"Mmm, there is. A normal parasite attack will disappear after a length of time has passed, but it should also be possible to cancel it with a purification ability. However, the ability level has to be the same or higher...And a master who could purify a parasite that's able to regenerate an entire body from the broken end of a wire..."

Here, Kuroyukihime and Fuko glanced at each other, their mouths stiffening in sync. Their faces soon returned to normal, however, and Kuroyukihime said in a clear tone, "All right, then. I'll handle this. Give me a little time."

"Thinking about it now..." Fuko opened her mouth next. "That time Corvus stayed at my house—"

Immediately, Kuroyukihime, Takumu, and Chiyuri all had the same question in reply. "Stayed?"

"This was in the Unlimited Neutral Field. When I stroked Corvus's back there—"

"Stroked?"

"This was with our avatars. Honestly, you have to let me tell the story. That time, I felt it, too, faintly. Something abnormal in one spot on his back. If we investigated that more closely—"

"C-come now, Raker! What do you propose when you say *investigate*?" Kuroyukihime's right cheek twitched, and Fuko grinned.

"Well, that's obviously a secret."

At this exchange, the mood in the room finally lightened, and Haruyuki exhaled heavily. He lifted his face and announced in a firm voice, "Uh, I know I did give in to that temptation once here, but the Armor disappeared thanks to Chiyu's power...and even if it's still parasitizing me right now, all I have to do is not call it again. Of course, I want to be 'purified' sooner rather than later, but..."

"Mmm, that's right. I believe in you. Naturally, you were

assisted by Chiyuri's ability, but at the same time, you yourself rejected the armor with your own will. And that's something that none of the others the Armor took over was able to do," Kuroyukihime said with a smile, before her face clouded intently in the next instant.

"Wh-what's wrong, Kuroyukihime?"

"Mmm...It's just...This might end up being not just our problem. Haruyuki, more than a hundred members of the Gallery watched from the stands as you summoned the Armor and fought Jigsaw, yes?"

"Y-yes..."

"In which case, regardless of the fact that it was only one battle, word that Silver Crow of Nega Nebulus is the owner of the sixth Chrome Disaster has likely already spread throughout the Accelerated World. From now on, we'll likely have people expressing strong opinions coming forward."

"Huh? What do you mean, 'strong opinions'?" Chiyuri cocked her head to one side, and Takumu explained quietly.

"People saying Haru should be Judged or punished."

"What?! Th-that's crazy, though!! I mean, Haru didn't even do anything wrong!!" Chiyuri shouted indignantly, and Fuko sitting next to her gave her a gentle pat.

"Bell, all of us here believe that. But, well...in the Accelerated World, there are many forces that have a very hostile view of Nega Nebulus."

"But, I mean, that's just awful." Chiyuri furrowed her brow tightly, as if saddened to her core.

Haruyuki flashed her his best smile, feeling something welling up in his heart. "It's fine, Chiyu. I mean, we've been up against the Kings other than Promi up to now anyway. This now is basically just another log on the fire."

"Mmm, that's precisely it." Kuroyukihime nodded firmly and stood up fluidly.

Smoothing the skirt of her school uniform, she moved over

to the large southern window. She turned around and looked at each of her four subordinates in turn with glittering eyes before the Black King announced resolutely, "Most likely, in the coming days, a meeting of the Seven Kings will be called for the first time in two and a half years. The first item on the agenda should be countermeasures for the fact that efforts to keep the Incarnate System concealed have been utterly ruined by Rust Jigsaw and the Acceleration Research Society, but there is no doubt in my mind that the topic of Haruyuki's transformation into Disaster will be brought up, likely by Radio, the Yellow King. But regardless of the demands they might make of me, I will protect you, Haruyuki. All-out war is what I seek, after all. Are there any objections to this policy?"

"None!" Fuko, Takumu, and Chiyuri sang immediately.

Haruyuki could only murmur in a trembling voice, "Thanks."

I'm so glad I can be here now. And I'm definitely going to protect this place, these friends. I'll protect them from any enemy, in the face of any adversity.

It was then as he etched these words into his heart. Chiyuri's curious voice found its way into his ears.

"Anyway, Kuroyukihime. Why are you wearing your uniform when it's Sunday?"

Gulp.

Haruyuki and Kuroyukihime froze.

"That's," Fuko said, the usual Fuko Smile popped onto her lips after she shot off a Raker Wink attack, "because Sacchi's closet is crammed with nothing but uniforms."

After that, they replenished their supplies of snacks and drinks at the shopping center on the ground floor and held a formal victory party. By the time they had laughed and chatted and all finished cleaning up together, the hands of the clock had rolled around to six PM.

Takumu and Chiyuri, with their early curfews, were the first to head home, and a few minutes later, Kuroyukihime, with Fuko in tow, turned toward the entryway.

"Sacchi," Fuko said in a quiet voice, just as Kuroyukihime was bending down to put on her shoes.

"Mmm?" She stretched out and looked back, black hair swinging. "What is it, Fuko?"

Fuko took a step forward from Haruyuki's side, who had come to see them off, and clasped her hands in front of her, as though she were looking for the right words.

After a moment, she began to speak hesitantly, in a tone with an unusually childish edge to it, almost as though they had gone back to being elementary school students. "Um...Um. At first, I was thinking I'd stay quiet until the next duel and then I'd surprise you, but...then I figured I should really tell you right away, so..." She took a deep breath.

The girl who had spent such a long time as the recluse of the Accelerated World lovingly enunciated each of the words that announced the end of those days.

"Um. My legs came back."

Obsidian eyes jumped up. From between slightly parted lips, a short breath slipped out. This surprise transformed into an expression that was half sob, half smile.

"I see," Kuroyukihime murmured and nodded. "I see...So you found it again. What you lost that day."

"Mm-hmm." Dipping her head lightly, Fuko took a step, then another, toward Kuroyukihime. She stretched out her arms, pulled her frozen friend toward her, and hugged her gently.

Unlike the time they had hugged at Shinjuku Southern Terrace two months earlier, the pair said nothing more than this. They simply, silently, warmly, held each other. Haruyuki felt that they were no doubt having a deeper spiritual exchange than even connecting their Neurolinkers directly with a cable. He could hear the glass wall that had been separating them break and crumble away.

Finally, Kuroyukihime slowly raised her head, looked straight at Haruyuki with damp eyes, and smiled. "The size of this miracle you have brought about...I can't even begin to express it in words. Thank you, Haruyuki."

Fuko looked back and grinned broadly, trails of tears glistening on her cheeks. "Corvus. You found the road to Hermes' Cord, you invited me, and then you took me to the other side of the sky...I will never forget this."

At their words, Haruyuki pulled into himself and shook his head fiercely. "No. I mean, I...It was just this thought that popped into my head...It was everyone in the Legion and Ash and Pard, too, who made it actually happen," he mumbled in a voice that was hard even for him to hear as he tried to sink into the wall behind him. *Gah, I'm ruining everything.*

Kuroyukihime and Fuko exchanged looks and grinned at the same time before suddenly walking toward him.

"Huh? Uh, um!"

He looked up at each of their faces in turn and tested his wall-walking skills again, but before he could succeed in that endeavor, Kuroyukihime's right arm and Fuko's left snaked out to wrap around him from both sides—

He had no memory of anything after that.

AFTERWORD

Reki Kawahara here. Thank you for picking up *Accel World 5: The Floating Starlight Bridge*.

First off, I have a confession. At the beginning of book three, I noted that there already existed a space elevator in the setting of *Accel World*, but my apologies! At that time, I hadn't done any kind of technical investigation into this. I simply wrote it because I got carried away with the vague idea that of course they would have space elevators at least in 2047, but then I thought that I should get around to making that the setting for this volume, and when I belatedly checked it out…I was fairly stunned and sort of stuck…

In fact, the so-called space elevator still hasn't left the realm of a thought experiment, and it definitely doesn't look like it will become a reality in the next thirty or so years. The details for this are explained by Kuroyukihime in the novel, so I'll omit them here, but I'll say that I did retort "An asteroid for a counterweight!" to the NASA person and grew quite pale.

Fortunately, there are some researchers who have put forth somewhat more practical ideas, and Hermes' Cord appearing in this volume is modeled on those. However, there is also apparently a huge problem with the hypersonic skyhook I used as a model…but what the problem is is not written in the book. So I'm going to act like I didn't notice it.

At any rate, this was a valuable lesson in "when you write about something, first check it out!" In the next book, a fairly young new character will probably show up, so I'm going to work hard, check into a bunch of things, and discuss with my esteemed friend A-yama-sensei.

I'm writing this afterword on April 10, that is, the deadline for the seventeenth Dengeki Prize. Which means a full two years have passed since I brought the envelope (well, it was actually an ExPack) with the first *Accel World* manuscript in it to the post office.

To be honest, at the time I submitted it, I thought if I won some kind of prize, that would be the finish line. I never thought that it would actually be a new starting point and that I would keep churning out manuscripts after that...Of course, I am super, super luckyyyyyy to be able to write these, but I can't help but be sort of baffled sometimes. Exactly where is the finish line on this Thunder Road?

And to my editor, Miki, who has been so kind as to guide little lost me with the deepest patience; my illustrator, HIMA, whom I am always messing with with my many troublesome requests; the manga artist Tatsuya Kurusu, who was kind enough to take on the design of the new avatars; and to you for sticking with me this far, giga thank you!!

Reki Kawahara
April 10, 2010

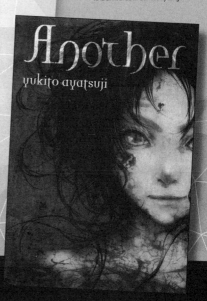

ACCEL WORLD, Volume 5
REKI KAWAHARA

Translation by Jocelyne Alen

ACCEL WORLD
© REKI KAWAHARA 2010
All rights reserved.
Edited by ASCII MEDIA WORKS
First published in Japan in 2010 by KADOKAWA CORPORATION, Tokyo.
English translation rights arranged with KADOKAWA CORPORATION, Tokyo,
through Tuttle-Mori Agency, Inc., Tokyo.

English translation © 2015 Hachette Book Group, Inc.

Yen On
Hachette Book Group
1290 Avenue of the Americas
New York, NY 10104

www.hachettebookgroup.com
www.yenpress.com

Yen On is an imprint of Hachette Book Group, Inc.
The Yen On name and logo are trademarks of Hachette Book Group, Inc.

The publisher is not responsible for websites (or their content) that are not owned by the publisher.

First Yen On edition: November 2015

ISBN: 978-0-316-29639-7

10 9 8 7 6 5 4 3 2 1

RRD-C

Printed in the United States of America

"Why are we playing this stupid game, Lee?"

Derek asked.

"Uh, game?" Lee muttered, her eyes downcast.

"Yes. Game. You looking at me the way you do, and me pretending I don't see. What's the point, when you're obviously attracted to me and—well, I suppose I might as well just say it. I'm attracted to you, too." Derek paused and then continued. "I think we might as well just go ahead and deal with this straight out. Get it out of our systems."

"Like a viral infection, you mean? Something that has to run its course?"

Derek gave her a reproachful frown. "You're behaving very strangely about this, Lee."

Maybe she was, Lee thought. Derek Taylor was her fantasy, and she'd had a safe, secret, one-sided, totally imaginary love affair with him. It had been great.

But he just couldn't leave it that way. Oh, no. He had to go and make it dangerous. Make it *real*

Dear Reader,

It's the most festive time of the year! And Special Edition is celebrating with six sparkling romances for you to treasure all season long.

Those MORGAN'S MERCENARIES are back by popular demand with bestselling author Lindsay McKenna's brand-new series, MORGAN'S MERCENARIES: THE HUNTERS. Book one, *Heart of the Hunter,* features the first of four fearless brothers who are on a collision course with love—and danger. And in January, the drama and adventure continues with Lindsay's provocative Silhouette Single Title release, *Morgan's Mercenaries:Heart of the Jaguar.*

Popular author Penny Richards brings you a poignant THAT'S MY BABY! story for December. In *Their Child,* a ranching heiress and a rugged rancher are married for the sake of *their* little girl, but their platonic arrangement finally blossoms into a passionate love. Also this month, the riveting PRESCRIPTION: MARRIAGE medical miniseries continues with an unlikely romance between a mousy nurse and the man of her secret dreams in *Dr. Devastating* by Christine Rimmer. And don't miss Sherryl Woods's 40th Silhouette novel, *Natural Born Lawman,* a tale about two willful opposites attracting—the latest in her AND BABY MAKES THREE: THE NEXT GENERATION miniseries.

Just in time for the holidays, award-winning author Marie Ferrarella delivers a *Wife in the Mail*—a heartwarming story about a gruff widower who falls for his brother's jilted mail-order bride. And long-buried family secrets are finally revealed in *The Secret Daughter* by Jackie Merritt, the last book in THE BENNING LEGACY crossline miniseries.

I hope you enjoy all our romance novels this month. All of us at Silhouette Books wish you a wonderful holiday season!

Sincerely,
Karen Taylor Richman
Senior Editor

Please address questions and book requests to:
Silhouette Reader Service
U.S.: 3010 Walden Ave., P.O. Box 1325, Buffalo, NY 14269
Canadian: P.O. Box 609, Fort Erie, Ont. L2A 5X3

CHRISTINE RIMMER
DR. DEVASTATING

Silhouette®

SPECIAL EDITION®

Published by Silhouette Books
America's Publisher of Contemporary Romance

For Christine Flynn and Susan Mallery,
who created a great pair of characters to be Lee's dearest
friends. You guys are such a joy to work with.
Here's hoping we do it again sometime.

And also for my dear sister-in-law, Millie Stratton,
who got me in to observe two clinics
and found the answers to all the questions I threw at her.

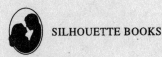 SILHOUETTE BOOKS

ISBN 0-373-24215-8

DR. DEVASTATING

Copyright © 1998 by Christine Rimmer

Printed in U.S.A.

CHRISTINE RIMMER

came to her profession the long way around. Before settling down to write about the magic of romance, she'd been an actress, a salesclerk, a janitor, a model, a phone sales representative, a teacher, a waitress, a playwright and an office manager. Now that she's finally found work that suits her perfectly, she insists she never had a problem keeping a job—she was merely gaining "life experience" for her future as a novelist. Those who know her best withhold comment when she makes such claims; they are grateful that she's at last found steady work. Christine is grateful, too—not only for the joy she finds in writing, but for what waits when the day's work is through: a man she loves who loves her right back, and the privilege of watching their children grow and change day to day. She lives with her family in Oklahoma.

The Pledge

Graduation day

We, the undersigned, having barely survived four years of nursing school and preparing to go forth and find a job, do hereby vow to meet at Granetti's at least once a week, not do anything drastic to our hair without consulting each other first and never, <u>ever</u>—no matter how rich, how cute, how funny or how smart—marry a doctor.

Lee Murphy, R.N.

Katie Sheppard, R.N.

Dana Rowan, R.N.

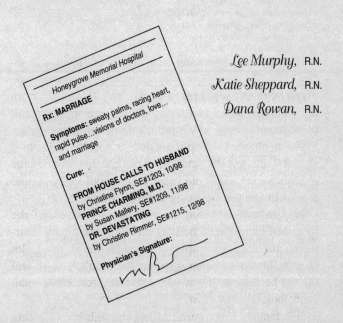

Honeygrove Memorial Hospital

Rx: MARRIAGE

Symptoms: sweaty palms, racing heart, rapid pulse...visions of doctors, love... and marriage

Cure:
FROM HOUSE CALLS TO HUSBAND
by Christine Flynn, SE#1203, 10/98
PRINCE CHARMING, M.D.
by Susan Mallery, SE#1209, 11/98
DR. DEVASTATING
by Christine Rimmer, SE#1215, 12/98

Physician's Signature:

Chapter One

Gold-shot hair gleaming, sky blue eyes intent and serious, Dr. Derek Taylor materialized on the other side of the clinic's front desk. Lee Murphy looked up from the computer screen on which she'd been trying to call up dear old Mr. Kelsey's prescription and lab records.

For a moment—a split second, a wrinkle in time—she saw the good doctor in a cocked hat and a blue military jacket with gold braid at the shoulders, his hand tucked inside the jacket right below his heart.

And instead of sitting in a creaky swivel chair, she imagined herself stretched out on a brocade divan, wearing an ankle-length Empire-style gown that showed a lot of pale, luscious bosom—bosom she didn't have in real life, to be honest, but what's a fantasy for if a woman can't look her best in it?

Her fantasy lover gazed at her through the brooding

eyes of a conqueror of continents. "Come here, Josephine...."

She saw herself sighing, deeply enough to expose even more imaginary bosom than her daring gown already revealed. "Ah, Bonaparte, you ask too much."

"Come here."

She sighed again—more deeply than before. And Napoléon Bonaparte took his hand from under his heart and held it out to her....

"Lee?"

Later for Bonaparte. Lee blinked to banish the fantasy. "Mmm?"

Dr. Derek Taylor smiled. Lord, he had a beautiful smile. A mouth to die for and beyond those perfect lips, two even rows of incredible teeth. *All* of him was perfect, actually. From that sun-shot hair to those blue, blue eyes to the five-o'clock shadow that sprouted in such manly fashion from his sculpted jaw.

For the past six months, since he'd taken over as attending physician at Honeygrove Memorial's Outpatient Clinic, Lee had been getting a lot of mileage out of all that perfection—harmlessly, of course, in her secret and wonderfully stress-reducing fantasy life.

He asked, "Didn't we get in some of those z-pack azithromycin samples last week?"

She nodded.

"Let me have a pack, will you?"

"Sure." Lee spun her chair around and wheeled it to the cabinet beneath the counter a few feet away. She worked the combination lock and came up with the antibiotic he'd requested. He moved around the end of the counter just as she straightened up with the card of tablets in her hand. Now, she could see all of him. In a blue shirt and maroon tie, gray slacks and white lab coat, the inevitable stethoscope slung around his neck, he looked good enough to eat—figuratively speaking. "Here you go."

He took the card from her. "Thanks."

Lee blew her bangs out of her eyes and smiled right back at the good doctor, a strictly professional, no-nonsense smile. "You're welcome."

He started to walk away. But then dear old Mr. Kelsey, who always got nervous when Lee left him alone in the examining room, poked his sweet, age-spotted head out the door of Room 3. "Lee? Where'd you get off to, Lee?"

Lee waved to him. "I'll be right there, don't worry."

The old man peered doubtfully in Lee's direction. She knew he couldn't see her. He was extremely myopic but would never wear his glasses. "You sure?"

"Positive."

Still frowning, but apparently somewhat reassured, Mr. Kelsey retreated into the examining room once more.

And Dr. Taylor spun back to face Lee. His gorgeous smile had vanished, all those perfect teeth were hidden from sight. "How long has that patient been in that room?"

"Well, Doctor," Lee hedged. "I only left him a few minutes ago. I'm just checking on his—"

"He's been in there for over an hour, hasn't he?"

She gave in and confessed, "Yes."

He demanded, "Why?"

Very patiently, she explained, "We talked, after I examined him. He's eighty-four and has developed some cognitive difficulties lately. Most worrisome, he's having some trouble getting his meds straight. There seems to be a small discrepancy concerning the various medica-

tions listed on his chart, so I was just looking them up
here to—"

Those fabulous bronze brows drew together over the
Paul Newman eyes. "Lee. We're getting backed up."

Doctor, she thought, "backed up" is the nature of the
beast. But she didn't say that. She only said, "I'll do
my best to move things along."

"Thank you," he said for the second time in five
minutes, though he didn't sound the least bit grateful.
Lee did not lose her smile, though she did shake her
head when he turned away and headed for Room 4.

A truly gorgeous man, she thought. And he took the
lead role in all her fantasies lately. But in real life, Dr.
Derek Taylor was just like nearly every other M.D. Lee
had ever known. He had a thing about control. He was
very, very organized. Very time-conscious. And he
wanted the rest of the staff at the D.P. Wiley Outpatient
Clinic at Honeygrove Memorial Hospital to be organized
and time-conscious, too.

Well, Lee Murphy *was* organized and time-conscious.
In her own way. Lee Murphy knew how to *prioritize*.
And sometimes rushing a patient through the clinic just
to keep on schedule helped no one. Sometimes a patient
needed advice, or a referral—or just someone to listen
and care. And that was her job as she saw it, to deal
with the whole patient.

Lee pushed the swivel chair under the counter and
returned to Room 3 where Mr. Kelsey waited. Ten
minutes later, she was showing the old man out, re-
minding him to keep up with his daily walks and to use
the new tricks she'd shown him to stay on top of his
meds.

She turned to slip behind the front desk again—and
almost ran into a tiny dark-haired sprite of a child.

''Mama's lost.'' Huge brown eyes looked up at Lee expectantly.

Lee set Richard Kelsey's chart down and knelt before the child. ''Where was your mama the last time you saw her?''

Instead of answering, the sprite stuck her thumb into her mouth and began sucking furiously.

Lee said, ''My name's Nurse Lee, what's your name?''

The sprite removed her thumb long enough to provide, ''Maweeah.''

Lee rose to her feet again. ''All right, Maria. Come on. Together, I'll bet we can find that mommy of yours.'' She held out her hand. Maria looked at it doubtfully for a moment, still sucking her thumb as if her life depended on it. Finally she took it. Lee led the child around the end of the high counter, where the clinic's clerk/medical technician could see her. ''Jack.''

Jack Yellowhand spun in his chair, tucked the phone under his chin and looked from Lee to little Maria.

''Mother missing,'' Lee said.

Before Jack could answer, Terry Brandt, one of the clinic's two L.P.N.'s, spoke up from over by the door to the copy room. ''Lenora Hirsch. Head trauma and facial injuries. She's in Room 5, waiting on Dr. Taylor to go over her X rays.''

Lee looked down at Maria. ''See? I told you we'd find her.''

Lee led the child down the hall, where she tapped on the door with the big number 5 on it. A small voice on the other side called, ''Come in.''

Lee pushed the door open and guided Maria over the threshold. ''Someone's been looking for you.''

The woman was sitting on the examining table, facing

away from the door. She turned. Her right eye was purple. Multiple lacerations circled her ear and a number of angry-looking, swollen bruises distorted her face. She glanced dully at the child. "Maria. Sweetheart, stay here." The woman forced a smile for Lee. "Thank you. I'll watch her better."

Lee closed the door and led Maria to the chair in the corner. "You sit right here." Someone had left a picture book on the windowsill. Lee scooped it up. "How about a little reading material?"

Maria's thumb made a popping sound as she pulled it from her mouth. "I like to wead."

"Good." Lee handed the book over. Maria bent her dark head. Tiny ankles crossed and dangling above the floor, she began studying the pictures.

Lee turned back to the mother. "Dr. Taylor should be in shortly with those X rays."

The woman nodded, still facing the door, not looking at Lee.

Lee asked gently, "What happened, Mrs. Hirsch?"

The dark head whipped around. Sable brown eyes as big as Maria's seemed to grow even darker with stark fear—before they once again shifted furtively away. "I...tripped. I fell. I am a clumsy person, that's all."

Right then, following two imperious taps on the door, Derek Taylor appeared, holding Mrs. Hirsch's X rays. At the sight of Lee, he looked distinctly perturbed. "Lee, could you help Paul with the phone triage?" Paul Uhana was their other L.P.N. "He's backed up again. There are a lot of patients on hold."

"Sure." Lee pulled a card from the pocket of her lab coat and handed it to Lenora Hirsch. "Those are my phone numbers. Both here at the clinic, and at home. You call me if you feel like talking. Anytime."

Those big dark eyes grew moist. "Yeah. All right…" And then she looked away again.

"Lee. *Please.*"

"Yes, right away, Doctor." Lee headed for the door but pulled herself up short before she got there. "I'd like a few words with you, in private, before you leave today."

Those fabulous eyes were like a pair of blue lasers, burning right through her. "A problem?"

"I'd prefer to discuss it then."

He shrugged. "Good enough."

The minute the phone situation was under control, a patient had a seizure in the waiting room. They ended up rushing the poor man over to the ER. And then Lee had some exams to perform, a couple of injections to give and two pap smears to take care of. She even wrote a few prescriptions. That was the nice thing about being a nurse practitioner in the state of Oregon; Lee was actually considered qualified to perform many of the duties only doctors could carry out in some other states.

Katie Sheppard, an R.N. in Memorial's telemetry unit and Lee's friend since high school, dropped by the front desk at three-thirty.

"Granetti's," Katie said in a voice that brooked no objections. "Five-thirty. Dana's already said she'd be there. We're going to settle on dates for good and all." Dana Rowan, another R.N. and also a friend since ninth grade, had moved up recently to administration. She was in charge of Memorial's OR.

Both Katie and Dana were planning to marry soon. And that was the problem. They wanted to be in each other's weddings—and still get married at almost the same time. This created some difficulty with honeymoon scheduling that Lee had yet to totally comprehend.

"Dates," Lee muttered gloomily.

Lee would dance at their weddings, not to mention spring for two more bridesmaid's gowns to wrap in plastic and stick in the back of her closet. But she saw no reason she should have to be there while they argued over who would get married when.

Katie said, "Oh, come on. It won't take long, I give my word. I'll be eating and running as usual, since I'm on duty at the clinic tonight." Katie volunteered her services at a free women's clinic a few nights a week. "And Dana's having dinner with Trevor." Katie put on her most pitiful expression. "Lee. We *need* you. We have to get this problem solved."

"You and Dana can solve the problem yourselves. You're the brides. I'm only the bridesmaid. You tell me the dresses you want me to buy. And you tell me when to show up at which church. And I'll be there. Both times."

"It's not that simple and you know it." Katie blew out her cheeks with a frustrated breath. "Please."

Lee looked away, out toward the waiting room, where several patients caught her eye and stared back at her pleadingly. She thought of a remark she'd heard a med tech make last week: You know you're in the medical field when you believe that the waiting room should be supplied with a Valium salt lick. "Katie, we're backed up."

"Granetti's," Katie said, undeterred. "Five-thirty."

What could Lee answer but, "All right, all right. I'll be there."

She managed to get a minute with Dr. Taylor before

he left to make rounds of his hospital patients at four-thirty. "I'm worried about the Hirsch woman."

He looked at her blankly.

She spoke in terms he'd understand. "Head trauma, lacerations around the right ear, multiple contusions—all over the face?"

The light dawned. "Ah. I remember now. And I can tell you that her X ray was negative and the wounds are clean. There shouldn't be any problems."

"I can tell *you* that I think there's more to it than that. I brought up her records."

He looked bleak. "And?"

"She's been treated for various injuries here five times in the past three years. Each incident had a different supposed cause. She fell down the stairs. She tripped on a toy. She ran into a door...."

"You suspect spousal abuse." He didn't even try to make that a question.

"I do."

"What do you want to do about it?"

"Let me take care of her, when she comes in to have the sutures removed. I'll see if I can get her to open up to me a little. If it turns out that what I suspect is correct, I'll give her some referrals where she can get help."

He granted her one of his gorgeous smiles. "All right, Lee. I can do that."

"Good," Lee said with satisfaction. This, after all, was why she'd pushed to get herself on staff here from the day she'd completed the extra two years of training that had made her a full-fledged N.P.

The clinic at Memorial had been established by a grant from a very rich Oregonian named D. P. Wiley. D. P. Wiley had had a dream, a dream of a clinic that would serve all the branches of Honeygrove Memorial,

from cardiac care to oncology. A clinic where a super-
vising family care physician would work hand-in-glove
with a top-notch nurse practitioner, providing every patient who entered the clinic's doors with the most thor-
ough kind of primary care. Also, the clinic was to serve
the indigent; no one could be turned away just because
they couldn't pay.

D. P. Wiley was now deceased. But his dream lived
on. On any given day, Lee saw patients of all ages, for
any number of ailments. She loved her work. Here, she
felt she really contributed to people's lives on a long-
standing basis. She worked with obese people, helping
them to establish diets they could live with. She caught
respiratory problems before they developed into pneu-
monia. She helped people like Mr. Kelsey find ways to
remember to take their meds.

And maybe, every once in a while, she could help
save a life just by pointing someone like Lenora Hirsch
in the right direction.

Lee worked until five-thirty—only a half hour after
her shift was technically over. And then she hung her
lab coat in her locker in the tiny dressing area off the
staff rest room. Minutes later, she entered the back door
of Granetti's Pub, which could be reached via a short
walk through the hospital's parking garage.

Her friends were waiting for her. Both of them were
grinning.

"We ordered you a Diet Coke." Dana indicated the
drink that waited in the empty space next to Katie. Lee
slid in behind it.

"And we've come to a decision," Katie announced,
as Dana pushed the basket of complimentary cheese gar-
lic bread across the table toward Lee.

"Eat some of that," Dana instructed. "Please. Katie and I each had one already. And someone has to protect us from eating any more. We do have our wedding gowns to get into, you know."

One piece, Lee thought, reaching for a big one and biting down. As usual, the bread was heaven. Sheer heaven. She chewed, swallowed, took a sip of the Coke her friends had so thoughtfully provided, then asked, "What decision?"

Dana caught Katie's eye. The two of them beamed at each other. Katie said, "We're going to have a double wedding."

Lee took another bite of that incredible bread and chewed thoughtfully, looking from one friend to the other. For some crazy reason, she found herself remembering the day she'd met them both.

It was the first day of school, freshman year, at Honeygrove High. In the cafeteria.

Lee had gone through the food line and then turned with her tray and looked out at the roomful of kids, all talking and laughing. All kids who *belonged*. She knew a lot of those kids from junior high school. And she knew that none of them liked her. She was uncool Lee Murphy, whose mother worked at the Valley Dry Cleaners. She didn't dress right and she wasn't good-looking and she never could bring herself to invite anyone home to the tiny run-down house she and her mother shared. The house that had no father in it. Really, there was nothing about her to make someone want her for a friend.

"You can sit here if you want to." The voice had come from her left. Lee glanced over.

A blond girl smiled at her, a slightly wavery smile. The girl was pretty, with blue eyes and clear skin. But her clothes were almost as tacky as Lee's. And Lee could see that she was scared—scared that Lee would turn her down. The girl lifted her chin. Defiance sparked in her eyes. "Well. Are you gonna sit down?"

Lee felt dizzy with gratitude. Not to have to sit alone for once...

She took the chair beside the other girl.

"I'm Dana. Dana Rowan," Lee's new friend said.

They started talking. Just like that. About who they had for homeroom and how much they liked biology and hated algebra. How they were both already thinking about careers in the medical field.

"Is it okay if I sit here, too?"

Lee looked up. A girl with curly hair and brown eyes stood next to their table. She had a gold bracelet on her wrist and she wore a skirt and knit shirt that were simple and smart and expensive. The kind of clothes that said her parents had money. The kind of clothes that should have meant she wouldn't waste her time on a couple of nobodies like Lee and Dana. But those brown eyes were soft. "My name is Katie."

And Dana said, "Hi, Katie. Have a seat."

Now, a grown-up Dana demanded, "Come on, Lee. Admit it. It's the perfect solution."

Lee put her memories away and smiled at her friend. Dana had come a long way from the insecure girl Lee had first met in the Honeygrove High cafeteria. Now, Dana dressed with style and carried herself with confidence. And since she'd admitted her love for Trevor MacAllister, everything about her seemed to glow.

Lee said, "Let me get this straight. Instead of a bridesmaid twice, I'll be the maid of honor for *two* brides?"

"Exactly," said Katie.

"Only one dress to buy to add to the others in the back of my closet. And only one church to show up at."

"That's right."

"My kind of compromise," said Lee. "And when is this momentous event to take place?"

"September 6." Dana sipped at her own Coke. "The same date as Katie's was supposed to be."

"Sounds good."

"And you'll wear the dress Katie originally chose for you. In fact, you can keep the fitting Katie already scheduled for you, a week from Saturday, at one."

"Fine."

Katie added, "We're going to design the ceremony together. Dana will choose the flowers—except for my bouquet, of course. And she'll use the florist I already hired, so my deposit won't go to waste. And Dana says Walter and Maggie would be thrilled if we held the reception at their house. There shouldn't be any problem if I just cancel the hall I booked." Walter MacAllister was Honeygrove Memorial's chief of staff. His wife, Maggie, gave terrific parties—and Trevor, Dana's intended, was their son. "The only thing I'll really be out is the invitations," Katie added with a sigh. "I picked them up at the printer's just last Friday."

"But I'm paying for the new ones," Dana chimed in. "So it's all going to work out beautifully." She glanced at her watch and pushed back her chair. "Gotta go. I told Trevor I'd meet him out front at six."

As Dana rushed off, Katie's food arrived. She glanced over at Lee. "Aren't you going to order?"

Lee shook her head. "It's my gym night."

Katie sprinkled Parmesan on her pasta. "You're so *admirable* with this exercise thing lately."

Lee suppressed the urge to look away. She had her

own secret motivation now, one that had her heading for the gym three times a week without fail. But she wouldn't have called it admirable, exactly. "It's good for me," she said, feeling extremely insipid as the words escaped her lips. "Very…stress reducing."

"Stress reducing," Katie echoed, rolling her eyes. "I could use a little of that myself."

Lee laughed. Katie was famed as a total pushover. Got a free clinic to run? Need someone to work your shift? Ask Katie. She never learned to say no. "Watch my lips," Lee teased. "*No*. Say it. *No*."

Katie waved a hand. "Go on. Leave me and my linguini in peace."

"Not completely in peace, I'm afraid," said a deep voice from behind Lee.

Lee didn't have to turn to know who it was: Dr. Michael Brennan, Katie's lifelong friend, and now her husband-to-be.

"Mike." A soft, private smile lifted the corners of Katie's mouth.

Lee greeted him, too. "Hi, there." Tossing a bill on the table, she pushed back her own chair and stood.

Mike slid into her place. "How's it going, Lee?"

"As well as can be expected, considering that Katie and Dana have been talking wedding dates again."

"Did they reach an agreement?"

"We did," Katie told him. "What would you say to a double wedding?"

Mike put an arm around Katie's chair. "I'd say, fine with me."

"I knew you would." Katie leaned his way and they shared a quick kiss.

Then Mike turned back to Lee. "Those two really broke your old vow with a vengeance, didn't they?"

Mike referred to the pact that Katie, Dana and Lee had each signed on the day that they received their baccalaureate degrees from the University of Oregon, a pact that said never, under any circumstances, would one of them marry a doctor. As it had turned out, both Trevor MacAllister and Mike Brennan had M.D. after their names.

Lee reminded Mike, "You know very well that the vow was always more of a joke than anything else."

Mike chuckled. "Sure it was."

Katie elbowed him playfully in the ribs. "Quit teasing Lee and order some dinner."

Mike glanced down at Katie's plate of linguini. "Mmm. That looks good."

Katie laughed and moved the plate farther away from him. "Get your own."

Lee left them, feeling glad for their happiness—and only a tiny bit envious.

As Lee got into her car, a certain thought rose, unbidden and delicious, to the surface of her mind: *Would* he *be there?*

She knew the answer. Of course he would. He worked out Monday, Wednesday and Friday nights without fail, unless some emergency came up at the hospital. A delicious shiver of anticipation skittered through her as she shifted her car into reverse and backed out of her parking space.

Ten minutes later, Lee parked her car a hundred feet away from the broad glass front of the Optimum Fitness health club. Lee had joined the club three months before, after one of those nights spent on the couch with a stack of videos and a carton of Häagen-Dazs. She'd looked at herself in the mirror the next morning and groaned.

Okay, so she had zero breasts and minimal cheekbones. Did she have to sport cottage-cheese thighs as well? She'd joined the club that very evening—and discovered that *he* worked out there, too.

An accident of fate, that's what it had been.

Lee got her gym bag from the trunk, pushed through the gleaming glass doors and waved at the hunk behind the front desk. It took her five minutes more to change into shorts, a tank top and jogging shoes.

And then she climbed the stairs to the running track, which followed the perimeter of the huge gym below. She performed a few rudimentary stretches, keeping near the wall, out of the way of the runners. Then she moved onto the track.

As she jogged along, she could look out the banks of windows that gave a nice view of Honeygrove, Oregon's minimal skyline—or she could peek down at the floor below and keep her eye on what was happening in the gym. She could check out the action on the cardio-fitness machines, as well as the varying weight-resistance equipment, from the Nautilus to the Universal. She could see the free-weight area, too.

Lee had made two circuits of the track before she spotted him. On one of the weight benches, doing biceps curls. He wore pricey white running shoes, blue shorts and a gray athletic shirt—the kind with no sleeves and no neck, leaving a lot of deltoid and trapezius exposed.

Oh dear, and what deltoids! The left one bunched and bulged every time he brought that dumbbell up. The sight was enough to cause hot flashes, even though Lee was only thirty and, as far as she knew, still reproductively sound. Sweat stained that gray athletic shirt, a tempting dark line of it, down the center of his chest, from those gorgeous pectorali majors down the linea alba. Unfortunately Lee couldn't see the sweat on his skin from up there on the track. But she could darn well imagine it.

She jogged on, her breath coming a little harder even though she wasn't running fast at all, her mind spinning off into her own private world of secret pleasures.

Oh, he'd look great in a loincloth.

Hmm. A loincloth...

As in Tarzan.

Why not?

A bed of jungle orchids, the high, strange cries of bright-colored, exotic birds. Monkeys chattering. A lazy boa constrictor twining the limb of a rubber tree overhead. Humidity. Serious humidity. And Tarzan—her own personal Tarzan, with his gold-shot hair, his blue, blue eyes, his to-die-for deltoids—pressing her down among the fabulous blooms.

"Ugh. Jane."

"Oh, Tarzan. Yes! Now! Please..."

"Slow joggers to the outside of the track."

"Huh?" Lee blinked and came back to herself as a tall, skinny guy ran past her. "Oh. Sorry," she muttered.

The other jogger turned and jogged backward long enough to grin, "Don't be sorry, just move to the outer edge."

"Right. Of course. I will..." She was still panting excuses as the man faced front again and took off.

Lee moved to the outside. Unfortunately, from there, it was hard to sneak glances at Derek.

As she thought his first name, she felt a small twinge of guilt. A twinge she immediately told herself to ignore. Away from the clinic, it should be all right to let herself think of him by his first name. What could it hurt? It was all only in her mind anyway.

She jogged two more laps and then slowed to a walk, her enthusiasm waning without all that male perfection to provide inspiration. Maybe she should finish her cardiovascular workout downstairs on one of the stationary bikes. From there, she'd have a decent view of the free-weight area.

Then again, maybe that would be carrying things just a little too far. She could tell herself it was all right to fantasize about Dr. Derek Taylor when she'd never, ever let herself get near him in any personal sense. But to actually coordinate her workouts so she could keep him in sight? No, that would be pushing the whole thing one step beyond what she considered acceptable.

Lee ordered her legs to get going. She moved into the center of the track and kept up with the main flow of runners for fifteen more minutes, not indulging in a single fantasy during the whole of that time.

Then, following the workout schedule that the club's fitness advisor had laid out for her, she went down the stairs to the main gym. By then, Derek had progressed to performing squats with a weighted barbell balanced across his incredible shoulders. Now that they were on the same floor, she could see the sweat on his skin. She wasn't quite close enough to make out each little bead of it. But the shine was there, so tempting, making her think of heat and wet and salt on her tongue.

Lee went straight to the Universal machine. Yes, the Universal just happened to be directly across from the place where Derek stood before the weight rack, alternately squatting, pushing himself to his feet and rising onto his toes. This time, it wasn't her fault that the view was so good. Blame the fitness advisor.

Lee grabbed the bar that hung from a chain and began slow, rhythmical pull-downs. Twenty feet away, Derek's incredible gluteus maximus tensed and stretched with each squat he performed.

What about....?

The Lady and Laborer.

Hmm.

She could see herself now. In her boudoir. Her *scented* boudoir. She would lie, sated, in a bed with white curtains, silk pillows and satin sheets. And he would stand naked before the high, mullioned windows that overlooked the grounds of her estate.

"Come back to bed, my darling...." she would murmur throatily.

He wouldn't move. No, he would stand there showing her only the powerful perfection of his back, his buttocks, his muscular legs.

"Please," she would sigh.

Still, he would remain motionless, except for one long, weary exhalation of breath.

And she would rise from her silken bower and tiptoe to him, her gossamer night rail trailing across the Aubusson rug, only to hover, unsure, a few feet from his imposing form.

"My darling..."

"No. You won't use me again this way, my lady." His voice would be low, rough, rumbling. He would remain obdurately turned away from her.

And she would dare to reach out one slender white hand, to lay that hand on his hard tanned shoulder, which would instantly tense even harder beneath her caressing touch. "Oh, please. Look at me." Stillness. All that warmth and ready power beneath her palm. "Vincent." Were laborers ever named Vincent? Did it matter?

He would whirl on her, grab her, grind his mouth

down on hers. And she would melt, surrender, sigh in abject need...

"Are you done with that bar, or what?"

Lee shook her head, stepped back, forced a dazed smile for a plump redheaded woman in a lime green leotard. "Oh. Yeah. Sure. Go ahead."

"Thanks." The woman moved in front of Lee and positioned herself for her own series of pull-downs.

Lee backed up a few more steps, trying to clear her mind enough to recall which exercise she was supposed to do next. She remembered. Those push things, where she sat on the bench and used her feet to push the bar that lifted the weight. She bent to move the pin so that she'd be pushing exactly eighty pounds.

She had the strangest feeling, as she shoved the pin in place, the feeling that someone was watching her.

She looked up.

And found those Paul Newman eyes locked right on her.

Very slowly, as she gaped at him, Dr. Derek Taylor smiled.

Chapter Two

It was nothing, Lee told herself repeatedly as she finished her workout and then headed for the women's dressing rooms and the showers. He'd spotted a colleague, he'd smiled.

No big deal. Happened all the time. He knew that she worked out there. He'd acknowledged her presence at the club more than once in the past, just caught her eye and given her a tight little nod, then gone on with his flexing and pumping.

This time was no different than all the others.

Except...

Well, this time, there *had* been something strange about his smile. Something unlike all the cool, detached smiles he'd granted her before. Something *knowing*.

Lee turned the shower knob all the way to cold and then stood there, shivering under the icy spray. "Chill out, girl," she muttered under her breath. "Chill out and get yourself a grip. The man's an M.D. He's got a serious case of blonde-of-the-week syndrome. You've seen the kind of woman he dates. No way he's going to suddenly decide to take an interest in you. You imagined it. It did not happen. Wipe it from the old memory banks. Now.''

"Everything all right in there?" A woman with a twenty-year-old body and a fifty-year-old face appeared at the entrance end of Lee's doorless shower stall.

Lee armed water from her eyes, wrapped her arms around herself to still her shivering and managed a sheepish grin. "Everything's fine. It's just my teeth chattering you heard, that's all."

The woman chuckled. "Whoever he is, I hope it works out."

Lee turned off the water and reached for her towel. "There's nothing to work out, I promise you."

"Whatever you say, dear. Whatever you say."

The woman moved on to the next stall and Lee got busy drying off.

A few minutes later, she slung her bag over her shoulder and headed for her car, giving the bemuscled front-desk attendant a second wave. She pushed through the glass door and stepped out into the warm July evening. Her car was about thirty feet away. She started for it.

But she didn't get far, because a voice straight out of her fantasies called from behind her, "Lee. Wait up."

Lee froze. She gritted her teeth. She reminded herself that nothing, absolutely nothing out of the ordinary had happened in the gym, and that nothing out of the ordinary was happening now.

She drew in a breath, carefully let it out, pasted on a smile and then turned to face him. "Dr. Taylor, I—"

"Look. This is stupid. We're not at the clinic now. How about calling me Derek?"

No! she thought frantically. How about not? But she kept smiling, somehow. "Um, well...what?"

His fine brow creased. "Excuse me?"

"You asked me to wait up?" She put a question mark after the statement, hoping he'd take the hint and get it over with, let her know what in the world he wanted, let her deal with it and then let her go home to her nice little house and the lamb chop in the fridge and the philodendron on the windowsill—which needed to be watered, now that she thought about it.

"Oh," he said. And then he smiled. Lord, he could send her right into a myocardial infarction with that smile of his. "How about dinner?"

She gaped. "Dinner?"

He shifted his gym bag from his left hand to his right. "Yeah. You know. The meal most people eat in the evening? And don't tell me you've had it already. I won't believe you."

She cast frantically about for an excuse to say no. But her brain seemed to have flat-lined right out on her. "Well, actually. I have to get home. I have a lamb chop. And a thirsty philodendron."

He laughed. Those gorgeous teeth sparkled. "You're kidding, right?"

She brushed her bangs out of her eyes. "No. I'm not. I really do have to—"

Right then, he reached out and took her arm. His grip was warm and firm. Arrows of awareness went zipping through her. What was left of her mind flew right out of her head.

"Come on. We can take my car. I'll just bring you back here afterward."

* * *

His "car" was one of those four-wheel-drive things. A deep, peacock blue with lots of shiny chrome. The kind of vehicle that would look equally appropriate on safari—and parked in front of some chichi restaurant. The kind of car you actually had to climb to get into. Lee sat in the deep embrace of the leather passenger seat and looked down at her own dusty little economy car as they rolled past it headed for who could say where.

"I hate Thai food," she muttered at him, just so she could pretend she had some say in this transaction.

He shot her another gorgeous grin. "All right. We'll skip that little Thai place I like so much."

"Thank you."

"What do you want, then?"

Out of this "car" of yours and far away from you. "How about just a sandwich?"

"You're easy to please."

If you only knew. "How about that place right there?" She pointed at a stucco building up ahead.

He turned into the parking lot. "This is Mexican. You like Mexican food?"

"It's fine."

He switched off the engine and turned to her, draping an arm over the steering wheel. "Lee, you seem hostile."

She stared at all that male perfection. He was wearing tan chinos and a polo-style shirt that clung lovingly to his broad shoulders and muscular arms. So close, in the limited space of the cab, she could smell him. He smelled of soap and a recent shower—and some maddeningly subtle aftershave. She wanted to lean closer, so she could smell him better.

She sat back. "I'm not hostile, just...wary. I don't know what you're up to here."

He lifted one of those sculpted, rock-hard shoulders in a totally casual shrug. "Just dinner." He tilted his golden head, his expression turning thoughtful, as if he were choosing his next words with care. Then he said, "And I think it's time we talked."

On reflex, she gulped. "Talked? About what?" The three words came out all breathless and squeaky.

He gave her a long, considering look, then leaned on his door. "Come on. I'm starving."

"But—"

He swung his legs to the blacktop and descended from the car before she had a chance to insist that he answer the question she'd just asked. He walked around the front of the vehicle and pulled open her door. "Let's go."

She glared at him. "You totally ignored my question."

"No, I just didn't answer it." He held out his hand to help her down.

She disregarded that hand and climbed down on her own.

The restaurant seemed pretty busy, but still Derek managed to secure them a corner booth next to a potted umbrella palm. They ordered immediately.

As they waited for their food, Derek made noises about what a good nurse she was—on the whole. Naturally he couldn't resist bringing up how he wished she'd think about shortening the consulting phase of her patients' visits. Lee made noncommittal noises as she crunched on chips and salsa and sipped white wine and wondered how in the world she'd managed to let herself go out to dinner with a doctor.

All right, it *was* only dinner. But still, it made her very nervous. Her fantasies aside—and they didn't count anyway, because they were totally in her own mind and thus no one's business but her own—she just couldn't afford to take any chances with getting near this man on anything but a strictly professional level. Katie and Dana may have found two exceptions, but the rule remained. Doctors were just plain deadly, at least when it came to personal relationships. Doctors, Lee knew from years of dealing with them, tended to be out of touch with their emotions, dictatorial—and unwilling to give their time or attention when it came to their own families.

And Derek Taylor was just like almost every other doctor Lee had ever known. A little overbearing, always ready to treat the symptom and move on to the next case, never willing to slow down and deal with each patient as a whole and complex organism. And egotistical to the max.

Across the booth from her, Derek lifted his bottle of Dos Equis and took a long sip. She watched his Adam's apple work as he swallowed. When he set down the bottle and leveled those eyes on her, she was struck for the gazillionth time with how downright incredible-looking he was.

Much too good-looking for her. At Memorial, med techs had been known to bump into walls at his passing, and L.P.N.'s to sigh in hopeless longing. He dated only spectacular-looking women. A few of them—always blond, inevitably beautiful—had wandered into the clinic looking for him under one pretext or another. Lee had thought what a match each of them had been for him, as gorgeous as he was. And perfectly color-coordinated too, with blond hair, blue eyes and blindingly white teeth. Nothing like Lee, who was so ordinary as to be virtually invisible to anyone who didn't know her personally.

And beyond the disparity in their looks, he was neat; she tended to be a slob. He was cool; she saw herself as caring.

Their food arrived. Lee realized as she picked up her fork and dug into her red chili burrito that she'd actually started to relax. No, this was not a match made anywhere but in her own overactive imagination. And whatever Dr. Taylor thought they needed to talk about, it couldn't possibly have anything to do with him as a man and her as a woman. She didn't want him except in her daydreams. And never, not in a hundred thousand years, would he be interested in someone like her.

Across from her, Derek chose a tortilla and carefully arranged his sizzling fajita meat on top of it. He rolled up the tortilla, brought it to his mouth and took a bite. As she watched him chew, she thought of Zorro, for some crazy reason.

Probably the mariachi music coming from the speakers suspended in the corners of the big, busy restaurant.

Could Zorro have blond hair and blue eyes?

Well, who cared? *Her* Zorro did.

Oh, she could see him now. A blond moustache, yes, caressing that finely shaped upper lip of his—and those blue eyes looking at her through a black silk mask.

And the sword. Oh my, that long, flexible sword.

He would send it zipping through the air and all of her clothes—the layers of red taffeta and black lace— would simply float from her body and drift to the floor around her dainty feet. She'd stand before him, clad only in red satin shoes, a black mantilla and an ebony comb. He'd make short work of each one of them, of course.

And then he'd—

"Lee."

Zorro vanished and Dr. Derek Taylor took his place. He was wearing that strange, knowing smile again, the same one he'd given her earlier, at the club.

Lee grabbed her wine and took a healthy slug of the stuff.

"Lee." He said her name again, as if he couldn't be sure she'd heard him the first time.

With the wine still trapped in her mouth, she pasted on a smile and made a questioning sound. "Mmm-hmm?"

"What the hell was that look you just gave me?"

Lee gulped. The wine went down wrong. She had to cough. For a few hideous seconds, she felt like an asthma victim caught without her inhaler. But then, blessedly, the choking fit passed.

"Are you all right?" he asked.

"Uh. Sure. Fine. Just fine." She started to knock back the last bit of wine, decided against it and reached for her water glass instead. Cautiously she sipped.

And he asked again, "That look you just gave me, Lee. What did it mean?"

She stalled by feigning innocence. "Mmm. What look?"

He set down his own fork, pushed his plate away a little and folded his beautifully shaped hands on the table in front of him. "Lee. You were staring at me. It appeared you'd slipped into a nearly trancelike state. You do it a lot, Lee."

She coughed again. Her heart was pounding in her ears and the capillaries at the surface of her skin had suddenly decided to start working overtime. Her cheeks burned. And, of course, he could see it. Why were Mexican restaurants invariably well lit? Fool, fool, fool, she chanted silently. What was the matter with her? To have let herself slip into a fantasy while he was sitting right across from her?

"Lee, let's face facts here." He took in a slow breath and let it out at the same speed. So tolerant, so forbearing. The good doctor dealing with a very sick patient in serious denial as to the severity of her illness. "I know you're—" he hesitated, treading so cautiously, looking for exactly the right words "— attracted to me."

The words came at her like a slap in the face. He knew! Oh Lord, he knew!

Her heart just stopped. Cardiac arrest. She needed CPR, an ambulance, a few heavy jolts from a defibrillator....

He went on, so calmly, "Look. It's all right." He paused long enough to flash that knock-'em-dead smile, this time with a rueful edge to it. "Well, to be honest, it wasn't all right at first. I was afraid that your, er, *interest* would interfere with our work. But it hasn't at all. You're always right there when I need an assist, and you're extremely conscientious when you handle a patient on your own. Yes, there remains the problem of your difficulty with time management. But I think you'd have that problem regardless, don't you?"

She put her hand against her heart and felt it pounding as if it would crack her chest right open.

Bronze brows met over that fine Roman nose. "Are you sure you're all right?"

"Uh. Hmm. Fine. Okay."

"Do you want some more wine?"

She waved her hand at him. "No. No wine. No more of that. No thanks." She looked down at her half-eaten burrito. She'd always loved a good red chili burrito. But after tonight, she'd probably never eat one again.

"Lee?"

She made herself meet those waiting eyes.

He tipped his head sideways and leaned a little closer to her across the table. His expression was infuriatingly calm and sincere. "Seriously. It's not a big deal. Okay, I admit that at first, all I wanted was for you to stop looking at me like that. But somehow—and I don't really understand how, since as far as I can see, no two people were ever more poorly suited to each other than the two of us—"

Amen to that, she thought grimly.

He continued. "—somehow, I guess I've grown accustomed to your looking at me that way. And today, at the gym, it finally hit me. Why the hell are we playing this stupid game?"

"Uh, game?"

"Yes. Game. You looking at me the way you do, and me pretending I don't see. What's the point, when you're attracted to me and—well, I suppose I might as well just say it. I'm attracted to you, too."

Chapter Three

"Huh?" Lee almost dropped her water glass. The thing slid through her fingers and clinked on the edge of her plate. Awkwardly, at the last second, she caught it by the rim and somehow managed to ease it to the table without spilling any.

Derek watched her struggle with the glass. And then he nodded, still rueful, a little abashed. "It's true." His expression said it all. He couldn't understand what in the world he saw in her. He considered her totally beneath him, since she was neither gorgeous nor blond. For goodness' sake, her eyes weren't even blue. "I don't know how it happened, but I'm attracted to you."

Amazing, Lee thought. The man really did have an ego every bit as hefty as the two-hundred pound barbell he bench-pressed each time he worked out. But then, he was a doctor, after all. Lee recalled an old joke she'd heard back in nursing school: Imagine an arrogant doctor. But I repeat myself...

Derek went on, a little bewildered, but still utterly sure of himself and his power over disease, injury—and the feminine gender. "I guess what I'm saying is, I think this is something we might as well just go ahead and deal with straight-out. I think we can see each other in private and still maintain a viable working relationship. Because I really do believe this is something we're just going to have to get out of our systems."

"Like a viral infection, you mean? Something that has to run its course?"

Lee had meant to inject a note of irony, but Dr. Taylor failed to pick up on it. "Yeah. You could say that. We could agree that whatever happens between us, we won't allow it to affect our work at the clinic."

"Whatever...happens?"

"Yes." He narrowed his eyes at her, in one of those reproving looks he reserved for patients who balked at the course of treatment he'd prescribed. "And what's the problem? Am I not making myself clear?"

"Well, no. I think I'm getting the picture just fine."

"You do?" He looked doubtful.

"Yes. You want us to...date." The word sounded so incongruous to her that she had to choke back a burst of hysterical laughter as soon as she said it.

He blew out a breath and gave her a reproachful frown. "Lee. You're behaving very strangely about this."

Strangely. He thought she was behaving strangely. Well, all right. Maybe she was. Derek Taylor was her fantasy. Her mind candy. She'd had a very good thing going with him. A safe, secret, harmless, one-sided, totally mental love affair. It had been great.

But he just couldn't leave it that way. Oh, no. He had to go and make it dangerous. Make it *real*.

And beyond that, there was the little matter of his attitude about the whole thing. His arrogance and his ego simply knew no bounds. It was written all over his too-handsome face; he thought he was doing her a big favor to give in and go out with her.

Well, she didn't need any favors from him.

What she needed was out of here, stat.

"Lee. Say something. Please."

Carefully she pushed her glass and her plate toward his, in the center of the table. Easy, she thought. Tread cautiously. Remember, you do have to work with the man.

"Lee?"

"I, um…"

"Yeah?"

"Well, Dr. Taylor—"

"Derek."

No. She was not going to call him that. *"Dr. Taylor,"* she repeated, a real edge in her tone.

They stared at each other. At last, he said too quietly, "Go on."

She reached for her shoulder bag a few inches away on the Naugahyde bench of the booth. She pulled it into her lap, all ready to go. And then, choosing each word with agonizing care, she told him, "Dr. Taylor, I'm sorry if you imagined I had some…romantic interest in you. But I promise you, I never intended for you to think I wanted anything more than a strictly professional relationship with you. I love my work. And going out with you is way too likely to cause problems—for me, for you, and most importantly, for the work we do."

His fabulous face had taken on a totally blank, disbelieving expression. She thought of how a Ken doll might look if Barbie told him she was leaving him for G.I. Joe. "You're telling me you won't go out with me." Clearly getting turned down was a new experience for him.

"Yes. I think it's for the best. I think that we—"

"Just a minute." The words were pure ice. She did her best not to flinch at the sound of them. And the blank look was gone, too. Suddenly he bore no resemblance to a Ken doll at all.

"Yes?"

"Are you saying you're not attracted to me in the least? That I imagined those looks you're always giving me?"

Lee knew what she should answer: That's exactly what I'm saying. But she just didn't have it in herself to tell a lie that big. So she hedged, "Whether I'm attracted to you or not isn't the issue here."

"I think it is."

"Well, I'm sorry, but I can't agree with you."

"You *are* attracted to me. Admit it. I just want the damn truth, that's all!"

She shot a look around. The diners in the booth behind him had both glanced up from their meals. "Keep your voice down, please."

"Fine. Sure," he whispered low and ragefully. "*Are* you attracted to me?"

Instead of answering, she fumbled in her purse and came up with some bills, which she set on the table beside her plate.

He looked at the money. "Don't insult me."

"I don't—what?"

"I brought you here. Okay, maybe it was one hell of a mistake that I did. And I can see that nothing's going to make you admit you've got a thing for me. Fine. We'll keep it strictly professional. But the damn check is mine."

"It isn't necessary, really. I don't mind paying my own—"

"Pick up your money and put it away."

The thread of steel in his tone could not be ignored. Lee scooped up the bills and stuffed them back into her purse. "I'd really like to go back to my car now."

"Fine." He signaled for the waitress, and she brought the check.

The ride back to the health club took place in a frosty silence that made it seem like January instead of July. Derek didn't say a word when they pulled into the parking lot. Lee pointed out where her car was parked and he stopped the big vehicle right behind it. Lee gathered her gym bag and purse, and then turned to him one last time, feeling she should say something that might somehow ease this awful situation. But what? She hadn't an inkling.

Gamely she began, "Dr. Taylor, I—"

His eyes met hers, cool and distant. "Don't make it worse. We'll just chalk tonight up to bad judgment on my part. Good night, Lee."

"I..." No other words took form. It came to her that there really was nothing more to say beyond, "Good night."

Fifteen minutes later, thinking of Lee and telling himself to forget her, Derek ran up the stairs to the condo he'd been renting since his move from Sacramento to Honeygrove six months before.

"Hey, baby brother." The voice came from the shadows in the little overhang to the right of the door. "Where the hell you been?"

Derek stopped a few steps short of the landing. "Larry?"

Grinning, Larry Taylor emerged from the shadows. He held a cigarette clamped in the corner of his mouth and squinted against the smoke that spiraled up toward the evening sky. "You been busy savin' lives—or out with some gorgeous babe?"

Derek thought of Lee again and didn't know whether to laugh or mutter something satisfyingly profane. "Nothing that exciting."

Larry grunted. "It was a babe, I'll bet. Who woulda thought you'd end up being so lucky with women? But then, you always did have the brains. And since you put on some muscle, you don't look half bad. And now they gotta call you Doctor. What more could a woman ask for? You're deadly, brother. Deadly." Larry took a final drag on the cigarette dangling from his mouth and then flicked the butt over the railing and onto the concrete walk below.

"Speaking of deadly," Derek said wryly, wondering what Larry wanted, wishing he could simply be glad to see him. "Those things'll kill you."

Larry pantomimed his hand as a pistol, cocking it, pointing it at Derek. "Gotcha, Doc. Bang." In the harsh light from the porch lamp, Larry's eyes looked bloodshot, the skin under them puffy and dark. He held out his beefy arms.

Masking his reluctance as best he could, Derek set down his gym bag and allowed his brother to embrace him. When Derek pulled back, Larry made a show of boxing him on the chin. "You *are* lookin' good. Been workin' out regular, huh? Watchin' the old diet, all that jazz?''

Derek picked up the gym bag again. ''Yeah, I guess so.''

The two men looked at each other, a long look. They hadn't seen each other in a year...not since their mother's funeral. Then, Derek had been finishing his residency at American River General. Larry had just gotten married—to a sweet, very young woman named Ellie. Larry and his bride had driven up from Bakersfield for the funeral.

And Larry had borrowed four hundred dollars from Derek, money Derek couldn't really afford to lend at the time. After all, med school hadn't been cheap. In fact, in spite of the scholarships he'd earned, Derek would be making payments on his education for several years to come.

''So. Where's Ellie?'' Derek asked.

Larry grunted. ''You don't want to know.''

Derek stared at his brother, fighting the urge to ask for more details. With Larry, if you asked for details, you always ended up knowing more than you wanted to about things you couldn't change anyway.

''Well,'' Larry said. ''Do I get to come in?''

Derek stepped past his brother and opened the door, then went around the small living area, flipping on lights.

Larry headed for the sofa, where he flopped down and stretched out. ''How 'bout a beer?''

Derek got a couple of cold ones from the fridge, passed one to his brother and sat in the chair opposite him.

Larry guzzled the beer, belched into a fist, then looked around. ''Nice.'' He tipped his dark head and wrinkled his brow in an expression that reminded Derek of their father. "But you're not exactly livin' large, huh?"

Derek shrugged. "I'm doing okay."

"Well, in a few years you will be, right?"

"Yeah, in a few years."

"You get that big Suburban you were always sayin' you would buy for yourself, as soon as you got your first real job?"

Derek nodded. "Bet on it."

"So you're not strapped or anything, right?"

Derek knew what was coming. No reason to put it off. He asked, "Why? You need a loan?"

Larry chuckled. "Well, little brother, now that you mention it…"

When Derek woke the next morning, Larry was gone. But he'd expected that. Once Larry got what he came for, he always moved right along. "No flies on Larry," their father, Mack Taylor, used to say, back before he succumbed to a non-Hodgkin's lymphoma, which he'd refused to have looked at until it was way too late.

Derek straightened the small second bedroom where Larry had slept, stripping the sheets from the bed, tossing them into the washer and carrying the empty beer cans to the recycling bin under the kitchen sink. Then he ate his breakfast, showered, got dressed and headed for the clinic. He told himself that things could be worse. Larry had come and gone. And he was only out another five hundred bucks.

But then he thought of Lee. He scowled.

He did not look forward to dealing with her all day.

In her little house on Hawthorne Way, Lee woke feeling groggy and apprehensive. She'd spent the night reliving the moment when Derek had told her he knew she was attracted to him.

As well as the moment when he'd said that he was attracted to her.

And then, there was the moment when he'd told her he wanted to go out with her.

Not to mention the moment when she had told him no.

So many moments to agonize over. No wonder she'd hardly slept at all. And now that it was morning, she had to face the prospect of working with him all day. She watered her philodendron and ate cornflakes for breakfast and told herself firmly that everything would be all right.

She and Dr. Taylor were professionals. It might seem awkward for a while, but they'd concentrate on work and treat each other in a strictly businesslike manner. Soon enough, they'd forget all about what had happened last night.

Lee had just taken a seat at one of the two computers in the small nurses' station around the corner from the front desk when Derek came in at nine. She caught sight of him as he went past on the way to his office at the end of the hall, where he would shrug off his sport jacket and pull on his lab coat as he did every morning.

She looked up and ordered a smile onto her face. "Good morning, Dr. Taylor."

He stopped. He turned. He looked straight at her. "Lee." He didn't sound friendly. And he certainly didn't smile. It was an acknowledgment, and nothing more. As soon as he'd given it, he stalked down the hall and disappeared into his office.

Lee stared after him, feeling snubbed—and worried. Had that been a sample of how her colleague and immediate supervisor would be treating her from now on? If so, it was not acceptable. And she should tell him as much.

Before she could talk herself out of it, Lee stood from her chair. She marched down the hall. When she reached the door to his small office, she knocked sharply.

After an endless ten or fifteen seconds, the door swung open. He scowled at the sight of her. If looks could kill, she'd be coding for certain. "What is it?"

She wanted to cringe and run. But she didn't. She spoke calmly. Firmly. "I'd like a word with you."

His lab coat dangled from one hand. He swung it over his shoulder and shoved his arms into it, then flipped the collar in place and settled his stethoscope more comfortably around his neck. "I have work to do. So do you."

Lee made herself stand taller. "This won't take more than a minute or two."

He glared at her some more. And then, at last, he stepped back. "Come in, then."

She did. But the space was very small. As he closed the door, his arm brushed her shoulder.

It was insane. Just that one quick, accidental touch sent ridiculous pops of sensation snapping along every synapse Lee possessed. And then there was the smell of that aftershave of his. And the warm, clean scent of his skin.

He'd already closed the door. He had no need to remain so close to her. But he didn't step back. He looked at her and she looked back at him. And somehow, through the sudden absurd sensual fog that seemed to have risen up out of the floor and surrounded them, she admitted her error. She shouldn't have come in here; the space was too small and he smelled too good.

''What is it, Lee?'' His voice was low. There was anger in it. And something else, something soft. Something way too intimate.

She flattened herself against the wall, her head hitting the frame of one of the documents that hung there. She had no idea which one. There were so many. Maybe the one that proclaimed him a bona fide family care physician. Or perhaps the one that said he'd graduated with honors from U.C. Davis. Then again, maybe it was the one that declared him a member of the Honeygrove Physicians' Association.

''I'm waiting,'' he said, still in that low, caressing tone.

''Could you, er, step back a little? Please?''

For a heartbeat or two, he didn't budge. And then he was moving away, around the corner of the desk that took up most of the limited space, to the swivel armchair behind it. He dropped into the chair.

Lee drew in a breath she hadn't even realized she needed and edged into the nearest of the two consulting chairs. She sat. They faced each other across the spotless expanse of the desk.

''Well?'' he asked.

She forced herself to begin. ''Look. I want you to know that I'm really sorry, for the misunderstanding last night. You were right, about me.''

''Oh, really?''

''Yes. I did behave strangely. I'm afraid that you took me completely by surprise. I honestly hadn't thought that you had any personal interest in me at all.''

''You hadn't?'' He seemed to sneer the words.

She refused to descend to his level. She kept her voice even and sincere. ''No, I had not.''

He made a low, disbelieving sort of sound.

She forged on. "Dr. Taylor, as I told you, I really don't believe in dating anyone I work with."

"I got that. Loud and clear."

"No, seriously."

"I'm perfectly serious."

"Just let me have my say."

He stared off at all those framed credentials on the wall behind her chair. "Fine. Go on."

"Well, I mean, if I had agreed to go out with you, we could tell each other that we wouldn't allow our relationship to affect our work, but these are *feelings* we'd be talking about. You can't make agreements about feelings."

"Maybe *you* can't."

"Oh, come on. Be honest."

"I am."

"Dr. Taylor. Think about what would happen when it's over."

He stopped staring at the wall over her head and actually focused those cold eyes on her. "Why should I think about that, Lee? This is all hypothetical anyway. Something that isn't going to happen, as you made perfectly clear last night. In fact, I really think it's inappropriate for the two of us to be closeted in my office discussing a nonexistent relationship when there are patients out there requiring medical attention."

She raised both hands, palms out. "All right. Fine. I get the message." He started to stand. She gulped in a breath. "One last thing, though."

He settled back with an impatient sigh. "What?"

"I want you to know that, if I've stared at you in the past, I promise you, I will not be staring at you anymore." She waited, hoping he might say something remotely congenial. But he didn't. He went on looking at her, his eyes hard and his jaw tightly clenched.

She wrapped it up. "Look, I just want to do my job and let you do yours and…get along. And I hope we can find our way back to the pleasant working relationship we had before."

Another awful, endless silence descended. At last, he asked, "Is that all?"

"Well. Yes. I suppose it is."

He stood. "Fine, then. I'd like a pleasant working relationship, too. I'm sure we can manage that."

You don't look very pleasant, she wanted to say. But what good would that do, beyond inviting him to sneer at her some more? "Okay, then." She rose to her feet. "I'll just…get back to work."

"An excellent idea." The words were innocuous, but not the tone.

She opened her mouth to retort. And then shut it before anything angry could get out. The whole point here, she reminded herself, was to get past last night and get back to the way things had been before.

Smiling resolutely, she turned for the door.

Through the rest of the morning he behaved just as he had when he sat across from her in his office. Barely civil. And as cold as the North Pole. In the afternoon, when things got busy, he barked at her twice, once for the usual—taking too long with a patient—and once because of some supplies that weren't there when he wanted them. His usual gorgeous smiles were not in evidence at all.

When he finally left to do rounds at four-thirty, Lee heaved a sigh of relief and went to grab a cup of coffee in the copy room, which also served as a makeshift staff lounge. Beyond file storage and the copying equipment, the room also boasted a table with three chairs around it, a coffeemaker, a small microwave and a cabinet shelf stacked with coffee, filters and cups.

Lee got her cup from the shelf and filled it with the strong, dark brew from the coffeemaker. She knew she really ought to take the time to nuke a little water for some herb tea. It was so much better for her than coffee. But she didn't. Sometimes nothing hit the spot like a good jolt of caffeine. And for days like today, the stuff really ought to be available in IV form.

Just as she sank into a chair at the table, Terry Brandt popped her head in the door. "Is he gone?" The other nurse made her tone low and theatrical.

Lee nodded.

Terry slipped inside, shut the door and leaned on it. "What was the matter with him today? I've never seen him like that. Did he even smile once?"

Stalling in order that she might avoid making a comment, Lee sipped her coffee. It had been sitting on the burner too long, as usual. She grimaced as she swallowed.

Terry folded her arms over her chest. "I mean, he's never exactly Mr. Warmth, or anything. But he's…amiable. And fair. The man was neither today. Were you there when the Bailey woman's chart turned up missing?"

Lee sipped some more and made a vague *uh-hmm* kind of noise.

"He lit into Jack about it. And then, a few minutes later, we found the darn thing. On the doctor's own desk."

Irrational as it was, Lee couldn't help feeling just a tiny bit responsible for Dr. Taylor's bad mood. She found herself jumping to his defense. "Maybe he had a rough night last night."

"I'm sure. One of his blondes probably had a bad hair day—and took it out on him."

Lee set down her cup. "Come on. Everybody's entitled to be a grouch now and then."

Terry groaned. "You're awfully generous, considering it seemed to me he picked on you worst of all."

"I'm tough. I can take it."

"Well, I guess so." Now Terry sighed. "Still, he's a total dreamboat, even when he's a jerk, don't you think?"

"I suppose."

Terry sighed some more. "Dr. Devastating, that's how I think of him. He's right up there with young Dr. MacAllister and Dr. Heartache himself, Mike Brennan—who, by the way, have both been snapped up by *your* friends."

Lee made a face. "So now it's my fault that my friends got the good ones?"

"No, not at all. I'm only pointing out that the good ones are limited. And going fast, if you know what I mean." She raised a hand and fluffed her auburn hair. "So. How do you think I'd look as a blonde?"

Lee made noise in her throat. "Temporary."

"Ah, yes. They do come and go, don't they?"

"Exactly."

"Still, who can blame a woman for fantasizing a little?"

Luckily Lee had just swallowed a sip of coffee, so she avoided a choking fit when Terry said that word. All day, she'd stood absolute guard on herself. Not a single fantasy had dared to creep into her head.

"Lee. Don't tell me you've never daydreamed about him. Just a little. Come on, tell the truth...."

Lee made another of those noncommittal noises.

And then, blessedly, someone pushed on the door that Terry was still leaning against. Terry turned and moved back. "What?"

Jack, the med tech and clerk, peeked in. "Are we still open here or not? I've got a sweet old lady with a duodenal ulcer waiting patiently for someone to check her vital signs."

"All right, I'm with you," said Terry. She followed Jack out.

Truly grateful to have escaped the other nurse's grilling, Lee got up and rinsed out her cup. There were still a few patients in the waiting room. And after they closed the doors, there would be paperwork to do. She wouldn't get out of there until six at the earliest.

Lee rubbed the back of her neck in an effort to ease the tightness there. She was running on no sleep and way too much tension caused by you-know-who. Once she got home, she'd have that herb tea she should have had right now. She'd brew a nice big pot of it and she'd zone out in front of the idiot box, sipping and relaxing. She'd go to bed by nine.

And tomorrow, she told herself, after she'd had a good night's sleep, after a little more time had passed, things would be better. Within a week, she felt certain, everything would be back on an even keel with the good Dr. Taylor and the clinic staff.

Chapter Four

Lee was only partially right.

Dr. Taylor's attitude did seem to improve with the staff in general. The next day, he made it a point to spread those fabulous smiles around, to praise Jack's efficiency—and to criticize more gently if things weren't where he wanted them *when* he wanted them.

But with Lee, he remained cold and utterly distant. Lee told herself that she could deal with that. It wasn't exactly the pleasant atmosphere she'd hoped they could foster. However, other than the deep-freeze looks he gave her whenever they had to speak for some reason or another, he left her pretty much alone. She could bear that.

And, quite gratifyingly, she managed to keep her imagination under strictest control. She indulged in zero fantasies. Really, it wasn't that hard. Who wants to fantasize about a man who hates you? Very off-putting.

And Lee took no chances. She didn't let herself get cocky concerning her own self-control. The gym had always been her favorite place to daydream. So, just to be on the safe side, she skipped her Wednesday workout. After all, she could see no sense in tempting fate.

She decided she'd wait a week or so to show up at Optimum Fitness again. And since Derek usually worked out on Monday, Wednesday and Friday, she'd go on alternate days. She felt certain that, with patience, discipline and good planning, she'd thoroughly vanquish her longing to spin sexy scenarios around Derek Taylor, M.D.

On Friday, four days after what Lee had come to think of as the debacle at the Mexican restaurant, a stunning blonde appeared at the front desk.

"Excuse me. I have a lunch date with Dr. Taylor." The woman's voice seemed to be composed of two parts velvet and one part thick cream. "I wonder if you could tell him that Felicia is here?"

Tucking the phone under his chin, Jack glanced up over the rim of the high counter. At the sight of the exquisite creature standing there, his mouth dropped open.

The blonde laughed, a laugh as creamy-velvety as her speaking voice. "Dr. Taylor. Is he here?"

"Uh. Oh, yeah. Just…have a seat. I'll let him know that you're waiting."

"Thank you." The blonde turned. Jack gaped as the woman walked away from him, slender hips swaying gently with each step. Lee, who happened to be standing beside the clerk, found that she was gaping, too. She watched the woman take a seat, watched her cross one fabulous leg over the other. Her skirt fell back a fraction, revealing a few extra inches of truly spectacular thigh. Above her sexy black high heels, her trim ankles fairly twinkled.

As she stared, Lee told herself she wasn't the least bit jealous. Not at all. And besides, after a nice lunch with a woman like that, Derek Taylor would forget all about being cold to his nurse practitioner just because she'd turned him down for a date.

Right then, the man himself came striding down the central hall from the direction of his office, straightening the collar of his sport jacket and shooting his cuffs. Lab coat and stethoscope were nowhere in evidence. He must have just shed them, in preparation for lunch with she of the velvet-and-cream voice.

"Felicia is here," Jack told him—rather unnecessarily, Lee thought. The woman had chosen a seat that faced the central hall. She must have seen the doctor come out of his office. And Derek clearly had her in his sights, since he stalked right by Jack, headed straight for her.

Felicia stood, her angel's face lighting from within. "Derek. It's so good to see you."

He grinned down at her. "Felicia, you're looking well."

She tucked her hand into the crook of his arm. "Come on. Let's get out of here. I want you all to myself."

They turned then, as one, and strolled across the dark blue indoor-outdoor carpet of the waiting room, headed for the door. Lee thought that they looked like royalty, two golden beings, set apart from the mere mortals surrounding them by virtue of all that blondness, those blue eyes, that aggressive good health.

"Wow," said Jack reverently, when the two were

gone. Then he flipped the phone back up to cover his mouth and started talking as if he'd never stopped.

Lee looked blindly down at the medical history form in her hands and ordered her eyes to focus on it. This is good, she silently told herself for the second time. This is just what the doctor ordered. After lunch with a woman like that, giving me the cold shoulder is going to seem really ridiculous to him.

She hoped he had a wonderful time, she honestly did. And she just knew things would start smoothing out between herself and him from now on.

Felicia reached across the console and put her hand on Derek's thigh. "That was a lovely lunch."

He looked down at her hand and then back up into those delft blue eyes. "I'm glad you enjoyed it."

Delicately she licked her upper lip. "Do you have to go right back to the clinic?"

He didn't. He'd purposely had Jack juggle his schedule so he'd have two full hours for lunch. The idea had been to thoroughly enjoy the company of a beautiful woman—and thus forget all about a certain nurse practitioner with poor time-management skills and a bad haircut who refused to admit she had a thing for him.

But it wasn't working. Felicia was nice. And absolutely gorgeous. She was also quite bright and sexy as hell. They'd enjoyed more than one mutually satisfying intimate encounter in the months he'd lived in Honeygrove.

But it hadn't really gone anywhere. Hell, the truth was, none of his relationships ever seemed to go anywhere.

Which had been fine with him until recently—like Monday night, maybe.

Felicia sighed and drew her soft hand slowly along his thigh. "Derek, is something troubling you?"

In his mind's eye, he saw Lee, staring at him, glassy-eyed, the way she used to stare all the time—until last Monday night.

"Derek?"

He blinked and ordered thoughts of Lee out of his mind for good and all. "What?"

"I asked if something is bothering you."

"Bothering me?"

She gave a small, throaty laugh. "Yes. Bothering you."

"No, nothing's bothering me. Nothing at all. Why?"

"You just seem…preoccupied."

"I'm not."

"Are you sure?" She pouted across the console at him.

To show her how *un*preoccupied he was, he leaned over and captured her mouth. She sighed and returned his kiss with considerable enthusiasm.

But the console was in the way. She retreated to her own seat and suggested softly, "Let's go to my house."

He stared at her. And it came to him.

He couldn't do it. He could not go to her place and fall into bed with her.

It seemed…wrong, somehow. And cheap. And unfair to both of them.

He could strangle that damn Lee Murphy. This was all her fault.

Dr. Taylor returned from lunch at exactly one o'clock. Lee came out of Room 6 just as he came stalking down the hall. She had to back up against the door to avoid running into him. "Oops. Excuse me." She tried a smile.

He granted her one swift, dismissing look. "Watch where you're going," he growled.

And then he marched on by, straight to his office, where he shoved open the door and closed it harder than necessary behind him.

Lee stared at that closed door, feeling grim. Even lunch with a beautiful blonde hadn't changed his attitude toward her. The prognosis for the future of their professional relationship did not look good.

Derek bent at the knees and hoisted the barbell to his chest. He breathed in. Exhaling, he raised the thing over his head. He adjusted his grip and lowered the bar behind his head, till it rested on his shoulders. Slowly, deliberately, he raised it, lowered it, raised it again, breathing rhythmically as he worked.

At last, when his arms and shoulders felt like rubber, he lowered the bar to his chest, bent at the knees and put it down again. He stood, armed the sweat from his forehead—and couldn't help glancing up at the running track overhead.

The glance became a long, hard stare.

He waited, watching for Lee to appear near the center rail, running slower than she should have, glancing over at him as she used to do, when she thought he didn't see.

She was avoiding the gym. She had stayed away both Wednesday and today. Because he was here. She didn't want to deal with him outside the clinic.

Hell, she probably didn't want to deal with him at work, either. But she had no choice about that. So she smiled at him and treated him so pleasantly during the day.

"Dr. Taylor, good morning," she'd chirp. Or, "Dr. Taylor, have a look at this X ray..." So cool. So professional. As if she really had no interest at all in him, other than as her colleague and immediate supervisor.

And maybe she didn't. Maybe he had imagined those steamy, yearning looks she used to give him.

Because she certainly didn't give him looks like that anymore.

With a low sound of fury, Derek turned for the slant bench. He raised it to an angle of sixty degrees. Then he climbed on, hooked his feet under the rung and started doing stomach crunches.

He was so busy thinking about Lee that he did thirty extra.

The rest of his workout was the same. He spent too much time between sets staring off toward the running track or over at the Universal, willing her to show up and furious when she didn't. And then, when he'd get back to business, he'd lose track of his reps.

Before he went home, he took a long, cold shower. He stood under the icy jets and told himself he was going to have to get Lee Murphy out of his mind.

But how the hell could he manage that? How could he forget her when she was always underfoot? He was the clinic's attending physician, and she was the charge nurse. Since the clinic was closed nights and weekends, they worked basically the same shift. He saw her five days a week for six to ten hours a day, depending on the patient load.

He needed a break. A getaway. A change of scene.

Dr. Walter MacAllister, chief of staff at Memorial, had a cabin up in the mountains somewhere not too far

away. There was a lake up there, too, as Derek understood it. Blue Moon Lake. A place where a man could
escape the day-to-day grind, do a little fishing, breathe
clean air. Walter often let other doctors he worked with
and some of the residents use it. In fact, a few weeks
ago, he'd offered it to Derek. Derek had demurred, but
asked for a rain check.

Maybe the time had come to accept the chief of staff's
generous invitation. Maybe what Derek needed was that
cabin, a fishing pole and a six-pack or two of beer. He'd
get away from town for a weekend, from the clinic, from
the gym—from all the various elements of his life that
lately seemed to have way too much of Lee in them.
The fresh mountain air would fill his lungs, and clear
her from his mind.

By the time he returned, he'd wonder how he'd ever
let her get to him in the first place.

Saturday morning, Lee lost control.

It happened because she glanced out the living-room
window and saw a man jogging by.

It was just a little after eight. Lee had carried her
second mug of Good Earth Original Blend tea from the
kitchen to the living room, where she planned to sit on
the sofa, sip her tea and thumb through her newest *Vic-
toria's Secret* catalog.

The blinds over the front window were still drawn.
She went to open them. As soon as she did, she caught
sight of the jogger. A well-built man in his thirties. He
wore the same type of shorts Derek always wore and the
same kind of athletic shirt—a gray one.

He didn't really look anything like Derek. His hair
was dark and he wasn't quite so tall. But at the sight of
him, Lee froze, transfixed.

The runner jogged on down the street.

But it didn't matter to Lee. By then, she didn't see him anyway.

By then, she saw Derek.

Derek turning into her front walk, approaching the steps, taking them two at a time, pounding on her front door.

"Lee," he would shout. "Damn it, Lee! Let me in!"

Oh, she shouldn't. She absolutely should not.

But how could she help herself? Drawing in a shuddering breath, she would take a step toward the front door. Her eyes would be wide, frightened, yearning...

"Lee!" More pounding. "I know you're in there!"

One trembling hand would fly to her throat. "Oh, no! Derek..." she would whisper on a torn gasp of dismay.

And then, as he continued his pounding and his shouted demands, she would take another step, and another, until she stood opposite him, with only the door and about six feet of scarred hardwood floor separating them.

And finally, he would be able to bear it no longer. He would kick the door open. The frame would splinter; the dead bolt would give. And the door would fly back, hitting the wall with a sound like a thunderclap.

They would stare at each other.

And he would whisper, "Damn you, Lee."

And then, in three long strides he would be on her, yanking her against him, kissing her so hard she would almost faint from the pleasure of it, then scooping her up against his chest. "Your bedroom. Where is it?"

"No, Derek, we can't. We have to *work* together. And you're so arrogant. And way too good-looking. And a *doctor*. We can't do this. It's impossible."

"Quiet. Don't argue." Of course, by then he would

have seen the tiny hallway behind her, the open bedroom door beyond. Purposefully, still holding her cradled in those powerful arms of his, he would stride toward it.

She would struggle. "No, Derek! Don't... We can't...."

"Stop it, Lee. You know it's what you want. What we *both* want."

"It's not, it's not..."

Again, his mouth would descend on hers, stopping her protests, stealing her breath and her will to resist. At last, he would pull away enough to whisper, "What do you say now?"

Only one word would come. "Yes."

Something hit the floor and shattered.

Lee blinked. She stood a few feet from her front door. Dazed, she looked down. Her mug lay on the floor in pieces. The fragrant tea had spattered everywhere, on the Keshan-style floor runner and the end of the sofa.

Oh, dear Lord, Lee thought in sudden, abject misery. Four days. She'd gone four entire days without a single fantasy of Derek.

But now, when she finally had one, he'd been playing himself. And she'd been herself.

That had never happened before. Always before, he was someone else—a figure from history or the movies, or some character she'd made up to suit a certain scenario.

And never, ever was she just her boring old self, with her minimal breasts and her flyaway hair and her scrubbed-clean, ordinary, round-cheeked face.

With a small cry, Lee spun on her heel. In the hall cabinet she found an old towel. She rushed back to the front door and knelt to blot up the tea. As she blotted, her eyes blurred. Oh, God. She was going to cry.

She closed her eyes. She counted to ten, swallowing back those foolish tears. Really, it was nothing to get worked up over. Yes, it was odd that they'd both appeared as themselves this time.

But it didn't have to *mean* anything. She wouldn't *let* it mean anything.

Lee set the tea-stained towel to the side. Carefully she began picking up the shattered pieces of the mug. She had two days off, today and Sunday. She wouldn't have to see him for a full forty-eight more hours.

Time off from him. Yes. It was just what she needed.

And surely, when they returned to work, he would start to treat her more civilly. By then it would have been a week since their awful encounter in the Mexican restaurant. A week had to be long enough for him to get over his anger at her and get on with his life.

But apparently, it wasn't.

In fact, on Monday, things got worse. He went beyond being merely cold and aloof. He began criticizing her work methods again.

Tuesday was worse than Monday. And Wednesday worse than Tuesday. As each day passed, he seemed to become more and more obsessed with what he considered the way she wasted time. It seemed to Lee that he was constantly commanding her to move her patients along faster and to get her charting done more quickly. He complained that the nurses' station wasn't organized effectively, that the toys in the waiting room were always finding their way to the examining rooms with Lee's patients—where *he* always ended up tripping over them later.

Lee gave up on practicing civility toward him, she stopped making herself smile at him, she didn't even try to speak to him cordially. She just did her best to stay out of his way.

It was no way to live, but what else could she do? He remained, as he'd been from the first, very civil in his persecution of her. He never raised his voice. He never stepped beyond the boundaries of technical courtesy. But he was hounding her, plain and simple.

Lee felt so frustrated. And alone. And by Thursday night, she knew she had to talk to someone. She thought it might be one of Katie's nights at the free clinic, so she tried Dana.

"You busy?" she asked, as soon as her friend picked up the phone.

"What's up?"

"I suppose Trevor's there, huh?"

"You bet. It's just him and me and take-out Italian. Later I'm going to show him my etchings."

"Oh, well. I don't want to bother—"

"Lee. What's the matter?"

"Honestly, you and Trevor just enjoy your dinner, all right?"

"Are you at home?"

"Dana, really, it's not right that you should have to—"

"I'll be there in fifteen minutes."

Dana was better than her word. Thirteen minutes later, she strolled through Lee's front door. She said yes to a Diet Sprite. They sat on the sofa in the living room.

Dana toed off her shoes and gathered her legs to the side. "All right. Spill it."

And Lee did. She told all—well, almost all. She did leave out the part about her fantasies. They were her business and hers alone, after all.

When Lee finally fell silent, Dana remarked gently, "So. Still holding firm on the old vow, huh?"

Lee closed her eyes, tipped her head back. "Yes. No..." She opened her eyes, faced her friend. "Okay, I'm willing to admit that there may be a doctor or two out there worth getting close to. After all, you found Trevor and Katie's got Mike and I've got no gripe with either of them. But Derek Taylor..." Lee sucked in a breath and shook her head. "Let me put it this way. If I ever met a man who is living, breathing proof that a woman should never get involved with a doctor, he's it."

"Why?"

"You really want to know?"

"I asked, didn't I?"

"All right. Derek Taylor doesn't converse, he gives directives. He dates women for their looks alone—about one blonde a week. And he's got an ego the size of Mount Hood. Are those reasons enough?"

Dana volunteered sheepishly, "Walter really likes him."

Lee groaned in frustration. "Of course Walter MacAllister likes him. Derek Taylor is a fine doctor and a credit to Honeygrove Memorial. As chief of staff, Walter MacAllister would naturally think he's just dandy."

Dana set her glass on the coffee table. "I guess I'll get nowhere suggesting you give the man a break."

"Dana, he honestly is *persecuting* me on the job."

Dana reached out and put her slim hand on Lee's shoulder. "Hey. I hear you. I honestly do. And from what you've just told me, I think you really are being treated unfairly."

Lee could hardly let herself believe her own ears.

Dana understood. *Someone* understood. "You do?" The words came out small and weak.

"Yes."

Lee sat up a little straighter. "Any suggestions as to how I can change the situation?"

Dana reached for her Sprite again, and took a small sip. "Call him on it."

Lee thought of that first morning after the Mexican restaurant ordeal. She'd tried to "call him" on his behavior then. Fat lot of good it had done. "I tried. He didn't listen."

"Try harder. I think, from what both Walter and Trevor have said about him, that he's an honorable man. I'd like to believe he doesn't truly realize what he's doing to you. So you're going to have to explain it to him. And if he doesn't snap out of it, then let me know."

"And?"

"We'll go to Walter."

"And tell him…?"

"Just what you've told me. Because, quite frankly, I think Dr. Taylor's behavior skirts awfully close to sexual harassment. And don't look so stunned. I didn't say it *was* sexual harassment—not exactly, anyway."

"Are you serious? I'm not even sure I know what constitutes sexual harassment."

"Shall I explain?"

Lee shot her friend a sideways look. "You sound so authoritative."

"Well, since I've moved into administration, it's part of my job to keep up on anything that has to do with employee relations. And the way I understand it, sexual harassment can take two forms, both of which are illegal. The first form occurs when submission to sexual advances is used as the basis for employment decisions.

The second form is called hostile environment harassment."

"And that is?"

"When a worker is subjected to offensive comments and unwelcome physical advances of a sexual nature on the job."

Lee shook her head. "No, Dana. Really. The first part of that doesn't fit at all. I was hired before he got there and he could complain about me, but he couldn't actually fire me. And as for the hostile environment idea—"

"Answer me this. Since you turned him down, how would you describe your working environment? In one word."

Lee sighed. "All right. Hostile. But listen. The man has made no advances to me, except that one. I said 'no way' and he didn't try again. And I swear to you, he would never make suggestive remarks to a woman on the job. That would just be so completely beneath him."

A tiny, knowing smile tugged on one corner of Dana's pretty mouth. "Considering you hate this guy, you certainly seem ready to jump to his defense."

"I didn't say I hated him. I just want him to treat me fairly at work."

"Okay, okay. So the situation is, you turned him down when he asked you for a date and—"

"He didn't *ask.*"

"Fine. You turned him down for a date. Yes or no?"

"Yes."

"And since then, he has been hostile and very close to insulting toward you in your working relationship with him. No, he does not make sexual remarks, obscene gestures or physical advances. But he's mad because you told him no—and he's taking his anger out on you."

"Yes," Lee said. "That's it. That's it exactly."

"So confront him with it."

Lee set her own glass on the coffee table, drew up both of her legs and rested her chin on her knees. "I know you're right."

"Look. Do you want to go to Walter with this right now?"

"No. No, I think it's only fair to Der...er, Dr. Taylor, that I try to settle this between the two of us, if I can."

"Good. Then do it."

Lee wrapped her arms more tightly around her legs and studied her bare toes. "I have to admit, I keep hoping that maybe he'll just...stop treating me this way. That I'll wake up tomorrow and things will be the way they were before."

"Well." Dana spoke kindly. "Maybe they will."

"But you think it's doubtful, don't you?"

Dana ran a hand back through her sleek honey blond hair. "I'm making no predictions. You just come to me, if you can't work it out. And we will talk to Walter. All right?"

"Thank you," Lee said softly, and couldn't resist adding, "you're the greatest, you know? And you look so...happy. You and Katie both. I mean, it's true what they say. Love makes a woman glow."

Dana pretended to groan. "I can't stand all this gushy stuff. What's gotten into you?"

"You're going to be a beautiful bride."

"Which reminds me—your fitting is this Saturday."

Now Lee was the one groaning. "Right. My fitting. Bridesmaid's dress number—what? Twelve or thirteen, I do believe."

"Now you sound more like your old self. And you know, Katie and I have been talking. We've been thinking that maybe instead of that deep teal for you, we'll go with magenta. With that dark hair of yours, magenta would be striking.''

''I've never been striking in my life, and I have no intention of starting now.''

''Don't put yourself down. I hate it when you do that.''

''Dana. Thanks for your help. Now go home to Trevor.''

''You don't like magenta?''

''Whatever you and Katie want, I will love.''

''We'll discuss it at length, on Saturday.''

''Oh, I'm sure we will.''

Dana leaned over and brushed Lee's bangs away from her eyes. ''I mean it. If you can't work it out with Dr. Devastating, you let me know. Okay?''

''Dr. Devastating. Terry Brandt called him that just the other day.''

''All the nurses call him that. And did you hear what I said?''

''Yes. But I still hope it doesn't come to that.''

Chapter Five

At a little after ten the next morning, when Derek had barely been at work for an hour, Lee found him rifling the papers at her desk area of the nurses' station.

She asked him, with seriously strained courtesy, "Is there something I can help you find?"

He held up a chart she'd been checking against some of the information in the hospital's computer files. "This should be back in records by now."

"I was just checking—"

"I don't want to hear your excuses, Lee. I want you to do your job."

Paul Uhana, the L.P.N. who handled most of the clinic's phone triage, was sitting just a few feet away, on the phone as usual. Even with a patient describing symptoms in his ear, he couldn't miss the blatant censure in the doctor's tone. He glanced up long enough to send

Lee a pitying look, and then cut his gaze away and spoke into the phone once more.

Lee drew herself up. "I think that remark was uncalled-for, Doctor."

Derek tossed the chart back on the counter. "Just get it back to records." And he turned and stalked away.

About a half an hour later, Paul caught her in the copy room. They were standing side by side as he poured himself some coffee and she heated water in the microwave for a mug of strawberry leaf tea.

"I never give advice," Paul said in that soft Jamaican lilt of his. "But I'm making an exception for you."

Paul rarely gossiped and *always* minded his own business. To Lee, that lent validity to whatever he might have to say. "I'm listening."

Paul leaned closer. "Dr. Taylor is a good man, I think."

The microwave beeped. Lee took out her mug and dropped in the tea bag. "All right. He's a good man."

"But he goes too far with you. We've all noticed. You ought to talk to him about it."

Lee found a stir stick and poked at the tea bag to submerge it fully. She was thinking of her conversation with Dana the night before. "I'm...working up to it." She tapped the stick on the edge of the cup.

The door opened then. It was Jack. "Paul. Patient for you on three."

"Coming." He gave Lee one last significant glance. "You should do it soon, I think. Very soon."

"I know," she said.

Alone in the copy room for a blessed few minutes, Lee sipped her tea and considered the suggestion both Paul and Dana had made.

That she talk to him. Get it out in the open. Make a

real effort to get him to understand that the way he treated her was totally out of line.

Would talking to him work?

It hadn't before.

But she had been a little...placating then. That had been the very first morning after she turned him down. She'd hoped more to smooth things over than anything else at that point. Now, she had honest complaints to voice.

Would he listen?

Maybe.

She did believe that, beneath all that ego and arrogance, there beat the heart of an ethical man. She'd worked with him for six months, after all. They had different working styles. He might be your typical control-freak M.D., but he wasn't totally uncaring.

She had seen him hold the bell of his stethoscope in his hand, warming it before he put it against an asthmatic child's thin chest. He sometimes told little stories when he gave an injection—silly stories about cars or animals or whatever might interest the patient—to distract them from the quick, cruel pain of the needle going in.

Until recently, and in spite of the differences in their two approaches to patient care, she had *liked* him. And she had enjoyed working with him.

And maybe Paul and Dana were right. Maybe she was going to have to stop hoping that Derek Taylor would just wake up one morning and decide to get off her back.

She would have to take action. And soon.

Derek was thinking along the same lines.

However, from his point of view, Lee was the one with the problem.

It drove him crazy, just to have to be around her. And

it wasn't anything personal—no, not personal at all. He'd simply had it up to here with her sloppy work habits and her refusal to consider better ways to manage her time.

True, her work habits hadn't really bothered him all that much until just recently. He *had* felt more tolerant of them before.

Before what?

He chose not to think about that. He focused on her transgressions.

She left toys in the examining rooms. And she was always holding charts back from records to check on things that didn't require checking. Her work area needed straightening.

And she left herself sticky notes. Derek hated sticky notes. Little yellow squares of paper, looking sloppy, stuck everywhere from computer screens to the cabinets in the copy room. A few days before, he'd sat down in one of the chairs in the nurses's station, having failed to notice that a sticky note had fallen onto the seat. He'd walked around for an hour or so with the number of a local women's shelter stuck to the back of his lab coat.

Unacceptable. That was the word for Lee's work lately. Unacceptable.

He would have to have a serious talk with her. There was no way around it. And he would have to do it soon.

The final straw came that afternoon.

The waiting room was packed. Derek, Terry and Jack were working their tails off trying to deal with the patient load. Sometimes, when they got seriously backed up, Paul would step in and help speed things along. But Paul was backed up, too. He sat at his phone in the nurses' station, taking one call after another.

Every examining room had a patient in it. And the patients in the waiting room were starting to complain.

And Lee had been closeted for half an hour in Room 2 with a woman who had come in for five minutes worth of suture removal. Every time Derek glanced at his watch, he grew angrier.

Lee was just going to have to get her priorities in order here.

Finally he'd had enough. He rapped on the door behind which Lee was busy wasting time.

After a minute, she stuck her head out.

He tried to compose his expression, tried to keep himself from scowling at her. "Lee. This is unacceptable. We have more than one patient to consider here and—"

She interrupted him in midsentence. "Is there an emergency?"

"Well, no. But—"

"Then I can't help you now."

He wondered at that moment if she understood the English language. "Did you hear what I said? We are running seriously behind and you will have to—"

"I'm sorry," she informed him, not sounding sorry at all. "I have a real crisis going on in here and I can't deal with you right now." With that, she shut the door in his face.

He stared at that door. At the big, white number 2 mounted on it at eye level. He wanted to kick the damn thing in. Just kick it in and get to her. Get his hands on her and—

"Doctor," Terry Brandt said, "I've run the diabetes stick and checked the vital signs on Mr. Ontkean in Room 5. He's ready for you now."

Derek closed his eyes. He sucked in a long breath. "Thank you, Terry."

He turned toward the room farther down the hall.

Right then, the door to Room 2 opened. He spun back to it.

Lee emerged, an arm wrapped tight around the patient, who had her face buried in Lee's shoulder. The woman's child—Mary or something, Derek couldn't quite call up the name—sucked furiously on the thumb of one hand while, with the other hand, she clutched the hem of her mother's skirt.

"Mama cwy," the child said around her thumb.

Derek confronted Lee. "What the hell is going on?"

At the sound of his voice, the patient—Hirsch, yes, that was her name, Lenora Hirsch—gasped and cringed closer to Lee.

Lee said, so carefully, "She's very upset. And she doesn't need to hear harsh words from an angry man right now." She rubbed the woman's back. "Come on, Lenora. Let's go. It's not far, I promise you. I'll take you there."

"Take her where?"

"The women's shelter over on East Main."

Derek stared from the patient to Lee and back again. He did remember Lee's suspicions concerning that patient. Clearly the woman needed more than medical help. But he also had a waiting room full of patients—and Lee Murphy was one quarter of his staff.

"You're needed here."

She didn't waver. "I'll be back in half an hour. I promise you." She started to guide the woman and child up the hall toward the exit.

He stepped into her path. "It's half an hour we don't have, Lee."

The Hirsch woman let out a strangled, frightened sob. Lee held her closer. "I'm sorry. There's no putting this off. This is the moment when she's willing to act. And I consider it part of my job to see that the moment doesn't get by her. Now, would you please step out of my way?''

Derek knew he was beaten. Rage and frustration churning inside him, he moved aside.

''Thank you,'' Lee said tightly, then lowered her voice to a soothing whisper. ''Come on now, Lenora. Let's go.''

Derek spoke to Lee's retreating back, keeping his tone even and very controlled, ''I want to see you in my office. Today, before the end of your shift.''

''Fair enough.'' She tossed the words back over her shoulder as she led the Hirsch woman and her child away.

Chapter Six

At 6:20 that evening, when the last patient had finally been seen, Lee knocked on the door to Derek's office.

"Come in."

Lee closed her eyes, rested her forehead against the door and mouthed the word, "Courage." Then she straightened her shoulders and turned the door handle.

Derek sat behind his desk. He'd taken off his lab coat but had yet to put on his jacket. He was writing something on a yellow legal pad. Beneath the starched cuff of his pale blue shirt, his tanned hand moved swiftly across the pad. He glanced up.

"Lee," he said. Cool. Professional. Totally self-possessed. He pointed with his pen. "Have a seat."

Lee slid into the same consulting chair she'd taken the last time she'd been closeted in here with him, when she'd told him as diplomatically as she could that she just wanted to do her job and get along. As it turned

out, diplomacy hadn't worked very well. Now she knew
she must steel herself to employ stronger tactics.

He wrote a few more lines, gold head bent, a frown
between those shining brows. Lee waited. He was the
one who had called this meeting, after all. He could take
charge of it, run it any way he wanted to—including
letting her just sit there and squirm while he scribbled
away.

Fine. She would sit. She would do her best *not* to
squirm. As soon as he got around to it, he would have
his say. And then she would have hers.

A few seconds later, he stopped writing. He looked at
what he'd written, frowned some more and then
shrugged. He set the pen and the legal pad to the side
of his desk blotter, taking an extra few seconds to place
the pen just so at the top of the pad and square the pad
up with the edge of the blotter.

Finally he folded his hands on the blotter and faced
her across the desk. "I think it's time we spoke frankly,
Lee."

She realized her own hands were gripping the chair
arms way too hard. She ordered them to relax and tried
a polite smile. "I think you're probably right."

His frown deepened. "I don't see this situation as humorous in the least."

So much for politeness. She scowled right back at
him. "Neither do I."

"Then why were you smiling?"

She decided not to answer that. He'd only said it to
intimidate her anyway.

He looked down at his folded hands, then back up at
her. "Lately I find it extremely difficult to work with
you. And the incident this afternoon with the Hirsch
woman was the final straw. You could see how backed

up we were, yet still, you insisted on walking out on your job.''

Lee longed to jump to her own defense. Already, her adrenal glands had kicked into gear, producing epinephrine, urging a fight-or-flight reaction. Her face felt hot with anger and her skin all prickly. Her heart pounded like an angry fist at the wall of her chest. Still, she clung to her original intention not to speak until he had said it all.

He continued, ''You've been—how else can I say it?—nothing but a problem lately. You're constantly holding charts back from records. Your work area is untidy, papers everywhere, in no order that I can see. And worst of all, you simply refuse to manage your time effectively when you're with patients. If some aging hypochondriac wants to bend your ear for an hour over nothing in particular, you let him—no matter how many other patients are out there, waiting for their turn with you.''

He fell silent, and just stared at her, as if daring her to speak. When she didn't, he picked up the pen that he'd set so neatly on the legal pad and turned it in his fingers, studying it, as if he'd just noticed something new about it that had escaped his notice up till now.

At last, he looked at her again, pinning her with that cruel blue stare. And then he tossed the pen down. ''All right. What I'm getting at here is that your work has become unacceptable. And you're either going to have to start improving or—''

Lee did speak then. ''Don't say it.''

His broad shoulders stiffened. ''Excuse me?''

''Don't tell me I should look for another job. Please.''

He leaned back in the chair, a very deliberate kind of

motion, and rested his elbows on the chair arms. "Why shouldn't I?"

"Because I'm not going to quit. And you can't fire me. I work for Honeygrove Memorial, not for you. You can place a formal complaint about me, but that's the most you can do."

He made a low, impatient sound. "I know that."

"Then don't suggest I go elsewhere. Because I won't. I love this job."

"You don't behave as if you do."

"That's an outright lie."

"No, it's—"

"A lie, Doctor," she said again. "And you know it is."

"I do not—"

"You do. You know. My work habits have not changed. I do things exactly the same way I always did."

"Of course you want to believe that."

"I believe it because it's true." She leaned forward in her chair, determined to get through to him. "Listen, if Lenora Hirsch had come in here on a busy Friday afternoon a few weeks ago, I would have done exactly what I did today. The difference is, a few weeks ago, you would have understood."

"No, I—"

She cut him off by repeating her own words more slowly, emphasizing each one. "*You would have understood.* Oh, you might have been irritated with me. You might have tried to talk me out of leaving—at first. But then you would have really looked at that woman. You would have seen how emotionally devastated she was. You would have admitted to yourself that her situation constituted an emergency and that she was clinging to me as her lifeline. You would have realized that my job right then was to take her to a place where she could get the help she needed.''

He was shaking his head. "No, that's not so. This is a medical clinic. We are not in the business of involving ourselves in the personal lives of our patients.''

"As much as we can, Doctor, we are in the business of *saving* lives.''

"You want me to believe that your walking out of here with that woman today somehow saved her life?''

"Yes, that is exactly what I want you to believe. Because it's true. Her husband's been beating her for years. On more than one occasion, he has threatened to kill her. At some point in the near future, I have no doubt he would have succeeded. He has managed, over time, to break quite a few of her bones—not to mention all the lacerations and mild concussions he's inflicted. She's terrified of him. Over the years, she's seen five or six different doctors. At least one or two of them must have suspected the real problem. But you know how it is. Who has the time to look into the cause of all these 'accidents' she keeps having? It's easier just to treat the injuries and move her along.''

Derek shifted in his chair. She could see that she was reaching him.

She pressed on. "It had to stop, that's what I'm telling you. And it had to stop today, when she finally broke down and was willing to take action.''

Derek looked off toward the file cabinet in the corner, and then, with some effort, back at her. "All right. Maybe I was too quick to judge you concerning the Hirsch woman.''

"You've been too quick to judge me in every instance—lately. Why is that, do you think?''

His big shoulders drew even tighter than before. "What are you getting at?" His voice was as flat and hard as his eyes.

She stared back at him without flinching. "You're angry with me, but not because of my work habits. Your real reasons are strictly personal."

His square jaw twitched. "That's absurd."

"No. It's the truth. Until that awful evening in the Mexican restaurant, when you said we should go out together and I said no, you never found it all that impossible to deal with the differences in the way we work. But since then, everything I do bothers you. Since then, I'm too sloppy and too slow and I have no idea what's urgent and what's not. Well, Doctor, I'm telling you that I have not changed. That my work habits are exactly the same as they've always been. The real problem here is that I said no and you can't deal with that."

"No, that's not—"

She ran right over him. "I turned you down. And you're furious with me for it. You want me out of here. You don't want to work with me. You don't want even to be around me. So you've set out to get rid of me, by convincing yourself that I'm no good at my job. Well, I happen to be damn good at my job, thank you. And I'm not going anywhere. And I think, as a basically fair man at heart, you'd better face up to this little trick you're pulling on yourself. You'd better admit that you're angry at me, and get over it. Because you have been harassing me, Doctor. And I want it to stop."

Derek stared at Lee.

Her hair was falling in her eyes and her face was flushed and she still wore her lab coat over one of those shapeless shirts of hers and a pair of baggy slacks. She shouldn't have held the least attraction for him.

But, damn it, she did.

He wanted to...touch her.

He wanted to get up, go around his desk, reach for her hand and pull her into his arms. He wanted to kiss her. And to take off that lab coat, that shapeless shirt, those baggy slacks. He wanted to make love with her, right here in his office. It was totally inappropriate.

But he wanted her naked. He wanted to see that look on her face again, that blank, hungry look that said she desired him.

What was it Larry had said? "Who woulda thought you'd end up being so lucky with women? You're deadly, brother. Deadly."

Of course, Larry had been joking—to an extent. But the fact remained, Derek Taylor did have a way with women. They might tell him no after a while, when they realized he had no plans to make things permanent. But he couldn't remember a single woman who had ever turned him down for a first date.

Except the woman sitting opposite him now.

Very quietly, he asked, "Do you honestly believe what you just said?"

Lee hardly dared to breathe at that moment. It looked as if she'd reached him at last. The cold mask of intolerance was gone. Sincerity—and something that might have been shame—shone in his eyes.

"Lee. Do you really believe I've been...upset with you personally, rather than with your work? Do you really see my actions as harassment?"

He looked so stricken, she found she wanted to soften the blow. But it was no time to start waffling. "I do."

A brief silence. Then he said, so softly, "Oh."

Silence again. He didn't seem to know what to say next. And nothing came to Lee, either.

Derek's chair squeaked as he leaned forward again, picked up his pen, threw it down. He glared at the legal pad as if something of life-and-death import was written there that he couldn't quite make out. Then, abruptly, he stood.

Lee watched him, unsure what he would do next, as he slid carefully out from behind the desk, stuck his hands into his pockets and turned away from her.

He stared at the wall. He held his head so tall and proud, his broad shoulders stiff and straight. She had the most dangerous, impossible urge—to rise and go to him, to put her hand on that broad back, between his shoulder blades. To murmur soft, soothing things.

But touching him would be worse than foolish; after the hard things she'd just said to him, it would be wrong. She had no right to give him any signals he might construe as provocative. Right now, a touch, even given in comfort, would be stepping over the line. Lee stayed in her chair.

At last, he turned. "Okay," he said gruffly, "maybe you've got a point."

It wasn't quite good enough. "Maybe?"

"Damn it. All right. I'm the one with the problem here. And I will…deal with it." He was scowling again. "Is that good enough?"

"Yes." She spoke gently. "That's just fine."

They shared a long look. His scowl faded. Lee dared to smile at him. She felt…so much lighter, as if she'd been carrying some impossibly heavy weight around with her and had finally been allowed to set it down.

Derek dropped into his chair again and rested his forearms on the desk blotter. "Look." His sexy mouth curved in a rueful smile. "Do you ever go fishing?"

She blinked. What did fishing have to do with anything?

He hurried to explain, eager and hopeful and so handsome it hurt to look at him. "You've heard about that cabin of Dr. MacAllister's, haven't you? It's up in the mountains, about an hour from here. And there's a lake there. Good trout fishing, or so everyone says. Yesterday, Walter gave me the key. I was planning to head up there tonight, but since we're getting out of here so late, it looks like I might as well wait until tomorrow. Anyway, I was thinking, maybe—"

She put up a hand. "Hey."

His smile deepened. "What?"

"It sounds like you're just about to ask me to spend the weekend with you at Dr. MacAllister's cabin."

"Well, if it sounds like it, that's because I am."

Lee shifted in the chair, not sure how to move on from there. Hadn't they been through all this? Hadn't she made it painfully clear that she wouldn't go out with him?

"Lee, come on. You might have fun. And it could be just a friendly trip, you know? Nothing romantic, if you're not interested in that."

He looked so…sweet. And vulnerable. Which made no sense at all. He was Dr. Devastating. The gorgeous man with the massive ego and a different blonde for every week of the year. Still, Lee found herself wanting to let him down easy.

"I don't think that would work," she said carefully. "I really don't."

He did a sort of double take, then looked down at the desk blotter and muttered, "I don't know what my problem is, when it comes to you. Because I should have this figured out by now, shouldn't I? You won't go out with me—even as a friend.'' He looked up, lifted an eyebrow. ''Right?''

She nodded.

He shook his head. ''I knew that.''

Idiot, he was thinking to himself. Moron. Cretin.

The damn woman had him tied in knots. It was an experience to which he was not accustomed.

Seeing his sincere confusion, Lee couldn't help feeling that she ought to explain further. ''Really. It just wouldn't be wise. The two of us getting involved romantically would only mean trouble in the end.''

He frowned again. ''I don't think it would necessarily have to be that way.''

She sighed. ''Derek, I—''

The frown vanished. ''Hey. You called me Derek.''

''—And I shouldn't have. It's just…it's been a rough day.''

He studied her for a moment. ''Yes,'' he said. ''It has. But things will get better. You'll see.''

She eyed him doubtfully. ''They will?''

''Yes. Somehow, I'm going to learn to live with the fact that you don't want to go out with me.''

She couldn't resist teasing, ''I don't think it should be *that* difficult.''

He actually teased back. ''Maybe you underestimate yourself.''

''And maybe you have a sense of humor, after all.''

He pretended to look pained. ''Ouch. You got us both with that one.''

There was really nothing more to say. She stood. ''You have a good time this weekend, Dr. Taylor.''

He shrugged. ''Yeah. A couple of days alone with the woodpeckers and the pine trees is probably just what I need to put things back in perspective.''

Chapter Seven

Walter MacAllister's cabin at Blue Moon Lake was a rustic structure sided in knotty pine and tucked up close into the side of a hill. It had a basement below and a high deck in front, which could be reached on one side by a set of stairs.

At nine-thirty Saturday morning, Derek parked in the clear space below the deck. He'd bought a few groceries before he left town. He put them away in the ancient refrigerator, and on a spare shelf in a kitchen cabinet. Walter had told him to go ahead and use anything he wanted from the pantry, which consisted of several built-in basement shelves, next to the stairs that went down from a door in the kitchen.

Unfortunately the basement light had burned out. Derek rummaged through several drawers, looking for a replacement, but didn't find one. So he got his flashlight from the Suburban and left it on the floor by the basement door, thinking that later, if he needed anything, he would go down there and check things out.

Once the food was taken care of, he tossed his change of clothes into a drawer of the bedroom's knotty-pine bureau. Next, he thought maybe he'd take a little nap. The truth was, he hadn't slept well at all the night before. The hard things Lee had said to him kept echoing in his head.

It really bothered him that they were all true. He knew he wasn't the nicest guy in the world. But, until yesterday, he'd always prided himself on being relentlessly honest and fair.

Unfortunately sleep didn't come any more easily in the morning than it had the night before. The minute he stretched out on the bed and closed his eyes, he saw Lee's face. Never mind a nap.

He put on swim trunks under his jeans and changed into hiking boots. Then he packed a light lunch and hiked around Blue Moon Lake, stopping midway to strip down to the trunks and swim in the icy water of a sandy little cove he found. He met a few other hikers on the way and exchanged greetings with them. But through most of the trek, he found himself alone. He tried to focus on the clean, unspoiled country around him and not to let himself wonder what Lee might be doing.

"I don't know," Dana said. "It's just so…"

"Magenta," Katie concurred. "So really, completely magenta."

Dana stepped back a little. "But we do want a strong color, for contrast, with the two of us all in white. And the boat neck is good on her. She has such well-shaped shoulders, don't you think?"

Katie nodded. "All those nights at the gym must be paying off."

If you only knew, Lee thought. "Too bad I can't exercise my way into a pair of breasts."

"Breasts aren't everything," Katie chided.

Lee let out a deep sigh and looked from one friend to the other in the gold-rimmed triple mirror of the bridal boutique. "Why are we making such a big deal out of *my* dress? You two are the brides."

Dana and Katie shared a glance, one that communicated how very patient they were being with Lee. "We want you to look just right," Katie said.

"After all," Dana added, "you're the only bridesmaid we've got."

The boutique owner, a tall fashion plate of a woman dressed all in black, appeared through the red velvet curtain from the front of the store. She had another long gown over her arm. "How about this one? It's simple. Clean lines. A quiet, understated elegance."

"Hmm," Katie said. "Emerald green velvet." She looked at Dana. "What do you think? It would provide that strong contrast we want."

Dana fingered the material. "I don't know. This green says Peter Pan to me. Is that what we're going for?"

Katie groaned. "Absolutely not."

"I'll find more options." Still carrying the green dress, the woman in black retreated through the curtain again. Dana and Katie turned back to Lee. Dana began fiddling with the wide neckline of the magenta dress, while Katie tugged on the hem.

"Hey you guys," Lee complained. "Do you have to keep rearranging me in this one, considering I'm not even going to be wearing it?"

Katie looked up at Dana. They both shrugged. "She's

right,'' Katie said. They helped her unzip and then, once Lee had stepped out of the thing, Dana hung it back on the hanger.

"Where's the next one?" Lee asked, when she stood before the mirror in her long half-slip and lacy lemon yellow strapless bra.

Dana said, "You know, for a woman who won't get near a pot of lip gloss or a mascara wand, you sure go all out on your underwear."

"She always has," Katie agreed, looking way too intrigued for Lee's peace of mind. "What does this tell us about her?"

Both of her friends turned to study her.

Lee said, "Look. I'm letting you dress me up however you want for your wedding. I'll do whatever it takes not to be an embarrassment to you, I promise. I'll get my hair done. And I'll even wear makeup. But don't start analyzing my underwear. That's one step over the line."

Dana arched an eyebrow. "Did you tell Katie about Dr. Devastating?"

"Dr. Taylor?" Katie piped up. "What about him?"

Lee frowned. "Hey. How did you know she meant Dr. Taylor?"

"There's only one doctor they call Dr. Devastating," Katie said. "And that's Dr. Taylor. And what's this all about?"

Lee aimed a glare at Dana. "You would have to bring it up."

"Come on." Dana didn't look the least bit guilty. "I want to know what's been happening since Thursday night, and Katie will, too—as soon as you tell her what's going on."

"What *is* going on?" Katie demanded.

Just then, the woman in black came through the curtain again. She had a whole stack of new prospects this time, a lot of them in velvet, and also something fuchsia, with gold beading on the bodice and a filmy chiffon skirt. "Try these. Maybe one of them will work for you."

Dana took them from her and hung them up.

"I'll be back to check on you in a few minutes," the woman said.

The three friends waited for her to vanish through the curtain.

Then Katie spun on Lee. "Come on. Tell all."

Lee made a stab at evasion. "Hey, I have to try on these dresses. You two *will* make a choice today, because I swear I'm not going through this again."

But Katie refused to let it go. "You can try on the dresses and talk at the same time."

Dana was grinning. "Come on. It's written all over you. You *want* to talk about it."

Lee looked from one expectant face to the other and realized she couldn't deny them. And Dana was right. She didn't *want* to deny them. She needed a couple of good friends to talk to—and here they were.

So, as they zipped and hooked her into one dress after another, Lee brought Katie up-to-date on what she'd already revealed to Dana. From there, she went on to tell them both about all that had happened Friday.

When she'd finished, Dana immediately suggested, "As soon as we're done here, you should get in your car and head for Blue Moon Lake."

"What?" Lee could hardly believe her ears. "You know I don't want to get involved with him. Why in heaven's name would I be insane enough to follow him up to Blue Moon Lake?"

"Because. He actually *admitted* he was in the wrong—and promised he'd do something about it."

"Well, he *was* in the wrong. And it was only right that he should do something about it."

"Lee. Stop. Think. This is the sign of a superior man. Men, as a general rule, will never admit they're wrong."

"Oh, please. Trevor would admit it if he was wrong. And so would Mike."

"And maybe you've noticed that we're marrying them," Katie suggested softly.

"Lee," Dana said, "it's about time you got past this fear of M.D.s you've got."

"No, it's not."

"The vow we made is dead. Buried. Over. Kaput."

"Of course it is. For the two of you."

"Look at it this way. He says he's willing to just be friends. Give him that much of a chance. Be his friend."

"Friends. Right. Katie and Mike were *friends*. And look what happened to them."

"Exactly." Dana took Katie by the shoulders and placed her squarely in front of Lee. "Look at this woman. This is a *happy* woman. She's not suffering at all since she and Mike finally admitted they're much more than friends. You could be happy like this. If only you'd let yourself."

"I am happy."

Dana set Katie aside and shook a finger at Lee. "You are impossible. That man is utterly studly. And I can see it in your eyes. You are crazy about him. And you just...well, you remind me of myself a couple of months ago, throwing away happiness with both hands, and feeling totally justified in doing it."

"Look. Could we just choose a dress—please?"

Katie put her hand on Dana's arm. "She's right. It's her life."

Dana let out a long, deep sigh. "I know." She scrunched up her nose at Lee. "Go on. Do it your way."

"Thank you," Lee said.

Dana turned her attention to the dress they'd just helped Lee get into—the fuchsia one with the chiffon skirt. "What is this? *The Nutcracker?* I swear, she looks just like one of the sugarplum fairies."

Katie shook her head. "Get her out of it. Where's the next one?"

"Right here." The woman in black came through the curtain again, bearing more dresses.

"Wait a minute," Dana said. "I think we should try the magenta one more time...."

Derek's hike around the lake took him several hours. It was near six when he came full circle to the cabin again. Since there was no phone in there, he got his cell phone from the Suburban and called home to check his messages.

There were none. And that depressed him a little. He realized that he probably ought to put in some effort to make a few friends, people who would call up out of the blue and leave how-are-you messages on his machine. People who would invite him over to their place for pizza or something. The women he dated never seemed to turn into friends, for some reason.

Maybe that was Lee's attraction for him. She'd seemed the kind of woman who would make a good friend.

However, he wasn't going to think any more about Lee.

He tossed a salad and fired up the stone barbecue,

which was built into the side of the hill not far from the stairs that led up to the deck. Once he'd eaten his dinner and cleaned up after himself, the shadows had lengthened enough for the fish to start biting. He got out his fishing gear and found himself a nice, flat rock beneath a pine tree right at the edge of the lake. He settled in, casting his line into the clear water and telling himself for about the hundredth time not to think of Lee.

He caught two nice trout and threw a couple of small ones back. He should have been having a nice time.

And he would have been.

If only he had someone to talk to.

Someone sharp-witted and funny. Someone who gave as good as she got. Someone like—

Derek swore, enunciating the expletive with great clarity, even though there was no one to hear it but the shining water, the tall trees and the darkening sky. At that moment, he almost wished his beeper would go off; he wore it hitched to his belt as always, just in case he might be needed, though he wasn't on call. If his beeper went off, he'd have some emergency to deal with. Something to get his mind off brooding about Lee.

Right then, he felt a tug on his line. He let the line play out a little, then began reeling it in.

In the end, Katie and Dana decided on the magenta velvet dress, after all. Next, the lady in black turned the shop's alteration specialist loose on Lee. Finally she was allowed to put her street clothes back on. The tailor promised that the dress would be ready within the week.

"Let's drop in at Granetti's," Dana suggested. "We could all use a glass of wine."

But Lee demurred. She wanted to run over to the shelter on East Main and see how Lenora Hirsch was doing.

Lenora cried and clung to her. Lee held the woman close and smoothed her hair and reassured her that even the toughest of times eventually passes.

At least, Lenora seemed firm in her determination to start a new life. And Maria had made a friend at the shelter—a little boy named Gary. They sat together on the floor in the big playroom downstairs, building an intricate structure with Duplo blocks, talking in low, very serious voices as they worked.

"Gai-wee, this will be the king's palace. All the pwincesses will live hewe."

"And the princes, too."

"Wight. The pwinces, too."

Maria looked up then, and noticed Lee. She beamed a happy, welcoming smile. "Nuss Lee. Will you wead to us?"

So Maria chose a Dr. Seuss anthology from the bookshelves that lined one wall. Lee sat on the sofa with a child on either side and read both *Yertle the Turtle* and her own personal favorite, *The Lorax*.

The children begged for more, and Lee couldn't say no. She ended up reading *Horton Hatches the Egg* and *The 500 Hats of Bartholomew Cubbins* as well.

At home, there was a message from Dana on her answering machine. It contained clear directions to Walter MacAllister's cabin up at Blue Moon Lake. "Just in case you decide you might like to go for a little drive," Dana's voice suggested archly at the end.

"Right. Sure." Lee quickly hit the Erase button.

But the directions really had been very simple. They seemed to stick in her mind.

If she wanted to, she'd have no trouble finding her way up there.

Not that she ever would.

*   *   *

An hour after he'd sat down on the rock and put his line in the water, it was full dark and Derek had seven trout. He'd have a feast for his breakfast tomorrow. He took the fish back to the cabin and cleaned them in the big concrete sink on the screened-in back porch. Then he got himself a beer from the fridge and sat on the comfortable old sofa in front of the potbellied stove in the main room.

He considered the idea of building a fire. But no. It really wasn't that cold. A fire would be cozy at first, but too warm in the end.

And this wasn't so bad, after all. A good hour and a half had gone by since he'd thought of…no, he wasn't even going to let himself say her name in his mind.

He glanced at his watch: 9:32. He'd tossed a Tom Clancy thriller in with his clothes when he packed his bag. It waited on top of the pine bureau in the other room. Maybe he'd go in there and stretch out on the bed and read himself to sleep. He set down his beer and started to stand.

He was halfway to his feet when he heard the noise. He froze, half crouched, listening. For a moment, he heard nothing but an owl hooting somewhere outside.

And then, there it came again. Bumping sounds. From below, in the basement. Someone—or more likely, some animal—was knocking things around down there.

In the kitchen, propped against the side of the refrigerator, he found a knotted walking stick made of a nice, solid hardwood. He gripped the thing, and hefted it. It would do. If whatever-it-was came at him down there, he could give it a whack or two and hope that would convince it to get lost.

The bumping noises continued, followed this time by

a series of rolling sounds. As if something—probably cans of something—had been pushed off the pantry shelves, bumped down the stairs and then rolled along the floor below.

Derek's flashlight was waiting right where he'd left it. He scooped it up, switched it on and carefully opened the basement door.

Silence. The skin on the back of his neck pebbled. It seemed he could feel whatever-it-was, down there in the gloom. Watching. Waiting.

He pulled the door all the way open and pointed the flashlight down the steep pine-plank stairs.

The light revealed nothing but a strange cloud of pale dust floating thick in the air.

But then the shaft of light fell on the concrete slab at the foot of the stairs. A dented can of corn lay there, on its side. He flashed the light farther out and spied a can of peaches and a can of…pinto beans, it looked like.

Derek took one step down. And then another. Three steps more and he came even with the pantry shelves. He shone his light in there. The first thing the beam picked up was a torn-open box of Bisquick. The floury contents had spilled out across the shelf.

Well, at least now he knew the source of the pale dust that still swam in the still, cool air.

He shone the light farther back on the shelf—saw a pair of shining eyes, a black bandit's mask—and that was it.

The animal leapt, shrieking, at him. He grunted and backed up, tripping on the damn walking stick that was supposed to be his weapon. The stick rolled down the steps as the creature tried to scramble past him.

Derek tripped over the scurrying animal with his right foot. It shrieked again. And then he was tumbling, banging his head on each step, headed for the concrete slab below.

His flashlight went flying and the world went black.

When he came swimming back to consciousness, Derek's first thought was that he couldn't see a thing. His second was a single word.

Raccoon.

A damn raccoon had gotten loose in the basement somehow. It had jumped him and tripped him. And now he was lying in the dark on the slab at the foot of the stairs with a killer headache, a throbbing right ankle and an aching right wrist. Groaning a little, he rolled to his back and sat, disturbing a can of something-or-other in the process. He heard it roll slowly away.

When he looked up, he could see the light from the kitchen bleeding through the basement door, which he'd left only slightly ajar when he started down. The stairs were so steep, the light faded to nothing just a few steps from the top. Down where he sat, the only illumination came from the dial of his watch. It was 9:43.

It had been after nine-thirty when he'd first heard the noises down here, which meant he hadn't been unconscious all that long. With his good hand, he felt around for his flashlight. He found another of those cans of peaches or pinto beans, but not the light he needed.

He wasn't sure what hurt most—his head, his ankle or his wrist. Carefully sitting there on the cold concrete in the pitch-dark, he examined himself by feel alone, grunting each time he touched a tender spot. His diagnosis: two bad sprains and a mild concussion. He'd also cut himself somehow. There was wet, sticky stuff on his forehead, back into his hair and down the right side of his face—drying blood from a shallow laceration about an inch in length, directly above the supraorbital notch. It was also just possible that his wrist had actually been fractured. But he wouldn't know for certain about that until he got himself back to Memorial and ordered an X ray.

Graphic images of raccoon vivisections scrolling through his mind, Derek rolled onto his knees. Slowly, painfully, trying not to put any weight on his bad wrist, he began crawling up the stairs.

When he finally reached the top, he rose to a kneeling position and shoved the door open wide with his good hand. Light poured in on him. He grasped the door frame and hauled himself to his feet—well, onto one foot, anyway.

What he needed, he realized as he limped into the kitchen, was that walking stick he'd dropped when the raccoon first shrieked at him. But damned if he had any intention of crawling back down those stairs to grope around for it.

Balancing on his good foot, he shoved the basement door shut.

Now, what?

He'd noticed a few other cabins nestled among the trees on his hike around the lake, but considering the condition of his ankle, getting to one of them would have been pretty damn rough. And then what would he do? Ask the occupants to interrupt their weekend to drive a stranger all the way to Honeygrove?

No, thanks.

Next, he considered calling Memorial for help. He shook his head at that idea. He'd be summoning an ambulance and emergency personnel all the way up to Blue Moon Lake for a couple of sprains and a bump on the head. Wasteful, he decided—not to mention damned embarrassing.

The Suburban was right outside. It had an automatic transmission. He should be able to make it down the mountain just fine on his own. He hopped into the bedroom, collected his keys and his wallet from the bureau and then hobbled around the place, turning off lights. He locked the back door, then stumbled out onto the front deck and locked that door, too.

Getting down those stairs was an adventure, but he did it. And then he hauled himself up into the driver's seat, groaning aloud when his right wrist bumped the steering wheel simultaneously with his right ankle hitting the base of the door frame. With a muttered oath, he dragged his injured ankle inside the cab and positioned it carefully on the floor. Then, cradling his sprained wrist against his body, he yanked the door shut, reached under the steering wheel with his left hand and stuck the key into the ignition.

By the light of the fat, full moon shining through the windshield, he caught a glimpse of himself in the rearview mirror. He looked like holy hell. There was drying blood smeared all over his face and a big, swollen purple contusion up near his hairline. He muttered more curses, thinking of that damn raccoon and how, once he got himself patched up, he would be back. With that rifle he never used, a .30-06 Springfield that had belonged to his father. A rifle of that caliber would blow the head off a damn raccoon, a thought that gave Derek immense satisfaction.

He turned the key. The engine hummed to life.

He had to use his left hand again, reaching across his own body to shift into Reverse. And then he had to steer with the same hand. It was challenging. Especially since he usually operated both the gas and brake pedals with his right foot. But, with a lot of swearing and a severe level of awkwardness, he managed to get the vehicle turned around and headed down the twisting, deserted road toward town.

The problem occurred on a certain sharp turn. He supposed he had let himself get going a little too fast for his limited range of motion. He meant to hit the brake, to slow himself down. But somehow his inexperienced left foot stomped on the gas. The Suburban seemed to leap forward, headed for the ditch that ran between the twisting, two-lane road and the mountainside. Desperately he fumbled for the brake.

But he was too late. Just as he found it, the big vehicle shot into the ditch, rolled along about a hundred yards and came to a metal-crunching stop with its grill half buried in the side of the mountain. On instinct, Derek braced both feet on the floorboards and gripped the steering wheel with both hands. Thus, at the moment of impact, he was treated to searing needles of pain shooting up his injured wrist and down through his bad ankle.

He pressed his lips together and hissed a string of curses through them. Then, for about fifteen seconds that seemed never-ending, he just sat there, rocking back and forth, moaning in agony and cradling his hurt wrist.

Finally the waves of pain at his wrist and ankle receded a little. He just wished the damn headache that pounded between his brows would do the same.

But it didn't.

The sudden stop had killed the engine. However, the lights were still working. Maybe, just maybe, he could back himself out of there and up onto the road.

He reached with his left hand again, shifting into Park

first and then turning the key. The engine started right up. Thank the powers that be for small favors.

He eased the gearshift into Reverse, gripped the steering wheel with his good hand and put his working foot on the gas. Slowly, steadily, he depressed the pedal. The engine revved higher. And higher still. The wheels grabbed, then spun.

And the Suburban remained, stuck firmly with its grill buried in the dirt.

With great difficulty, Derek shifted into first, then back to reverse again, hoping the change of gears might jog the vehicle loose. No such luck.

After several minutes of spinning wheels and grinding gears, he was forced to give in. It would take a tow truck to get the damn vehicle out of that ditch.

So he'd have to call a tow service.

It was at that moment that he remembered he'd left his phone back at the cabin.

"Good going there, Taylor. Really great work," he muttered darkly to himself.

Then he turned off the engine and shoved the key into his pocket. He left all the lights on, including the warning blinkers. That way, if and when anyone came along, they'd see what had happened. Just maybe, they would stop.

Getting out of the Suburban was even more fun than climbing in had been. He sort of slithered to the sloping edge of the ditch and then crawled up the bank to the edge of the road.

He estimated it was about fifteen miles to the main highway. And only about five to the cabin where he'd left his phone. But someone was bound to come along eventually—weren't they?

He couldn't be sure. All he knew was that he hadn't

seen a single car since he'd started the aborted drive down the mountain. Under ordinary circumstances, he'd jog right back up to the cabin and make a phone call. But these were hardly ordinary circumstances.

With a great deal of effort, he managed to lower himself to a sitting position at the side of the road. The night had grown chilly. Derek sat there and shivered, waiting.

Twenty minutes went by. Twenty minutes he would have sworn was two hours if he hadn't had his watch to tell him otherwise. Twenty minutes—and at the end of that time, he was still sitting and still shivering. His head still throbbed and his ankle and wrist still ached.

And no one had come along to rescue him.

Finally he couldn't stand it anymore. He struggled to his feet and started back the way he'd come, hobbling along, head pounding, wrist throbbing and ankle screaming in protest every time he had to put his weight on it.

He didn't get far at all before he heard the sound of a car's engine behind him. The relief he felt at that moment was very sweet indeed. He turned, just as the sweep of headlights appeared around a bend in the road and bathed him in their blinding beams. He put up his good hand to shield his eyes and squinted into the glare.

The car had already slowed—no doubt because the driver had spotted the marooned Suburban back there about two hundred yards or so. It eased to a stop just as it came parallel with him. Half blinded by headlight afterimages, Derek squinted harder, studying the car. It looked familiar.

Right then the driver's door swung open. And damned if wasn't Lee Murphy who got out.

"Derek," she cried. "Good Lord, what's happened to you?"

Chapter Eight

A hallucination. He was suffering from delusions brought on by head trauma. He closed his eyes and, in spite of the way it played hell with his headache, he shook his head.

But when he looked again, she hadn't vanished as he'd expected her to do. Instead she was flying at him around the end of the car. "Are you all right?" she demanded, and then went right on, giving him no chance to answer, "I saw that big thing you drive stuck in the ditch back there." She reached him then, and visibly reined herself in. She took his arm, very gently, and put on that calm, soothing voice she always used with her patients. "How badly are you hurt?"

He breathed in the scent of her. She always smelled fresh, he realized. Like soap and sunshine.

"Derek?" she asked carefully. "Do you know who I am?"

"I sure as hell do."

"Then can you tell me how seriously you're hurt?"

"Mild concussion," he muttered. "A couple of severe sprains, of the right wrist and the right ankle. A few cuts and scrapes."

"That's all?"

He scowled at her. "Isn't it enough—and what are you doing here?"

She let go of his arm and turned to open the passenger door of the car. "Let's get you to Memorial where they can—"

"Wait. Answer my question."

She left the door shut and faced him with a sigh. "Derek. Your condition may not be critical, but you do need medical attention."

"I know that. I am a damn doctor, after all. Answer my question."

"You have to—"

"Just answer me."

She shoved her bangs back away from her face and glared at him good and hard. "If I answer you, will you get in the car?"

He tried to look sincere and appealing, though he supposed all the dried blood on his face spoiled the effect. "I promise." She was still eyeing him distrustfully. "Come on, Lee. Just tell me why you're here."

"It's crazy. I shouldn't be."

"But you are."

"I almost turned and went back five times on the drive up here."

"But you didn't."

"I should have."

"Lee. You didn't. You're here. Why?"

"Because I...well, you said we could be friends."

"I did?"

Her head bobbed up and down in an emphatic nod. "Yesterday. In your office. You said—"

He put up his good hand. "All right. I said it. And that's why you're here? You drove most of the way to Blue Moon Lake after ten at night just to tell me you want to be my friend?"

Her scrubbed-clean face kind of crumpled into a sheepish little grin. "Crazy, huh?"

He actually felt himself smiling, even though it hurt to do it. "Not really."

Now she looked hopeful. Adorably so. "It's not?"

"No. It's not crazy." He was thinking that it was a start, at least.

She looked down at the ground beneath their feet and then back up at him. "So. Will you be my friend?"

He pretended to have to think about it. "If I say no, will you get back in your car and leave me all alone out here for the bears to kill and the buzzards to pick clean?"

"Oh, stop it. I don't think there are any bears around here at all."

"But would you leave me here?"

"Of course not." She turned for the passenger door again. "Come on. Let's get you over to Memorial."

"Lee."

She froze, facing away from him, her hand on the car door. "What?"

"I would love to be your friend."

She still didn't turn to him, but she did lift her head. She seemed to be staring out over the top of the car, at the shadows of the trees across the road. "You would?"

"Yeah."

"Well." Her voice sounded small and soft. He

guessed that she was smiling—just a hint of a smile. "Okay, then. We'll be friends." A slight breeze came up. It stirred the trees so they whispered and sighed. Lee pulled open the car door and stepped back. "Now," she said briskly, "will you please get in?"

He limped the two steps it took to get into position and she helped him lower himself into the seat.

"We'd better stop at your car and let me turn off the lights," she suggested. "It's well off the road, so no one's going to hit it, and that means there's no reason to run the battery down. Tomorrow, we can see about having it towed out of that ditch."

He leaned his aching head back against the seat and let out a long, tired breath. "Whatever you think."

It was well after midnight before they released him from the hospital. By then, he had an elastic bandage on his ankle, which had been sprained, a lightweight resin cast on his wrist—which had sustained a simple fracture at the distal end of the radius bone, damn it—and two butterfly strips taped over his right eye to close the gash there. He also had a big bottle of codeine to help him handle the pain.

Lee drove him to his condo. She helped him up the stairs, though he probably could have managed it himself. However, he liked leaning on her. He liked it a lot. No way was he going to argue with her if she wanted to give him a hand.

She took his key from him and opened the door, stepping right inside and switching on a light. "This is nice," she said.

"What?" he asked, innocently, "You and me alone like this?"

"I was referring to your apartment. It's attractive."

"Why, thank you very much. But it's a condo. I think."

She looked at him knowingly. "Had enough codeine, have we?"

"Doing all right, yes. Will you put me to bed, please?"

She shot him a sideways look that brimmed with suspicion, but then she slid up nice and close to him, wrapped his left arm around her shoulder and assumed the responsibility for holding him upright once again. "Which way?"

"Through that arch there."

Slowly but surely they hobbled across the living room, under the arch and down the short hall to his room. She took him straight to the bed. "Sit." She flicked on the bedside lamp. "Do you have anything in your pockets?"

"Is this a quiz?"

She held out her hand. "Come on. Your wallet, keys, anything too lumpy to sleep on."

He reached into his hip pocket and pulled out his wallet. "You have my keys."

She took the wallet from him and set it, along with the keys, on the night stand, beneath the lamp. "Give me the watch." He held out his arm and she slid the watch free. She put it by the lamp, too. Then she volunteered, "I'll take your other boot off for you."

She knelt before him and he found himself looking down at the top of her head as she started unlacing his left boot. "What happened to the other one, anyway?" he asked, as he glanced at his right foot, which was bare except for the elastic bandage applied to stabilize the sprain.

She glanced up. "It's down in my car, along with your

other sock and those loaner crutches they let you take home.''

''Do you know you have freckles across the bridge of your nose? Very light freckles, just a few of them, kind of sprinkled there. I never really noticed them before.''

She didn't answer, just went back to her work, removing his boot and then his sock, too. That done, she rose and stood over him. ''Do you have to go to the bathroom?''

He shook his head. ''I took care of that when they finally let me wash my face. You didn't answer me, about the freckles.''

She reached for the extra blanket that he always left neatly folded on the steamer trunk at the foot of the bed. ''Stretch out on the bed. Come on.''

He looked down at himself. ''Except for my shoes, I'm still fully dressed. And I'm dirty.''

''You need rest. You can take a bath in the morning.''

''There's blood on my shirt.''

She dropped the blanket and planted her hands on her hips. ''If you insist on a bath tonight, fine. Good luck. I'm outta here.'' She started to turn.

''Wait.'' He hoped he sounded really, really pitiful.

She turned back. ''Well?''

He hoisted his legs up onto the bed and stretched out. ''Satisfied?''

She picked up the blanket again and carefully spread it over him. Her badly cut hair curved along her cheek as she did it, as dark as night against her pale skin. Then she pulled his codeine from her pocket and set it on the nightstand, along with his watch, keys and wallet. ''Don't go crazy with these.''

The bed felt good, really good. ''I won't.''

"I'll go down and bring up your boot and your crutches before I go."

"I owe you. Big time."

"You certainly do. You can start paying me back by never questioning my judgment again. Especially at work."

Work. He hadn't even thought of that. "Hell. What about the clinic?"

"Don't worry. Dr. MacAllister will find some last-year residents to stand in for you. We'll manage, I promise you."

"It shouldn't be long before I can walk on this ankle. Then I can come in, anyway. I can see patients, though I'll probably need more assistance than usual, to work around this damn wrist."

"Derek. We'll have all day tomorrow to find someone for Monday. And now is not the time to worry about it, anyway." She reached over and turned off the lamp. "Get some rest."

Though light still spilled in from the hallway, the near-darkness soothed him and the codeine made everything hazy and soft. "Lee?"

"What?"

"You didn't say, about the freckles. Do you know you have those freckles?"

She gave no answer for a moment. But then she admitted in a voice very close to a whisper, "All right. Yes. I know."

"Will you check on me? In the morning?"

"Hey. What are friends for?"

Derek smiled and closed his eyes. "There's an extra key in that little wooden case on top of the dresser. Take it with you."

"All right. I'll do that."

A moment later, he heard her tiptoe out. And after that, the world seemed to just fade away.

Lee went down to her car and got the boot, the sock and the crutches. She carried them back up and started to leave them just inside the front door.

But really, if he was going to get any use out of those crutches, they should be where he could reach for them, near the bed. So she tiptoed down the hall again and into his room, where she tried to be absolutely silent as she set his boot and sock in the corner and propped the crutches against the wall on the far side of the nightstand.

Apparently she wasn't quiet enough. Derek moaned a little and whispered, "Lee?"

She whispered back, "I was just putting your crutches here. Go back to sleep."

"My throat's so dry, all of a sudden. I wonder, could you get me some water?"

"Sure. Be right back."

When she returned with a full glass, he'd already propped himself up to a sitting position. She handed him the glass. He drank. Then she took it from him and set it where he could reach it easily during the night.

"Now, lie back down," she instructed.

He obeyed. She straightened the blanket around him again.

"Lee?"

"Go to sleep."

"Do you know what did this to me?"

"Yes. You said at the hospital that you fell down the basement stairs at Walter MacAllister's cabin."

"I did fall down the stairs. But I had help."

"Derek. You need sleep."

"A damn raccoon jumped me."

She shook her head and let out a noise that sounded suspiciously like a barely restrained laugh. "Oh, Derek, come on."

"It's true. At the cabin. I heard it knocking the canned goods around in the basement. I went down to investigate and it jumped me. I tripped. And that's how I fell down the stairs." He reached up and grabbed her arm with his good hand.

Lee gasped at the contact, partly in surprise at the abruptness of the action—and partly because of something she refused to examine too closely.

"Lee. Are you *really* my friend?"

"Yes." She peeled his fingers away and tucked his hand beneath the blanket. "And you are going to sleep now."

"There's a rifle in that closet." His hand was out from under the blanket again, pointing.

"Derek—"

"It's on the top shelf, in a wooden case. The shells are in a box right next to it. If you're really my friend, you'll get it down and load it and drive up to Blue Moon Lake and eliminate that animal from the raccoon gene pool."

Lee did laugh then, in pure disbelief. "Derek. Forget it. I'm not murdering any innocent little raccoon."

"Innocent? That animal is about as innocent as Ted Bundy. Killing it wouldn't be murder. It would be a public service."

"Stop it."

"Listen. If you don't kill it, I'll do it myself. As soon as I can use this damn wrist of mine."

Without pausing to think about it, she brushed his hair back from his forehead. "Derek. Will you settle down?"

His eyes changed, turned soft and smoky. Lee pulled her hand away and stepped back. "I am leaving now. And you are going to sleep."

"Yes, nurse."

"Good night."

He waited until she was halfway to the door before he murmured, "Good night, Lee," to her retreating back.

Lee drove home smiling. After all, she'd helped a friend. And tomorrow, she would help him some more. She'd arrange to have that huge vehicle of his towed back to town. And she'd contact Dr. MacAllister so he could make sure there would be someone to cover for Derek on Monday.

It was a little after two when she let herself in her front door. She went straight to the bathroom, where she washed her face and brushed her teeth. Then she took off her faded jeans and Fruit Of The Loom T-shirt. Underneath, she was wearing a rose-beige silk teddy edged in oyster white lace.

Lee left the teddy on. She liked the feel of silk against her skin. Also, a teddy was comfortable to sleep in. It never hampered movement, since there really wasn't much to one. She climbed into her big, comfy four-poster bed, turned off the light and snuggled down.

Morning came so swiftly. It seemed to Lee that she'd barely shut her eyes before the sun was shining in the window. She stretched and yawned and the sheet slipped down.

How surprising. Instead of the rose-beige silk teddy she'd gone to sleep in, it seemed she was wearing a leopard-skin demibra and itty-bitty string bikini panties to match. She looked down at the underthings and sighed.

Lee loved sexy lingerie. Her friends might tease her about it, but she didn't care.

As far as Lee was concerned, provocative underwear was her own little secret she kept to herself, every bit as personal and private as her fantasies. Nice undies made her feel good. Very good. And undies, like fantasies, were one hundred percent harmless. You couldn't get infectious—not to mention deadly—diseases from your underwear, or from your fantasies. And neither would ever break your heart. They didn't even raise your blood sugar levels or make you fat.

Sighing some more, Lee pushed the sheet away completely. Yes, she really did like this leopard-skin look—although, now she stopped to think about it, she couldn't remember ever seeing this particular bra and panties before.

But what did it matter? She was wearing them now.

With a lazy index finger, she traced the string of the bikini, where it clung so high up on her thigh that it was almost at her waist. And then she drew her finger up, over her tummy and between her breasts.

"Lee."

She looked up from watching the progress of her own finger. What a surprise! Derek was leaning in the open doorway to the hall.

Chapter Nine

"Derek," Lee said. "You should be in bed."

"I was just thinking the same thing." He came away from the doorway and started walking toward her.

"You're not limping," she whispered. "And there's no cast on your wrist."

Now he stood right by her, at the side of the bed. "My ankle is fine and I don't need the cast anymore. Thanks to you, I'm completely healed."

He laid his right hand—the one with the now-healed wrist—on her left thigh. His touch was so warm, it completely distracted her from the miraculous nature of his sudden recovery. She looked down at that hand, so tanned and fine, with those little gold hairs she'd always admired dusting the back of it.

Slowly, with his fingers spread to cover the entire top of her thigh, he ran his hand upward, until he reached the notch where her legs joined. Lee hitched in a small gasp.

His thumb was now caught between her thighs, nudged up to rest against the leopard-skin panties and the tender mound beneath. She watched, her breath trapped somewhere high in her chest, as he slid his hand over, onto her right thigh and slipped his other four fingers in where his thumb had been, against that silky, leopard-skin fabric.

On instinct, she pressed her knees more tightly together.

"Lee," Derek whispered reproachfully.

Her thighs relaxed. His fingers stroked—so lightly, rubbing at the silken fabric of the panties. Lee closed her eyes and tossed her head on the pillow, moaning low, her heart pounding hard and deep. Her body felt all quivery. Beneath the panties, there was such wetness and heat.

And then he slipped one finger under the elastic of the panty leg. He touched her, that finger sliding in, parting her, stroking the feminine center of her.

Lee cried aloud.

...and sat straight up in bed.

She dragged in a breath, shoved her bangs out of her eyes and looked around.

It was still dark. The clock on the dresser said it was three-thirty.

Somehow, she'd kicked the covers off.

What *had* she been dreaming?

Something sexy, that was certain. Her body still hummed with sensual excitement.

With a sigh, she reached down and pulled up the covers. Then she lay her head on her pillow and waited for sleep to claim her again.

* * *

Lee let herself into Derek's condo at nine the next morning. She heard noises in the kitchen and followed the sound. Derek was there, balancing on his good leg as he tried to crack an egg into a bowl.

"What are you doing?"

He looked over his shoulder at her—and he smiled. "You came."

"I said I would, didn't I?" His hair looked wet and he wore different clothes. "I see that you managed to take a bath."

He grunted, his smile fading. "Barely."

She'd stopped at a bakery on her way over. Now, she set the bakery bag on the table and went to stand beside him. "Give me that egg."

He handed it to her.

"Scrambled?" she asked.

"Sounds great. I'll make the coffee." He started to hop down the counter.

She pointed at the table. "Sit down. Now. I'll take care of the coffee."

So he hobbled over to the table and lowered himself into a chair. "Thanks." He scooted another chair around and put his bad ankle up on it, then reached for the bakery bag. "What's in here?"

"Cinnamon rolls. Help yourself."

He took one out, using his left hand, and bit into it. "Mmm. Good."

She watched him chew. "How do you feel this morning, anyway?"

He swallowed. "Like someone really big and mean beat me up and then threw me off a cliff."

"Maybe you should be in bed."

"Lee. It's not *that* serious, and you know it."

"You do have to stay off that ankle, if you want to be able to get around on it anytime soon."

He pointed at the appendage in question. "It's elevated, isn't it?"

"It seems to me you were standing on it just a minute ago."

"Okay, okay. I will stay off it. As much as I can. And if you insist on making the coffee, would you do it now, please?"

"I'd be glad to, if you tell me where it is."

"In that upper cupboard to your left. The filters are in there, too."

Ten minutes later, she poured his coffee and served his eggs.

"You probably ought to call Dr. MacAllister," she suggested as she sat down herself.

"I already did. And I managed to catch him, too. He says not to worry. He'll find people to cover for me for as long as I need to be off my feet."

"I told you it would all work out."

He looked at his outstretched ankle with obvious displeasure. "I hate hobbling around. And I don't like it when someone else does my work for me. I have certain procedures I like to see followed. And no matter how conscientious another doctor is, things tend to become...unorganized."

She licked the frosting off the top of a cinnamon roll. "Well, now. What are you worried about? I'll be there, won't I?"

He grunted at her. "Exactly."

She drew in a breath and straightened her shoulders. "Excuse me, Doctor, but I do believe you just implied that I am not organized."

He lifted his right hand, very carefully, and scratched

his bruised forehead with some effort, due to his immobilized wrist. "Would I imply something like that about you?"

She made a face at him, then got up to fetch the coffeepot.

Naturally he wanted to help with the dishes. She shooed him into the other room with clear instructions to sit down and elevate his ankle. Then she loaded the dishwasher herself. When she joined him, he was seated on the sofa with his leg up on the coffee table, talking on the phone to a towing service. When he hung up, he told her that the Suburban would be towed to a local garage.

Lee left around noon, to visit the gym and buy groceries. And it just seemed natural that she might as well go ahead and pick up something she could cook for Derek's dinner.

They had chicken with saffron rice and a salad. And afterward, she hung around and watched an old movie with him on the Classics channel. It was fun and relaxing.

She supposed Dana had been right. There was no reason in the world why she couldn't be friends with Derek Taylor. In fact, when she found a message from Dana on her machine that night, she called her friend back and told her just that.

Dana said, "Well, I think we're getting somewhere here."

"And where's that?" Lee asked suspiciously.

Dana only laughed and told Lee to have a good time.

During the week that followed, Lee stopped in at Derek's condo after work every day. He always seemed so glad to see her. He'd only been in Honeygrove for six months, after all. He hadn't had time to make many friends.

While she was there, she would run a load of laundry for him, or straighten up the kitchen, or take care of any errands that couldn't wait. And then they'd inevitably end up either ordering takeout or throwing something together from what he had on hand.

True, sometimes she couldn't help thinking how attractive Derek was, couldn't stop the occasional bone-melting fantasy from rising up out of nowhere. But he was such a hunk. Even a friend had a right to a secret daydream or two.

Twice, he got calls from other women while she was there. That didn't bother Lee. His romantic life was his own concern. And he didn't really seem all that interested in those phone calls, anyway. He'd exchange pleasantries for a moment or two and then say he had to go.

On Wednesday night, he told her a little about his childhood. They were sitting on his sofa, side by side. He had his bad ankle propped on the coffee table with a pillow beneath it. He told her that he'd been a skinny, unpopular kid.

She laughed. "Oh, no. Not you. I don't believe it."

He didn't argue, only bent forward and pulled open a drawer in the coffee table. He brought out a stack of old photos and filed through them until he found the one he sought. "Look at that." He gave her the picture, then put the rest back into the drawer and pushed it shut.

Lee stared at the thin, pale-haired boy with the deep-set, haunted looking eyes. The boy appeared to be around eight or nine. He stood in a weed-ridden yard in front of a run-down clapboard house. He looked nothing at all like the man sitting beside her. And yet Lee did recognize him. There was something in those eyes, in the stubborn set to that small, strong jaw.

"Do you have any brothers or sisters?" she asked, as she bent forward to set the picture on the coffee table.

"An older brother. His name's Larry."

"What's he like?"

He gave her a vague answer, and seemed reluctant to say more. She asked about his parents and he told her that they were both dead.

Again, she glanced at the photo that lay faceup on the coffee table. "I still can't believe that's you. You look so…" She sought the right word.

He supplied it. "Scared. And shy. To tell you the truth, I still find myself fighting shyness all the time. I guess it's a lifelong battle, if you're cursed with it." Her disbelief must have shown on her face, because he insisted, "It's true. I'm shy."

"Derek, come on. You want things done your way and you make no secret of it. And you certainly don't seem to have any problem getting dates."

"A naturally shy man can be quite capable of giving instructions. And as for dates, well, *most* women find me attractive. Or they have since high school, anyway, when I started working out and discovered the big secret of getting women to go out with me."

"What big secret?"

"I ask them."

She knew she shouldn't, but she found herself teasing, "You said *most* women find you attractive. Why the emphasis on the word 'most'?"

He laid his left arm along the back of the couch and leaned toward her a little. "You know damn well why. When I asked you, I got nowhere."

"I wouldn't say you *asked*, exactly."

"Okay, I was a jerk."

She just couldn't let it go at that. "And then, for almost two weeks, you tormented me."

"I said I was a jerk. But I've learned my lesson. I'm a very intelligent man, in all modesty."

"Yeah. Right. Modesty. Hah."

"All right. Maybe I'm not exactly the most humble man in town. But I can admit my mistakes and take steps to change my negative behavior. And that's what I've done when it comes to you—just in case you didn't notice."

"I noticed." She spoke more gently. "You're doing very well."

He leaned closer still. "How well is very well?"

All of a sudden, she could have sworn she heard warning buzzers going off somewhere nearby. She slid a few inches toward her end of the sofa—and away from him. "What do you mean?"

He only leaned in even closer than before. "I mean, when are we going to get past this 'just friends' routine?"

"Well, I…um…"

"Yes?"

"Derek. It's not a routine. It's…"

His gaze scanned her face as he finished her sentence for her. "…all you want from me?"

"Well, yes. I mean, I *like* being your friend. And I hope you like being *my* friend."

He stared at her intently for a moment more. Then he retreated to his own side of the couch.

"Derek, I—"

He waved his cast at her. "Never mind. Let it go."

She was only too glad to do that. They sat for a few moments in silence and then she found herself talking about her own childhood. About her unhappy mother and the father she never knew at all.

"He was a doctor, actually," she heard herself confessing. "A plastic surgeon."

"Was? Is he dead now?"

"No. He's still very much alive, as far as I know. I suppose I just enjoy thinking of him in the past tense."

"Why?"

Lee shrugged. "He lives back east now. He's in private practice, repairing the ravages of time on the faces of Philadelphia society matrons. Or at least, he was living in Philadelphia the last my mother heard."

"Your mother's still alive, then?"

Lee nodded. "She lives pretty close. In Salem. She manages a dry cleaners there." That more than answered his question. She should have let it go at that. But she didn't. Her mouth opened and she heard herself volunteering more. "My mother's still carrying a torch for my father. It's pitiful. He *used* her. Used her and then just walked away. And she doesn't even blame him for it. She only thinks she wasn't good enough for him."

Derek asked gently, "How did your mother meet your father?"

Lee had made herself a cup of peppermint tea a little while before. She picked up the cup from the side table and sipped, wondering what had come over her, to reveal so much. Now she wouldn't be able to drop the subject without making a big deal out of her own reluctance to continue.

"Lee? Are you going to answer me?"

Carefully she set the cup down. "My father did his residency here, at Memorial. My grandmother had fallen and broken her hip, and my mom took her into the ER. And there was my father-to-be. My mother thought he was the handsomest man she'd ever seen. And she couldn't believe it when he asked her out. Pretty soon, they were living together. She gave him everything. Love, sex. Total adoration. She always considered him way above her. He came from a well-to-do family, he was a professional. The Murphys never had much, and my mother never went beyond high school."

"So she adored him and they lived together. Then what?"

"She got pregnant—about the time he finished his residency. He immediately took a job at a hospital in San Francisco. He did not invite my mother to go along. She had me and we waited for him to come back. Then she learned that he'd married someone else."

Derek winced. "He does sound like a complete rat."

"When it came to my mother and me, he certainly was."

Derek's left arm still rested on the back of the sofa. He caught a swatch of Lee's hair and gave it a tug. "So you don't trust doctors, is that the message I should be getting here?"

She tipped her head away from him, so that her hair slid free of his gentle grip. "That's not so. I'd trust a good doctor with my life. And I know very well that not all doctors are like the one who fathered me."

"Then what *are* they like?"

Again, the truth just seemed to slip out. "Like Katie's father."

"Katie? That's your friend in the telemetry unit?"

"Right. But I shouldn't have said that."

"Why not?"

"It's Katie's private business."

"Come on. I can keep a confidence. And I'm only trying to understand."

"Understand what?"

"This hang-up you have about doctors."

She shifted uncomfortably against the couch cushions. "It's not a hang-up."

"Tell me about Katie's father."

Their eyes met. Locked. Lee was the first to glance away.

She said, "Katie's father is Dr. Randall Sheppard."

Derek nodded. "I think I've met him once or twice. A pediatrician, right?"

"Yes. Dr. Sheppard is an excellent doctor. Very well respected. I'd even go so far as to say he's beloved, by the children he treats, and by their parents."

"What's so bad about that?"

"Nothing. The problem lies in his relationship with Katie—or more correctly, his *lack* of relationship with her. Because he never had time at all for his daughter. She spent her whole childhood longing for him to notice her. He never did. He's always been too busy playing God for his patients, making himself one hundred percent available to everyone except the members of his own family." She turned to pick up her tea, took another sip and set it down again. "What I'm telling you is that I find most doctors to be dictatorial, career obsessed and emotionally distant, at least from the people they're supposed to be close to."

"And that's how you see me?"

"Yes," she answered immediately, and then, to be fair, had to add, "at least until very recently."

One side of his mouth tipped ruefully upward. "So we're making progress, right?"

She decided she'd better drive the point home once and for all. "Derek, you're a doctor. And I really do believe that makes you a bad emotional risk."

"Well." That rueful smile had vanished. "Thanks."

"In fact, I once made a vow that I'd never marry a doctor." As soon as she said that, she wanted to grab the words and hide them behind her back. What was the matter with her? She just couldn't keep her darn mouth shut tonight.

And naturally, he had to know more. "A *vow?*"

"Yes. A vow."

"Explain."

"Why did I know you were going to say that?"

"Come on. Tell me more."

"Oh, all right. I made a vow. With Katie Sheppard and Dana Rowan.

"Dana Rowan. That would be the administrative nurse for Memorial's OR."

"Right."

"I suppose her father was a heartless M.D., as well."

"No, as a matter of fact, he wasn't. But he did desert her mother when Dana was pretty young."

"Men are so terrible."

"I did not say that."

"But you thought it." She only looked at him. And he prompted, "So you, Katie Sheppard and Dana Rowan made a vow…"

"That's right. On the day we finished nursing school."

"You went to nursing school together?"

"Yes. Up on the hill, U. of O. in Portland. We met in high school and there was something…special, between us, from the very first day. We all wanted to go into the medical field, too."

"But not to be doctors."

"That's right. We all chose nursing. And on the day

that we graduated from college, we swore that we'd never, ever marry M.D.s.''

''Oh, come. This has to be a joke. You didn't actually make a *pledge*.''

''We did. We actually made a pledge.''

''Did you sign it in blood?''

She shot him a tolerant glance. ''No, just plain ink. And it *was* a joke. Sort of.''

''I'm not following.''

''Well, we all knew we'd never be foolish enough to marry M.D.s, and so it was serious in that sense. But mostly, over the years, we've just kidded each other about it.''

''But I thought I heard that your friend Katie's marrying Mike Brennan, and that Dana Rowan is engaged to—''

She cut him off before he could finish rubbing it in. ''Yes. All right.''

''All right, what?'' He looked way too smug.

She was forced to admit, ''As it turns out, Katie and Dana are marrying doctors, after all.''

''So they've both broken this pact of yours.''

''Yes. But I won't.''

He was shaking his head.

''All right,'' she grumbled. ''Whatever you're thinking, say it.''

''Well, what if you end up like those two friends of yours?''

She answered without missing a beat. ''I won't.''

''But speaking hypothetically—''

''No. There's no point in what-ifs here. I won't be marrying an M.D.''

He leaned her way again, and his hand brushed her

shoulder, so lightly it might have been completely un-intentional. "Has one asked?"

"Of course not."

"Then you've got nothing to worry about, have you?"

Thursday night after work, Lee paid a short visit to Lenora and Maria Hirsch. Then she picked up some Chinese food and drove to Derek's. When she got there, she noticed his Suburban, looking like new, parked in the carport beneath the stairs.

"I see you got your wheels back," she said a few minutes later as she bustled around his kitchen getting the table set.

"Yeah." Derek sat at the table, his leg resting on a chair, watching her serve the meal. "A mechanic from the shop where I had it repaired drove it over here this morning."

She poured herself a Diet Coke. "You want a beer?"

"Sounds good. I'll get it." He started to push himself to his feet.

"Stay off that foot."

He dropped back to a sitting position, but couldn't resist arguing, "Lee, it really is getting better."

"I know. Because you've been staying off it." She returned to the fridge and found the beer. "The car looks good as new."

"It should," he said glumly. "It cost enough to fix. I can't wait to get my next insurance bill." She set his drink in front of him as he lowered his voice to a threatening growl. "And all because of a damn raccoon." An evil gleam came into his eyes. "Are you sure you won't change your mind and go get my revenge for me?"

She slid into a chair. "Forget about it."

WELCOME TO THE
CASINO!
Try your luck at the Roulette Wheel ...
Play a hand of Twenty-One!

How to play:

1. Play the Roulette and Twenty-One scratch-off games, as instructed on the

opposite page, to see that you are eligible for FREE BOOKS and a FREE GIFT!

2. Send back the card and you'll receive TWO brand-new Silhouette Special Edition® novels. These books have a cover price of $4.25 each, but they are yours to keep absolutely free.

3. There's no catch. You're under no obligation to buy anything. We charge nothing — ZERO — for your first shipment. And you don't have to make any minimum number of purchases — not even one!

4. The fact is, thousands of readers enjoy receiving books by mail from the Silhouette Reader Service™ before they're available in stores. They like the convenience of home delivery, and they love our discount prices!

5. We hope that after receiving your free books you'll want to remain a subscriber. But the choice is yours — to continue or cancel, any time at all!

So why not take us up on our invitation, with no risk of any kind. You'll be glad you did!

Play Twenty-One For This Exquisite Free Gift!

THIS SURPRISE MYSTERY GIFT COULD BE YOURS FREE WHEN YOU PLAY
TWENTY-ONE

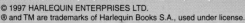

It's fun, and we're giving away *FREE GIFTS* to all players!

PLAY ROULETTE!

Scratch the silver to see where the ball has landed—7 RED or 11 BLACK makes you eligible for TWO FREE romance novels!

PLAY TWENTY-ONE!

Scratch the silver to reveal a winning hand! Congratulations, you have Twenty-One. Return this card promptly and you'll receive a fabulous free mystery gift, along with your free books!

YES!

Please send me all the free Silhouette Special Edition® books and the gift for which I qualify! I understand that I am under no obligation to purchase any books, as explained on the back of this card.

Name (please print clearly)

Address   Apt.#

City   State   Zip

Offer limited to one per household and not valid to current Silhouette Special Edition® subscribers. All orders subject to approval.   PRINTED IN U.S.A.

(U-SIL-SE-12/98)   **235 SDL CKFL**

The Silhouette Reader Service™ — Here's how it works:

Accepting free books places you under no obligation to buy anything. You may keep the books and gift and return the shipping statement marked "cancel." If you do not cancel, about a month later we'll send you 6 additional novels and bill you just $3.57 each, plus 25¢ delivery per book and applicable sales tax, if any.* That's the complete price — and compared to cover prices of $4.25 each — quite a bargain! You may cancel at any time, but if you choose to continue, every month we'll send you 6 more books, which you may either purchase at the discount price...or return to us and cancel your subscription.

*Terms and prices subject to change without notice. Sales tax applicable in N.Y.

If offer card is missing write to: Silhouette Reader Service, 3010 Walden Ave., P.O. Box 1867, Buffalo, NY 14240-995

BUSINESS REPLY MAIL

FIRST-CLASS MAIL   PERMIT NO 717   BUFFALO NY

POSTAGE WILL BE PAID BY ADDRESSEE

SILHOUETTE READER SERVICE
3010 WALDEN AVE
PO BOX 1867
BUFFALO NY 14240-9952

NO POSTAGE
NECESSARY
IF MAILED
IN THE
UNITED STATES

He picked up the moo-shoo pork and poured some onto his plate. "It doesn't matter what you say, I'm still going to get that raccoon."

"Derek." She looked pleadingly across the table at him. "Can we talk about something else. Please?"

He met her eyes for a moment, then shrugged. "Fine. Tell me how you're barely managing without me at the clinic."

She launched into a report of what had happened at work. Then they talked about Lenora and Maria, who were still in the first tough stages of making a new life.

"Lenora says her husband—Otto's his name—tracked her down, at the shelter."

"Was he violent?"

"No, he's apparently in a remorseful phase right now. He cried and begged her to come back to him. He swore it would never happen again."

"Did she believe him?"

"I think she really wished she could. But she's staying where she is."

"That's good, don't you think?"

"I do. And she's really working hard to make a new life. The people at the shelter helped her sign on for a job-training program. She starts this coming Monday, learning to be a supermarket checker at Superserve-Mart—the one just around the corner from Memorial."

"So things are improving for her, then?"

Lee nodded. "And because of the day care program at the shelter, she'll be able to leave Maria in good hands while she's on the job." Lee smiled to herself. "Lenora even suggested that the two of us might go out to lunch sometime, since the store is so close to the clinic." Her smile faded. "It's too bad she's so terrified of her husband. She says all his tears and apologies mean nothing,

that he always feels bad about what he's done—for a
while. But then, eventually, he gets angry again. And
then he becomes violent. She's afraid he'll come after
her when he gets to the violent stage.''

''Well, at least now she's got people around her who
understand the problem. And if he did try to hurt her
again, he'd end up in jail.''

''I keep telling myself that.''

''What does that mean? You don't believe it?''

''I just worry about her. Who knows what a man like
that will do?''

Derek reached out then—across the table. He snared
her hand. She didn't pull away, though his touch always
made her feel things a woman probably shouldn't feel
with just a friend.

''Lenora Hirsch was lucky,'' he said, ''that you saw
the signs. That you followed up on what you saw.
You're one hell of a nurse, Lee.''

Dr. Derek Taylor rarely gave a compliment. So when
he did give one, it meant the world. ''Derek?''

''What?''

''Can I get that on tape?''

On Friday, she made eggplant Parmesan. And she
brought over a thriller she'd rented at a local video store.
Derek produced a nice bottle of Chianti to go with the
eggplant and then made sure to fill their glasses again
when it came time to watch the movie.

The thriller lived up to its billing. It started with an
edge-of-your-seat helicopter chase. Derek seemed very
absorbed in it. He sat in his usual spot, with his ankle
propped on a pillow, sipping his wine, his gaze glued to
the tube.

Lee felt happy and relaxed. The workweek had been

a tough one, but it was over at last. And Derek's ankle was healing well. He planned to be back on the job Monday.

She shot him a grin that he didn't catch, since he was so caught up in the movie. She'd probably never admit it to him, but she'd actually missed his presence at the clinic.

Yes, he was demanding. But he always drove himself just as hard as he did his staff. The residents who were filling in for him did their best, but they couldn't approach his efficiency or his skill. And they were always asking Lee to look things up and track things down for them, which slowed her progress with her own patient load.

Lee smiled, and sipped her wine. She glanced at the movie. The helicopter chase had ended. The hero was being given instructions for a top-secret mission. Lee allowed her glance to drift over to the man beside her again.

He didn't notice. His gaze never left the TV as he leaned forward and set his wine down. Lee did the same, setting her glass beside his, watching him as she performed the action. And then she sat back again, just as he did.

Sometimes, lately, she actually forgot how gorgeous he was. She just thought of him as Derek, her friend. And his spectacular looks didn't even occur to her.

But right now, watching him when he didn't know it, she found she couldn't resist cataloging his various perfections, from the rich gold of his hair to his strong, straight nose to the shape of his left ear.

Lee let out a sigh—only a small one.

Yes. It was a truly fine ear. An ear with good color— not too red and not too pale. An ear that was neither too large nor too small. An ear that heredity had determined would stay close to his head, as perfect in shape as some lovely shell.

Well, of course, every ear was like a shell, but Derek's was an especially fine-looking specimen.

The kind of ear a woman would enjoy kissing.

Lee could almost imagine herself kissing Derek's ear. Right now, it would be so easily accomplished.

She would simply hitch her leg up onto the cushions, laying her arm across the sofa back at the same time. Then she would lean his way enough to run her tongue slowly along the helix—that tempting outer ridge. He might shiver a little, when she did that.

And she would laugh, a whispery sound. And then her tongue would go roaming, following the whorling shell-like pattern. Around once. Twice. Until finally she found her way to the entrance of the dark canal, the external auditory meatus, there at the heart of his outer ear.

Yes. She would taste him there. With her tongue. And then she would pull back enough to take his earlobe—so lightly—between her teeth.

He might even moan then, a very low moan, faint and quickly controlled.

And then he'd turn to her.

He would say her name, on a ragged intake of breath.

He'd reach for her. And she would—

"Lee."

Lee blinked. Swallowed.

Because he *had* turned.

"Lee."

"Uh, yes?"

"You're not watching the movie."

"Well, um, I am. I mean, I was. I mean—"

"Lee, I know that look."

"What look?"

"The one on your face."

"There's no 'look' on my—"

"Lee."

"What?"

"I thought we were friends."

"We are."

"But friends don't lie to each other."

"I wasn't ly—"

And that was as far as she got. Because he reached out with his left hand, cupped the back of her neck and brought her mouth to his.

Chapter Ten

Oh, my goodness, the man knew how to kiss!

He had one leg up on the coffee table and one hand hampered by a cast.

And those little disadvantages didn't even give him pause.

His mouth met hers, coaxing and commanding at the same time. She felt the scratchiness of his end-of-the-day beard and the lovely, contrasting softness of his lips. And she smelled him, warmth and man and the lingering hint of that lovely aftershave he wore. At her nape, his fingers rubbed and caressed—and held her captive at the same time.

A pretty willing captive, actually. She let out a tiny moan and when she did that, her mouth opened just a little. Enough that his tongue slid inside.

She moaned louder. He kissed her more deeply, his tongue roaming the moist recess beyond her now quite definitely parted lips. On the video, someone had started firing a machine gun. The *rat-tat-tat* sound jarred her enough that she froze.

She made herself pull away a fraction. And she whispered with breathless urgency, "Derek—"

And that was all she managed to get out. Because he caught her mouth again with his.

Though gunshots still echoed from the television, she hardly heard them now. She sighed in surrender and kissed him back.

The problem was, it felt so wonderful. She knew she should stop. But she didn't want to stop. All those months and months of fantasies had suddenly exploded into searing, incredible life. It was terribly disorienting.

She raised her hand, thinking—with the tiny part of her mind still capable of reason—that she would push him away. But her hand didn't do what she told it to do. It grasped his hard shoulder and held on, making it all the easier for him.

Easy enough that he didn't need to keep holding her in place with his one good hand. He brought that hand around to the front of her. In a single long, burning stroke, he dragged it down her chest, over the slight curve of her right breast, all the way to her waist. He pushed the hem of her shirt out of his way.

And then he was touching her bare skin, all the while continuing to kiss her so hungrily, drinking from her lips. Her head spun in absolute delight and she went on moaning and clutching his shoulder, making no move at all to get him to stop.

He caressed her, that clever hand of his touching her as if he couldn't get enough of the feel of her, as if he were memorizing the curve of her waist, the shape of each rib beneath skin that felt as if it had somehow managed to catch fire and burn.

Out of control. That was how she felt. As if she were a fire, blazing out of control. It was just like her fantasies.

Well, maybe not just like her fantasies. In her fantasies, Lee always knew what would happen next, since she was the one making them up.

But not now. Oh, not now. Now, anything could happen. Because Derek was here doing this, too.

On the television, a loud engine roared out, and a man and a woman shouted at each other. Lee didn't care.

Derek gathered the hem of her shirt in his fist and pushed at it, impatiently. Before she could really think about what she was doing, Lee had lifted her arms. He thrust the shirt up to her elbows. Somehow, she caught the hem and shimmied it up the rest of the way, pulling it over her head and then tossing it to the carpet by her feet.

Derek made a low, approving kind of sound in his throat. Lee opened her heavy eyes and saw that he was looking at her breasts. His slight smile told her he was pleased, which surprised her somewhat. Really, there wasn't enough there to get all that excited about.

But then again, today she wore her seafoam blue stretch satin bra. It really was a gorgeous piece of lingerie. Evidently Derek liked it as much as she did. The bra had bikinis to match—though since she still had her jeans on, Derek couldn't see them.

Yet.

Lee looked down. Yes, the bra was very pretty.

Even if there wasn't much filling it.

She glanced up again—and met Derek's eyes.

And the full impact of what was happening hit her like a blow to the solar plexus.

"Oh, no," she heard herself whisper.

"Oh, yes," he replied.

She hitched in a tiny gasp and raised both arms to cover herself.

"No." He caught her right wrist with his left hand. "Don't do that. Don't hide."

"Derek, I—"

He let go of her wrist then, roughly, almost tossing it away.

"Derek…"

He growled, angrily, "Don't tell me you want to stop."

I won't! the traitor in the back of her mind cried. I won't tell you that. I don't want to stop. I never, ever want to stop.…

She had to force herself to speak firmly. "I *do*. I want to stop."

On the TV screen, the man and the woman were shouting again. Derek leaned forward and snatched the remote off the coffee table. He pointed it at the television and the screen went blank. He tossed the remote back down and turned to her again. His jaw was clenched, his fine mouth a grim line.

Quickly Lee scooped up her shirt from the floor, yanked it on over her head and smoothed it down to cover herself. He watched her, not moving, looking terribly annoyed.

Finally she couldn't bear the heavy silence for another second more. "Derek, listen. I am sorry. I didn't mean for this to happen."

He let out a poignant expletive and then he challenged, "I'm not sorry. Not in the least. I'm sick of this stupid game we've been playing. And I think it's about time that it stopped.''

"Game?" she murmured weakly. "What do you mean, game?"

"You know damn well what I mean." Now his mouth had curled into a snarl. "I mean the 'let's be friends' game.''

"It's not a—''

"Don't," he commanded. "Do not try to tell me that all you want from me is friendship. I've seen the way you look at me, the way you've looked at me for months now. Are you going to try to tell me that you look at every man that way?''

"I—''

"Just say it. If it's true, then say it. Do you look at other men that way?''

She closed her eyes, and turned her head away.

But he caught her chin, made her face him. "Do you?''

She shoved at his hand. He let go. And then, since she knew she could no longer evade this particular question, she met his eyes straight on. "No. I don't look at other men the same way I look at you.''

"You want me.''

She nodded.

"I think the least you can do, at this point, is to say it out loud.''

"Fine. All right. I want you.''

"Exactly. And I want you. And we're both single. Hell, we even *like* each other. There is no damn reason in the world why we shouldn't make love.''

"Yes, there is. There are several reasons, as a matter of fact.''

"Name them.''

"We have to work together."

"At this point, that's completely irrelevant."

"It is *not* irrelevant. One way or another, if we became intimate, it would end up affecting our working relationship."

"Lee. The fact that you want me and I want you has already affected our work as much as it's going to. It's too late to go back on that score, I'm afraid."

"No, it's—"

"At this point, it's a nonreason, Lee."

"It is not. Look at the way you've treated me already. You were absolutely insufferable to me. You made my working life hell for almost two weeks."

"How many times do I have to tell you I know I was a jerk? I was totally in the wrong. And I won't be behaving that way again."

"You say that, but—"

"You've run this particular *reason* into the ground. Is that because you have no others?"

"Derek. Please. You don't want an...intimate relationship with someone like me."

"Oh, here we go. First, you tell me how I'm going to be treating you at work. And now you tell me what I don't want."

"All right, fine. *I* don't want that kind of relationship with you. I'm sure to take it more seriously than you would. And I'd get hurt in the end."

"You have no way of knowing the outcome of this. No way in the world."

"Oh, come on. All indications point to me getting my heart broken if I get involved with someone like you."

"What damn indications?"

"Derek, your girlfriends are still calling here."

"And I say 'how are you' and hang up. And besides,

you and I are supposed to be just *friends*, remember? Why shouldn't I date other women?''

"No reason. No reason in the world. I accept the fact that you like to date a lot of women. I just don't want to be one of them.''

He forked his right hand back through his hair, wincing at the slight pressure on his bad wrist. "Lee. Why are we arguing about this damn other woman thing? I don't *care* about any other woman. I could give you my word—and easily keep it—that as long as you and I are together, you would be the only one.''

She closed her eyes, took in a breath and let it out very slowly. Then she looked at him once more. "Look. Can we please just let this go?''

"No. I want you to run this whole thing down for me. I want to know the rest of the reasons you think we can't be more than friends.''

She sighed again. "Derek…''

"What does that sigh mean? Have you run out of reasons? Well, let me help you. Let's see. We've covered how badly I treated you at work and all those women I've dated that I don't even want to see anymore. What's left? Oh, I know. We're down to the truly ridiculous now, down to the ultimate in flawed logic. Your daddy was a bad man. And your daddy was a doctor. Therefore, all doctors are bad men.''

"Derek, it is not that simple.''

"It is. Just look at your own friends. They made that absurd never-marry-a-doctor pledge with you. And they've both had the good sense to break it. And hell, I'm not even asking for *marriage* from you. I'm only asking you to quit pretending that we're nothing more than friends.''

She longed for him to understand. "Please. I just...I really don't think I can do that."

He must have picked up on her honest confusion, because his hard expression eased a little. He spoke more softly. "Lee. You're blaming an entire profession for the behavior of one man."

"I don't think so. I've known a lot of doctors, and they do tend to be—"

"I know, I know. You've said it all before." He sounded weary. She dared to hope he might give up and let her be. But he didn't. "Let me ask you something."

She eyed him warily. "What?"

"Have you ever been married?"

She frowned, not sure why he'd ask such a thing—and wishing he hadn't.

"Just answer me. Have you?"

"No."

"How many really serious relationships with men have you had?"

Now, she felt uncomfortable looking in his eyes at all. She turned her gaze to the dark TV. "I've dated."

"That's no answer."

"What are you getting at?"

"Lee. Are you a virgin?"

She shot him a glance, then stared at the blank screen again. "Why are you asking me this?"

"I'm right, aren't I? You've never had sex with a man."

She surged to her feet, realized how foolish she looked and dropped back to the couch once more.

He was relentless, though he spoke so very carefully. "Lee, you're what? Thirty years old?" He waited. She gave him a tight nod, though she still couldn't bear to look him in the eye. He pressed on. "All right, you're thirty. You've never been married—or even come close to commitment with a man. You haven't let down your guard enough to have sex even once. Maybe it's more than just doctors you're afraid to get near. Maybe your father's desertion has left you afraid of *all* men. Do you think maybe that's possible?''

She stared numbly at the TV.

"Lee. Come on, look at me."

Reluctantly she turned his way. And then she made herself smile, though her mouth wouldn't stop trembling. "You're right," she whispered. "You're right about all of it. I don't want to take a chance on getting hurt by a man. And especially not a man like you. As a friend, I can deal with you. I...I like you so much, as a friend. But as far as any more..." Her darn lip kept quivering. She bit the inside it of it, to make it stop. "Oh, Derek, everything about you is all wrong for me."

Those blue eyes seemed to drill right through her. "Why, Lee?"

"We're just...so different."

"No, I don't think so. Not really."

"Yes, we are."

"No. We're not."

"Derek. Look in a mirror. You're one of those golden, perfect people that the rest of us stare at with envy— and longing. Do you know how all the nurses at Memorial drool over you? And then look at me. Nobody drools over me—unless they happen to be teething, I mean."

He looked irritated. "This is absurd."

"No, it's the truth. You're just...out of my league in every single way."

"I am not."

"Now, who's the one that's lying?" She stood again,

and this time, when she got upright, she stayed on her feet.

"Lee—"

"No. We just…we don't agree on this, Derek. And we're not going to get anywhere by debating it to death."

He gazed up at her. She hadn't the faintest idea what he might be thinking. He didn't seem angry—more like troubled. Or hurt. "You're leaving." It was a prediction, not a question.

"Yes."

He lifted his left hand to gesture at the TV. "Take your video with you."

She thought of how much he'd seemed to be enjoying the movie, until he'd turned and caught her staring at him. "I could leave it, if you—"

"Take it." The words came out on a growl. He drew in a slow breath, and spoke more gently. "Please."

She went to the VCR and ejected the cassette, then slipped the thing into its plastic sleeve. That accomplished, she picked up her purse and fumbled around in it until she found the key he'd told her to keep last Saturday night.

He watched her set it on top of the TV. Then he actually smiled—a gorgeous, rueful, Dr. Devastating smile. "Thank you. For everything, this week. You were terrific."

Her throat felt tight. "Um. You're welcome." She headed for the door.

Just before she reached it, he said her name. She turned back to him. He said, "If you change your mind, you know where to find me."

"I won't."

He only shrugged.

She turned again and kept going until she'd walked out the door.

Chapter Eleven

The weekend was awful.

Lee tried to keep her mind off thoughts of Derek. She picked up her bridesmaid's dress at the bridal boutique and visited Lenora and Maria.

And she tried not to obsess about work on Monday, tried not to long for the sight of Derek—at the same time as she dreaded the thought of having to spend her working day at his side.

No matter how it turned out, it would have to be difficult.

What if he began treating her harshly again? She imagined all kinds of slights and cruel attacks. She worried that she would be forced to go to Dr. MacAllister and complain, after all.

But then she would remember how he'd sworn he would change. She would recall the week of friendship they'd shared, all the things he'd told her about his childhood, about himself. She would remember the way he'd smiled at her and thanked her for taking care of him, in spite of the fact that she'd just rejected his advances and told him she could never be any more than his friend.

Thinking of that, of their week of friendship, she knew in her heart that he wouldn't go back to harassing her again.

But it didn't really matter. However he treated her, working with him was going to be difficult.

When she arrived on Monday morning, Jack told her that Dr. Taylor was expected in at last. The two residents had been relieved of their temporary clinic assignments.

"Maybe things'll get back to normal around here, now," Jack said.

Lee looked at him doubtfully. "Normal. What's that?"

Jack chuckled. "Good question."

When Derek made his appearance, Lee was standing at the front desk scanning the charts that had come up from records for the day. She heard the door to the waiting room close and she knew, though she couldn't see at first from where she stood, that it would be Derek.

She heard footsteps—slightly halting ones. And then he came into view, walking tall and proud without a cane or crutches, hardly limping at all.

"Welcome back, Dr. Taylor," Jack said.

Fabulous teeth gleamed. "It's good to be back." He held up his cast. "Slightly handicapped, but we'll work around it."

"You bet," said Jack.

The blue gaze swung her way. "Lee." He was still smiling. Cordially. Pleasantly. *Warmly* even. "How was your weekend?"

She forced air through ridiculously stiff vocal cords. "Uh. Fine. It was fine."

"Well, good." He gave a brief, the-doctor-approves kind of nod and then went down the hall toward his office, pausing at the nurses' station to exchange greetings with both Terry and Paul on the way.

The day that followed could almost have been called uneventful. Yes, one of the geriatric patients wandered out to the waiting room without remembering to put her clothes back on. Also, a three-year-old boy got away from his mother, causing a minor panic until they found him crouched in a corner of the copy room. And, as always, they got behind on the patient load around two and didn't get back on schedule until after four.

But such incidents were par for the course. As a whole, the clinic ran that day like a well-oiled machine. Everyone mentioned more than once how good it was to have Dr. Taylor back.

It was the same on Tuesday. And Wednesday, too.

Lee was absolutely miserable.

Derek treated her with respect and a strictly professional friendliness. He was calm and collected and unerringly fair. He never shot her a single hard look for the way she indulged her patients; he said not a word about her sticky notes or the occasional chart that somehow found its way into her area of the nurses' station.

Lee should have been content. She knew it. He had kept his word to her. He wasn't letting the things that had happened between them affect their working relationship in the least.

Everything had turned out for the best.

And still, she was miserable.

She spent every day at his side—and yet she missed him as if she never saw him at all.

On Thursday, just doing his job, he saved the life of an eight-year-old girl.

The mother had brought her in thinking it was some kind of flu. The child felt shaky, craved liquids and candy, was cranky and hard to manage. Jack had the mother filling out the history form when the little girl suddenly went completely out of control, falling to the floor, making loud nonsense noises, twitching and gasping like someone in the throes of an epileptic seizure.

Everyone came running, but no one could get her settled down enough even to take her vitals.

That was where Derek stepped in. He scooped the moaning, twitching little body against his broad chest, wincing a little as her slight weight put pressure on his bad wrist. She vomited all over him. Gently he smoothed her hair away from her small, sweating face. He looked up, and into Lee's eyes. "Come on." He turned for the examining rooms, Lee right behind.

Between them, he and Lee managed to get a blood pressure reading, heart rate and temperature.

At one point, as they worked over the thin body with fierce and mutual concentration, Derek had looked up. "Do you smell it?"

The strongest odor in the room right then was the vomit splattered all over his shirt and lab coat. It was hard to get beyond that.

"Her breath," Derek instructed.

Lee brought her head down close to the child's mouth. Right then, the child exhaled strongly. And Lee caught it: that sweet, fruity smell, of a body exuding the sugar it couldn't absorb.

They said it in unison: "DKA." Diabetes ketoacidosis.

"Let's get a normal saline going," Derek said then.

"And oxygen. Then call for a gurney. We'll get her over to ER."

They wheeled her down the hospital halls together. She was unconscious by then.

Results from the crash lab showed glucose at 800. But of course, by that time, they already had her on an insulin drip.

The child woke up fifteen minutes later. She stared at Derek. He smiled. And, very faintly, she smiled back.

Lee returned to the clinic and the rest of their patients, while Derek lagged behind to study the lab results more thoroughly. When he came back himself, he went into his office, got himself a fresh shirt and a clean lab coat and disappeared into the staff rest room.

A few minutes later, he emerged wearing the clean shirt and lab coat, with the dirty laundry clutched in his left fist. Lee saw him come out and couldn't help thinking of the way the child had smiled at him, with such shy, exhausted trust. She didn't realize she was staring at him until he caught her eye and winked at her.

Lee shook herself. She lifted an eyebrow.

He took her meaning and nodded. She read the nod as if he'd spoken aloud. The little girl would pull through.

It occurred to her that sometimes, lately, they didn't even have to talk. A lift of an eyebrow, a gesture, the slightest movement of a hand would do to say all that needed to be said.

They both moved on to the next order of business.

That night, Lee dreamed of him. She dreamed he came to her bed and made love to her.

She dreamed it was wonderful.

And in the morning, when she woke, she remembered all of it.

In detail.

She picked up the phone beside her bed. And set it back down quickly, before she actually let herself punch out his number.

That day, Friday, the fantasies came back.

They all centered around the simplest thing. In them, she would approach him. She would say, "I was wrong," or "Give me another chance," or "Let's start again. Please."

And each time, he would slowly extend his hand.

Twice, he caught her staring, in the middle of one of those fantasies.

Both times he inquired, "Something the matter, Lee?"

Of course, he knew. She could see it in his eyes.

And she almost believed that if she said, "Yes, I'd like you to make love to me, please," he would have instantly replied, "Fine," and then added without missing a beat, "But right now, would you take the vitals on the congestive heart failure in Room 1?"

She'd say, "Of course." They'd go right back to working with the eerie mutual precision they seemed to have developed lately. And then, when the day was over, she would go home with him.

But in reality, all she said was, "Nothing's the matter. Nothing at all."

And he simply shrugged and turned away.

At a little after three, Lenora Hirsch came flying into the clinic as if the devil himself was after her.

Lee was seated at her computer in the nurses' station when she heard Lenora speaking frantically to Jack. "Lee. Where's Lee? I need to see Lee...."

Lee shot to her feet and ran toward the other woman's voice. The minute Lenora spotted her, she burst into terrified tears. "Oh, Lee. You have to help me. Otto's following me. He's been following me all day. He was outside the market when I got off my shift."

Lee reached Lenora. "Shh. Settle down. It's all right—"

Lenora grabbed Lee and held on tight. "Lee, he won't leave me alone. I know how he is. He's not sorry anymore. Now, he's going to try to—"

Right then, from the waiting room behind them, someone let out a loud gasp. And a woman screamed.

At the same time, a man shouted, "My God. He's got a gun!"

Chapter Twelve

The man standing just inside the waiting room door was overweight and balding. He wore a short-sleeved white business shirt, rumpled and stained with sweat at the armpits. His slacks were blue and his shoes were brown wing tips. He'd pulled his red-and-white striped tie loose and undone the top two buttons of his shirt.

The silver gun in his hand wasn't very big. But it looked pretty deadly to Lee.

He pointed it at Lenora. "Come on, Lenora. We need to have a little talk. Right now."

Lenora cowered against Lee.

Lee said, "Mr. Hirsch—"

That was as far as she got. Otto Hirsch swung the gun on her. "You shut up, you bitch. You've done enough. I ought to—"

"Put the gun down."

It was Derek. His voice came from behind Lee. Lee

didn't turn to glance at him. She kept her eyes forward—on Otto Hirsch and his little silver gun.

Otto Hirsch was clearly a man at the frayed end of a short emotional rope. Dark circles ringed his eyes. His skin had a gray cast. Sweat beaded on his upper lip and trickled down the side of his face. And the hand that held the gun was shaking.

"Put it down," Derek said again.

Hirsch shook his head. With his free hand, he wiped his brow, then the beads of sweat on his upper lip. "That's my wife and this is a family matter. Lenora, you come on now. I've got a few things to say to you and I—"

Lenora actually spoke up then. "No." Her voice trembled, but Lee could hear the stark determination in it. "I'm not going with you, Otto. I'm not going with you ever again."

"Don't talk back to me." The gun in Hirsch's hand shook even harder than before. "Don't you ever, ever talk back to me." He pointed the thing, as best he could, at Lenora's heart.

And then Derek stepped forward.

Lee breathed the word, "No..." but Derek paid no attention to her. He put himself between Lee, Lenora—and Otto Hirsch's little silver gun.

"Get out of the way," Hirsch growled. "Or I'll shoot you first."

"I don't think so," said Derek. And he started walking—right toward the gun Hirsch held in his hand. He didn't stop until the short, silver barrel touched his chest. And then, very gently, he lifted his good hand and wrapped his fingers around the barrel. "Let go," he said. "Just let go now. Give yourself a chance for a life someday."

"No. No, I can't do that. That's my wife over there."

"Not anymore. It's over. Let go."

"I can't."

"You can."

"No…"

"Yes."

Sweat ran into Hirsch's eyes. It seemed to Lee that no one—not a single patient in the waiting room, not herself, Lenora, Jack, or Terry, so much as breathed at that moment.

"Let it go," Derek said, so softly, one more time.

Lee couldn't look. She closed her eyes. She waited for the sound of that gun going off.

It didn't come.

Lee dared to look again.

And could hardly believe the evidence of her own eyes.

Otto Hirsch had let go.

Hospital security arrived in minutes. They took Hirsch away. Not long after that, two representatives of the Honeygrove Police Department appeared. As soon as they'd taken statements from everyone. Lee drove the shaken Lenora back to the shelter.

Miraculously, by the time Lee returned to the clinic, things seemed to have gone right back to business as usual.

"We're even on schedule, more or less," Terry announced. "Can you believe it?"

Lee gave her a quelling look. Anyone who worked in the medical field could tell you: never mention things like being on schedule or how quiet it is. Disasters inevitably occur if you do. "I'll pretend I didn't hear that."

Terry chuckled. "Sorry. I take it back."

Lee kept thinking about Derek, kept seeing him in her mind's eye stepping right up to Otto Hirsch's little silver gun. "Where is Dr. Taylor?"

"With a patient. You want me to—"

"No. I'll catch him later."

At five, when things seemed to actually be winding down, Lee gathered all her courage and went to knock on Derek's door, behind which he'd vanished about twenty minutes before.

He didn't answer.

Terry walked by. Lee jumped back from the door as if she'd been caught doing something she shouldn't. "I was just—"

Terry shrugged. "He left already."

"He did? But I thought—?"

"Uh-uh. He's gone." Terry kept walking, sending the rest back over her shoulder as she went. "Took off to do rounds about ten minutes ago. Said he'd see us on Monday."

"Monday?" Lee called after her. "Are you sure?"

Terry called back, "That's what he said."

Lee left the hospital at five forty-five. Overhead, the sky was silvery-gray. There was rain on the way. Her car just seemed to point itself in the direction of Derek's condo and didn't stop until it got there. She pulled into the guest parking area, not too far from the steps that led up to his front door. Jumping right out, she headed for the stairs and took them two at a time, knowing she didn't dare slow down or she might never let herself get there.

She rang his doorbell.

He didn't answer.

She rang again.

Nothing. A pair of long, skinny windows flanked the door, but both had curtains over them, so she couldn't see if he was in there. And really, she knew he'd gone somewhere. He would have answered if he was inside—even if only to tell her to get lost.

Lee turned and ran down the stairs, pausing to glance at his parking space before she got into her car. It was empty.

She climbed in her car and slammed the door and felt awful. She kept thinking of blondes. Beautiful blondes. Of how he was probably out with one right now.

No reason he shouldn't be.

In fact, there was every reason in the world that he *should*. A man liked to go out with a beautiful woman. Especially if the woman said yes now and then.

Lee started up the car and drove home. She watered her philodendron and opened the refrigerator and looked at the chicken she'd planned to skin and broil that night. The phone rang just as she was carrying the bird to the counter.

It was Dana. "Hi. Just checking in. What are you up to?"

"Getting ready to broil a chicken."

"I heard about the excitement at the clinic today. Apparently Dr. Taylor was a hero."

"Yes. He was."

"So tell me, how's your love life?"

Lee leaned against the counter and began wrapping the phone cord around her index finger. "If there's one thing I admire most about you, it's your subtlety."

"Come on. Katie and I have left you alone for almost two weeks. But now I can't stand it anymore. How is it going with him?"

Lee had no idea where to begin, so she only sighed

and continued looping the cord around her finger until she'd covered the entire digit.

"Hmm," Dana said. "Sounds like the friendship thing pretty much ran its course."

Lee pulled her finger free of the cord. "You could say that."

"Are you…ready for the next step?"

Lee turned around and studied the fryer she was about to dismember. "Even if I was, it wouldn't matter. He's not home. Probably out with some beautiful blonde or other."

"Wrong."

Lee stood up straighter. "How would you know?"

"Because I know where he is."

Lee understood then. "Blue Moon Lake."

"Very good. My future father-in-law just happened to mention this afternoon that Dr. Taylor was giving the cabin another try."

Lee smiled, thinking of a certain raccoon—and then she frowned. "Maybe he took someone with him."

Dana let out a ladylike snort. "Oh, come on. Have a little faith."

"In what?"

"Him. Yourself."

Lee began wrapping the phone cord again. "You're a fine one to talk about faith." She referred to how Dana had had no faith at all in Trevor, back a couple of months before.

Dana said, "We're not talking about me right now— and besides, I got smart. I got past my fears."

So you think I should go up there? Just get in my car and—"

"Lee."

"What?"

"Do you *want* to go up there?"

She sucked in a big breath. "Yes."

"Then put the chicken back in the fridge, dig that old fishing pole of yours out of the hall closet and get moving."

It was twilight when Lee got to the cabin. Overhead, the clouds kept growing thicker, a blanket of gray, blotting out the still-dim stars. The first drops of rain had spotted her windshield.

She parked her car next to Derek's Suburban, in the clear space below the deck. Then she grabbed her small bag from the back seat and ran up the plank stairs.

No one answered her knock. She tried the door. It was open. She called, "Derek?" No answer. She stuck her head in, called his name again and then cautiously entered, dropping her bag next to the door.

She made a quick tour of the place. He wasn't there. He must have taken his pole down to the lake. The fish would be biting about now.

Since she felt uncomfortable at the idea of waiting there in the cabin for him, she wandered back outside and stood at the deck railing, looking off toward the lake that gleamed through the pines. The wind came up, just a gust of it, and then quickly died to nothing.

Lee shivered a little and wrapped her arms around herself as the random drops of rain began to fall more steadily, and ever more thickly, but without the fanfare of thunder and lightning. It was a true Oregon rain, the kind that seemed as if it might just go on forever, not dramatic at all, merely continuous. The drops drummed the deck and whispered in the tree branches. The world looked misty and dim.

Lee just stood there, hugging herself, staring off toward the lake. The water drenched her hair and her T-shirt. It ran in little streams down her nose and over her cheeks. It made rivulets down her neck and arms.

She tipped her head up and caught some in her mouth. It tasted fresh and misty, like the air. And then, when she looked out over the lake again, she saw him. He seemed to materialize out of the misty rain, carrying a fishing pole and one of those old-fashioned woven tackle baskets with the hole in the top where you can drop the fish inside.

He saw her car first. And then his gold head—drenched, like hers—shot up. His eyes found her, waiting there at the railing above him. For a moment, he froze, staring, the rain drumming down, thick and cold, a silvery veil between them.

And then he was walking fast, toward the stairs, up them, across the planks of the deck to her side. He held his dismantled pole and the tackle box in his good left hand and he simply stood there, the rain pouring down on him, looking at her.

"You're soaking wet," he finally said.

"So are you."

"Did you bring a fishing pole?"

"Mmm-hmm. It's in the trunk of my car." She watched the rain drip off his sculpted nose. He still had that bruise, on his temple, from the fall down the stairs. The cut over his eye was almost healed. She wanted to reach up and touch it. But she didn't quite dare. "You took a big chance today, with Otto Hirsch."

"It was a calculated risk."

"A dangerous one."

"But necessary—and is that why you came, to talk about Otto Hirsch?"

"No."

"Good."

They looked at each other some more. Lee knew they should go inside, but she felt no desire to move. "Did you catch anything?"

He frowned at her.

"I mean fish. Did you catch any fish?"

"Trout. Four nice-size ones. I would have caught more. But the rain started really coming down. I gave up."

"Understandable."

"You like trout?"

"I love trout."

"I had seven more. Two weekends ago. But they spoiled, because I forgot all about them and left them here, after my little run-in with that damn raccoon. Today, when I got here, I had to throw them away."

"That's too bad."

"I still want to kill that rodent."

"A raccoon is not a rodent and you know it."

"I don't care what it is. I just want to get my hands on it."

"Derek, you're never going to see that animal again."

"If it's lucky, I won't."

"Did you...bring your rifle?"

He grinned then. "Can you believe it? I forgot it."

She carefully suppressed her own grin of relief.

He held up the tackle box. "We can have these for dinner.... Did you have dinner?"

She shook her head.

"Or breakfast?" He lifted both eyebrows. "There is going to be breakfast, right?"

"I'd like that."

They stood there for another few seconds, under the

shimmering veil of the rain, staring at each other. At last, he suggested, "We should go inside."

She pushed the soaked hair from her eyes with a hand that hardly shook at all. "Yes. All right. Let's go inside."

Chapter Thirteen

Once he'd led her inside, Derek kept walking, out to the back porch. Lee felt strange trailing after him, so she waited, standing all at loose ends, near the cold potbellied stove in the main room.

He came back a few seconds later, minus the fishing gear. He flipped on the kitchen area light and a standing lamp in a corner, one that had a shade painted with snowcapped peaks, a lake and leaping trout. He studied her face for a moment, then his gaze strayed downward, to her breasts. She glanced down, too. Through her wet T-shirt, she could see her bra. It was red-and-white striped. Shyly she looked up at him again.

He gave her a crooked grin. "We need towels, I think."

Since she was making a puddle on the floor, she didn't argue. "A towel would be great."

He disappeared again, this time into the bedroom, and

came back with a pair of towels. He handed one to her. She rubbed herself down with it, blotting up the worst of the water, as he did the same with the other towel.

"I could build a fire," he said after a minute. "There's plenty of wood on the back porch."

The room was cool; the towel had helped, but still her hair and clothes remained wet. "A fire sounds—" she stopped herself before she said the word *great* for the second time "—nice. Very nice."

He turned and headed for the back porch again.

Five minutes later, the window in the stove glowed red as the fire caught.

Derek shut the stove door and gestured at the big, worn couch. "Sit down."

She sat.

"Do you want a blanket?"

"No. I think the fire will be enough."

He actually seemed to be rocking uncomfortably on his heels. "I, uh, should clean those fish I caught."

"I'll help." She shot to a standing position.

"No. Relax. I can handle it."

She sank back to the couch as he disappeared for the fourth time. Lee sat and stared at the stove, thinking that this wasn't exactly how she'd expected things to go. He was Dr. Devastating, after all, and presumably quite adept at seducing women. She'd imagined that he'd sweep her right off her feet, carry her to the bedroom and proceed, with his expert kisses and caresses, to set her whole body aflame.

Right now, the only thing flaming was the wood in the stove.

Slowly the warmth filled the room. By the time Derek

reappeared, carrying a platter with four trout on it, Lee
was no longer shivering.

"Hungry?" he asked.

She was too nervous to be hungry, but she decided
not to tell him that. She gulped and nodded. "Sure."

In the refrigerator, he had a bottle of Chardonnay and
the makings of a salad. Lee opened the wine and put the
salad together, while Derek breaded and fried the fish
on the cabin's ancient electric range. They didn't talk
much as they prepared the meal. Lee watched him from
the corner of her eye, noticing how well his wrist seemed
to be healing. He used his hand almost as if it didn't
pain him at all now. And of course, the plastic cast was
removable. He even took it off during the messy fish-
breading process, and then clasped it back in place when
it came time to throw the fish into the pan.

As they worked, Lee began to get the oddest feeling
that they had simply picked up their friendship where it
had left off. That he didn't intend to make love with her
at all.

The meal was a silent one. Lee drank a little more
wine than she should have, feeling more edgy by the
second, wondering what was going to happen next.
When the food was gone, they cleaned up. By then, it
was after ten.

They retired with the last of the wine to the sofa in
front of the potbellied stove. Outside on the roof, the
rain still drummed—a steady, whispery presence, like
some huge, shy animal, purring deep in its massive
throat.

Lee slipped off her shoes and gathered her legs to the
side. Staring at the fire in the stove, she sipped her wine.

"Lee?"

"Mmm?"

He reached over and took her wineglass from her fingers. She dared to meet his eyes. They gleamed now like the lake in the misty rain. No man with only friendship on his mind looked at a woman the way he was looking at her. The lead ball of disappointment that had formed in her stomach turned into a thousand fluttering moths of pure apprehension.

He asked, "Do you think maybe you've had enough?"

"Enough?"

"Wine."

She let out a small, breathy laugh. "I guess I have." She watched him set her glass next to his, on the small table at his end of the couch.

He turned back to her, drawing the leg nearest hers up onto the sofa. "You're nervous."

No sense in denying it. That breathy laugh had already betrayed her. She nodded.

A smile teased at his beautiful mouth. "Me, too."

"No, you're not. You *can't* be." The words kind of popped out of her, and then she couldn't stop herself from explaining them. "I mean, you do this sort of thing all the time, don't you?" She put her hand over her mouth. "Oh, why did I say that?"

He didn't look upset. "Blame it on the wine—and I meant what I said. I'm nervous, too."

"Really?"

"Really." He reached out his hand, the one with the cast on it, and slid his finger under the hem of her T-shirt. She held back a gasp. He asked softly, "What changed your mind?"

She looked down as he idly ran his fingers back and forth along the shirt hem. "A hundred things."

"I hope you're not going to tell me it's gratitude."

"Gratitude?"

"For this afternoon. For the way I stepped in with Otto Hirsch."

She pondered that idea—though it wasn't easy to think right then. The man would not stop fiddling with the hem of her shirt. "I *am* grateful. And you were wonderful. But that's not why I'm here."

"It's not?"

"Uh-uh."

"Then why?"

"Mostly, I...missed you, I guess you could say."

His eyes looked so soft. Soft and tender. "You saw me every day."

"Still, I missed you. And, from the absolutely fair and professional way you've behaved all week, I've come to accept the fact that you were right."

He instantly agreed with that. "Well, of course I was." And then he frowned a little. "What was I right about, exactly?"

"About how it doesn't...it wouldn't have to interfere with our working relationship. To have an affair."

"Is that what this is going to be?" His voice had gone as soft as his eyes. "An affair?"

She put on a sheepish expression. "Well, I really was hoping for a little more than a one-night stand, if you don't mind."

He chuckled. "I see."

Boldly she inquired, "So, what do you say? Will it be an affair?"

He nodded decisively. "All right. An affair. That's what we'll call it."

She wanted to ask, "And how long is this affair going to last, do you think?" But she knew how insecure and inexperienced that would sound. She'd already confessed her virginity to him. No point in proving it with every word she said. She kept her mouth resolutely shut.

He looked down at the hem of her shirt, still held so lightly between his fingers, and then back up at her. "Since we're having an affair now, would you mind taking this shirt off?"

Her pulse was practically galloping. "I...sure." Carefully she took the hem of the shirt from him and pulled the thing up, over her head and off.

The moment was a truly strange one. There she sat, Lee Murphy, nurse practitioner, minus her shirt, smiling rather shakily at Dr. Devastating. Her too-small breasts pointed right at him beneath the skimpy cover of her bra.

He said, "I knew it. Candy canes."

She looked down at her peppermint-striped bra.

He said, "I could see your bra. Earlier. When your shirt was wet."

She met his eyes again. "I like...interesting underwear."

"I noticed." He reached out, and touched the side of her face. "I'm glad you drove up here."

All her nerves seemed to be humming, purring, drumming like the rain on the roof overhead. "Me, too."

"Let's go to the bedroom."

"All right."

She stood, and so did he. He took her hand and they turned for the other room.

They got about two steps before they heard the clanging sound.

Both of them froze. "What was that?" Lee asked in a whisper.

"The garbage cans." Derek was scowling. "That damn raccoon. It's in the garbage cans down by the side of the house. It's after those spoiled fish." He turned for the back porch door.

Logically, since he'd failed to bring that rifle of his, there wasn't much he could do but scare the creature away. Still, Lee didn't like the look in his eyes. She held on tight to his hand. "Derek. No."

Outside, there was more clanging. A clattering sound. And then silence.

He tried to yank free of her grip. "Lee. Let go."

"Derek," she reasoned desperately, "you can't be sure it's that raccoon."

"I'm sure."

"What if it's...a bear?"

"It's not. There are no bears around here and you know it."

"But it could be. A big, hungry brown bear. With sharp teeth and long claws...."

"It's a damn raccoon, Lee. Let go of my hand."

"Oh, please. Stay here."

"I want that animal dead."

"Derek, please..."

"Shh." He listened. There was no sound but the rain.

"Derek." She took the hand she'd refused to release and wrapped it around her bare waist. Instinctively that hand took hold. His blue eyes narrowed—and then he yanked her close.

He spoke right into her upturned face, his breath fanning warm across her cheek. "What are you up to?"

She put her hands on his chest—catching his shirt in her fists so he couldn't escape without exerting great effort. "Distracting you."

He closed his eyes, and looked very put-upon. "I knew it."

"Leave the raccoon alone," she whispered. "Please?"

His hand was moving, rubbing up and down her back. "If I do…"

"Yes?"

"Are you going to make it worth my while?"

Even though she didn't want him to hurt the raccoon, she felt guilty about making promises she had no idea how to keep. "As you know, I am not terribly experienced at this."

"You're experienced."

"No. I told you, I'm—"

"Lee." His voice was like a caress, soft and arousing, full of promise and heat. "I've watched you. While you were watching me. I'm not talking about what you've actually done. I'm talking about what you've *thought* about doing." He nuzzled her hair. "I believe you have an extremely active fantasy life."

She licked her lips, and sighed. "You do?"

"Absolute—"

Right then, more banging sounds came from outside. Something hit the ground and rolled—probably one of the trash cans. Derek stiffened and let out a sort of low growl.

Lee slipped her arms up and around his neck. "Kiss me."

He growled again. "This isn't fair."

"Come on, Derek. Kiss me, please…."

With a muttered curse, he covered her mouth with his.

Chapter Fourteen

Lovely. His mouth on hers felt absolutely lovely.

Lee let out a small, gleeful cry and parted her lips. His tongue came inside. She sucked on it eagerly.

He yanked her closer and moaned into her mouth. At her bare back, his left hand started moving. It swept in one long caress, from the curve of her waist, up to her nape and back down again—all the way down, over the roundness of her bottom and then under, lifting her, pulling her even closer than she already was.

Oh, he felt wonderful. So broad and strong. His afternoon beard abraded her cheek, as rough as his lips were soft.

Then his mouth left hers to slide over her chin and down her neck. His other arm went around her. He held her in place as his lips caressed her throat and his good hand moved between them, to touch her small breasts through her bra.

Lee stiffened, cried out—and then melted as he rubbed his palm against her nipple, bringing it instantly to a hard, aching peak.

Outside, there was more clattering.

Derek muttered something.

Lee took his golden head and guided it downward. He found her nipple through her bra and sucked it. She groaned and pressed him close.

He went on kissing her, sucking her. She held his head and pressed herself up toward his mouth.

And then, again, that mouth went roaming. He kissed his way down the center of her stomach, lowering himself to his knees as he did it.

He looked up at her, his eyes burning into hers, as he unsnapped her waistband and tugged on her zipper.

"More candy canes," he whispered as he pulled the jeans open and revealed what was beneath. He stuck out his tongue and he licked her, on the smooth section of flesh between her navel and the red-and-white bikinis. Once he'd licked her, he blew out a breath, making goose bumps, making her clutch his head again and push her hungry body toward him.

At last, she felt his mouth—there, where she'd never let herself believe it would really be. Just as in so many of her fantasies, he found her through the fabric of her panties. He tugged on her jeans, and then pushed them out of his way. His hands wrapped around the backs of her thighs and he went on kissing her for the longest time, nipping and scraping lightly with his teeth, through the silky peppermint stripes.

In the end, though, he wasn't content with kissing her through her panties. He pushed on her jeans impatiently. They were stuck somewhere below her knees, keeping her from parting her legs to his satisfaction.

Clutching his broad shoulders for support, Lee wiggled her legs free, first one and then the other. He took the jeans and tossed them away, over somewhere near the potbellied stove.

And then he was taking her panties away, too. She stiffened her knees, or they surely would have buckled. Her blood sang in her ears as he parted her with his fingers, touching her where no man had ever touched her before. Desperately Lee grasped his shoulders, her body moving without any conscious command from her mind.

And then, at last, his mouth was there, where his hand had been. His tongue found her, stroking all along the wet, secret heart of her. She felt the end coming, rolling up, like some underground spring, bursting to the surface and bubbling over, so she trembled and quivered and cried out her joy.

As the waves of pleasure faded, her knees did give out. She collapsed across his shoulder. He chuckled. She lightly pounded his back with a weak fist. "You're laughing—and I may never walk again."

He made a low, satisfied sound in his throat. And then, very carefully, he stood, with her over his shoulder.

She looked down at the floor. "Uh. This is what is known as the caveman approach, right?"

Cans rattled outside again. Derek swung toward the sound.

Lee said to the beautifully formed small of his back, "Do not even think about it. Take me to your cave. Now."

He grunted and carried her to the bedroom.

There, he dropped her on the bed, switched on the lamp—a table lamp, but still with the obligatory leaping trout on the shade—and took off all of his own clothes.

She watched as he did it, enjoying the sight, wishing with one tiny corner of her mind that she was one-fifth as gorgeous as he was.

But Derek didn't seem to mind her lack of beauty. Maybe he'd seen so many lovely women naked that he was enjoying the variety of having someone really ordinary in his arms. He came down on the bed with her and he stroked and kissed her as if she were the most fabulous woman alive.

He had condoms with him. When he produced them, she teasingly accused, "So. You *were* expecting someone this weekend, after all."

He replied, "I was hoping that a woman with interesting underwear would just happen to show up." He grinned. "And she did." His eyes narrowed a little. "And I'll bet you brought protection along yourself."

She nodded. She was a nurse, after all. As he was a doctor. They'd both seen firsthand what lack of care in sexual matters can mean. "Let's use yours first," she suggested.

He willingly obliged, rolling the thing down over himself. And then he stopped. He looked at her tenderly. "I guess this will probably hurt a little, for you."

She sighed. "Probably."

He was careful, and gentle. And slow. Still, it did hurt. At first.

But then, gradually, since he took so much time with her, she felt her muscles begin to relax. He started to move faster then, and she wrapped her legs around him and went with him.

The hurt came back, he pushed into her so hard. He seemed to have forgotten gentleness, as his own pleasure took him. Lee moaned and held on, aware of so much at once, the feel of his powerful body crushing hers, the smell of his skin. His broad chest, which was covered with a light pelt of crisp golden hairs, pressed so tightly to her breasts.

He cried out. And then went still.

Overhead, the rain drummed. The warmth from the stove in the other room had reached every corner of the cabin by then. The bedroom was toasty warm. And Derek's skin was moist against her own.

Slowly his breathing evened out. He nuzzled her neck, whispered, "Lee...sorry...got a little rough..."

She cradled him closer, stroked his muscular back. It really did feel good, just to hold him.

But then he rolled to the side and slipped out of her. She sighed at the loss of him. And then she felt his hand, the left one, high up on her thigh. She looked down and saw the blood smears there.

"Sorry," he whispered again.

And then he moved, scooting down, laying his head on her thighs over the red smears. She put her hand on his head, threading her fingers through the gold strands. He turned his head. Beard-stubble scraped her lightly as he kissed the red stains.

He looked up at her. Their eyes met. And she thought for just a moment that none of this was real. Because surely this had to be the ultimate fantasy: Dr. Devastating kissing the evidence of her recent virginity from her thighs.

He slid up her body again, and pulled her close. She sighed and snuggled against him. He idly stroked her hair.

For a few beautifully contented minutes, they just lay there.

And then she realized what he was doing. Listening.

"Forget it," she commanded, "that raccoon is gone."

"I don't know what you're talking about," he said, sounding about as innocent as it was possible for a scheming man to sound.

She grumbled, "Right. You don't know. Humph."

And then he jumped from the bed and strode to the bathroom—my goodness, his buttocks were truly incredible. A couple of decades of squatting with a barbell across his shoulders had certainly paid off.

He returned minus the used condom and carrying a damp towel. Gently and tenderly, he wiped the stains from her thighs.

"Better?" he asked when he was done.

"You're not fooling me, Derek. I know you're just buttering me up so I'll go outside with you and reconnoiter the raccoon damage."

He stared at her for a moment, clearly trying to decide whether to keep up the considerate lover routine or just give in and admit the truth. The truth won. He tossed the towel back across his shoulder and held out his hand. "You're right. I want to see what that diabolical marsupial got up to. So come on. Put your clothes on."

"A raccoon is not a marsupial, Derek. That's an opossum you're thinking of, I'm sure."

"Who gives a damn? Get dressed."

Five minutes later, they stood out in the pouring rain again, by the side of the cabin. In the spill of light from the cabin window, they saw a pair of overturned garbage cans and a little trail of soggy trash leading off into the trees. The smell of spoiled fish was very strong.

"See?" Derek said, sounding terribly self-righteous. "It made off with my rotten fish." He turned accusing eyes on Lee. "If you hadn't distracted me—"

She put up a hand. "Gotcha. Next time, no lovemaking."

He reached for her then, pulled her close and rubbed his beard against her cheek. "Never say no to lovemaking because of a raccoon." She squealed and pretended to beat on his chest. "Never say no to lovemaking because of a raccoon," he growled again.

"Okay, okay. I will never say no to lovemaking because of a raccoon. I solemnly swear I will not."

"Good." He released her and grinned. "You're soaking wet, just like you were a couple of hours ago."

"So are you." She let out a resigned little sigh. "And I guess we might as well pick up the trash before we go in and get dry. If we don't, more animals will get into it and drag it all over the place."

Together, they slogged through the mud, picking up the rained-on trash. Then Derek trooped over to the Suburban and came back with a fistful of bungee cords. "This'll fix 'im," he muttered, as he hooked the bungee cords together, securing the lids tightly to the cans.

"Derek, I think you're going a little overboard about this."

"Next time, I swear I'm bringing my rifle."

"Can we go inside now?"

He linked the last bungee cord to the network of them he'd already hooked together. Then he looked up. "You need to dry off."

"Thank you for noticing."

His eyes had started gleaming. "I'm going to dry you off."

"This could be interesting."

"It will be. Wait and see."

That time, they didn't need towels. They stripped off their wet clothes and got into bed. They were both dry within minutes.

And covered with sweat a few minutes after that.

Derek asked her to tell him her fantasies.

She tried to pretend she didn't know what he was talking about. But she couldn't keep up the fiction for long. He could be very persuasive when he had his hands on her.

She ended up describing the one she liked to call the Maid and the Master.

"I have on a black dress," she said—and had to pause to let out a moan. "Derek, if you're going to keep doing that with your hand, I'm afraid I can't—oh!" She moaned again.

He said, "Go on. A black dress…"

"But, Derek—"

"A black dress."

"All right. Umm. Yes. It's a maid's dress. High neck, long sleeves. A white frilly apron. I'm dusting the Ming vases in the library."

"The Ming vases?"

"Yes. They're…oh! Very rare. I'm using a feather duster. It's an extremely delicate job."

"I'd imagine."

"Oh, Derek.…"

"Go on. You're dusting the Ming vases."

"And, um, you come in through the carved mahogany doors. *Big* doors. *Double* doors. But I don't hear you. You enter so quietly. Your shoes are of the finest, softest leather and you move like a cat. Carefully, so that I don't hear, you shut the doors."

"And then what?"

"You come up behind me."

"Behind you." Very gently, he guided her over onto her stomach.

Lee hitched in a gasp. "You pull up my dress."

"Just like that, I pull up your dress?"

"You're the master. That's what the master does."

"Hmm..." His hand strayed slowly, over the curve of her bottom. She gasped some more. He commanded, "Keep going."

"Oh, my!"

"I pull up your dress..."

"I'm...not wearing underwear."

"*You?* With no underwear? What a disappointment."

"You've ordered me not to wear underwear. In the past."

"I get it. I'm a guy who makes my desires known."

"Yes. Oh. You are."

His hand was driving her crazy. "Keep talking," he whispered.

"I can't...think. I can't...um..."

He pulled away for a moment. She knew why but didn't turn to look. She heard him tear the foil pouch, felt the movement of the bed as he slid the condom on.

He said, "Lee?"

"Um?"

"Go on, Lee. I come up behind you..."

"Oh. Yes. You...come up behind me. And you lift up my black dress and I drop the feather duster with a small, surprised cry. It rolls away across the parquet floor. You say, 'You should be more careful, Marielle.'"

"Marielle?"

"That's my name, in this fantasy. Marielle."

"Okay. Marielle. What happens next?"

"I bend over."

"You bend over."

"I..." Right then, he slid into her. Lee cried out, "Oh!"

"Like this?"

"Uh-huh..."

"Marielle?"

"Yes? Oh!"

"Like this?"

"Oh, Master."

"Answer me, Marielle."

"Oh, yes. Oh, my. *Exactly* like that..."

Chapter Fifteen

They spent most of that weekend in bed. They did, however, get up to go fishing at dawn and at dusk. And to eat now and then. And to check out a disturbance that occurred in the basement on Sunday morning.

It was the raccoon, or so Derek insisted, though by the time they got down there, whatever had created the racket had disappeared. There remained only a few cans of vegetables on the concrete slab at the foot of the stairs. They watched as one, caught in the flashlight's beam, slowly rolled off the slab and onto the dirt floor.

Derek made Lee hold the flashlight for him so he could change the burnt-out ceiling bulb. "Next time, I'll catch that damn critter," he muttered, as the two of them stacked the cans back on the shelves.

Then he took the flashlight and went around the perimeter of the basement floor, looking for what he called the "point of entry." He didn't find it.

"Maybe you ought to tell Dr. MacAllister about this," Lee suggested. "After all, it is his cabin."

Derek shot her a dark look and muttered, "This is between that raccoon and me."

They returned to Honeygrove in the late afternoon, in their separate cars.

Derek called her about five minutes after she walked in her door. "I've never seen your place, do you know that?"

She felt a warm glow all through herself. An hour away from her, and he already wanted to be back at her side. "Are you angling for an invitation?"

"No, I'm not angling. I'm asking straight-out. Let me come over."

He spent the night at her place and left early enough the next morning that he could go home to shower and change.

That day, at work, everything went just fine. They stuck to their roles of doctor and nurse. They kept things strictly professional. Or they tried to.

But still, Lee had to admit, there *was* something in the air between them. A certain extra warmth. An electricity, a feeling of promise that hadn't been there before.

Terry even remarked on it, when she caught Lee briefly in the copy room. "Something's going on between you and Dr. Devastating."

"What makes you think that?"

"Oh, come on. Another woman can see it. I'm green with envy. I mean, you're not even blond." Terry laughed. Lee could see the rest of what she was thinking in her eyes. *And you're certainly no great beauty, now are you?* She went on, "What is it with you and your friends, anyway? Three true hunks in this hospital, and you guys get them all."

Luckily Paul came in then and Lee was spared having to come up with a suitable reply. Lee told herself not to let Terry's comments bother her. She honestly did feel confident that neither she nor Derek would let their affair interfere with their work.

Derek was still doing rounds when Lee left for home. They'd made no arrangements to spend the evening together. And Lee told herself that was fine. They were having an affair, after all. It wouldn't last forever and they didn't have to spend every moment side by side.

She stopped in to see Lenora and Maria. Lenora seemed different. Not happy, exactly. But more at peace, more self-possessed than Lee had ever seen her. Otto would be locked up for a while, and Lenora said she felt safe for the first time in years because of it. Whatever happened when he came up for trial, it looked certain that he'd be required to get counseling before he could go free. Lenora hoped that would help him.

In any case, she was determined to get on with her life.

Maria begged for a story before Lee left. She went and got the Dr. Seuss book and her friend named Gary. Lee read them two stories and then said she had to go.

Lee drove home feeling good—at first. But then gradually, she realized that she felt a little sad. A little let down.

Because Derek hadn't called.

She wanted to pick up the phone and call him herself.

But she hesitated. Maybe he wanted a little time alone. She could understand that.

She would leave him alone.

She called Dana, mostly as a distraction, to keep herself from calling Derek.

But then, of course, Dana wanted to hear all about the

weekend. And Lee told her everything—well, not quite *everything*. But enough that Dana ended up announcing, "You're long gone in love, I can tell it."

"No, I'm not," Lee replied automatically, and wondered why she sounded so totally unconvincing.

"You are."

"I told you. We're having an affair."

"Sure, you are. And you're also in love. And I expect to be hearing wedding bells—in harmony with mine and Katie's."

"Dana. Stop it."

"You know I'm right."

At that moment—thank heaven—the line clicked. "Dana, gotta go. I have another call." She punched the flash button. "Hello?"

"How about a Meat Lover's Supreme?"

She felt so happy to hear his voice, she immediately forgot the question.

"Pizza," he prompted. "Meat Lover's Supreme?"

"Uh...sure."

"Deep dish or regular?"

"Deep dish."

"You have any beer?"

"I do."

"Be there in half an hour."

"You're on."

They sat on her couch and shared the pizza and drank their beer straight out of the can as they watched a TV movie starring Valerie Bertinelli. The movie was almost over and they had progressed to necking as if they were a couple of teenagers when the phone interrupted them.

Lee would have let her machine get it, but Derek simply was not the kind of man who could bear to let a phone go unanswered. He pulled away regretfully,

picked up her remote phone from beside the pizza box
and handed it to her.

"Lee. It's Mom."

"Hi, Mom," Lee said cautiously, wondering why she
already felt depressed when all Ina Murphy had said so
far was hello.

Derek, on the other hand, looked alert and interested.
Too interested.

"How have you been, honey?"

"Fine, Mom. Just fine."

"I don't want to bother you, but I thought I should,
you know, give you a call. See how you're doing."

"Well, I'm doing great. How about you?"

A deep sigh. "Just tired all the time, you know? My
back has really been acting up lately. And those migraines I get, well, I hope you never have to suffer with
migraines. Some people just aren't as healthy as others.
You know what I mean."

Lee knew. Too well. All her life she'd heard it; some
people aren't healthy. Some people aren't lucky. Or
good-looking. Or successful. Some people—like the
Murphys—just have no luck.

"Well," Lee said, resolutely cheerful, "I hope you're
feeling better soon."

"We both know I won't be."

Derek was watching, still showing an excess of interest.

"Mom, can I call you tomorrow?"

"You're busy. I knew it. I shouldn't have—"

"Mom, it's all right. I have...company, that's all."

"Company. Oh. Well, isn't that nice?" She sounded
sad and very lonely. Lee felt terribly guilty.

"I'll call you tomorrow. I promise."

"That will be fine, hon. I'll talk to you then. Good-bye." The line went dead.

Derek said, "Your mom, huh?"

Lee pushed the Off button and set the phone down. "Yes. That was my mom."

"Great. When do I get to meet her?"

"Meet her?" Lee gaped at him. Dr. Devastating wanted to meet her mother.

That should have made her happy. After all, a man didn't ask to meet your mother unless he was pretty darn interested.

But she wasn't happy.

"Lee?"

She studied his face. Lord. He was so incredibly good-looking and he carried himself as if he had the world at his feet. A man with *success* written all over him. She thought of Ina, who wasn't attractive and didn't dress well. Who complained every time she opened her mouth. Who had somehow ended up old way before her time.

And then Lee felt small. Small and petty and not understanding at all of her poor mother.

"Lee, come on. I really want to meet her."

"Derek, I don't think—"

"Call her back right now and invite her to my place. For dinner. Seven-thirty this Friday night." He picked up the phone again and held it out to her.

Ina said she'd come. "If you're sure you want me."

Lee reassured her that they did. She suggested that her mother come to her house first, at six-thirty or so. They could drive over to Derek's together. And then, afterward, Ina could go back to Lee's for the night. "How does that sound?"

Ina said, "Well, it's hard for me. I'm so tired after work. But I'll make it somehow."

"Good."

"After all, this must be important. You hardly ever date. This Derek must be someone very special."

"Well, I—"

"What does he *do,* anyway?"

"He's a doctor. Family Practice. We work together, at the clinic."

"A doctor. *You,* Lee? Dating a doctor? You always swore you would never—"

Lee had no desire to hear any more in that vein—especially not right at that moment, with Derek sitting next to her, seeming to drink in her every word. "Mom, I really have to go now."

"Oh, well, of course you do. I'm so sorry to keep you."

Lee stifled the urge to shout, "Mother, I'm the one who called you!" and instead told her mother that she loved her. With a sigh of relief, she punched the Off button again.

Derek took the phone from her. "That wasn't so hard, was it?" He set it back on the table again.

"No," she lied brightly. "That wasn't hard at all."

Wednesday night, they went to the gym together. It was Derek's first time back there, after his run-in with the raccoon. He had to modify his workout, with his wrist still in a cast, but he said it still felt good to start getting back into his old routine.

After they finished at the gym, Derek took her out to dinner at a little Greek place he liked. They had salads with goat cheese sprinkled on them and stuffed grape leaves with the main course.

They also ran into one of his old girlfriends, a woman striking enough that the people at the other tables stopped to stare as she walked by. The woman lit up like a thousand-watt bulb when she caught sight of Derek. She stood by their table and sighed and laughed and told him he really should give her a call soon.

He only smiled. "Andrea, this is Lee Murphy."

The woman barely glanced Lee's way. "Hi." Her big violet eyes zeroed in on Derek again. "I am serious." She shook a slender, red-tipped finger at him. "You had better call me."

He shook his head. "As a matter of fact, I'm pretty much spoken for."

"Spoken for?" She cast a swift glance at Lee. Lee read the look. It said, "What in the world is he doing with someone like you when he could have *me?*"

Lee wanted to mutter, "He's with me because I'm funny and smart and darn good in bed." However, somewhere deep in her heart, Lee couldn't help wondering right along with Andrea.

Once Andrea was gone, Derek said softly, "Lee. You do know I'm not going to call her, don't you? I told you once that there wouldn't be anyone else. And I meant what I said."

Lee tried to make light of it. "Derek, it's no big thing. Really." She knew that it shouldn't be. That, at least for now, Derek really would prefer to be with her than the beautiful Andrea. But the sight of the woman—and the stubborn insecurities the woman aroused—still depressed her.

He leaned a little closer across the table, "You don't look as if it's no big thing."

"Can we just drop it, please?"

"I don't think we should drop it, if it's bothering you."

"It isn't," she lied—a lie he saw for exactly what it was.

He set down his fork. "Lee. What did you expect me to *say* to her? Would you have been happier if I'd told her, 'No, Andrea. I'm not going to call you, so would you please get lost?'"

"Of course not. You did nothing wrong."

"Then why do you look so damn bleak?"

"I don't mean to look bleak."

He shook his head and swore under his breath—and then, thank goodness, he picked up his fork again. "Eat your stuffed grape leaves."

She did as he instructed. They endured a few minutes of uncomfortable silence, and then he looked up and asked her a question—something innocuous, about the workday just past. She answered. They shared a smile. And the beautiful Andrea was forgotten.

They were walking out to the Suburban when Derek's beeper went off. It was the hospital. He dropped her off at the health club where she'd left her own car, and went to deal with the emergency.

He showed up on her doorstep at eleven-thirty, looking tired and frustrated. "We lost old Mr. Carthage."

The eighty-five-year-old had been diagnosed with pancreatic cancer—far advanced when the problem was detected.

Lee took Derek's hand and pulled him over the threshold.

He said, "The prognosis was poor. We knew this was coming."

She said, "But you still feel like hell about it. I know."

His hand slid up her arm.

With a sigh, she stepped up close and rested her head against his broad chest. He slipped his arm around her, rather awkwardly. For some reason, he was keeping his right hand, the one with the cast on it, behind his back. He kissed her hair. "I shouldn't have shown up here. I should have let you sleep."

She looked up at him and smiled. She felt sad, about Mr. Carthage. And at the same time, she felt a little better about herself and Derek. Yes, they might be having a torrid affair—something straight out of her fantasies that wasn't going to last. But they did share more than just sex. They really were friends. And he felt he could come to her in the middle of the night like this, after losing a patient. He knew that she would understand.

She stepped back and snared his left hand again. "You look so tired. Let's go to bed."

He hung back. "Wait."

She gave him a puzzled smile. "What?"

"Come here." He pulled her over to the couch. "Sit down."

She dropped to the cushions. "Derek. What is it?"

He cleared his throat. "I...well, I've been trying to do this all evening. But we ran into Andrea in the restaurant, and that kind of put a damper on the mood. And then I got the call from the hospital..."

She was starting to get worried. "What? Tell me. Whatever it is, it's all right."

He blew out a long breath. "God. I'm nervous as hell."

Alarm skittered through her. "Derek. What is the matter?"

He stuck out his right hand. She saw then that he was holding a tiny blue velvet box.

And she knew. She couldn't believe it, but she knew.

She whispered, "Derek. You're not...?" and ran out of words.

He nodded. "I am. I'm proposing. Will you marry me, Lee?"

Chapter Sixteen

Katie held Lee's hand and admired the small diamond shining there. "It's really lovely."

Lee sighed. "I just can't believe it. Derek's ring. On my finger."

Dana, who sat in the chair across Lee's coffee table from the other two, spoke up then. "So. He asked you last night?"

Lee nodded.

"I told you that this was going to happen." Dana made a show of smoothing her hair. "And was I right?"

"You were," Lee conceded.

"It's all anyone talked about at Memorial today," Katie said.

Lee groaned. "I know. Terry Brandt has the eyes of an eagle. She spotted the ring when I walked in the door. And she knew it was Derek, without me saying a word. She went nuts. She said she just couldn't believe it. First you and Mike. Then Dana and Trevor. And now me and Derek. She thinks it's not fair. She insists that we got all the good ones.''

''And we did,'' Dana said cheerfully.

''I'm with Terry,'' Katie said. ''I mean, in that it's hard to believe. Here we are, each of us thirty years old. Confirmed single women. Or so everyone thought. And then, in the space of a few months, we all end up engaged.''

Dana laughed. ''To doctors. Which just goes to prove that it really is true. Never say never.''

Katie still held Lee's hand. She gave it a squeeze. ''When's the big date?''

''Come on, we haven't gotten that far yet. He just asked me.''

Katie turned to Dana. The two shared a look. ''Well?'' Katie asked. ''What do you think?''

Dana shrugged. ''Fine with me.''

They both grinned at Lee. ''Get married with us,'' Katie said.

Lee wasn't prepared for that suggestion. She pulled her hand free of Katie's and let out a weak laugh. ''Oh, come on.''

''What does that mean?'' Dana put on a wounded expression. ''You don't want to get married in the same ceremony with your two dearest female friends in the whole wide world?''

Lee knew that Dana was teasing. Still, she hastened to reassure her. ''It's not that. Not at all.''

''Then what is it?''

''Well, you two are getting married on September 6. That's hardly a month away.''

''So?''

''It's too late to add another bride.''

"We can swing it."

"Oh, come on. I know you two have it all planned, just the way you want it."

Dana said, "Yes, we do. And we'd like it even better if you went in with us."

"You've already sent out the invitations."

"So we'll send out announcements letting everyone know that instead of two brides, they get three."

"But...what will you do for a bridesmaid, if I'm one of the brides?"

"Oh, come on. With three brides, who needs a bridesmaid?"

"I've already bought my bridesmaid's dress."

Katie and Dana exchanged another look. Then Katie joined the argument in that calm, reasonable tone of hers. "You haven't worn that dress yet. The boutique will take it back, and happily—especially considering you'll tell them that you want a wedding gown instead."

"But I—"

"Wait a minute," Dana said.

And Katie nodded. "Yes. I think we're going to have to slow down here."

"Please," Lee muttered gratefully. "Let's."

"Do you want your own wedding?" Dana asked. "Is that it?"

"No. That's not the problem at all."

Katie said, "Lee. If you *do* want your own wedding, it's okay. There's nothing wrong with that."

"No. I mean it. It's not that. I can't think of a nicer way to get married than with the two of you. But I just..." She glanced from one dear face to the other. "A month is a little too soon for me."

Katie made a sympathetic sound and patted Lee's

shoulder. "Are you trying to tell us that you're feeling overwhelmed right now?"

"I just…I can hardly believe he asked me. I certainly didn't expect him to. We only really got together last weekend. And I have to admit, until last night, I've been telling myself to enjoy it while it lasts, you know?"

Katie asked, very gently, "Do you love him?"

Dana made a humphing sound. "Of course she does."

Katie frowned. "Come on, Dana. Let her say it for herself."

"Sorry." Dana actually looked sheepish. "You're right." She turned to Lee. "Well? Do you love him?"

Lee gulped. "I do."

Dana made a face. "You don't exactly sound thrilled about it."

Lee struggled to explain. "I'm scared. It only really hit me last night, after he popped the question. I was sitting right here, on the edge of the couch, and he was standing over me, looking down at me through those Paul Newman eyes of his and I thought, 'Oh, my Lord. I'm in love with him. He's everything I swore I'd never let myself get close to—he's domineering, he's always sure he's right. He's ten times better looking than I've ever dreamed of being, and other women will not leave him alone. And worst of all, he's got M.D. after his na—'"

"Wait a minute." Katie cut in. "Let's go back a little bit here. You make it sound as if *you're* not good-looking. And that is not true."

"I said that he's ten times better looking than I am. And it *is* true."

"But—"

Lee stopped Katie with a look. "Your loyalty is a beautiful thing. May I continue?"

Katie waved a hand. "Oh, all right. Go on."

"Thank you. What was I saying?"

Dana prompted, "You realized you loved him...."

"That's right. And I also realized I was going to say yes. And I did. I said yes. But I still don't believe it. And I need a little time, to get used to the idea. Please understand."

Katie made a sympathetic, tongue-clucking sound. "Of course we do."

"But if you change your mind—"

Both Lee and Katie swung quelling glances at Dana. Katie even shook her head.

Dana put up both hands. "I know, I know. It's your life. Live it your own way."

Friday was the dinner with Ina.

Lee's mother arrived right on time, at six-thirty. Just like Terry Brandt, she spotted Lee's engagement ring immediately. Her eyes went wide. "An engagement ring? From the *doctor?*"

"His name is Derek, Mom," Lee said, trying not to be hurt that her mother found the idea of someone wanting to marry her so difficult to accept. "And yes. We're going to get married."

"My goodness," said Ina. "You. Getting married. And to a doctor. I would never in a thousand years have imagined that happening."

"Well, imagine it. Because it's true."

Lee gave her mother a few minutes to settle into the spare room. Then Lee asked if perhaps Ina would like a cup of coffee or something before they went on to Derek's.

Ina looked doubtful, though she'd always been a big

coffee drinker in the past. "I've started to think the caffeine is what brings on my migraines."

"Well, how about herb tea then?" Lee suggested brightly. "That can't hurt you."

"That doctor of yours probably wouldn't appreciate us showing up late."

"We won't be late, I promise you."

"No. I think we'd better just go on, I really do."

Ina was silent at first during the drive. She sat there so stoically in her flowered polyester shirtwaist and off-white cardigan sweater. It seemed to Lee that her mother always wore that sweater, at all times of the year, in every kind of weather. She wore it when it was snowing, and she wore it now, in mid-summer, when it was eighty-five degrees outside.

Out of nowhere, Ina asked, "Hon, now that you're going to be the wife of a doctor, don't you think you ought to at least do something about your hair?"

Lee's hands tightened on the wheel as she held back a snappish reply. She shot a glance at her mother, who was staring straight out the windshield, gripping her cheap plastic purse in her lap as if someone was going to grab it if she relaxed her guard for so much as a nanosecond.

"What exactly do you think I should do with my hair, Mom?"

Ina sighed, a weary sound—though she continued to stare straight ahead and clutch her purse as if it were trying to get away from her. "Oh, you know. Fix it up a little. Go to a good beauty shop and see what they can do. Sometimes I think that's where I went wrong with your father. I just didn't take enough pride in my appearance. Of course, I don't know what he ever saw in me, anyway. He came from such a good family and I was—''

''Mother. Let's not get started about him. Please?''

Ina hunched her shoulders and clutched her purse even tighter. ''All right. That's fine. I just thought…a visit to the hairdresser, you know. It can't hurt.''

Lee tried to lighten the moment by making a show of blowing her bangs out of her eyes. ''You're probably right. I could use a haircut.''

''Of course, it's none of my business.''

''It's all right. Really. As I said, you've got a point.''

''I shouldn't have said anything.''

''Mother. It's all right.''

Ina subsided into silence after that, staring straight ahead, holding on to her purse for dear life. Lee silently prayed that she'd heard the last ''helpful hint'' of the evening.

When they got to the condo, Derek treated Ina like a queen. He helped her off with her sweater and even managed to convince her to let him take her purse. He served them a predinner glass of red wine. As they sat in the living room, sipping, he asked Ina if Lee had told her the good news.

''Yes,'' said Ina stiffly. ''Lee told me that the two of you are planning to get married. I hope you'll be very happy.''

Derek sent Lee a warm look, a look that went a long way toward easing her anxiousness. ''I know that we will.''

Ina asked, ''What happened to your hand?''

Briefly, Derek explained about the ill-fated visit to Blue Moon Lake a few weeks before. Then he inquired after Ina's health.

Lee shot him a *you'll be sorry* glance, but he only smiled.

And Ina was off and running about her sore back and her fallen arches, her irregular heartbeat and her killer migraines. Derek listened patiently to the bad-health litany, and then asked her if she felt she had a good doctor.

"I *love* my doctor. I've been seeing him since I moved up to Salem five years ago. He's a G.P. I like to see one man for everything. And if he thinks I need a specialist, then, well, he lets me know. His name is Stover. Dr. L. V. Stover." Ina peered hard at Derek, as if expecting him to tell her he knew all about Dr. Stover and considered him one of the best.

Lee came to his rescue. "I doubt if Derek's met your Dr. Stover, Mom. He's never lived in Salem and he's been in Honeygrove for less than a year."

Ina arched a brow. "Oh? And where are you from, then?"

"Sacramento. I was raised there, went to school at UC Davis and did my internship and residency at American River General."

"Oh, really? I suppose your family is hoping you'll come back home to stay soon."

"I have no family left, except for an older brother. And he doesn't live in Sacramento anymore."

"Well, I know how you young doctors are. Always on the lookout for a better opportunity. You'll want your own practice, I'll bet. That's where the good money is."

"To tell you the truth, I enjoy my work at the clinic."

Ina looked doubtful. "Wait till a better offer comes along, I'm sure you'll change your mind then."

Derek tipped his head and his blue gaze grew pensive. Lee thought he was deciding whether to disagree or not. In the end, he only shrugged. "I suppose time will tell."

For dinner, Derek served them steaks and salad and baked potatoes slathered in sour cream and sprinkled with chives.

Lee teased him that he cooked just like a man.

"Well, he is a man, honey," her mother said. Then she smiled at Derek, a smile chock-full of admiration.

Lee told herself to be pleased that Ina liked Derek so much. But still, she continued to feel edgy and uncomfortable.

And she was glad when the evening finally came to a close.

Derek walked them down to the car and helped Ina into the passenger seat. Then he went around with Lee to her side of the car. He pulled her into his arms right there, by her door.

She murmured, half chiding, half pleased, "Derek..."

"Kiss me."

She did, a little reluctantly at first, since her mother was waiting in the car a few feet away. Her reluctance passed swiftly, as the kiss curled her toes and weakened her knees.

Before he let her go, he whispered, "Maybe you could make your mom comfortable at your house—and come on back here."

"Derek. You can get along without me for one night."

"But I don't *want* to get along without you for one night."

"Derek..."

"All right, all right." His strong arms dropped away and he opened her door for her. She slid into her seat and buckled up.

At Lee's house, Ina said, "Well, I guess I'll go ahead and get ready for bed." She trudged straight to the guest bedroom and closed the door. Lee stood in the living room for a moment, wondering why she felt so let down. The evening had gone better than Lee had expected. And Ina was tired.

And really, Lee and her mother had never had all that much to say to each other. In fact, Lee had always felt like more of a burden to her mother than anything else. She was the love child that Ina had felt duty-bound to raise. Ina had fed her and clothed her as best she could, and then seemed just a little bit relieved when Lee grew old enough to strike out on her own.

Lee had no reason to expect Ina to want to stay up past her bedtime now, to have a mother-daughter chat about Derek and marriage and what the future might hold. Besides, Ina's opinions always set Lee's teeth on edge, anyway. Some people looked at the world through rose-colored glasses. But Ina Murphy seemed to view everything through a dingy gray fog. Whatever Ina might say to Lee about her upcoming marriage, Lee probably wouldn't like.

So it was all to the good that Ina marched off to bed. In the morning, Lee would fix them breakfast. The breakfast conversation would be limited to requests for more coffee and remarks on the weather. Ina would leave before ten, eager to get back to her apartment in Salem. Being away from home made her nervous. She worried that someone might break in and steal all her things—or that a pipe might burst or the place would burn down.

Lee dropped her shoulder bag on the couch and headed for the kitchen. She would brew herself a nice cup of tea and watch the late news. And she would stop wishing for more than her mother could give.

She'd just pulled the mug full of hot water from the microwave when Ina spoke from behind her.

"I'm going to bed now."

Lee turned. Ina had changed to her green quilted robe and her battered old slippers. Her face was shiny with night cream. Lee knew she should murmur a simple "Good night, Mom." But something inside her just wouldn't let well enough alone.

"Why don't you sit down? I'll make you some tea."

Ina pursed up her mouth. "Didn't I tell you, I can't take the caffeine?"

"I have herb tea, Mom. How about chamomile? It's one hundred percent free of caffeine."

Ina shook her head. "I don't really like chamomile. It tastes like some kind of weed to me."

Lee resolutely kept her smile. "All right. Good night, then."

Ina started to leave—and then turned back. "Lee."

Lee looked up from dipping a tea bag into the hot water. "Um?"

"I, well, I really do hope you're going to be careful about all this."

Lee felt tension, like a tightening cord, drawing her shoulder blades back. "About what?"

"About that doctor of yours."

"What do you mean, Mom?" Lee kept her voice light, though her stomach had suddenly decided to tie itself into a big, hard knot.

"Well, I'm just saying that I would hate to see you get hurt the way I've been hurt."

Lee set her tea on the counter. "What are you getting at?"

Ina sighed. She lifted a hand and fiddled with one of

the big plastic buttons on the front of her robe. "Oh, dear."

Lee spoke more strongly. "Just say it. Just go ahead and say it."

Ina stopped fooling with the button. She clenched her hands at her sides. "Oh, Lee. You're getting mad at me."

Lee folded her arms over her middle and leaned back against the counter. "I want you to say what's on your mind."

Ina took a deep breath. "Well, I just…I worry, that's all."

"About me and Derek?"

"Yes. Oh, don't get me wrong. I thought he was wonderful. I honestly did. And such a gentleman, too."

"But?"

"Now, honey…"

"Go on. Tell me. You think he's wonderful, *but*…"

"Well, he's just starting out, isn't he?"

"So?"

"Things are bound to change for him over the next few years."

"How?"

"Well, I'm sure he's got loans to pay back, from medical school and all. He'll start thinking how much quicker he could get rid of those, how much nicer he could live, if he found himself a fancy private practice somewhere." Ina lifted her hand again, found that button, and began twisting it. "That clinic you work at together will start to seem like a dead end to him. He'll want different things than he thinks he wants now."

"You mean he'll stop wanting me."

"Honey, all I'm saying is, he's barely finished his residency and—"

"You make him sound like a child, Mother. He's in his thirties, for crying out loud."

"Barely in his thirties, I'll bet."

Lee realized that she didn't know Derek's exact age. "What does it matter? Thirty is old enough to be sure of what you want. *I'm* thirty, for heaven's sake."

"Well, but…he's so *handsome*. He must have a lot of women after him. And let's be honest. You're…" Ina stopped twisting that button. She dropped her hand to her side again and looked away. "Oh, listen. Never mind."

But Lee couldn't stop herself from prompting, "I'm what, Mom?"

Ina chewed her inner lip, the way she always did when she was really upset. At her sides, her hands clenched and unclenched. "Oh, I never should have said a word about this. I can see that. I should have kept my big mouth shut."

Lee demanded for the second time, "I'm what, Mom?"

"Honey…"

"I'm ordinary? Is that what you were going to say? I'm plain? I'm ugly?"

"No. I did not say you were ugly."

"But you don't think I'm good enough for a man like Derek, a *doctor* like Derek."

Ina coughed. "Well, now. Whatever. You know what I mean."

"No. No, I do not know what you mean. I think you'd better tell me."

"Lee, all I'm saying is, you have a good job. You can take care of yourself. Much better than I ever could, that's for certain. You've always seemed perfectly happy, leading an independent kind of life. Why go and complicate things, that's all I'm asking? Why get your hopes up over someone who's so…different from you?''

"So far out of my league, you mean? So much *better* than me?"

"Lee…"

"That is what you mean. Isn't it?"

Ina quit clenching her hands and began rubbing them nervously down the sides of her robe. "I've really made you mad. I can see that. And I didn't *want* to make you mad. I just wanted—"

"What, Mother? What exactly did you want?"

"For you to be careful. For you not to rush into anything."

Lee stared at her mother across the width of the small kitchen. She reminded herself of the facts: Ina was a fearful person, a person who worried incessantly, who always felt ill, who never, ever saw any glass as more than half-empty. Ina was a woman who had taken one big chance in her life—on Lee's father—and ended up pregnant and alone as a result.

Naturally she would see Lee's situation as paralleling her own.

And doesn't it? a scared, small voice in the back of Lee's mind kept asking. Aren't her situation and mine very close to the same?

Ina lifted both hands and pressed her fingers to her temples, "I have to get my medicine. I feel a migraine coming on." She turned and shuffled toward the spare room.

Lee just couldn't let her go like that. She followed after her, made her lie down and got the Fiorcet tab for her, along with some water to wash it down.

"Thank you, honey," Ina said with a weary sigh, as Lee turned off the light. Then she spoke from out of the darkness. "You probably shouldn't listen to me. You know how I am. I worry. I worry way too much."

Lee smoothed the dry, wiry hair away from her mother's forehead. "It's all right. Just get some sleep."

"Yes. Sleep. That would be good...."

Breakfast the next morning went pretty much as Lee had expected. No sensitive subjects were broached. Ina remarked that it looked as if it might rain later.

"I just hate to drive in bad weather. I need to get on the road, see if I can get home before it really starts coming down."

Lee didn't even bother to point out that the weather channel had predicted a light drizzle at worst.

"I hope everything's all right at my apartment," Ina muttered. "You just never know, if you go away, what you'll find when you get home...."

Ina left at nine-fifteen. Lee stood on the sidewalk, waving as her mother drove away. Then she returned to the house and thought about calling Derek.

But really, hadn't they been spending too much time together lately? They didn't have to act like Siamese twins just because he'd asked her to marry him. They worked side by side Monday through Friday and then, for the past week, they'd spent every night excluding last night wrapped in each other's arms. They needed to have their own lives, didn't they?

Lee cleaned up the breakfast dishes, got her gym bag and headed for Optimum Fitness. She arrived back home at a little before noon. The phone was ringing as she let herself in the door.

It was Derek. "What does a guy have to do to get his fiancée to call him?"

Lee felt the flush of pleasure at the sound of his

voice—and then a certain wary defensiveness. "I call you."

"Not as much as I call you."

"I didn't know we were keeping score."

A silence. "Hey. Is this a stupid thing to argue about, or what?"

Lee flopped onto the couch. "You're right. Let's not argue. How old are you, exactly?"

"Thirty-three. Why?"

"I just realized I didn't know."

"Well, now you do. Feel better?"

She didn't, not really. But she found herself chirping pertly, "Much."

"What are you doing?"

"Talking to you on the phone."

"No kidding. What I meant was, where's your mom?"

"She left."

"Do you think she enjoyed herself last night?"

"Sure. As much as my mother is capable of enjoying anything."

He chuckled, the sound low and rumbly and warm. "I've got to admit, she's no optimist."

"She's a hopeless hypochondriac, not to mention obsessive-compulsive. But it's not as if she's a bad person. And she hasn't had an easy time of it in her life."

"I thought the dinner went pretty well, though. Didn't you?"

Lee thought of Ina, standing in the kitchen doorway, rubbing her hands down the sides of her robe and telling Lee that she wasn't good enough to marry Derek. "It went fine, yes."

He was silent again, then he asked, "Is something going on here that I should know about?"

"Why?"

"You don't sound right."

"Oh, really? And just how should I sound?"

"It's not how you *should* sound. It's whatever you're thinking that you're not saying."

"There's nothing." It was a bald lie. But really, Lee had no desire at all to reveal to Derek what her mother had said last night. It was all just stuff she'd already said to him herself, back before they'd become lovers: that, in the end, he wasn't going to be satisfied with someone like her, that what they shared couldn't last. What good would it do for her to tell him that her mother had the same doubts as she did?

No good at all that Lee could see.

Better to simply forget it, to put it behind her.

"Lee, are you *sure* there's nothing wrong?"

She forced a lighter tone. "Positive. And I'm sorry I didn't call. And when can I see you again?"

"I thought you'd never ask. Come over here."

"When?"

"Now."

"Well, I've got some laundry to do and I—"

"Lee. No man wants to hear how a woman would rather do laundry than rush to his side."

"I wouldn't rather do laundry. But it does pile up, you know?"

He made a low, aggravated sound. "When can you get here?"

"About four?"

"I guess that'll have to do."

That night, after dinner, when they were sitting on Derek's sofa with their arms around each other, Derek suggested, "Let's set a date."

Lee knew what he meant, but still she stalled. "A date?"

"For the wedding. You know. You in a white dress. Me in a black tux. Lots of flowers. A long walk down a church aisle."

"You want to set a date already?"

A crease formed between his perfect brows as he pulled away enough to look down at her. "Lee. That's what I just said. Let's set a date."

"But, Derek, I..." She tried to think of the right words to say.

"What?" Impatience tightened the corners of his mouth.

"I really think we should take it kind of slow."

He pulled back a little farther. "What does that mean, kind of slow?"

"It means we shouldn't set a date right away."

"Why not?"

"Well, this is all happening so fast, don't you think?"

He considered her question, then shook his head. "No, not really. We've known each other for almost a year."

"Seven months."

"Almost a year," he said, running right over her, his tone playful. "And you've been absolutely nuts about me for...how long would you say?"

"Derek." She tried to sound firm. "Don't flaunt your ego at me. It's your most unattractive feature, if you want to know the truth."

He grew more serious. "I know what I want, Lee. You. As my wife. Now."

"But...how long will you want that?"

"For the rest of our lives."

"How can you be sure about that? Maybe I'm just

kind of a...novelty for you. Someone different than your average gorgeous, shapely blonde.''

He got that stiff, the-doctor-knows-everything look he used to wear often, back before she really came to know him. ''I would not be asking you to marry me if you were just a *novelty*.''

''Well, of course you wouldn't consciously *think* that I was just a novelty. It might be something you wouldn't even realize, until you started getting bored with me and—''

He sat back all the way, to the far end of the couch. ''What the hell is going on?''

''I just...I don't want to rush this. I want to take it slow. Please.''

''You are not a damn *novelty* to me.''

''All right. Fine. I'm not a novelty. But I still don't want us to rush into marriage.''

He looked at her for a long time. Then he asked, ''How long do you want to wait?''

''A few months?''

''Before we even set a date?''

''A lot of people stay engaged for a year or more.''

''That's no kind of argument, and you know it.''

''Derek. Please...''

''You're not being straight with me.''

''Just give me more time.''

Again, he was silent. But then, finally, he nodded. ''All right. We won't set the date yet. You take the time you need. But don't take too long.'' He smiled, rather ruefully. ''I might start to think you don't really want to marry me at all.''

Chapter Seventeen

The doorbell rang at two-thirty the next morning. Derek and Lee were sound asleep in Derek's bed. He sat up as Lee yanked the covers over her head. The bell rang again.

Derek swung his feet to the floor. He reached for his Jockeys, which he'd slung over a corner chair, along with his slacks and shirt.

"What's goin' on?" Lee peeked out at him from under the covers. He got the Jockeys on and then couldn't resist stopping long enough to find her soft mouth and kiss it. She sighed and nibbled his bottom lip.

The bell rang again.

She reached out those slim, pale arms of hers and wrapped them around his neck. "Mmm. Kiss me again like that."

"Lee. The doorbell…"

"Don't answer it."

Regretfully he peeled her arms away. "Have to." He planted one last kiss on her nose. "You know how I am about phones and doorbells."

She canted up on an elbow and watched him through droopy eyes as he yanked on his slacks and zipped them up. "Hurry back."

"I will." He grabbed his shirt and pulled it over his head as he started for the door.

It was ringing steadily when he reached it. He looked through the peephole.

His brother, his face wreathed in cigarette smoke and distorted to fun-house proportions by the peephole glass, squinted back at him. The bell went on ringing. Larry must be leaning on the damn button.

Swiftly Derek shot back the dead bolt and turned the knob lock. He flung open the door.

Larry stopped pressing the doorbell. He was weaving on his feet. His mouth turned up in a goofy, pie-eyed grin. "Hey, li'l brother." The cigarette dangling from his lips bobbed up and down with every word. "Was beginnin' to wonner if you were even home."

Derek took him by the arm and pulled him inside.

"Whoops, where're we goin'?" Larry brayed out a laugh. Derek led him to the couch, where Larry immediately dropped into a sprawl. Derek switched on the table lamp near Larry's head. Larry let out a moan. "Whoa. The old eyes don' wanna deal with that one." He squinted up at Derek, then looked down, crossing his eyes as he studied the cigarette hanging from his mouth. "Got an ashtray?"

Derek took the few steps to the kitchen area and grabbed a saucer from the cupboard. He marched back to Larry. "Here."

Larry stubbed out the cigarette. "So. How 'bout a beer?"

"I'd say you've had enough." Derek set the plate on the side table. "Did you *drive* here?"

Larry answered with his favorite response. "You don' wanna know."

As usual, Larry was dead right. Derek did not want to know if his brother had been driving around falling-down drunk.

Even through his alcoholic fog, Larry must have read the disapproval on Derek's face. He groaned, "Aw, c'mon. Don' go all self-righteous on me. I can' take that right now. Things haven' ezackly been goin' my way." Larry let out a long, sad sigh and then rubbed his jaw, hard, as if checking to see if it had gone numb on him.

"I'll put you in the guest room. You can sleep it off."

"You don' wanna party?"

"No, thanks." He took Larry's wrist and gave it a tug. His brother grunted, but did stand up. Derek wrapped Larry's arm around his own neck. "Come on."

"Sush a stick-in-the-mud. Always have been. Never wanna party. Never wanna have some fun. Too busy bein' the good one. The shinin' hope of the Taylor fam'ly."

Derek started down the hall. Larry muttered and complained the whole way. When they got to the spare room, Derek took him straight to the bed and eased him down on it. "Here you go. Stretch out."

"Huh?"

Derek guided Larry to a prone position, then he turned on the lamp.

Larry groaned again. "You would haveta turn on that damn light."

"Just let me get your shoes off, and then I'll turn it off."

"Right. With the damage already done..."

Derek eased off his brother's run-down tennis shoes and slid his smelly socks away as well. Larry allowed all this, though he muttered and moaned the whole time. Then Derek got the extra blanket from the closet and spread it over him.

"Ellie divorced me," Larry was mumbling. "Got the papers...Friday, it was. I think. I didn' go to work. Prob'ly lost my job. Piece of garbage job anyway. I don't give a damn."

Derek wasn't surprised to hear either bit of news. "It's all right. We can talk about it in the morning."

"No. S'not awright. I did love her. Sweet li'l Ellie. Bu' she caught me. Makin' a mistake. With 'nother woman. She wouldn' believe me when I said I was sorry. She had to go and divorce me. Drove all the way from Fresno to tell you 'bout it. Tha's where I'm livin' now, did I tell you that? Fresno."

Derek pulled the blanket smooth, and tucked it under Larry's feet. "Go to sleep."

"Sleep? I don' wanna sleep. I tol' you. I wanna have a good time."

"Derek?" Lee's voice came from the doorway. Derek turned and saw her standing there, wearing the dark blue terry-cloth robe he kept on the back of his bathroom door. "Is everything all right?"

"More or less." Since she was looking at him so doubtfully, he explained, "This is my brother, Larry. He'll be sleeping over."

"Whazzat?" Larry demanded. He lifted his head and squinted at Lee. "Some woman? You got some woman here with you, s'why you won' party with your big bro?''

"My fiancée, Larry. So watch your mouth. Her name is Lee. You can meet her tomorrow. Right now, I want you to—''

Larry wouldn't shut up. "Fiancée. You got a fiancée? You're kiddin' me.''

"No, I'm not kidding. Put your head down and go to sleep.''

"Whadda you need with a damn fiancée right now? You're jus' gettin' started. An' besides, you got the women lined up for you. Gorgeous women.'' He squinted harder at Lee. "Hell. This one ain't even up to your stan'ards. She's too skinny. An' she needs a haircut.''

"That's enough, Larry.'' Derek shot Lee an apologetic glance. She stuck her hands into the pockets of the robe and gave him an it's-all-right shrug in return.

"Sorry.'' Larry let his head drop down and released a 90-proof sigh. "Got a big mouth. Got no class wha'soever. But I had a bad week. An' my wife jus' divorced me.''

"Just go to sleep, will you?'' Derek turned off the light.

"Yeah. Sure. Sleep. Fine…'' Instantly loud snores filled the dark room.

Derek moved toward the doorway, where Lee was waiting for him. She fell back to clear the way for him. He stepped into the hall, shut the door and pulled her into his arms.

She allowed the embrace, but barely. He cursed his brother's thoughtless mouth as he kissed her hair and breathed in the sweet, clean scent of her. "I'm sorry. My brother's a real ass.'' Her arms went around his waist then, and hooked at the small of his back. He smiled. "That's better."

"Does he...drop in like this often?" she whispered against his shoulder.

"He appeared about a month ago. And before that, it was a year since I last saw him. This is the first time he's showed up drunk, though. Usually he waits to get blasted until after he gets in the door."

"Charming."

He took her by the shoulders and looked into her eyes. "That's not all you should know about him, if I'm going to be honest."

"God, there's more?" Her voice tried to be light.

He confessed, "He always hits me up for money before he takes off again."

Her expression turned a little bit sad. "Do you give it to him?"

"Yes. I do."

"Can you afford to?"

"Not really, but he is my brother, my last living blood relation. And things just never seem to work out for him."

She went on looking at him. Those eyes of hers, not quite blue and not quite gray, seemed to see straight into his soul. "You feel guilty. Because you've done well and he hasn't."

"Maybe." He slid his left hand down her arm and captured her hand. "Let's go back to bed."

She allowed him to pull her along, down the short hall to his bedroom. When they got there, he kicked the door closed and caught hold of the tie of the blue robe.

She hung back, not quite resisting him, but not falling into his arms, either. He looked into her eyes again. She peeked out at him warily, like some lost waif, from under the dark strands of those shaggy bangs of hers. He knew that Larry's thoughtless words had gotten to her. But would she admit it, if he pressed her on the point? Doubtful.

He gave it a try. "Are you upset, about the things my idiot brother said?"

A muscle in her cheek twitched, but she resolutely shook her head.

He tried once more. "Sure?"

She nodded. And then she smiled. "Positive." The smile looked just a little bit forced. But he'd apologized once for Larry, back in the hallway. And now he'd given her two more chances to open up about it.

What the hell else could he do, if she wouldn't talk about it?

Those knowing, pale eyes regarded him. He stared into them, thinking that he'd never felt about a woman the way he felt about her. He saw so much now when he looked at her. Tenderness. And humor. A good, caring heart. An honest, incredibly imaginative, unfettered sexuality. And great dignity.

He saw what real beauty was.

"What are you thinking about?" she demanded, still hanging back.

"You and me." He gave the tie a light tug. But she didn't give in and come into his arms.

"What about you and me?"

He tugged on the tie again. Instead of bringing her closer, the tie came loose and slithered off her.

"Derek. What about you and me?"

The sides of the robe had fallen open. Her slim body gleamed at him in the light from the bedside lamp. She had slender, firm legs and a tiny waist. Very small breasts with soft, shell pink nipples. He knew she thought that her breasts were *too* small. He didn't think that. Why should he? They were *her* breasts.

"Derek?"

He reached out, touched one. She hitched in a tender little gasp.

He whispered, "You're so beautiful, Lee."

She stepped back as if he'd slapped her.

"What's the matter?"

She put up a hand. Those pale eyes had gone dead. "Look. Don't, okay?"

He felt injured, in the worst kind of way. Rebuffed. Still, he tried again. "I mean it. You *are* beautiful."

"I am not. And don't say I am. Please. Let's just…be honest with each other, at least."

Anger welled in him. He carefully kept it in check and spoke reasonably. "Have you noticed how lately it seems that everything I say is wrong?"

"That's not so."

"I think it is."

"Just let it go, all right?"

He didn't want to let it go. But he knew that whatever he said next, he'd probably live to regret. They'd end up in a fight.

And he didn't want to fight with her. He wanted to hold her, to touch her.

He reached out. She feinted back a step, avoiding his hand—and came up against the door.

The robe was still open, wider than before. He let his gaze sweep down, over her breasts and her belly, the dark triangle between her thighs, the long, firm legs, all the way to her bare, pink feet. He looked at her toes for a moment. She wiggled them—in apprehension, maybe.

Or just possibly, in invitation. He glanced up again.

Her eyes were waiting. And they had changed. That dead look had left them.

He knew what she was thinking. The same thing he was thinking.

His anger and hurt broke apart, melted away. What remained was the slow, thrumming heat of desire. "Where are you going to go now?"

She lifted one shoulder in a shrug that made the robe fall open even more. "Go to bed." A tiny, unwilling smile was trying to pull at the side of her mouth.

He dropped the tie on the floor and pointed a thumb back over his shoulder. "That bed?"

She nodded. "'I like that bed."

"It's my bed."

"Well, I know that."

"If you sleep in that bed, you'll have to sleep with me."

She frowned, as if considering that point. Then she nodded again. "I understand."

Very slowly, he reached out for the second time. This time, she didn't try to get away. He grasped the edges of the robe in either fist and pulled her toward him.

She melted against him with a soft little sigh. He slid his arms inside the robe with her, around her smooth, bare waist. Her body pressed along his, soft and warm, slim and firm.

She kissed his neck, then whispered. "Your wrist does seem to be healing well."

"Almost as good as new."

"Can we get into that bed of yours now?"

"In a minute." He was already lowering himself to his knees.

Lee left about nine the next morning. Derek knew that under better circumstances, he could have talked her into hanging around for a while, enjoying a slow, lazy Sunday with him.

But today there was Larry to consider. He could appear from the spare room at any minute, looking like hell and smelling of stale booze. Who could guess what he might do or say? No wonder Lee just wanted to get out.

And that was probably the best thing she could do. Derek needed to have a few private words with Larry about his rotten remarks the night before. Maybe, if luck was with him, he could write Larry another check and send him on his way before Lee even had to deal with him again.

Larry got up at eleven-thirty. He shuffled barefoot, past Derek, who sat on the sofa with the Sunday *Statesman Journal.* Neither brother spoke. Derek went on reading and Larry headed for the kitchen. When Derek had finished his newspaper, he folded it neatly and left it on the sofa.

Then he went to the other room, where Larry sat at the table, smoking a cigarette, hunched over a half-full cup of black coffee. Derek got him a saucer to use as an ashtray and then slid into the chair across from him.

Larry knocked his ash onto the saucer and looked up. In the bright light of morning, he wasn't a pretty sight. How he could see through all the broken blood vessels that crisscrossed his jaundiced eyeballs was a mystery to Derek.

"Don't even start on me," Larry growled.

"You're in my house. Drinking my coffee. And it was my fiancée you insulted last night. I think I've got a right to start on you, but good."

Larry grunted and sucked on the cigarette. He blew

smoke up toward the ceiling. "Damn. That was real, then? That skinny, dark-haired woman in the big blue robe?"

"Her name is Lee."

"Uh. Lee. Got it." Larry stubbed out the cigarette and tried on a smile, one that kept slipping into a grimace. "Sorry."

Derek rested both elbows on the table and rubbed his eyes with his fingertips.

"Hey," Larry said. "What the hell happened to your hand?"

"It's a long story. Look, Larry. Maybe you ought to get some help, you know?"

Larry's beefy shoulders straightened a little. "Help? What kind of help?"

"Some kind of counseling. Maybe check into a center where they'll get you sober and teach you how to stay that way."

Larry lifted his coffee cup. "Forget it." He slurped coffee, then set the cup down hard. "I don't need any damn help. I need a decent woman and a good job, that's all."

"And how do you think you'll get either one of those, when you cheat on your wife and don't show up for work?"

Larry swore and pushed himself to his feet. "I don't need to hear this from you. You're my brother. You're supposed to be on my side."

Derek looked up at him, and wondered why he'd bothered to try to get him to see that he was killing himself. "How much do you want this time?"

A crafty light came into the bleary eyes. "Five hundred?"

Derek winced. "Larry. You just hit me up a month ago."

"How 'bout four, then?"

In the end, they settled on three. And Larry was gone within the hour. Derek couldn't muster much more than relief to see him drive away.

He wanted to see Lee. He wanted to tell her all about Larry and the mess Larry had made of his life. He had a feeling Lee would see it all more clearly than he did. She might even have some decent suggestions as to what Derek could do to really help his older brother.

He called her. But he got her machine. "Call me," he said, and hung up.

He spent a half an hour cleaning his place, and then he got his gym bag and went to the club. He worked out for an hour and a half—hoping in the back of his mind the whole time that Lee might show up there.

She didn't. He took a long, hot shower, got dressed and went home. When he got there, he found that she hadn't called. And she didn't call in the next two hours.

It probably shouldn't have bothered him. They spent a hell of a lot of time together, after all. She had a right to a Sunday without him now and then.

Still, it did bother him. It felt to him as if she was pulling away from him. She wouldn't set a date for the wedding. She seemed on edge a lot of the time, and inevitably ready to take offense at anything he said. And, even though she wouldn't admit it, he was always the one who called her.

Worst of all, every time he tried to talk to her about the situation, she stonewalled him.

But what more could he do? If she wouldn't talk, she wouldn't talk.

By five-thirty, Lee had neither called nor appeared at his door.

He picked up the phone to call *her* again. And then he slammed it down, grabbed his keys and headed for her place.

She answered her door within fifteen seconds of his loud knock.

He glared at her. "Where have you been all damn day?"

She fell back a step and put a hand on her neck, her eyes going wide with surprise at his harshness.

He felt like a complete heel. He moved back a step himself, giving her some distance as he mentally counted to ten. "Look. I called. I thought you'd call back."

She said nothing for a moment, then she asked, "Do you want to come in?"

He let out a long breath. "Yeah. Yeah, I do."

"Well, come on, then." She ushered him through the door and then shut it behind him. "I did get your message, about ten minutes ago, when I finally got home. I was just about to call you."

A damn fool. That's what he was. "Oh. Well. I see." There were shopping bags, a lot of them, lined up on the couch. "You spent the day shopping?"

"Most of it."

"What did you buy?"

She waved a hand, vaguely. "Oh, nothing much."

"Looks like plenty of stuff to me."

"Well, I needed a few things. Oh, and I also dropped in to see Lenora and Maria."

"How are they doing?"

"Okay. She got all excited when she saw the ring."

That made him feel marginally better. "She did?"

"Yeah. She says she just had a feeling about us. And she was glad to know she was right."

Was she? he found himself thinking. Was she right? But he didn't say it. No need to borrow trouble.

She asked, "How did it go with your brother?"

A few hours ago, he'd wanted to tell her all about Larry. Now, somehow, the urge had vanished. "I gave him three hundred dollars. And then he left."

"Was he…all right?"

He shrugged. "Sure. As all right as any alcoholic ever is the morning after a big drunk."

She sighed then. "Oh, Derek. He really should get help."

"You think I haven't told him that? It's like talking to a wall."

"Maybe if you—"

He really didn't want to hear it, not at this point. "Look. I've had enough of Larry about now to last me a lifetime. Let's talk about something else, all right?"

She studied his face. "But he's all the family you've got, and I think that you—"

He didn't let her get another word out. "Drop it. Please."

She closed her mouth and just looked at him. Reproachfully. Again, he felt like a jerk. But then she put on a smile. "Tell you what. I'll make dinner."

He forced a smile of his own. "I'd like that."

"Just let me put my shopping bags in the spare room."

He tried a little teasing. "You still haven't told me what's in them."

She teased right back. "And I'm not going to, either."

Relief washed through him. The evening would be all right, after all. "Why not?"

Her smile turned mysterious. ''A woman has a right
to a secret or two.''

''What does that mean?''

''Forget it. I'm not telling you now.''

''When, then?''

''You'll see....''

Chapter Eighteen

The next morning, Lee pretended to be sick. When the alarm went off, she rolled over and moaned, "Oh, Derek. I feel awful."

He canted up on an elbow and leaned over her, his handsome face tight with concern. "What's wrong?"

"My throat's all scratchy and my head aches."

He laid a hand on her forehead. "No fever."

She tried to look miserable, even let out another moan. "I just ache all over."

"Congestion?"

"Not yet. But I really feel awful."

He said what she'd intended for him to say. "You'd better just stay in bed today."

And she—so regretfully—agreed with him. "All right. Maybe I can beat this before it really takes hold."

He got up and found her some Tylenol in the medicine cabinet. Then he put on his clothes. Before he left, he disappeared for a few minutes and returned with a pitcher and a glass. "Here. Ice water. Drink lots of liquids, okay?"

"I promise."

He set the glass and pitcher on the nightstand and then stood by the bed and looked down at her sympathetically.

"Don't kiss me," she said, playing her role to the hilt. "I could be contagious."

He felt her forehead again. "I'd still say you don't have a fever." She moaned some more and stirred around under the covers, as if her body ached so much she just couldn't get comfortable. He frowned at her in concern. "Don't get out of bed unless you have to."

"Yes, Doctor." She let out a long, sad sigh.

"I'll call you around noon, to see how you're doing."

Her pulse accelerated. Having him call her wasn't part of her scheme. "You know, as soon as I give Jack a call to let him know I won't be in, I thought I'd turn off the ringer of the phone in here. Uninterrupted rest, that's really what I need."

Derek reached for the phone and turned off the ringer himself. "I'll tell Jack you won't be in. And I'll be back as soon as I finish my rounds tonight."

She granted him a wobbly, pitiful, sick-person smile. "I'll be here."

"I'll lock the door on the way out. And tonight, I'll just let myself in, so you won't have to get up."

"You have your key?" she asked. He held it up for her to see. She'd given it to him the day after he proposed, just as he had given her back the key to his place. "Good," she said. "See you tonight."

He left at last.

She waited to throw off the covers until a full five minutes after she heard his Suburban start up and drive away.

Lee managed to get a ten-thirty appointment with someone named Margie at the Savoir-Faire Salon.

"So what can I do for you today?" Margie asked brightly, once she had Lee trapped in her big black chair with a plastic apron cinched tight around her neck.

Lee looked at Margie in the mirror. She was tiny, with unbelievably red hair cut in a very short shag. She wore a tight purple shirt and a short, tight black skirt. She could have been anywhere from twenty-five to forty. With all that makeup on, who could say for sure?

Lee felt a sharp stab of apprehension. Maybe she should have called Dana or Katie and asked for their help and advice. They would at least have given her referrals to their own hairdressers.

But then they'd just want to know why she'd suddenly decided to pay attention to her looks. One way or another, they'd pry the truth from her. She'd end up detailing all of her foolish, embarrassing insecurities. They'd get her to reveal everything, to go into all the grim details—from the depressing advice her mother had given her to the awful middle-of-the-night scene with Derek's brother, where he'd said she was skinny. And needed a haircut. And not up to Derek's standards at all.

Then they'd pry from her how Derek had actually tried to make her feel better by lying to her. That he'd looked right in her eyes and told her she was beautiful.

Beautiful.

She still felt awful every time she thought of that.

Then, once they'd made her tell all, they'd defend her. They'd say she looked just fine as she was. That her mother saw the worst in every situation and that Derek's brother needed therapy. That the last thing she should do was to listen to a hopeless pessimist and a ne'er-do-well drunk.

She'd tell them that she knew they were right. And at the same time, down inside, she'd be thinking that Ina Murphy and Larry Taylor might both need counseling, but the harsh things they'd said still rang true.

And Lee intended to do something about the problem. She would make a few changes. A few...improvements. And she would do it now and get it over with, before she got cold feet and talked herself out of it.

Derek loved glamour and beauty in women. She knew it. She'd *seen* the women he'd chosen before he'd run into her.

Lee couldn't give him beauty.

But glamour...

Well, she could at least take a shot at it. She'd get her hair fixed and buy some makeup. She'd put on some of the new, provocative clothes she'd bought yesterday.

And she'd meet Derek at the front door looking stunning—please God—when he came home from Memorial this afternoon.

"Er...are you all right?" Margie asked.

"Why?"

"You have a sort of blank look on your face. And you didn't answer my question."

Lee met Margie's eyes in the mirror again. "What question?"

"The question of what I can do for you today?"

Lee gulped—no mean feat, with the tie of Margie's plastic apron cutting into her windpipe. "I want a total and complete makeover."

Margie's brown eyes widened. "You were so smart to book four hours."

"I expected it would take some time."

"Hmm. You'll want a shampoo and cut..." Margie began.

"...And a perm. And I want some advice about makeup. Can you do all that?"

"Hair is my department. But the salon does have a cosmetics consultant. I'll turn you over to her as soon as you and I are done."

"Fine."

"Would you like to see our manicurist, too? You could get a good nail wrap from her."

"Yes. I want long nails."

"And you know, Lee, sometimes it helps to start with a massage and mud wrap—to make you feel pampered. What would you say to that?"

Lee considered, but then shook her head. "Let's just stick to the exterior improvements, all right?"

"Whatever you'd like."

"I'd also like my hair color changed."

"To what?"

"Blond."

Periodically throughout the day, Derek found himself wishing he hadn't unplugged Lee's bedside phone. He wanted to call her, just to see that she was doing all right.

He couldn't help worrying about her. In spite of her lack of fever, she'd really seemed miserable that morning. He hoped she'd stayed in bed the way he'd told her to, and kept getting the liquids down.

The director of nursing had found a temp R.N. to cover for Lee. And the patient load that day wasn't too bad. Derek finished his rounds by four forty-five and dictated his remaining patient summaries quickly. At five-fifteen, he pulled out of the hospital's parking lot.

Halfway to Lee's place, he stopped at a café and picked up a quart of chicken soup. It was quarter of six when he let himself quietly in her front door.

"Hello, Derek."

He pushed the door shut behind him and stood there, clutching the container of soup, gaping at the strange blond woman in the tight red skirt.

Her red lips vamped a smile. "What's that?" She pointed a long, crimson nail at the container in his hand.

"Soup," he croaked.

"Oh, Derek," she simpered. "You brought me soup."

That was when the truth hit him.

In total disbelief, he heard himself whisper, "Lee?"

She came sauntering up to him on red high heels. He found himself staring at her chest, which somehow, between that morning and that moment, appeared to have grown a pair of ripe, round-looking breasts.

She slipped her arms around him and tipped her face up to his. Those breasts that belonged on someone else brushed his chest. She smelled…different. Wrong. Of some musty perfume that wasn't her at all. "Surprise," her red mouth whispered.

This close, he could see the makeup, so thick on her face. She actually had shadows painted on, to make her nose look thinner and her cheekbones more prominent.

"What do you think?" she asked huskily.

He thought he couldn't breathe. "You said you were sick." It came out sounding like an accusation.

A shadow of hurt moved across her face, under all that paint. "Derek. I asked what you think of my new look."

He didn't want to answer that. No way. He accused again, "So you weren't sick, then. Right? It was all a big act."

Her lip started to quiver a little. Then it stopped. She assumed that come-hither smile again. "I wanted to surprise you."

He took her by the upper arms and peeled her off of him enough that he could meet her heavily made-up eyes. "Well. You succeeded. I'm surprised."

She stared at him for a moment and then she pulled free of his grip. "You hate it."

He knew with stunning clarity that whatever he said next would be wrong.

She stumbled backward a little, on those heels that she wasn't used to wearing. "You hate it." Her voice went shrill. "Just say it. Just tell me the truth."

"Lee—"

"Just tell me! Just say it. I want to know."

So he told her. "All right. I hate it. You look like hell."

She gasped and put her hand against those too-red lips. From behind that fringe of false eyelashes, her eyes went wide, brimming with hurt.

He felt like a jerk. Why lately, with her, did he always end up feeling like a jerk? "Lee," he tried one last time. "What is going on with you?"

She blinked, took her hand away from her mouth and drew her shoulders back. "Nothing."

"That's pure garbage. Something is wrong."

"There's nothing. Really. I only wanted to please you. I wanted to try to be the kind of woman you like so much."

He let out a short, succinct expletive and then pointed the soup at her. "Look. I didn't ask you to do this. I didn't even *hint* that I wanted you to do this. I told you the other night what I thought of you, just as you are.''

Her eyes went as hard as chips of ice. "Right. You said I was *beautiful*.''

"And you are, damn it. Or at least, you *were*.''

She whispered furiously, "Liar.''

He felt as if she'd kneed him where it would hurt the most. He plunked the damn soup down on the coffee table and then threw up both hands. "This is a setup. No matter what I do, I lose.''

"That's ridiculous,'' she hissed.

"No, it's the truth. Something really stinks here. Any fool could see that something's eating you, but you keep saying it's not. And now you've gone and done this...*thing* to yourself. And if I say it looks fine, then you know I'm lying. And if I go ahead and say I hate it, then you can call me a damn heartless creep.''

He knew he'd hit a nerve with that. Her eyes shifted away. "That's not so. I told you. I only did this to please you.''

"Like hell you did.''

She sank to the couch then, and hung her fake blond head. And then she said the words that he knew had been hovering in the back of her mind for days now. "Derek, maybe this isn't going to work out.''

He felt a great stillness then. An emptiness that echoed, down deep inside. Out of that stillness, he heard himself ask, "What isn't going to work out?''

She looked up, into his eyes. "You and me.''

He wanted to grab her, shake her, shout at her. But he only said in a flat voice, "You mean you want to break off our engagement.''

She was already tugging on her ring. "Yes. I do. I

think it's for the best." She slid it free of that red-tipped finger and held it out to him.

He made no move to take the damn thing from her, only asked, very reasonably, "This is what you've been after all along, isn't it?"

Those perfectly arched eyebrows that someone had painted on her forehead drew together as she frowned. "No. No, of course not."

"Lee. Ever since I asked you to marry me, you've been pulling away."

"No, I—"

"Yeah. You have. And I can't for the life of me figure out why. I may have been a pompous ass until you came along, but I've done my damnedest to make a change. And the last thing I want now is for *you* to change. I love you, Lee. Just the way you are. Or *were*."

Her face started to crumple then. He could see the tears coming, though she bravely bit them back. "Oh, Derek. I—"

"What? You what?"

"I just…can't do this. I can't be what you want."

"But you *are* what I want. Why won't you believe me?"

"Because real life is no fantasy. Because in real life, you'll get tired of me, I know it."

"Damn it, Lee. Haven't we been through this?"

She swiped at her eyes with the back of her hand. "Yes. I know. We have."

"I told you you're no novelty to me."

"I know you did."

"But you never heard it, did you? You never believed."

She bit her quivering lip and shook her head.

Derek understood then what futility really was. "You

know, there's not a hell of a lot of hope for us, if you refuse to believe the things I say."

"I...I know that."

"You know it," he repeated her words, feeling weary to his core. "But still, you don't believe me."

She closed her fingers around his ring and wrapped her other hand around her tight fist. "I wish I could believe you."

"But you don't."

"Oh, Derek..." She seemed to have no idea how to go on. Instead she peeled her outer hand away and held out the one with the ring in it again. "Please. Just take it."

He looked at the damn thing. "Don't do this, Lee."

"Just take it."

"Don't give me so little credit, don't treat me like I'm not even really here. Like I'm someone you made up. Some...fantasy of yours. Someone without enough guts or substance to stick by you, someone who doesn't even know his own mind."

"I just...I can't...."

"You've said that. You've said it over and over again. And always, in the end, you found out you could."

"Not this. Not...forever. Forever doesn't last."

"That's something your mother would say. You're not your mother, Lee."

"I know that."

"I don't think so. Not deep down. It looks to me like, deep down, in the most secret part of yourself, you believe that you're just like your mother. And where does that leave me? Except to play your dear old dad all over again, and walk out on you?"

She only stared at him, pale eyes shimmering with

barely held back tears. Then she looked down at the floor again.

"Look at me, damn it," he commanded.

Her head bobbed up and she met his eyes.

"I can't keep trying, Lee. Keep knocking myself out. I can't reach for you and reach for you, if you won't reach back."

"I know," she got out on a whisper.

His anger flared again. "You know. You know?"

She winced as if he'd slapped her, then she whispered once more, "I do. Yes. I know."

He stared at her, hopelessness rolling over him. At that point, finally, he ran out of anger, out of arguments, out of the will to keep trying to get through to her. He asked, softly now, "Is this really what you want?"

She nodded.

"All right, Lee. I'll give you what you want." He extended his palm. Into it, she dropped the shining circle of gold with its single gleaming diamond.

He stuck the thing in his pocket and left her there.

Chapter Nineteen

Lee's tears, so tightly held in check while Derek loomed above her, dried to nothing without falling as soon as he walked out the door.

She sat there on the sofa, her hands clasped stiffly in the lap of her tight red skirt, for the longest time.

Eventually she kicked off the silly red high heels. She stood, very carefully, the way a drunk would stand, extremely conscious of the possibility that she just might lose her balance and end up toppling to the floor.

Once she was on her feet, she aimed herself at the small bathroom in the tiny hall between her bedroom and the spare room. There, taking great care not to look in the mirror over the sink, she stripped off the red skirt and matching jacket, the black garter belt and stockings, the tiny red bikini panties and the padded bra.

She turned on the shower and waited for the steam to rise. When it did, she got under it.

She took a cloth and the soap and she worked up a lather. And then she scrubbed her face until it burned. She poured on shampoo and lathered every last bit of spray and mousse out of her hair. Then she rinsed, for a long time, watching the soap foam run down the drain. Finally she turned off the water and reached for a towel.

She dried herself roughly, scouring the drops of water from her skin. And then she got the little pair of manicure scissors from the bathroom drawer and sliced off those silly long red nails. Tomorrow, after work, she'd buy some remover and get rid of the red polish.

She froze, with the little scissors poised to cut the nail from her pinky.

After work.

Dear Lord.

How would she get through that? Working with Derek, every single day…

A small, tight sob escaped her. She sucked in air and held it.

She *would* get through it. Somehow. And if it turned out to be impossible, she'd examine other options.

And there was certainly no point in dwelling on it now.

Slowly, she let out the breath she was holding. She cut off the last long red nail and pulled open the drawer to put the scissors away.

Right then she caught sight of herself in the bathroom mirror, from which the film of steam had started to evaporate.

Her face was her face again—though it looked scrubbed almost raw.

But her hair. Oh, God. It was the color of wet straw.

And it corkscrewed out in electric, Medusa-like tendrils all around her head.

* * *

"Whoa," said Terry the next morning. "What happened to your hair?" Then she glanced down and saw Lee's ring finger. "Never mind. Forget that question. You okay?"

Lee lifted her chin. "I'm just fine."

Derek came in at his usual time. He said hello to Lee and she said hello to him. They shared a forced smile and then he went down the hall to his office, as he always did.

The day went as well as could be expected. Derek treated her with great civility and she returned the courtesy. Still, she felt as if she'd lived through some natural disaster by the time the day finally drew to a close.

Dana and Katie were waiting on her doorstep when she got home that night. They'd heard that the engagement was off through the hospital grapevine. She let them in and they fussed over her hair and tried to offer comfort for a while. But she wasn't talking and they knew she didn't really want company right then.

They left around seven, with admonitions that she should call them the minute she needed anything at all.

Once they were gone, she got out the bottle of remover she'd bought on the way home and rubbed the red polish from her chopped-off nails.

Wednesday and Thursday went much the same as Tuesday had gone. Lee moved through the days, doing her job, dealing politely with Derek and telling herself that it would work out, that she'd get used to seeing him every day.

That the longing and the awful emptiness would pass.

Thursday night, her mother called. "I hope everything's going all right with you and your doctor, honey."

Lee didn't feel up to telling her mother that she could

stop worrying about Derek getting tired of her. So she lied. She said everything was going just fine. There would be time, a little later, to tell Ina that she had one less thing to worry about, her daughter wouldn't marry a doctor, after all.

Friday, when the day was finally over, Lee dropped in to see Lenora. Maria was downstairs, playing with her friend Gary, so Lee and Lenora had some time alone.

It was good to be with Lenora. She didn't even mention Lee's horrible hair. She looked at it and shrugged. And that was that.

"We're moving," Lenora announced. She and another woman at the shelter had decided to rent a small house together. "It's not far from here, so Maria can still go to day care at the shelter, where she's used to it." The other woman had two small daughters of her own.

"That's wonderful," said Lee.

And Lenora reached across the distance between them and put her hand over Lee's. "You saved my life."

"Oh, no…"

"Yes. You did. You brought me here when I was finally ready to come. And then your Dr. Taylor, he faced Otto down, and saved me again." Lenora frowned at Lee's hand, and then looked up into her eyes. "Where is your ring?"

Lee's throat clamped shut. The tears that had not come on Monday, for some insane reason, took that moment to rise again.

Lenora's dark eyes were full of sadness and knowing. "You gave it back to him."

Lee gulped, sucked in air. "I'm…an independent type. I don't think marriage is for me."

"You were the one that broke it off, then?"

A torn sound escaped Lee. "Yeah. That's a shock, isn't it? That *I* broke it off with him?"

"Like that old song, right?"

"What song?"

"You beat him to the punch."

"Oh, no. I didn't. I mean, that isn't how it was."

Lenora waved a hand in front of her face. "Hey. I understand. You were just...too scared to try. Right? So you decided to give up before you even really gave it a chance."

Lee felt the damn tears, pushing so hard. She gulped again, in a vain effort to swallow them.

Lenora smiled. "We get counseling here, you know? And we learn that sometimes the hardest things to escape are the horrible voices of fear and doubt inside our own heads."

The tears kept pushing. They wouldn't be kept back. Lee swallowed again, but it did no good at all. They ran over, down her cheeks. She heard herself sob.

Lenora reached out her arms.

And Lee found herself wrapped in them.

Lenora said, "Go ahead. Cry. Yes, you just cry...."

Lee told Lenora everything—about her mother's doubts and Larry Taylor's derision. About how she never could quite make herself talk about it all with Derek. And about the awful makeover that had been the final straw.

When she was done, Lenora said, "Go find him. Ask him to take you back."

Lee let out a laugh that was almost another sob. "He's taken me back several times already. He'd be crazy to take a chance on me again."

Lenora smiled her patient, knowing smile. "Well, maybe that's a chance *you* really need to take."

Lee went to Derek's house straight from the shelter.

She ran up the steps to his door with her heart trip-hammering against her breastbone.

Larry Taylor sat on the top step, his legs drawn up to his barrel chest and his head on his knees.

"Larry?"

With a groan, he lifted his head and peered at her through slitted eyes. "Uh. Lee. Right?"

She nodded.

"What the hell did you do to your hair?"

On reflex, she reached up and touched it. She gave a hank of it a tug, which accomplished nothing. It was still straw-colored and still sticking out from her head in an electrified frizz. She sighed and dropped her hand. "You don't want to know."

He laughed then, as if she'd said something really humorous. "I can relate to that."

She gestured at the dark condo. "I take it he's not home."

Larry grunted. "I'd say you've got that right."

"What are you doing here?"

Larry put his head down again. A shudder went through him and he groaned. Lee waited for the shuddering to stop. But even after it did, he said nothing. She had a sudden suspicion that he might have dropped off to sleep.

"Larry?"

"I lost my job." He spoke to the step. "They kicked me out of my apartment. I got no damn place to go." At last, he lifted his head again and looked right at her. "I haven't had a drink in twenty-four hours."

She took a minute to stare back at him good and hard. Then she nodded, a nod of acknowledgment that he'd taken a first step toward helping himself. "Okay."

Another convulsive shiver went through him. "I don't feel so hot." He shuddered some more, holding onto his drawn-up knees as if a tight grip might make the shaking stop. "You despise me, huh?"

She shook her head and spoke gently. "No, Larry. I don't despise you."

"I'm a pig."

"I do not despise you."

He grunted again, shuddered some more. "I need a cigarette." He closed his eyes. "Last time I was here, Derek said I should get help. I been thinking about that. I was kind of hoping that maybe he would tell me someplace to go."

"You mean rehab?"

He opened his eyes, blinked twice and then nodded. "Yeah. Rehab. That's what I mean."

Lee bent and took his arm. "Come on. I know a place. It's not too far from here. They'll help you there."

He hung back. "Look, I gotta tell you. I got no money."

"Don't worry about that now. We'll get the money somehow."

"We?" He actually smiled. "Hey, that's right. You're marryin' Derek. That makes you family."

I *hope* I'm marrying Derek, she thought. But what she said was, "Yes. Now, come on."

An hour later, she'd checked Larry into detox. For a while, he wouldn't be allowed to see anyone, but Lee promised she would be there, the minute he could have visitors.

"You and Derek," he stated. "Together, right?"

She took a huge leap of faith and answered, "Right."

Then she went back to her place and packed a bag. She didn't even bother to call Dana and ask if Walter MacAllister had given Derek the keys to the cabin for a third time.

She just followed her heart up the twisting mountain road to Blue Moon Lake.

It was past dark when she got there. The Suburban was parked below the front deck and the front door was unlocked.

As she had two weeks before, she made a circuit of the rooms.

She found Derek sitting at the top of the basement stairs with a rifle across his knees. She went and sat beside him.

He turned very slowly and looked at her. "If you aren't here to stay, then just get up right now and go on back home."

"I'm here to stay."

His beautiful eyes narrowed with suspicion. "This is it. If you change your mind this time…"

"What?"

He looked at the door frame over their heads, as if he might find an answer there. "Hell. I'll turn this damn rifle on myself, I suppose."

She dared to lay her hand on his arm. "Please don't do that. I love you."

"I think the question is, when will you believe that *I* love you?"

"I do believe it. Or at least, I'm learning to."

He looked at her doubtfully.

She confessed, "All right. I'm still pretty terrified. But I'll stick it out. I'll…tell you what I'm thinking.

I'll…reveal my most ridiculous inner fears. If you'll just give me one more chance.''

"You'll have to marry me. Soon. You'll have to set a damn date for the wedding and stick with it.''

"Yes, Derek. I will.''

His gaze ran over her. "You'll let me tell you you're beautiful.''

She managed not to flinch. "Yes. I can do that. I can.''

"And I guess your hair will grow out.''

"Of course it will.'' She drew in a deep breath. "By the way, I just took your brother to the Crossroads Center.''

"You're kidding, right?''

"No. I found him on your doorstep tonight. He said he hadn't had a drink in twenty-four hours and he'd come to ask you to help him check into rehab.''

"So, since I wasn't there, you took him yourself.''

"That's right.''

"What is it with you? Relentlessly doing the right thing, going the extra mile for the hopelessly lost.''

She thought of the way he'd always been there for his brother, the way he'd stepped in front of Otto Hirsch's gun. "We're alike that way.''

Those blue eyes seemed to see straight into her heart. "We're alike in a *lot* of ways, if you bother to look beneath the surface.''

"I'm working on it. Be patient with me.''

"I'm not a patient man.''

"Well, *you* can work on *that,* then.'' She glanced down at his right wrist. "Your cast is gone.''

"I don't need it anymore.''

She indicated the rifle. "And what are you doing with this thing?''

His firm jaw got firmer. "I heard that animal. Down there, in the basement, about a half an hour ago. And this time, I didn't come empty-handed. When he moves again, I'll get him."

"Derek," she said tenderly. "Let me have that rifle." He pressed his lips together and gripped the thing harder at barrel and stock. "Derek." She made her voice whisper-soft, and then she bent closer. She blew in his ear. Right into that external auditory meatus she admired so much. "Please. Let me have it."

He made one of those low, growly sounds.

Carefully, she took hold of it. She gave a tug. He held on at first. And then grudgingly he let go.

"Is it loaded?"

"Give it back." When she didn't move, he said it again. "Give it back. I'll unload it and put it away."

"Promise?"

He looked infinitely put-upon. "Lee. You're going to have to start believing that I'm a man of my word."

She handed him the rifle. He rose with it and left her. When he returned to stand above her, the rifle was nowhere in sight. "Come on. Close that door."

She stood and pushed the door shut.

"Come here."

She went to him. He cradled her face in his warm hands. "God. I missed you."

"I missed you, too."

"Don't do that to me again."

"Never. I swear to you."

"I love you, Lee."

Down below them, something dropped. Then it bumped. And then it rolled.

Lee said, "Oh, no…"
Derek said, "You'd better kiss me now."
So she did. She kissed him. He gathered her close.
And the creature in the basement escaped once again.

Epilogue

The vow, tattered and heavily seamed from years of handling, of folding and refolding, sat open on the silver tray.

The three brides, Katie, Dana and Lee, each in her long white gown and filmy veil, stood in a circle around the small, spindly-legged table on which the tray sat.

"Read," Dana said.

And Katie read, "We, the undersigned, having barely survived four years of nursing school and preparing to go forth and find a job, do hereby vow to meet at Granetti's at least once a week, not to do anything drastic to our hair without consulting each other first and never *ever*—no matter how rich, how cute, how funny, how smart, or how good in bed—to marry a doctor."

A moment of reverent silence ensued.

Then Dana asked, "Lee, have you got the matches?"

Lee held up the small cardboard box and gave it a shake.

"Good," said Dana. "Do it. They'll be starting the wedding march any minute now."

Lee opened the box, produced a match and struck it with a flourish. The scent of sulfur burned the air and the flame leapt up, strong and bright. Lee lowered the match toward the tattered paper on the tray.

But before flame could touch fuel, Katie caught Lee's arm. "Wait."

Lee turned toward Katie, and Dana did, too. "What?" they demanded in unison.

Katie's soft eyes looked misty. "If you guys don't mind, I think I'd like to say a few words first."

Lee blew out the match and tossed it on the silver tray beside the vow. "Okay. Speak."

"And make it quick," Dana advised. "We don't have all day here."

Katie coughed nervously. "Do you think we could...hold hands?"

Dana made a noise in her throat.

Katie shrugged. "Too corny, huh?"

And Dana grinned. "No, of course it's not."

Lee tucked the box of matches into the bodice of her gown, where there was plenty of room. Then she reached out to find a friend's hand waiting on either side. "Okay, say it, whatever it is."

Katie coughed again. "All right. Um. Well. Today, we burn our old vow before we each make a new one—to love, honor and cherish our husbands. Husbands that, somehow, incredibly, all turned out to be doctors. But still, I have to say I think it's appropriate that certain aspects of the vow remain in effect, to remind us—"

Lee knew what was coming. And she didn't want to

hear it. After all, Dana's hairdresser had worked miracles to repair the damage. Beneath her veil, Lee's hair didn't look half bad. Lee let out a put-upon groan. "Oh, come on…"

Katie repeated, "To remind us…"

Lee glared at Katie, and Katie stared right back, unwavering. Lee was the one who dropped her gaze. "All right, all right. I suppose I deserve this. Say it."

And Katie did. "…to remind us that drastic changes in hairstyle really aren't a good idea."

"Okay, okay. I get the message."

"Good," Katie said. Then her expression turned soft again. "Also, we should remember to get together often, one way or another." Katie looked from Dana to Lee and back to Dana again. Suddenly her eyes had gone beyond misty. They shone with happy tears. "Because I never, ever, want to lose touch with either of you."

"Agreed," Dana said huskily.

"Me, too," Lee concurred.

"Now," said Dana. "Do it." She let go of Lee's left hand as Katie released her on the right. Lee fumbled in the top of her dress and finally pulled the matchbox free.

For the second time, she removed a match and struck it. The small flame exploded into life. She lowered it slowly toward the vow.

The flame kissed the paper, licked along the edge and burst into brightness.

In less than a minute, only ash remained.

And right then, beyond the door of the tiny space off the narthex that the church had let them use as a dressing room, the wedding march began.

* * * * * *

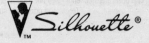

Take 2 bestselling love stories FREE

Plus get a FREE surprise gift!

Special Limited-Time Offer

Mail to Silhouette Reader Service™

3010 Walden Avenue
P.O. Box 1867
Buffalo, N.Y. 14240-1867

YES! Please send me 2 free Silhouette Special Edition® novels and my free surprise gift. Then send me 6 brand-new novels every month, which I will receive months before they appear in bookstores. Bill me at the low price of $3.57 each plus 25¢ delivery and applicable sales tax, if any.* That's the complete price, and a saving of over 10% off the cover prices—quite a bargain! I understand that accepting the books and gift places me under no obligation ever to buy any books. I can always return a shipment and cancel at any time. Even if I never buy another book from Silhouette, the 2 free books and the surprise gift are mine to keep forever.

235 SEN CH7W

Name	(PLEASE PRINT)	
Address	Apt. No.	
City	State	Zip

This offer is limited to one order per household and not valid to present Silhouette Special Edition® subscribers. *Terms and prices are subject to change without notice. Sales tax applicable in N.Y.

USPED-98   ©1990 Harlequin Enterprises Limited

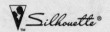

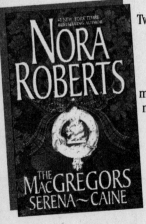
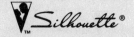

For a limited time, Harlequin and Silhouette have an offer you just can't refuse.

In November and December 1998:

BUY **ANY** TWO HARLEQUIN
OR SILHOUETTE BOOKS and
SAVE $10.00
off future purchases

OR BUY ANY THREE HARLEQUIN OR SILHOUETTE BOOKS
AND **SAVE $20.00** OFF FUTURE PURCHASES!

(each coupon is good for $1.00 off the purchase of two
Harlequin or Silhouette books)

....

JUST BUY 2 HARLEQUIN OR SILHOUETTE BOOKS, SEND US YOUR
NAME, ADDRESS AND 2 PROOFS OF PURCHASE (CASH REGISTER
RECEIPTS) AND HARLEQUIN WILL SEND YOU A COUPON BOOKLET
WORTH $10.00 OFF FUTURE PURCHASES OF HARLEQUIN OR
SILHOUETTE BOOKS IN 1999. SEND US 3 PROOFS OF PURCHASE AND
WE WILL SEND YOU 2 COUPON BOOKLETS WITH A TOTAL SAVING OF
$20.00. (ALLOW 4-6 WEEKS DELIVERY) OFFER EXPIRES
DECEMBER 31, 1998.

....

I accept your offer! Please send me a coupon booklet(s), to:

NAME: _____

ADDRESS: _____

CITY: _____ STATE/PROV.: _____ POSTAL/ZIP CODE: _____

Send your name and address, along with your cash register
receipts for proofs of purchase, to:

In the U.S.	In Canada
Harlequin Books	**Harlequin Books**
P.O. Box 9057	**P.O. Box 622**
Buffalo, NY	**Fort Erie, Ontario**
14269	**L2A 5X3**

PHQ4982

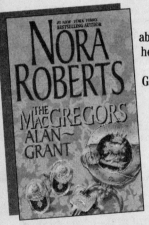

COMING NEXT MONTH

#1219 A FAMILY KIND OF WEDDING—Lisa Jackson
That Special Woman!/Forever Family
When rancher Luke Gates arrived in town on a mysterious mission, he had everything under control—until he lost his heart to hardworking ace reporter Katie Kincaid and her ten-year-old son. Would Katie still trust in him once she learned a shocking secret that would forever alter her family?

#1220 THE MILLIONAIRE BACHELOR—Susan Mallery
During their late-night phone chats, Cathy Eldridge couldn't resist entertaining a pained Stone Ward with tall tales about "her" life as a globe-trotting goddess. Then a twist of fate brought the self-conscious answering-service operator face-to-face with the reclusive millionaire of her dreams....

#1221 MEANT FOR EACH OTHER—Ginna Gray
The Blaines and the McCalls of Crockett, Texas
Good-natured Dr. Mike McCall was only too happy to save Dr. Leah Albright's ailing kid brother. And, as an added bonus, the alluring, ultrareserved lady doc finally allowed Mike to sweep her off her feet. But would their once-in-a-lifetime love survive the ultimate betrayal?

#1222 I TAKE THIS MAN—AGAIN!—Carole Halston
Six years ago, Mac McDaniel had foolishly let the love of his life go. Now he vowed to do anything—and *everything*—to make irresistibly sweet Ginger Honeycutt his again. For better, for worse, he knew they were destined to become husband and wife—for keeps!

#1223 JUST WHAT THE DOCTOR ORDERED—Leigh Greenwood
A hard-knock life had taught Dr. Matt Dennis to steer clear of emotional intimacy at all costs. But when he took a job at a rural clinic, struggling single mom Liz Rawlins welcomed him into her warm, embracing family. Would Liz's tender lovin' care convince the jaded doctor he *truly* belonged?

#1224 PRENUPTIAL AGREEMENT—Doris Rangel
It was meant to be when China Smith blissfully wed the only man she would *ever* love. Though Yance had proposed marriage for the sake of his son, an enamored China planned to cherish her husband forever and always. And she wasn't about to let a pesky prenuptial agreement stand in her way!